# Praise for Peter Elbling's *The Food Taster*

**Peter Elbling** is a writer, actor, and director who has worked in television, film, and theater. He lives in Venice, California.

**Visit www.peterelbling.com**

# The Food Taster

### Peter Elbling

A PLUME BOOK

PLUME
Published by the Penguin Group
Penguin Group (USA) Inc., 375 Hudson Street, New York, New York 10014, U.S.A.
Penguin Books Ltd, 80 Strand, London WC2R 0RL, England
Penguin Books Australia Ltd, 250 Camberwell Road, Camberwell, Victoria 3124, Australia
Penguin Books Canada Ltd, 10 Alcorn Avenue, Toronto, Ontario, Canada M4V 3B2
Penguin Books (N.Z.) Ltd, Cnr Rosedale and Airborne Roads, Albany, Auckland 1310,
New Zealand

Penguin Books Ltd, Registered Offices: 80 Strand, London WC2R 0RL, England

Published by Plume, a member of Penguin Group (USA) Inc. This is an authorized
reprint of a hardcover edition published by The Permanent Press. For information
address The Permanent Press, 4170 Noyac Road, Sag Harbor, New York 11963.

First Plume Printing, June 2003
10  9  8  7  6  5  4  3  2

 REGISTERED TRADEMARK—MARCA REGISTRADA

The Library of Congress has catalogued the Permanent Press edition as follows:

Elbling, Peter.
    The food taster / Ugo DiFonte; translated by Peter Elbling.
        p.   cm.
    Fictional memoir of medieval Italy written by Peter Elbling and ostensibly translated
from Italian.
    ISBN 1-57962-047-7 (hc.)
    ISBN 0-452-28434-1 (pbk.)
    1. Father and daughters—Fiction. 2. Master and servant—Fiction. 3. Peasantry—
Fiction. 4. Poisoning—Fiction. 5. Nobility—Fiction. 6. Cookery—Fiction.
7. Italy—Fiction. I. Title.

PS35555 L19 F66 2002
813'.54—dc21                                                        2001036618

Printed in the United States of America

PUBLISHER'S NOTE
This is a work of fiction. Names, characters, places, and incidents either are the products
of the author's imagination or are used fictitiously, and any resemblance to actual persons,
living or dead, business establishments, events, or locales is entirely coincidental.

for Dimitri and Simon

**i**

March 1534

For years after my mother hanged herself, I wished I had been older or stronger so that I could have stopped her. But since I was only a child who could not even reach her waist, I had to watch helplessly until it was over.

The day before, we had celebrated the feast of San Antony stuffing ourselves on roast pig, cabbage, beans, polenta, and dried chestnuts. We stuffed ourselves because the plague had been walking through the valley for weeks, striking whomever it pleased, and no one knew if they would live to see the sun rise.

Now it was evening and Mama and I were staring at the hilltops where my father and my older brother, Vittore, were lighting bonfires. I preferred to stay with my mother. I liked it when she scratched my head, put her arms around me, and called me "my little prince." Besides, that afternoon that bastard Vittore had banged my head against a tree and it still hurt.

It was dark, there was no moon, but I could hear my father's bellowing over everyone else's. The wind teased the fires this way and that as a man teases a dog by pulling on a stick in its mouth. Then the flames shot straight into the air, and for the blink of an eye I could see the men standing like ants on the top of the hills. Suddenly, one of the bonfires toppled over and bounced down the hill, a huge fiery ball, spinning over and over, faster and faster, leaping in the air, flattening bushes and crashing into trees as if the devil himself was guiding it.

"Holy Mother of God!" my mother cried. "It will eat us alive," and, grabbing my arm, she pulled me into our house. A moment later the flaming wheel passed right over the spot where we had been standing, and in the center of its fire I saw the face of Death staring straight at us. Then it disappeared down the hill leaving a trail of burning leaves and grasses behind it.

"Maria? Ugo? Are you all right?" my father shouted. "Are you hurt? Answer me!"

*"Stupido!"* my mother screamed, racing out of our house. "You

could have killed us. *C'è uno bambino qui*. May the devil piss on your grave!"

"I missed," my father yelled to much laughter. My mother kept on shouting until she ran out of curses. They say I take after her because I use my tongue as others use a sword. Then my mother turned to me and said, "I am tired, I want to lie down."

When my father stumbled home, the sheepish expression on his face pulling his big curved nose even closer to his pointed chin, my mother had boils the size of eggs under her armpits. Her eyes had sunk into her head, her teeth were rising up from her gums. Everything I loved about her was slipping away in front of my eyes so I clasped her hand tightly so she would not vanish completely.

When the sun rose, Death was waiting in the doorway. My father sat on the floor by the bed, his big face in his hands, weeping silently.

"Vicente, lay me outside" my mother whispered. "Go. Take the boys with you."

I climbed up the chestnut tree outside our house and straddled one of the branches. My father lay my poor mama on the ground and placed a bowl of polenta and water next to her. My brother Vittore told me to come down to watch the sheep with him.

I shook my head.

"Come down!" my father yelled.

"Ugo, my angel, go with him," my mother pleaded.

But I would not. I knew that if I left I would never see her alive again. My father tried to climb up after me but he could not, and since Vittore was afraid of heights he threw stones at me instead. They hit my back and cracked my head, but though I cried bitterly, I stayed where I was.

"Go without him," my mother said.

So my father and Vittore climbed the hill, stopping every now and again to shout at me, but the wind twisted their words until they were no more than the cries of a distant animal. My mother coughed up blood. I told her I was praying for her and she would soon get better.

"*Mio piccolo principe*," she whispered. She winked at me and said she knew a secret cure. She took off her shift, tore it in half, threw one end up to me and told me to tie it round the branch. I was happy to help her. It was only when she wrapped the other end around her neck that I sensed something was wrong. *"Mamma, mi dispiace!"* I cried, *"Mi dispiace!"* I tried to untie the knot but my hands were too small and besides my mother was making it tighter by jumping into the air and pulling her knees up to her chest. I screamed for my father, but the wind threw my cries back in my face.

The third time my mother jumped there was a crack like a piece of wood snapping. Her tongue shot from her mouth and the smell of shit curled up to me.

I do not know how long I screamed. I only know that, unable to move, I stayed on the branch all night, whipped by the wind, ignored by the stars and engulfed by the stench of my mother's decaying body until my father and Vittore returned the following morning.

## ii

Until the death of my mother, I had known only one sort of hunger, but now my heart was emptier than my stomach and only night brought my weeping mercifully to an end. Then I prayed to join her because after she died my father became more bitter than wormwood. Nothing I did pleased him. He said I burned the polenta. He said I let birds escape from his traps. Whatever I did or said made him angry. "You have your mother's tongue," he shouted at me. "You will come to a bad end."

To avoid his temper I spent my days minding our flock, sometimes taking Vittore's turn. Vittore was five years older than me and looked older still because he was tall and thin. He had a long nose like my father, but my mother's small flat chin which threatened to crumble under the weight of his face. When he boasted how he had won at cards or screwed some girl, my father clapped him on the back. When they went fishing I had to spend the night alone with the sheep. I did not mind. I knew them all by name. I talked to them. I sang to them. Christ! Later on I even fucked one of them. I am not proud of it, but it is the truth and what is the point of writing all this if I do not write the truth? Besides, *all* shepherds have fucked sheep and if they say they have not, then trust me, they are liars and they will burn in hell. Anyway, compared to Vittore, I was a saint. Whenever the sheep saw him coming, they would run the other way.

I built fires to warm myself at night, and if the sheep did not talk to me they did not beat me either, although I was nearly bitten by a wolf who snatched a lamb. I was blamed for that, too.

Five years after my mother died, famine struck our valley. Our crops died, our chickens were too thin to lay eggs, and since our sheep belonged to the lord of the valley, we were forbidden to even eat their turds. I had often prayed for sleep to forget my hunger, but now my stomach ached all the time and my knees were so weak I could not stand. My father made a pie out of chestnut flour and grass and baked it on the stones by the fire. He sang a song which went,

> Cut the loaf of bread in half
> The first half to eat,
> The second to shove up my *culo*
> To stop what I ate from coming out.

I dreamed my mother was making my favorite pies stuffed with figs and apples. The smell of the hot apples excited me and I asked her if I could have a small slice. She smiled and broke off a piece of crust for me. But as I reached out for it I woke up to find that my father and Vittore were already eating. "Where is mine?" I asked.

My father pointed to a small black glob of pie on one of the stones. "That is it?"

"You were asleep."

Tears welled in my eyes.

"Do you want it or not?" Vittore shouted at me. I grabbed it. His hand closed over my fist.

"It is mine," I screamed. The pie burned my palm but I would not let go. My father shouted "*Basta!*" and opened my fist up. The piece had been squeezed into a ball half its size. He broke it in two and gave half to Vittore. "He is bigger than you," he said. "Now eat before I give it all to him."

"One day I will have as much food as I like," I shouted. "You will be starving and I will not give you a crumb."

"You are no son of mine," my father said, and smacked me across the face. The pie flew out of my mouth. Vittore laughed and my father joined in. My father's words carved themselves into my heart even as the picture of the two of them laughing etched itself into my memory. No matter how many things have happened to me since then, I have never forgotten that moment. My mother used to say, "He who bears a grudge will be buried beneath it." But I thank God for giving me a grudge! I thought of it every single day and prayed for the time when I could have my revenge. Now God in His mercy has rewarded my patience.

# iii

After my mother died, my father carried the weight of his sorrows on his back. In time they bent him double. When he could no longer walk to the pastures, Vittore inherited the flock. Since I had cared for them so often I asked Vittore for a few sheep to start my own farm somewhere else. He refused. That cursed, miserable *fallo!* (prick) I knew better than to ask him again, so the next morning before it was light, I bundled my clothes together, and without a word to Vittore or my father I left. I was about fourteen although I cannot be sure. I remember standing on top of the hills watching the clouds scurry across the skies as if they were late for church. I said, "They are blowing away my old life," and my spirits lifted immediately.

The sun was shining, the hills were dizzy with the smell of rosemary and fennel. God had blessed me! I began to sing and I would have sung all the way to Gubbio where I hoped to find work, had I not seen a girl on the path in front of me.

I noticed her hair first of all. It was as dark as the soil and tied in a plait which swayed down her back like a great horse's tail. I do not know why, but I wanted to grasp it in my hands. I wanted to bite it and rub its silky warmth against my face. Can you blame me? I was fourteen. I had spent all my life with sheep.

I did not know what to say to the girl so I crept behind a mulberry bush to see her better. She was about my own age with big dark eyebrows that matched her hair. Her lips were red and full, her nose straight and her cheeks as round as apples. She was wearing a loose blouse, but I could not see her breasts or if she had any. Her hands, which were quite small, were picking fennel and blue geraniums, lifting them up to her nose to smell before placing them in her basket. I had heard people talk and sing about love, but until that moment I did not know what it was. Now, as if I was suddenly bewitched, every part of me ached to be close to her.

The girl was singing to herself, a song about a woman waiting for her sweetheart to return from the war. At first, my heart was crushed because I thought she was singing about a real person. Then I remembered my mother used to sing about a woman waiting for her lover to come back from the sea, she had grown up in Bari, and I knew my father had never even seen the sea.

Although this gave me courage, I still did not say anything for the girl seemed so at peace and I did not want to frighten her. In truth, I feared she might be angry if she knew I had been watching her so I sat quite still as bees buzzed around my face and the stones cut into my thighs. A scorpion even crawled over my legs, but I hardly breathed.

I followed her back to her house, and all afternoon I hid in a nearby glade of oak trees, planning what I would say to her on the one hand, and on the other fighting with my feet, which wanted to run away. But as the sun sank behind the hills I was afraid that if I did not speak soon I never would. So I banged on her door and when she opened it, I asked her to marry me.

"If you had asked me on the hillside," she said slyly, "I might have said yes. But you waited too long." And she closed the door in my face!

*Potta!* I wanted to kill myself! But Elisabetta, for that was her name, had smiled before she closed the door so when her father, a small man with hands as large as cabbages, returned that evening, I told him I was looking for work. He asked me if I knew how to cut wood and I said I was the best woodcutter he had ever seen. He spat on the ground and said that if I was as good a woodcutter as I was a liar, he would never have to work again.

My days were filled with hard work, but Elisabetta's father had always wanted a son and he treated me kindly. If I did not eat well, at least I did not have to give my food to Vittore and my father. And in the summers, when we left off woodcutting and went to the plains north of Assisi to help with the wheat harvest, I ate like a pig. We were fed not once, but seven times in a day! There was as much pasta as we liked, bread shaped like *falli* and *bocche sdentate* (mouths without teeth), fried calves' liver, plenty of roast chicken and, of course, polenta. We drank and danced till we could not stand. A couple of the women lifted their dresses and showed off their *culi. Jesus in sancto!* That was it! The men leaped on them and screwed them in front of everyone.

The third summer, I took Elisabetta's hand and we walked to the trees on the edge of the field where the air was heavy with the scent of sage and thyme, and I asked her to marry me.

For a time we were happy. Then Elisabetta's father cut his thigh with a blow from his axe. It did not heal well and gangrene set in. Elisabetta became pregnant. Her father knew he was dying and wanted to live long enough to see his grandchild, but the good man passed away before that could happen.

One evening I came home to find Elisabetta screaming in pain. Her beautiful hair was matted with sweat. Her lips were black with dried blood where she had chewed them. She was in labor all day and all night. The midwife, a gnarled old woman said, "She is too thin. I can save one or the other."

"Save Elisabetta," I said, "we can always have more children."

When she heard that, Elisabetta lunged forward and grasped my arm. "Promise me you will take care of the child," she cried. "Promise!"

When I pleaded with her, she shook my arm and shrieked, "Promise!" so loudly that I did as she asked. No sooner had I done so than Elisabetta expelled the baby to the world and her soul to heaven. My Elisabetta for a blob of bloody, crying flesh.

I did not look at the suckling for two days. I blamed it for Elisabetta's death and, because I wanted to leave it for the wolves, the midwife hid it from me. On the third afternoon she put Miranda— that was the name Elisabetta had breathed before she died—in my arms. Oh, *miracolo!* What a miracle! That tiny life turned my sorrow to a joy I did not know existed! She was Elisabetta all over again. She had the same big, dark eyes, the same dimples in her cheeks, the same straight nose. She was already biting her bottom lip just as her mother used to! For months after, I prayed that God would forgive me for what I had said.

Miranda was a year old when I heard that Vittore's flock had died and that he had left the valley to become a soldier. I thought—my father will be lonely. This will be a good time to take Miranda to him, it is his first grandchild, he will be pleased to see her.

I got blisters upon blisters walking to my father's house and many times on the way I cursed myself for starting the journey. But when I saw his hunched-up figure sitting in the sun—he had become so much smaller—my pains were drowned in a sea of tenderness. Holding Miranda in my arms, I ran to him, crying, "Babbo! It is me, Ugo!"

He did not recognize me right away, his eyesight was failing, but when I came close and he knew who it was, he shouted at me for not coming to see him sooner! Even then it was my fault!

He was hungry and cold and had little money. "Where is Vittore?" I asked, pretending I did not know.

"Fighting for the Venetians," my father boasted. "He leads hundreds of men."

"Anyone who puts Vittore in charge of anything is a fool," I replied.

"You are jealous," my father shouted. "He has won honors. He will be a *condotierro*."

I was about to say, "You stupid ass! It is your own fault you are in this mess. Vittore ruined you and you know it. But instead you pretend he is a captain in the army. Screw you." But that is not really what I wanted to say.

In truth, I did not want to say anything. I wanted him to say something to show that he was glad to see me. I wanted him to cradle his only grandchild in his arms and kiss her face and squeeze her cheeks as other grandparents did. I wanted him to show Miranda off to his neighbors and proclaim that she was the most beautiful child in the whole world. But he did not. All he did was sniff at her and sneer, "A girl."

# iv

After that I stopped cutting wood and raised vegetables in the valley of Corsoli. Most of them went to the palace, just as most of everything did. However, there was still enough left over to eat and sell in the market. I also had a goat, a sheep, some chickens, God's blessings, and Miranda, whom I loved more than life itself.

My Miranda! *Che bella raggazza!* A heavenly angel. Her lips were the color of rich red grapes and she had blushed apple cheeks just like her mother. Her skin was soft and she had light brown almond-shaped eyes that peeked out from beneath her thick, dark eyebrows. She often frowned even then, but this only endeared her to me even more. Her hair was thick like mine, but lighter in color. She loved to laugh and sing. And why not? She had the most beautiful voice even as a child. Clear and bright as a bird's in springtime. It was a mystery to me how she knew so many songs! Some, of course, she learned from me, but others must have been borne on the winds from churches in Assisi or festivals in Urbino. She only had to hear a melody once and I swear she could repeat it perfectly months later.

As they say, "He who makes himself laugh is never alone," and so she was never lonely. The animals adored her, sometimes knocking her to the ground in their eagerness to be near her. Then they would turn her cries to giggles by licking her tears away. When she was no more than three years old I saw her pretend to fall down just so they would do that. She could imitate all the birds and bleat so like our goat that it used to chase her round the farm. When she did this I would pick her up, squeeze her cheeks and say, "These are the prettiest apples in all of Corsoli," and tickle her till she begged me to stop.

When Miranda was eleven years old her breasts sprang up like young buds and she started her monthly courses. I used to take her to the market, but the boys would not leave her alone, so she often stayed at the Benedictine Convent, where the nuns stroked her hair and fought over who would teach her to read and write and spin wool.

One evening, as the sun was sinking behind the mountain, I was returning from the market with my friends Jacopo and Toro, when we were attacked by bandits. Jacopo fled, but Toro and I could not because we were sharing the same horse. Swearing loudly, Toro jumped down and drove his sword into the belly of one of the bandit's horses, causing it to rear up and fall on its rider. Since my knife was too small to fight against their swords, I threw my purse in the air, shouting, "Here is the money." I had tied another purse with most of the ducats to the horse's belly for safekeeping. Two bandits chased after it and I turned around to help Toro. But just then the fourth bandit was pulling his bloody sword from Toro's stomach. The effort made the bandit's hood jerk backward and I saw a thin gaunt face which, even though it had been over ten years since I had seen it, I recognized immediately. Vittore!

I shouted his name and he sprang toward me, but God sent an angel to protect me for I escaped his sword and rode into the forest as fast as I could. Suddenly I feared I might never see Miranda again, even as I had feared I would not see my mother the day she had fallen sick.

The nuns were at Vespers. The abbot Tottorini said it would be a sin to take Miranda from the convent, but I pushed him to the ground and ran through the convent opening every door until I found Miranda—in *his* room. Luckily for him, that fat bastard disappeared before I could find him.


"You brought me home to starve me," Miranda accused me a few weeks later. I had not planned it that way, but my traps were empty, our crops had withered, and our animals were too sick or thin to eat. We did not even have a few lousy chestnuts to make bread! "Sad is the person who is born poor and unfortunate," my mother used to say, "for he must have spit on his hands if he wants to eat and God knows how many times he will fast without a vow."

At dawn I led Miranda to the woods and told her to imitate a bird. When a finch perched on a tree close by, I killed it. I told her to do it again, but she shook her head.

I said, "What difference does it make how we catch them?"

She did not answer.

"If we do not eat we will die," I shouted at her.

She sang to please me, but the birds heard the tears in her voice and flew away.

I cooked the finch with some greens and told Miranda she could eat if she wanted, but if she was going to weep she had to go outside. She left. Despair overcame me. I thought of going to Corsoli to find work, but I was not a craftsman and I did not belong to a guild. I had no skills. I called Miranda to me. She looked fearfully at me from beneath her dark brown eyebrows. I held her in my arms—she was so thin I could put both my hands around her chest—and told her the story of how I met her mother, until she fell asleep.

I awoke as the sun's first rays were rising over the hills. I walked to our dried-up vegetables and fell on my knees saying, "Holy Mother, I ask your help not for me, but for my Miranda who will surely die unless she eats soon."

Before the words were out of my mouth the ground beneath me trembled. I could not see anything, but I could hear branches smashing and the yelping of hunting dogs. Suddenly, a most magnificent stag shot out of the trees, its eyes wild with fear, its black tongue hanging out of its mouth. It came so fast that before I could move, it leaped right over me and disappeared into the oaks on the other side. The next instant the air was filled with bloodthirsty cries and shouts that chilled my heart. I ran back to the hut just as a hundred hounds tore out of the forest, barking and snarling and howling, followed by a huge man on a black horse—Federico Basillione DiVincelli, Duke of Corsoli.

I had only seen Duke Federico once or twice and then from a distance, but that was the safest way to see him. Everyone knew he had killed his father and poisoned his brother Paolo to become duke. Before that he had been a *condotierro*—he had once slain thirty men single-handedly in battle—and had served princes all over Italy and Germany. It was also known that he had betrayed everyone he served. Because of this he had left Italy and spent five years in Turkey in the service of a sultan. Rumors swirled about him: he always wore silk, he feared the number seven because that was the day on which he had killed his brother, and he had once forced a woman to eat her own child. I did not know if any of this was true or not but *potta!* When I saw him face to face, I believed everything I had heard.

To begin with, his features were at war with one another. His face was round like a pie, but his nose, which cut his face in two, was as thin and as sharp as a sword. His eyes were small and fierce like a hawk's, but his bottom lip hung open like a dead fish. He had a thick bull neck but small hands.

But it was not just the way he looked that frightened me. I have seen stranger-looking men. There is a miller not far from Gubbio who has a third ear growing under his right one and a woman in Corsoli who has no nose. No, it was the arrogant way Duke Federico rode across my farm, as if not just the land but the very air itself belonged to him.

Do not ask me how, but the duke's horse nearly impaled himself on one of my bean stakes and reared so fiercely that Federico almost fell off. He drew his sword, cursing and yelling, and hacked the few shriveled beans I had left into a thousand pieces. Then he looked up and saw me standing in the doorway of my hut.

"*Avanzarsi!*" he shouted, his voice like two knives scraping together.

*Sono fottuto*, I thought, I am as good as dead. I whispered to Miranda, "Do not come out till after they have gone," and then I walked across my dusty, trampled plot to the duke. By this time the other hunters—there must have been a dozen or so—had ridden up and they sat on their prancing horses, in their dark green hunting jackets and big black boots, staring down their noses at me. The dogs bared their teeth and barked as I walked past them. A huge mastiff wearing a ruby-studded collar leaped up and would have bitten me if Duke Federico had not shouted, "Nero!"

I knelt in front of the duke, but as his sword was in his hand I decided it was better not to bow my head.

"Who told you to put your farm in the middle of my hunt?" Duke Federico demanded.

"No one, Your Honor. Begging a thousand pardons—"

"I lost a stag because of you," Federico said, and raised the sword above his head. I heard a scream and Miranda came running out of our hut and threw herself about my neck. Since the duke had served with the Turks, I knew he would not think twice about killing children, so I tore her arms from me and shouted, "Go away! Go away!"

A hunter with a long gray beard and a sad face said, "He could be useful."

"Useful?" Federico asked. "How?"

"He could take Lucca's place, Your Excellency."

"Yes," I said, rising to my feet. "I will take Lucca's place."

Federico's eyes opened wide and he laughed in a high shrill voice. The hunters immediately joined in, while I stood there, Federico's sword poised above me, Miranda's arms around my waist, thinking that must have been God speaking since I did not know what I was talking about! "Take him," Federico said, and looking at Miranda, he added, "And take her, too."

Since the hunter with the long gray beard sat Miranda in front of him on his horse, I did not mind running uphill with a rope tied around my neck for several hours. Each moment I stayed alive was a gift from God. He had performed a miracle. I was going to take Lucca's place. As I have written, I often went to Corsoli for market, but this time I saw things I had not noticed before or did not remember: the huge, gray stone wall of the West Gate, the houses huddled together along the streets winding their way to the top of the city, the sound of horses' hooves ringing on the cobblestones. We rode through the Piazza Del Vedura with its splashing fountain, through the Piazza San Giulio, and more winding streets, and then up the Weeping Steps to the Palazzo Fizzi. The palace stood on our right and, facing us across the piazza, the Duomo Santa Caterina with its beautiful golden Madonna above the door, to whom I whispered a prayer for Miranda's safety.

From the outside, the Palazzo Fizzi looked like a castle, but the inner courtyard was lined on three sides with columns and arches. That is what little I could see of it. Christ on a cross! It was as if the usual market had been moved inside. There was food everywhere! More food than I had ever seen in my whole life. Here women were tending to bubbling cauldrons and roasting spits; over there young girls sorted baskets of fruits and vegetables; and in the middle a group of men were carving up animal carcasses.

"What saint's day is this?" I asked a hunter. He said San Michele and the duke's birthday and then cuffed me on the head for not knowing. *Potta!* How was I to supposed know? There had been so many new saints in the past few years that I did not even know there was a San Michele.

We had just reached the stables when two soldiers dragged a man in front of Duke Federico.

"Did he confess?" The duke roared.

The soldiers nodded. But the man sobbed, "Your Excellency, it is not so."

The duke swung down from his horse and told the man to stick out his tongue. The courtyard had become silent, and glancing about me

I saw that every window had filled with faces. The man slowly, timidly stuck out his tongue. Duke Federico gripped it in his left hand, pulled his dagger with his right, sliced it off, and threw it to Nero.

Blood shot out of the man's mouth and onto Duke Federico's boots. Duke Federico turned to the other hunters. "First, he lies to me, then he bloodies my boots."

The man wailed piteously, his hands reaching to Nero, who, having eaten his tongue, was now busily lapping up his blood. Federico kicked the man. "Be quiet," he yelled and walked away.

But the man could not be quiet. As if they sympathized with his sorrow, the cauldrons, the spits, the prancing horses, and barking dogs all stilled so that his cries bounced off them and off the walls of the palazzo. Federico stopped, his back to the man.

I muttered, "Please God, make him be still."

But the man's good sense was captive to his terror. Tears streamed down his face, blood poured from his mouth, and agonized sobs continued to burst from his lips. Federico pulled his sword and, without looking, whirled about and stabbed the man through the back so that the point of his sword went right through his heart and came out blood red on the other side. All the hunters applauded. I felt Miranda's body stiffen and I pressed her face into me so she would not scream. A curly-haired youth—who I had noticed was staring at Miranda—nodded his head as if to say I had acted wisely.

Duke Federico pulled his sword from the man's back, wiped it on his body, and strode into the palace. The same soldiers who had brought the man out now dragged his body to the wall at the back of the courtyard and threw it down to the valley below. I could feel it bouncing off the cliffs, hear the bones crunching on its way to the bottom. In another moment the servants were back at work as if nothing had happened, but as we entered the palace I felt a great wind of hatred snap at the back of my neck.

Miranda and I were locked in the tower on the other side of the palace. The cell had iron doors with large locks, a tiny window near the ceiling, and a few wisps of soiled straw.

"Where are we, Babbo?" Miranda whispered. She was still trembling from what she had seen.

"In Duke Federico's palace."

"But this is not the palace."

"That is because they are preparing a grand room with beds and servants for each of us," I said as gaily as I could.

"But why?"

"Why? Because I am to take Lucca's place. Did you not hear the man?"

She thought for a moment and then said, "But who is Lucca?"

I did not know and when I did not answer I feared she would start weeping. I gathered her to me and looking in those soft dark eyes I promised her that God had not made us only to abandon us. I told her to recite all the prayers she had been taught, and while she did that I asked God if perhaps He had not mistaken us for someone else, and that if He had, could He not correct His mistake before it was too late.

Eventually, we ran out of prayers and so we huddled together in the corner of the cell and became so still that all I could hear was the beating of our hearts and at one moment I swear they stopped too.

"Please," I begged the guards when they came to take me away, "do not leave my daughter alone here."

A guard said, "We will do whatever we want." But the captain, who had a good heart said, "I have a daughter, too. I will take her upstairs."

I was led to a room with a large tub of sweet-smelling water and told to scrub myself and wash my hair. Other servants hurried by preparing for the banquet. The curly-haired youth passed by carrying a basket of apples. "Hey!" I called out, "Where's Lucca?" but he ignored me. The gray-bearded hunter looked in and said to the servants, "Make sure his hands are clean." The stupid idiots scrubbed my hands till they were raw and would have drawn blood had I not threatened to pull them into the tub with me. I was dried off and my hair brushed. Then I was shaved and given a pair of red hose, a white shirt, a jerkin, and a pair of shoes. When I had dressed, the servants held a mirror in front of me. They laughed, saying, "He does not recognize himself."

They were almost right. I recognized myself not because I knew what I looked like, but because I looked so much like my mother. My hair was straight like hers, I had her almond eyes, the left one slightly larger than the right. I do not remember what my nostrils looked like. Miranda says they are fleshy, but only my mother could have known if they were that way when I was born or if they became that way because of what I do. And yet, I was not that different from the men around me, thinner certainly, but no bigger or smaller. And so from appearances only, I did not know why I had been allowed to take Lucca's place. "Whose clothes are these?" I asked.

"Lucca's," the servants replied, and told me angrily I had no business asking questions.

Except for the shoes, which fit me perfectly, Lucca was bigger than me in every way. I was lost in his jerkin, the sleeves of the shirt were too long and so were the hose. Despite this I was pleased. It was still better than my shift. A guard took me to Miranda who was now in a pleasant room overlooking a garden of flowers.

"Babbo," she gasped, "you look like a prince!"

"This Lucca must have been somebody," I said. "Who knows, perhaps he has a daughter. Then you will get some new clothes too."

The sun had long stopped shining when the guards came for me again. I kissed Miranda and told her I loved her and to trust in God. I was led upstairs along silent stone hallways lit with fiery sconces. I heard noises followed by smells of food, both of them growing stronger and stronger till we turned a corner and then, O blessed saints! What a sight! A corridor crowded with servants, all handsomely dressed in red and white, holding platters of the very food I had seen earlier, but now cooked and roasted and boiled and stewed and fried in a hundred different ways.

In front of me, servants held more platters and upon each one was a swan with a silver crown on its head, its eyes so bright, its plumage so alive, that I said to myself—These are the best-trained birds in all of Italy. Holy Mother! What an innocent I was! They were not alive at all, but as I later found out, each one had been flayed so carefully that the feathers remained on the skin. Then after the insides were removed and the stomach stuffed with egg whites and finely chopped meats, the birds were roasted to perfection. Then the feathers, the feet, and the beak were cleverly gilded back on with saffron-colored paste. A miracle all of its own!

More servants carried aloft spit-roasted legs of goat, tender slices of veal, quail with eggplants, and still more platters of fish covered in parsley and dill. *Oi me!* I felt weak. The smells invaded my nose, they captured my brain, they seduced my stomach. Years of hunger which had become part of my flesh, pangs of starvation which had burned into my bones awakened with so great a cry that I had to clutch the wall or I would have thrown myself at a servant who was carrying a leg of mutton.

A short fierce man with bushy eyebrows and a goiter by his left ear angrily pushed past me and ran from one dish to another sniffing, tasting, and stirring. This was Cristoforo, the chief cook at that time. Then came the whistling of pipes, the beating of drums followed by laughter and barking and the frantic bleating of a sheep! The bleating stopped and a great roar rang through the halls.

The curly-haired youth walked by with a bowl filled with lettuce. "You *saw* Lucca," he said. "He was the one who had his tongue cut out."

I thought I would faint. My miracle had turned into a disaster. When he passed again I grabbed his arm. "But why?"

"For trying to poison Federico. He was the food taster."

"The food taster!" And I was taking his place! I wanted to rip my clothes off, jump through a window, and run until I reached my farm. But there were guards everywhere and now someone was shouting, "*Adesso!* We go. Now!" Trumpets blared and then we were marching toward the great hall and I was fourth in the line!

O my soul. That morning I thought I was at Death's door and now I was entering paradise. The smell of orris and rosemary was everywhere. Colorful banners and beautiful tapestries hung from the walls. There were long tables covered in white tablecloths and vases of flowers arranged so artfully as to make nature herself jealous. Seated at the tables were guests dressed in the finest silks and linens and velvets all trimmed with beaten gold. Jewels of every kind hung from necks and wrists, and sparkled against snow-white bosoms. Musicians played joyfully. Dogs rose from under the tables to watch us. A dwarf, covered in sweat, sat on top of a dead sheep. We stared straight ahead, our heads held high, although I was squeezing the cheeks of my *culo* together because of what I had just been told.

By this time we had reached Duke Federico's table at the far end of the hall. Dressed in a robe of red ermine with puffed sleeves, the duke was leaning back in an enormous chair watching us with his little beady eyes. A gold medallion with his face engraved upon it lay upon his chest. A servant placed the platter with the largest swan in front of him. The guests stopped their chatter. Nero yawned at the duke's feet. Cristoforo, the cook, stepped forward, a long knife in his right hand and a short spear with two points in the other. Squinting his eyes, he studied the swan, took a breath, and, stabbing it with the spear, lifted it into the air to the height of his chest. Then, first touching the bird with his knife to measure his aim, he cut six perfect slices off the right breast, zip, zip, zip, all while the swan was held by the spear and all so neatly that the pieces fell onto the duke's plate in one row as if they had been placed there by hand. *"Stupendo! Meraviglioso!"* everyone shouted. Cristoforo bowed.

Someone pushed me forward so that I was standing opposite Federico, the six slices of reddish brown meat wallowing in their own juices between us. Then Cristoforo picked up the platter and handing me a knife, said, "Taste it."

# vi

*"Che bruta sorpresa,"* my mother would have said. "The unhappy surprise." Unhappy? *Oi me!* The slices of swan grew so big I could see nothing else. I thought I saw maggots feasting on them, worms slithering through them, green pus oozing from the sides. I looked at Federico. A river of saliva sat on his fat bottom lip. I could feel everyone's eyes on me—nobles, knights, wives, courtesans, servants. I remembered the hatred on the servants' faces earlier in the courtyard. Could one of them have poisoned the food? Miranda had already lost her mother and without me her life would be worthless. Although I did not wish to annoy Federico (God knows I wanted to do everything I could to please him), I put the knife down and said, "Thank you, Your Excellency, but I already ate."

The duke blinked, stared at me, then blinked again. His face quivered with rage. His teeth gnashed, his bottom lip fell to his chin.

"Taste it! For the love of God, taste it!" Cristoforo screamed.

Federico pushed back his chair, leaned over the table and snatched up the knife. All around me people cried, "Taste it! Taste it!"

I had no doubt that Federico was as good with a knife as he was with his sword, so I quickly picked up a slice of swan's breast and bit into it.

I had only eaten meat a few times in my life; pork on the feast of San Antony, a few chickens, and once a sheep that had become lame when we were driving the flock. Whenever my father ate meat he said, "This is the way meat should taste," just because it *was* meat. But the times I ate it were so far apart I could never remember what it tasted like from one time to the next. But this breast, this breast, I have never forgotten. When my teeth sank into it the flesh fell apart in my mouth. The juices trickled over my tongue like brooks in springtime. Someone groaned with pleasure. It was me!

Duke Federico slammed his fist onto the table. "Swallow it," he yelled. He did not have to tell me twice! I would have eaten the whole bird if I had had the chance. My throat opened, my stomach reached up to pull the food down, and yet the breast did not move. As much as one part of me yearned to swallow, another part did not. This other part of me said, "What if the breast *is* poisoned? How soon will I feel it? What will it feel like? Is it too late?" Something tickled my throat. Perhaps it was just my imagination, but when I felt that, I tried to pull the meat out of my mouth. Platters crashed to the floor, dogs barked, the guests rose in panic. Then my hands were grasped behind my back and the meat forced down my throat as if I was an animal.

I once saw a miller die from drinking bad water. He rolled over and over on the ground trying to tear his stomach out with his hands. His eyes bulged, his tongue grew thick in his mouth. He screamed he would leave his mill to the man who brought him a knife to end the fire in his belly, but his wretched wife forbade us. His cries lasted until morning and then he lay silent, his lips gnawed away by his frantic teeth.

But this meat did not burn my mouth, nor did it tear at my throat. My stomach did not feel as if it was being torn apart by a griffin's claws. I did not feel anything other than a wondrous sensation. Every part of my body sighed with satisfaction. Sconces flickered, flared up, and died down. Eyes darted from me to the duke and back again. When several moments had passed and still nothing had happened, the duke grunted, pulled the platter toward him, picked up the other slices with his hands, and ate them. That was the sign to the guests to begin eating. One moment every eye in the hall was on me, and the next I was invisible.

"Do you want to get me killed?" Cristoforo shouted when we returned to the kitchen. He was so angry his goiter had turned as red as his face. "Just do what you are told or I swear if Federico does not kill you *I* will."

I later found out being Federico's cook could be as precarious a position as a food taster, for when it came to food Federico was more suspicious than an old fool with a young bride, and would strike first and ask questions afterward. Cristoforo did not have time to continue his ranting, for the kitchen servants were busily preparing more dishes. Every now and then my stomach rumbled and I thought— This is it! This is the poison! But when I did not fall sick, I realized the rumbling was just my stomach getting used to having food inside it. The curly-haired boy, whose name was Tommaso said, "Stay close by. Federico will need you again."

I stayed by the serving table, where the meats and other foods were prepared, and watched as the guests nibbled at dainty little sausages, chewed on chicken legs, gobbled down slices of veal, and sucked the marrow out of bones. The color of their sleeves changed from red to mustard to brown as they dragged the food through a half-dozen different sauces. They spoke of politics and art and war. When someone sneezed, a hunchback with a big head, big ears, a black beard, and eyes that bulged beneath his spectacles began a discussion about table manners.

Just as I was walking behind him, he said, "In Venezia they get rid of snot like this," and holding his nose between his thumb and fore-finger, the little toad turned away from the table and blew a huge wad right onto my leg. Everyone laughed. I was furious because I had just been given this pair of hose and I did not know when I would get another.

Five more times I was called to taste the duke's food. I remember salted pork tongues cooked in a blood-red wine, fish galantine, vegetable ravioli delicately sprinkled with cheese, a farinata, a thick pudding of wheat grains with almond milk, and saffron for the venison. There were also capons. Capons with fritters, capons with lemon, capons with eggplants, capons cooked in their own juices. They loved it all! God in heaven! How could they *not* have loved it! As for me, each time I had to taste something I feared I would die. My stomach growled like an angry bear, but nothing happened.

So after tasting dish after dish without any ill effect, I said to myself—Ugo, perhaps the food is not poisoned. And since this might be the only time you taste food like this, why not enjoy it!

Just then Cristoforo served Federico a platter of flaky-crusted yellow pastries bursting with cream and sprinkled with sugar, called Neapolitan spice cakes, and best of all, pear tarts wrapped in marzipan. My mouth filled with enough saliva to drown an ox. I prayed Federico would choose the pear tart first. He did. Steadying myself not to show my excitement, I raised the tart to my mouth and bit into it.

O saints be praised! To those who say cooking is not as great an art as painting and sculpture, I say they have their head up their *culo*. It is far, far greater! A sculptor's work is eternal, but a cook's greatness is measured by how fast his creations disappear! A true master must produce great works every day. And that sniveling creep Cristoforo was a master. If you can imagine a warm doughy base crumbling against the sides of your palate, the sugary pulpiness of a soft brown pear lying on your tongue like a satisfied woman, Eden's succulent juices filling up the canals between your teeth, you would not even be close! You would think that I, who had never tasted such a delicacy, would have gladly surrendered myself to this pleasure, maybe even risked death and grabbed another bite. But I did not. Believe me, it was not because I did not want to, but because I *could* not! Something had changed in me. I received no pleasure from the tart at all. None. *Niente!* My taste buds had been robbed of all power of enjoyment. I left the table staring at the pear tarts and spice cakes with such disappointment that tears came to my eyes.

It is the same to this very day. Meals which have inspired men to poetry, women to open their legs, and ministers to reveal state secrets leave me unaffected. Even when I am not tasting for the duke, when I am here alone in my room, a single candle illuminating my solitude, with only bread and cheese for sustenance, I feel nothing. But it is a small price to pay. For if I had been allowed to enjoy food all these years, in time I would have become less vigilant, and the duke's enemies wait for such moments. No, much as I want to enjoy food, I love life even more.

It was now so late that the birds were awakening, but the banquet was still not finished. A thin man with yellow teeth, huge eyebrows, and a runny nose stood up to speak, and I noticed the servants slip quietly out of the hall. I tried to follow, but they closed the door in my face and I heard them giggling on the other side.

The thin man cleared his throat and began by saying, "Septivus, the lowest of all orators, gives you, Duke Federico Basillione DiVincelli, the greatest of all patrons, his warmest thanks."

I do not remember exactly what Septivus said that night, but I have heard so many of his speeches since then I could recite them in my sleep. First, he praised Duke Federico as if he was Jesus Christ and Julius Caesar rolled into one. Then he said that if Cicero had been here he would not have said, "We should eat to live," but, "Let us live to eat," because this was the most magnificent banquet he had ever seen. "It frees our senses and by eating the fruits which

God bestowed upon the Garden of Corsoli, we ingest paradise itself."

As if it was not bad enough that I could not enjoy the food, now I had to listen to this fool praising it! "This magnificent feast," Septivus cried, "not only puts us in harmony with nature, but also joins our hearts with those sitting beside us. Today, injuries are healed, quarrels are forgotten, for food is man's greatest healer."

I could hear my father shouting, "What the devil is that idiot talking about?"

Then Septivus went on to praise the mouth because in return for food it nurtured words. "These words, spiced by the food, celebrate the union between man and nature, man and society, and the body and the spirit. Did Christ not say, 'This is my body, this is my blood?' This blending of body and spirit leads us to another hunger which God alone can fulfill!"

He paused to sip some wine. "In the truly successful banquet the conversation is neither too stupid nor too intelligent, but flows so that everyone can join in." He waggled his finger. "For there is nothing worse than one person dominating the table with a long, boring speech which undoes all the pleasures the stomach has—"

"That is right. Nothing," Duke Federico said. "I am going to bed." He lurched to his feet and stomped out of the hall like a drunken ox. Within a minute the room was empty.

The pink fingers of dawn were already reaching over the hills when Tommaso said, "Now *we* eat," and led me to the servants' hall.

I wonder what Septivus would have said about the servants' meal. Meal? This was not a meal. Meals are prepared in a kitchen. This was prepared in a graveyard! For every breast of quail or capon served at the banquet, we were given a beak or a talon. For every goat leg, we were given a hoof. For every sausage, a horn or tail. No one spoke. No one made a speech or cracked a joke. Instead we crammed around the table, the pale yellow light of our candle of pigs' grease lighting our weary faces, and used what little strength we had to pretend that what we were eating was as delicious as what we had served. Suddenly, I remembered Miranda. "My daughter, I must find her—"

"She has already eaten," Tommaso said, sucking on a scorched black chicken's claw as if it was the tastiest morsel in the world. "Have some dessert." He dumped a bowl of figs, grapes, and plums onto the table, each piece so spoiled and rotten I could hardly tell one from the other. Then grabbing some bruises in the shape of an apple, he said, "Come, I will take you to her."

With a cocky stride, he led me through a maze of hallways and staircases, biting into his apple and spitting out the pips, until we came to a small room across from the stables in which three boys were fast asleep on their pallets. Miranda was curled up on another under a tattered blanket.

I grasped Tommaso's arm. "Thank you for your kindnesses."

He was looking at Miranda's face, which even in the ill-green light of the sconces was soft and beautiful. "*Buona notte,*" he replied and, cocking his head to one side, he left, whistling to himself.

I lay down next to Miranda and cradled her to me. Her fresh, strong smell enveloped me, and I pressed my face against hers and thanked God for keeping her safe from harm. But although I was exhausted I could not sleep.

*Oi me!* I have slept with sheep, goats, pigs, but all of them together were not as bad as the wretched stink in that room. Nor was it just the smell, but the yelling and arguing and weeping of the boys as they thrashed about, tossing from one side to another, kicking their legs backward and forward as they tried to outrun their nightmares.

But even if everything had been quiet and that pisshole had smelled like a Turkish harem, my mind refused to be silenced. I wanted to know how Lucca had tried to poison Federico. I wanted to know why, if I had to taste food, God did not allow me to enjoy it. I wanted to know, if someone did sprinkle poison over the meat or coated a pudding with it, how could I tell? *Potta!* How could I stop them?

However starved I had been on the farm, at least I was free. Now I was a bird trapped in a net waiting for Death, the eternal hunter, to collect me. And that day could be tomorrow! Or the day after. Or the one after that. Any meal could be my last. My heart beat so loudly it rang in my ears. I stood in the doorway to the courtyard to clear my head. The palace was silent. The moon was fading and the face in it barely visible. But then before my eyes, the face changed to that of my father and then my cursed brother Vittore. Vittore laughed. "Ugo's in the middle of all that food and he cannot taste it!" The food I had eaten welled up in my throat.

After I vomited, I picked Miranda up in my arms and carried her out of her room. People were sleeping everywhere, curled up against one another in the hallways and alcoves, and under benches. Every room was crowded with huddled forms, some under blankets, some without. Miranda opened her eyes and when I told her we were going back to our farm, she pulled my arm and said, "No, I like it here, Babbo. I had meat—"

"But Miranda," I whispered. "They have made me Duke Federico's new food taster. His old one, Lucca, was the man who had his tongue cut out."

The sleep fled from her eyes. I stood her up on her feet. "Babbo, I do not want you to be poisoned."

"No, nor do I. That is why we must—"

Suddenly, there was a growling and in the moonlight I saw Federico's dog, Nero, his teeth bared, his ears pricked back lumbering toward us. Miranda, who loved animals, was as scared of him as I was, and hid behind me.

"Nero!" said a voice from the shadows. My heart leaped out of the window. Duke Federico was limping toward us.

"*Scusi*, Your Honor," I bowed deeply. "My daughter had a dream—"

"You are the taster," the duke said.

"*Si*, Your Excellency."

"Come here." I hesitated and he repeated. "Come here! Do not worry, I try not to kill more than one person a day." Putting his weight on my shoulder he grimaced and lowered himself onto a nearby bench.

"Now pick up my foot." It was bandaged and swollen with gout and I did not know where or how to grasp it. "Underneath!" he snarled. "Underneath!"

Praying that I would not drop it, I picked up the foot as he instructed (it did not help that Nero's mouth was inches from my face), and raised it toward the bench.

"Careful!" Federico shouted and Nero barked loudly.

Sweating so much I could hardly see, I gently laid his foot down as if it was a newborn child. Federico leaned his head back against the wall and gave a great sigh. I did not know whether to leave or stay where I was. Then he said, "What are you doing?"

I realized he was not looking at me, but at Miranda who was stroking Nero's massive head. She immediately withdrew her hand.

"You like dogs?" the duke asked.

She nodded. "I like all animals," and she reached out her hand to Nero's face again. O blessed saints! Was there ever a braver child?

"I should have had a daughter," Federico grunted. "My eldest son will want to kill me soon enough."

I wanted to ask him if he thought his son might poison him, but just then Federico scratched his big toe and cursed with such anger I decided it best to remain silent. Then, as if he had forgotten we were there, he said harshly, "Go back to sleep!"

We hurried to our room.

Miranda was soon breathing quietly, but I lay awake thinking. Although it was true Federico was vicious and cruel, he had good reason to be so if people were trying to poison him. However, as they say, "A coin has two sides," and I had seen a glimpse of the other. He liked children, maybe not his own, but small girls anyway. Or at least he did not dislike them. Surely, this was a good omen. He also said he tried not to kill more than one person a day. It was a jest of course, but in every jest is a kernel of truth. *Potta!* There had to be or otherwise Corsoli would have long ceased to exist.

I marveled at the path God had led me on that day. He had given me the opportunity to serve a great duke; to rise to a better position than my father or my brother could have ever dreamed of. Surely that was why Federico had killed Lucca. Why the stag had run across my farm and why the man with the gray beard had spoken when he did. God had answered my prayer and saved Miranda from starving. I vowed to return His love by being the best food taster Federico had ever had.

# viii

I must have slept after all, for when Tommaso woke me the sun was shining and the guests were preparing to depart. "I have something for you," he said.

I left Miranda sleeping and followed him through the crowded hallways. He walked with the same cocky attitude he had the previous night, greeting everyone, be they footmen, courtiers, or servant girls, in a loud, high voice. It had not yet broken, which made his cockiness seem all the more ridiculous. After we passed them, he would say, "That washerwoman was a slave from Bosnia," or "He is a thief," "She is a gossip." According to Tommaso, everyone was a thief or a gossip except him.

Tommaso led me into the kitchen where the servants ran to and fro attending to the rows of ovens and cauldrons. Against the back wall were spits for small birds and another for larger animals. Knives and spoons stuck out from a bale of hay in the corner and on a nearby table lay tools for chopping, spearing, and mincing. There were also rows of pots for stewing and baking, ravioli wheels and sieves of all sizes, rolling pins, mortar and pestle, presses, jugs, whisks, graters, spoons, ladles, and a dozen different utensils which were a mystery to me.

Tommaso climbed to the top of a cabinet and threw a leather pouch down to me. I untied it and three stones and a piece of bone tumbled onto the table. The stones were small, dark, and round and looked like a thousand others I saw every day except these were smooth to the touch. "What are they?" I asked.

"Amulets. They belonged to Lucca."

A kitchen boy picked up the smallest black stone. "This is not an amulet. It is a sheep's turd."

The other boys laughed. At any other time I would have too, but because Tommaso had said they belonged to Lucca I could not even smile.

"It is a good-luck charm!" Tommaso said, snatching it from the boy. "This," he picked up the bone, "is a piece of unicorn's horn. If you dip it in wine and the wine is poisoned, the bone changes color."

"To what?"

He shrugged. "All I know is the unicorn has to be killed by a virgin so they are hard to find."

"No, they are not!" said a boy pointing to Tommaso, and the other boys burst into fits of laughter again.

Tommaso turned bright red. "Shut up!" he shouted, but the boys kept repeating *"vergine"* over and over.

I put my hand on his arm. "Take no notice of them."

He turned toward me, eyes blazing, and tried to compose himself. "Federico's goblet is made of gold and silver. If someone puts poison in it, it changes color and the wine bubbles like boiling pasta."

"Who is boiling pasta?" That cursed cook, Cristoforo, had returned flailing the air with a long wooden spoon. The boys tried to dodge his blows, but he was faster than he looked and beat several of them about the head and arms. Tommaso scooped up the amulets. "Come on, I have to piss." We slipped outside, passing a boy who was sitting on the ground tearfully rubbing his head. "I would have given you worse!" Tommaso said, and trod on his leg.

As we walked through the hallways, Tommaso again greeted whomever we met as if they were old friends.

"You know everyone," I said.

"And why not? I was born here."

I grasped his arm. "Do you know if Lucca really tried to poison Federico?"

He jerked himself free and did not answer. We reached a portion of the rampart which jutted out over the edge of the mountain. Men were pissing and shitting into a trough which ran through a wall and out into the valley. Some were talking about the banquet, boasting about what they had said or done; others walked about silently, still caught in the web of sleep.

We were surrounded on three sides by hills, and on top of each hill a tiny village glinted in the morning sunlight. Below us lay the town of Corsoli, the streets winding between the towers and then reappearing again like streams in springtime. Beyond the walls, the occasional traveler moved toward the city like a bustling ant. Yesterday I had looked just as small and unimportant, but today, God in His mercy had placed me on the roof of the world.

"Hey, *contadino*," Tommaso said. "If you want to take a shit, the straw is over there."

"My name is Ugo!" I said loudly. I had been called a peasant all my life, by the guards when I came to the city, by the merchants who cheated me, by tax collectors, even by the priests. Now that I was in the palace I wanted to be called by my right name.

"All right, *Ugo*." Tommaso pointed to the top floor of the palace. "That is where Duke Federico lives. Giovanni the hunchback, Federico's brother-in-law, lives below him."

"The one who spat on me?" I asked. Tommaso nodded. He told me that Giovanni was Corsoli's ambassador for the wool trade and without his contacts the valley would starve. "He wants to be a cardinal," Tommaso went on. "But Federico will not pay because every *scudo* he gives to the pope, the pope will use to attack Corsoli. So Federico hates the pope and everyone hates Federico."

"Perhaps Lucca and Giovanni—"

"Your nose is for sniffing, not poking," he warned me. "It does not concern you."

"But it does concern me. *Potta!* If some fool decides—"

"There is a ten *scudi* fine for swearing," Tommaso interrupted, holding out his hand. "Give me ten *scudi*."

"Ten *scudi!* I do not even have one."

Tommaso nibbled the nail of his little finger (all his nails were bitten to the quick), and his brown eyes stared at me from beneath his thatch of curly black hair. His eyes were a little too close together and his two front teeth too big for his mouth. His face had several pock-marks. My mother had warned me each mark was a lie the person had told. "You owe me then," he said. "Come on, this way."

Sometimes after the rains, when the grass sprouted up through the earth and the flowers burst into bloom, I had dreamed of a huge garden full of cauliflower, garlic bulbs, cabbages, rows of carrots like marching soldiers, and so on. Now Tommaso led me to a garden filled with every type of vegetable I had ever known and many I had only heard of. Beans, garlic, cabbages, carrots, onions, curly lettuces, eggplants, mint, fennel, anise, all neatly arranged in rows with little paths between them. "This is where I work," Tommaso boasted. "It is only for Federico and his family."

"You are in charge of all of this?"

"Me and an old woman. But I do all the work. Not even the pope has a garden like this. You have never seen anything like it, have you?"

I said I had not. He prattled on about how important his job was and would have gone on for hours had I not interrupted him saying, "Tommaso, you have lived in the palace all your life. You know everyone. I do not care what happens to me—I trust God will protect me—but my daughter, Miranda. She is young. She—"

"You want my help?"

"You work with the food. I wondered—"

"Do you want me to help you?" he repeated, folding his arms.

"Yes, but I cannot pay you. Whatever we agree—"

"How old is Miranda?"

"Ten, I believe."

Tommaso cocked his head to one side. "Marry her to me when she is thirteen and I will be your eyes and ears in the kitchen."

"Marry her?" I laughed.

His face turned red. "Do you not think I am good enough?"

"No, it is not that. It is just that she is a still a child."

"My mother was married when she was fourteen."

"Then when Miranda is fifteen," I said.

"Twat!" he spat on the ground. "I gave you amulets! I fed your daughter out of the goodness of my heart. You see how much I know about the palace. You ask for my help and this is how you repay me?"

In the blink of an eye he had worked himself into a rage, waving his arms about and turning as red as a beet so that I barely recognized him. Other people were looking over at us. I remembered my mother saying "Hot heads lead to cold graves." I said to myself—much can happen in four years—my whole life had changed in four minutes—so why not agree with him. "Fourteen then. When she is fourteen."

Tommaso stuck out his arm. I took hold of it. "We will not tell anyone now."

He shrugged. "As you will."

He started to pull away, but I held him fast. "You must be good to her because if you harm her, I will kill you."

"I will treat her as a princess," he said, "as long as she behaves like one."

Just then two serving boys called to us. They said Tommaso was wanted in the kitchen and I had to taste the duke's breakfast.

"What has Tommaso been telling you?" a serving boy asked as we climbed the stairs to Federico's chambers.

"About the palazzo and the people who live here."

"What have you been telling him?" asked the other.

"Nothing. I have nothing to tell."

"Just as well," he said, and the first one nodded his head in agreement.

Something gripped my insides. "Why?"

"*Niente*," they shrugged. "Nothing."

I wanted to know more, but guards were leading us through Federico's apartment to his bedroom.

After we had been searched for weapons, the serving boys knocked on Duke Federico's chamber. His doctor, Piero, answered. A short fat Jew, Piero was bald except for a few stray hairs on the top of his head. He smelled of fat, which he mixed with ground nuts and rubbed into his scalp to keep those same few hairs from falling out.

"Breakfast, My Lord," Piero laughed. He laughed after everything he said whether it was funny or not.

"Food!" roared the duke. "I have not shit for three days and you want me to eat more food?"

Piero's right cheek began to twitch. Another voice, lower and calmer, said something I did not hear.

"Oh, bring it in," came the duke's voice again.

We entered the duke's bedchamber. It was unlike any room I had ever seen. The floor was covered with thick carpets of many colors and tapestries hung from the walls showing men and women making love. In the center of the room stood a bed big enough for my whole family to have slept in. It was surrounded by deep red velvet curtains and covered with silken cushions and sheets that shone in the sunlight. The bed was raised up from the floor and when the duke sat up, as he was doing now, he was as tall as any man standing next to him. His thin, wispy hair lay like thin strands of wet pasta about his head, his eyes were runny and his face blotchy, and a great mass of hair poked out of his nightshirt. He did not look like a duke at all, but like a fishmonger I knew at the market.

The duke was listening to the solemn gray-bearded man, Cecchi, his lawyer and chief adviser, who was saying, "I told him since it was your birthday you assumed the horse was a gift, and it would not reflect well on your friendship if he were to ask for it back."

"Good," Federico said. "I will ride him later. Bernardo!" An untidy-faced man with scraggly hair and shifty pale blue eyes, Bernardo spat a mouthful of fennel seeds into his hands, scurried over to the bed and lay some charts in front of the duke. "Your Honor, Mars is on fire while Mercury and Saturn are cold. Now since Mars—"

"But is that good?" demanded the duke, slamming his hand on the chart.

"It is good for war," said Bernardo slowly. "Otherwise it is better not to do anything."

The duke sank back on his cushions. "If it were up to you, I would stay in bed all day."

Bernardo frowned and stuffed some more fennel seeds into his mouth as if this would prevent him from having to answer.

"Your Honor," said Piero, stepping forward on tiptoe, "I think—"

"You think?" said the duke. "You do not think. You do not know how to think. Leave me! All of you. Leave me!"

"Not you," the serving boy muttered to me. He gave me the bowl and followed everyone else out of the room, leaving me alone with Duke Federico.

Because we had spoken in the hallway during the night, I thought the duke would remember me, so I bowed and said, "Good morning, Your Excellency. I hope you slept well and that God brings you many blessings."

He stared at me as if he had never seen me before. "You are not here to talk to me," he yelled. "You are here to taste my food. Have you?"

"No, I—"

"What are you waiting for?"

I lifted the lid and saw a bowl of bubbling polenta covered with raisins. The steam sprang out, burning my face. There was only one spoon. As I raised my hand, the duke yelled, "Clean them," and pointed to a pitcher with a handle shaped like a naked woman.

Christ on a cross! Before last night I never washed my hands from one month to the next and now I was washing them twice in one day. I soon discovered Federico was so afraid of being poisoned that he insisted everything had to be clean. He changed clothes several times a day, and if he saw even a shadow of a spot on his clothing or a tablecloth or a curtain, it had to be washed again. I did not understand what that had to do with poisons, but no one was asking me, and if that is what he wanted who was I to tell him he was wrong?

I poured water into the bowl and rubbed my hands in it. Out of the corner of my eye, I saw the duke clamber out of bed and pull aside a beaded curtain. He raised his nightshirt and sat on a chair with a chamber pot underneath. He grunted and groaned and farted like a cannon. I pulled the amulet bone out of my pouch and dipped it into the porridge to see if it changed color. But I did not know how long to leave it in or if I should ask the duke's permission before I did so. What if he said no? He farted again, a great smelly fart all the perfumes of Arabia could not have hidden. I dipped the bone into the polenta.

The duke moaned. His back was toward me, his nightshirt raised above his waist. He was bending down staring at the chamber pot between his legs. I was so startled by his huge white *culo* that I dropped the bone into the porridge. I put my hand in to take it out, but the polenta was so hot I nearly screamed in pain.

"What are you doing?" asked the duke. I had stuffed my fingers into my mouth. "Tasting, Your Honor."

The duke climbed back into the bed. For the second his back was turned I dipped my hand into the water. "Give it to me," he said.

I gave him the bowl of polenta. The duke lifted a spoonful up to his mouth and swallowed it. I prayed he would not scoop up the bone.

"The last taster used amulets and stones and horns," he said. "Do not use any of them. I want you to taste EVERYTHING." He swallowed another mouthful and made a face. "Go. Take that with you." He pointed to the chamber pot. My thoughts were jumping around like a bat caught in the daylight. If the duke found the bone I would say that Cristoforo had put it there. I picked up the chamber pot. "Take this, too," he said, and handed me the bowl of porridge. By a blessed miracle, he had not seen the bone.

As soon as I was outside I pulled out the bone. It had not changed color so the porridge was not poisoned. But what color would it have changed to if it *had* been poisoned? And if the bone had changed color, what should I have done? Would Federico have made me taste it anyway? Each question led to another, and none of them led to an answer.

# X

In the months that followed it became obvious that although many people feared and hated Federico, none were brave enough to kill him. Every moment of his life was protected either by a taster like myself or by guards who accompanied him wherever he went. They were posted outside his room and below his window. They listened for malicious gossip and wandered through the town looking for assassins. They looked under his bed before he slept. *Potta!* They would have looked up his *culo* if he suspected someone was hiding there. He also employed spies. Anyone could become a spy if they had useful information, and so even as the weather changed from one season to another, the climate of fear was always present in the palace.

The only people who did not fear Federico were Giovanni the hunchback and his sister Emilia, Federico's wife. Giovanni I have talked about so I will tell a little of Emilia, but only a little since she herself was no more than a small ball of fat with a voice of a crow and breasts which stuck out of her *camora* like pigs' bladders. She spent her time collecting paintings and sculptures, planning her flower garden, and writing letters to her relatives in Venezia and Germany, complaining how Federico consorted with the town whores. The whores claimed Emilia tried to poison them. Whether it was true or not I did not know, but I was glad I did not have to taste *her* food.

Even though Tommaso was now my eyes and ears in the kitchen, I still feared tasting the capons or kid or venison, asparagus, eggplant, peeled cucumbers dressed with salt and vinegar, fava beans, sweetbreads, pastas, almonds in milk, pies, tortes, and the thousand other dishes Federico ate.

Anyone reading this might think that I soon became fat, but since I only ate a little of every dish and many of them, such as apples and cherries, were for cleansing the bowels, added to which I did not enjoy what I was tasting, it is a wonder I did not starve to death. As it is, I am as thin now as when I first arrived in the palace five years ago. However, in two months' time when the wedding is over, I will sit down at the table and eat to my heart's content. Not just one helping either, but as many as I can. But to return to my story:

What eased my nervousness during the meals was listening to Septivus read. It was from Septivus that I heard of Julius Caesar, from whom Federico claimed he was descended, and also of Socrates, Homer, Cicero, Horace, as well as parts of the Bible. Or at least the beginnings of these stories; for if Federico became bored he would order Septivus to start a new tale. So it was not till Miranda taught me to read that I discovered that Odysseus arrived home safely or that Julius Caesar was assassinated!

Even if Federico was not bored he changed his mind so often that no one could tell what his mood would be from one moment to the next, except of course when he had not shit or when his gout flared up. Then he was more dangerous than a hungry wolf. For putting seven raisins in his polenta, a kitchen servant was flogged. For disagreeing with him, a kennel keeper was thrown down the mountain. It was best to avoid him, but as if he knew that he demanded that we stay close. We hopped from one leg to the other trying to guess which way to jump in case one of Federico's rages descended upon us.

Not that it was that different when he was in a good mood. Then he amused himself by throwing gold coins down into the streets of Corsoli to watch the peasants fight in the mud for them or he encouraged the courtiers to jostle for his favor. I remember one evening Federico had finished a new recipe of fried artichoke bottoms—I hated new recipes because I did not know what they were supposed to taste like—when instead of calling on Septivus to read, he pushed away his trencher and said, "I have been thinking that the world is shaped like a triangle. What say you?"

O my soul! I could hear the courtiers' brains clanging around in their heads as if a madman had been let loose in the campanile of Santa Caterina! They scrunched their faces up and stared at their half-eaten artichokes as if the answer lay among its leaves. Piero's tic started violently.

Septivus said, "To the immortal Dante, three is the highest number because it represents God the Father, Christ His Son, and the Holy Ghost. Thus it is only right that our world would reflect the Holy Trinity and be a triangle."

Federico nodded and bit into an orange.

Cecchi scratched his beard and furrowed his brow. (He always looked as if he had witnessed some tragedy that was forever replaying itself in front of his eyes.) "I must agree," he said. "Our lives are divided into three—past, present, and future. Since we are a mirror of the universe, it is only natural that the universe would also be in three. What I mean is, three sides, as in a triangle."

This was also clever for since Federico had not objected to Septivus's answer, Cecchi was wise to climb on its back.

"I too agree," Bernardo said, spitting some fennel seeds over his shoulder, "but for sounder reasons. In numerology, to which astrology is closely related, three is the highest power. Now it is well known that the stars, the moon, and the sun govern the earth; therefore, the earth reflects the wisdom of the heavens and thus the earth is unquestionably a triangle."

"Not just a triangle," Piero giggled, terrified he would be left out. "But a special triangle that has two long sides and one short side. And Corsoli," he said, when everything had become so quiet we could hear Federico's orange digesting, "is at the topmost point."

Federico stared at him as if he had spoken in Greek. Then he looked around the table, gobbled another piece of orange and said, "It was a stupid idea."

Again everyone was still. Then they burst out laughing, slapping their sides and wiping their eyes as if it was the funniest thing they had ever heard. Federico raised the tablecloth to wipe his chin, and I, who was standing behind him and a little to one side, saw him smile.

Piero said, "If my good friends will allow me to speak for them, let me say the duke has made us all feel very foolish. However, we do not hold this against him; indeed, we welcome this feeling of ridicule because of the skill with which the joke was delivered."

The others nodded. Federico swallowed the piece of orange. He snorted, coughed, his eyes bulged. His face turned purple and he made a harsh scraping noise at the back of his throat. He lurched to his feet, arms flailing. Bernardo ran toward him, but Federico's elbow struck his face and knocked him down. Drool dribbled from Federico's nose; his eyes were glazed over. He threw himself first one way and then the other while the courtiers watched paralyzed with fear.

I had been waiting for a moment whereby I could prove my loyalty and so as he whirled away from me, I hammered both my fists into the middle of his back as my mother had done to my father when he had choked on a chicken bone.

A piece of soggy, mangled orange flew out of Federico's mouth and he fell face forward onto the table. Everyone looked at me—some with fear, others with surprise. Raising himself up, Federico turned around, eyes and mouth wide open. I thought he would thank me, but Piero and Bernardo (whose nose was pouring with blood) ran in front of me crying, "It was necessary to save your life, Your Excellency. Please sit down. Drink this. Rest, lie down," and so on, as if they had been the ones to save him!

Federico pushed them aside and staggered from the hall, Piero, Bernardo, and other courtiers trailing behind. Only Septivus and Cecchi remained. Septivus looked at me, a half smile displaying his little ferret teeth. He sighed and shook his head.

I said, "Did I not—"

"Yes, you did," Cecchi said quickly and followed after the others.

"But since it was I who saved him," I said to Tommaso later when we were playing cards, "I should be the one who is rewarded. I will tell him at breakfast."

"Save your breath," Tommaso shrugged and dealt another hand of piquet.

I threw my cards down. "Why should Piero and Bernardo be praised for what I did?"

"Getting close to Federico is more of a curse than a blessing."

"How would you know?" I was annoyed that he did not care for my welfare.

He stared at me, his eyes flitting from side to side. "Oh, do what you will," he said, and throwing his cards in the air, he kicked over the table.

# xi

It was not the first time Tommaso and I had argued. Christ! You could not ask him if the sun was out without getting into a fight with him. Not long after I had promised Miranda to him, he had complained to Cristoforo that he needed help in the garden. Cristoforo, who was only too pleased to do me ill, agreed Miranda would be a good helper. The days were growing shorter and the sun, having spent its summer strength, hid its weakened face behind a blanket of sullen clouds. Miranda often returned to our room muddy and cold. She did not complain, but at night when I held her shivering body close to me, her tears escaped under the cover of sleep. I told Tommaso she would get sick if she did not work inside the palace.

"Where? In the laundry?" he shouted. "So the lye can blind her?"

His shouting no longer had any effect on me, and besides I suspected the true reason he wanted Miranda to work in the garden was because he feared someone in the palazzo might steal her affection. I think it was for that same reason that he, who could not keep a secret any more than I could keep an ant on a string, did not tell anyone of their betrothal. I beseeched God, saying, "For all that You have given me, please take it away if it will ease Miranda's troubles."

God in His mercy answered my prayer.

One evening Septivus was reading the poetry of Catullus when Federico interrupted, saying, "I would rather be put on the rack than listen to this."

"A child would better understand," Septivus mumbled as we left the hall, to which I said, "I know such a child," and told him how Miranda had learned to read and write at the convent and could also sing and spin wool.

Despite his huge eyebrows which gave him a fierce expression, Septivus was gentle in nature for he said, "I only teach the children of courtiers. But if she is as you say, perhaps I can make an exception. Send her to me."

I ran to the garden and, without a word to Tommaso, pulled Miranda from her work and took her to the library. Before she went into Septivus's room I told her to remember everything the nuns had taught her and all would be well; then I pushed her inside. I pressed my ear to the door. I heard her speaking softly, reading perhaps, and then her small clear voice broke into song. Some moments later the door flew open and Septivus emerged, steering Miranda by the shoulder. "I will speak to Cecchi," he said. "She can start tomorrow."

In my haste I had not told Miranda why I had acted so and now she cried out, "Start what? What must I do?"

Septivus told her she would be studying with the other children.

"And not work in the garden?" she asked, her face lighting up like a candle in the darkness.

"Only for a little while each day," Septivus replied. "I will arrange it."

"You see how God protects those who serve Him," I said as I led her back to the garden. "Now you must honor Him by studying hard. It will also be good to meet the other children. One day you will become a maidservant. You will be seen by fine, wealthy men." I had not told her about my pledge to marry her to Tommaso, and if Tommaso said anything I would deny it. If Miranda could better herself then why should she not? As I had predicted, much could happen in four years.

Miranda, however, could not contain her excitement and, as I left, I heard her telling Tommaso that he would no longer be able to lord it over her since she would soon be a princess.

But the next day Miranda sat in the corner of the room picking at the scabs on her knees and refused to go to her class.

"But why? Yesterday you were so excited."

She would not answer. I said if she had not changed her mind after I had pissed I would drag her there myself. On my return I passed the garden where Tommaso was pulling up carrots and cabbages. I told him of Miranda's refusal to go to the class and asked him if he knew why.

He shrugged and opened his eyes wide to show his innocence. "But," he added, "she is right not to go. She will become vain and forget those who helped her."

I leaped across the path and jerked his head up by the neck. "Tell me what you told her or I will give you a blow your children will remember."

"I told her they will make fun of her because of her clothes," he stammered.

I boxed his ears and he ran away, swearing he would revenge himself. Then I found Miranda, pulled her dress from her shoulders, and took it to the laundry.

When my eyes got used to the sting of lye and the billowing clouds of steam, I saw that the dim shapes laboring over the boiling pots were mostly young girls no older than Miranda. There was also an older half-blind crone and the tall blonde woman whom Tommaso had told me was the slave from Bosnia. Their faces were red and sweaty, their arms and hands pink, rough, and wrinkled. I asked if one of them would be kind enough to wash Miranda's dress.

The tall blonde one, Agnese, who had a wide face and mouth, but a nose no larger than a button, raised her arm and pushed her hair out of her sad gray eyes in a way that moved something in me. Without saying a word, she took the dress from me and washed it. When she had finished I saw colors in it I had never seen before. I thanked her and returned it to Miranda. She kissed me over and over with delight, dancing around the room, holding the dress to her as if she was a princess. I lay on the bed, tears forming in my eyes, and resolved to do everything I could to make her happy even if it cost me my life.

The next day Miranda went to her classes. Except for Giulia, Cecchi's daughter, who was lame in one leg, the other children ignored her. This did not disturb Miranda for she enjoyed her lessons and practiced them in our room, especially the lyre, which she loved best of all. She still worked in the garden every day—Tommaso saved the dirtiest work for her—but since he often slipped away to his friends in the kitchen, Miranda did likewise, spending time in Giulia's apartment playing with her dolls.

Indeed, Tommaso seemed to have forgotten about Miranda altogether. The wind had whipped the peach fuzz from his face, hairs sprouted on his upper lip, and his voice no longer cracked. He swaggered around the palazzo in a new blue velvet jacket and matching blue hose, boasting how he would soon be a courtier. Of course, the kitchen boys teased him and threatened to cut up his jacket so he wore it all the time, even sleeping in it. It soon became shabby. He feared he would ruin it but was afraid to take it off. Eventually, he had to wash it and then hid it so it could dry. Someone must have been watching because when he returned, the jacket had been slashed into a thousand pieces. He fell into a maddened rage, weeping and threatening to kill whomever had destroyed it, which made the kitchen boys, who I am sure had cut it up, tease him even more.

I came upon him sitting by the stable. His face was puffy and red, and he was cradling the remains of his beloved jacket in his arms as if it was a dead child. I assured him he would soon get another but he burst into tears and fled from me.

The whole palace laughed at him, even Miranda, although when we were alone she surprised me by saying, "I wish I could buy him another because I cannot bear to see anyone so unhappy."

I still had not told her of her betrothal, and the longer I waited, the more difficult it became. But now that she felt so inclined toward him, I believed this might be the right time and was about to tell her so when she went on to say, "If only he did not boast so. I hate that." And the moment passed. I needed to ask someone's advice and so I sought out Agnese the laundrywoman.

In truth, I just wanted to talk to her. I had given her a ribbon for washing Miranda's dress, but one of the other washgirls had returned it to me, saying, "She still mourns her husband and her child."

"Tell her I will turn her mourning into dancing," I replied, but Agnese's ears were deaf to my words.

The underside of her arm and her pale sad eyes floated to me in my dreams and sometimes, when I walked past the laundry to glimpse her through the steaming white mist, my *fallo* got so hard I had to pull my shirt out to cover it. I spent hours thinking of ways to approach her and then one night, as I was carrying the remains of a platter of Federico's, I stuffed a piece of uneaten veal under my shirt, took it to the laundry, and offered it to her.

"*Non e velenoso*," I said, and took a small bite to show her that the meat was not poisoned. The other girls urged her to taste it. Agnese reached out her hand—her fingers and wrists had a muscular beauty to them—and put a small piece in her mouth. She chewed it, closing her eyes, moving her jaws slowly up and down as if she was not used to doing so. At last, when she had chewed all the juice out of it, she swallowed it and gave a little burp. Then she tore the rest of the meat into equal pieces and shared it with her friends. She made a space for me on the bench and I sat beside her in the dark, surrounded by the bubbling cauldrons and piles of laundry, watching the girls devour the veal. They did not talk and joke as the guests had done at the banquet. They savored each bite as if they might never have another, and when they had finished they said a prayer of thanks, kissed me on the cheek, and went back to their washing.

"*Grazie. Multo grazie*," Agnese said to me with such sincerity that my knees felt weak. I wanted to throw my arms around her and kiss the sadness from her eyes, but I simply nodded and said, "*Prego*."

In the weeks that followed, I snatched capon legs, slices of pork, a chicken neck, a wing of a bird, and small round cakes of dough with fennel seeds. I loved the way the girls stopped their washing the moment I arrived. I loved the way Agnese's eyes widened when she saw me. I loved the way she licked her lips to make sure she had not missed a crumb, how she patted her stomach when she had finished, leaned against the wall and pushed the hair off her forehead.

On the Feast of the Ascension I stole a fennel sausage, two roasted birds, and some roast lamb bathed in rosemary and garlic. "I could get hanged for this!" I said to myself, but I did not care. The girls shrieked and kept running to the door to see if someone was coming to arrest me. Agnese laid her hand on my arm (it was the first time she had touched me), and said "*Attenzione*."

"Do not worry about him," the old washerwoman laughed. "He could steal a halo from an angel."

Afterward, Agnese offered to wash my shirt because it was stained with sauce. Another girl offered to wash my hose, but Agnese would not let her. From then on she often washed my clothes and, no doubt because of her love for me, they fit me better than ever. I did not see how I could be any happier, but one morning at breakfast, Federico cuffed his serving man, saying, "Why can you not be clean and neat like Ugo?"

*Jesus in sancto!* Federico had noticed me not because I saved his life, but because my clothes were clean! I hurried to thank Agnese for my good fortune. No sooner had I started talking than she put her hand over my mouth and pointed to the girls who were taking their midday nap. Her hand was warm and I bit gently into the fleshy part of her palm. She gasped, but did not draw her hand away. I licked the part I had bitten. She looked at her palm and then into my eyes as if deciding something. Then, taking me by the hand, she led me through the sleeping forms, out past Emilia's garden, and we began climbing the hill behind the palace.

# xii

Agnese did not tell me where we were going and I was glad for the silence, because I was overcome with such longing that my mouth would have made a fool of me had I spoken. God's almighty eye beat down on us, causing us to bow our heads and place our hands on our thighs to push us higher. A herd of goats sleeping beneath the outstretched arms of a fig tree barely glanced at us as we passed. A salamander darted across a rock and disappeared into a patch of purple geraniums. Finches and robins sang from the trees, and in the distance a small gray cloud sailed across the blue sky, pulled by an invisible breeze. The hill was steep so I offered Agnese my hand, but hers was as strong as mine, and when I slipped it was she who stopped me from falling. We climbed higher, our breathing joining us together until not only our breath, but our footsteps and our thoughts, became one; and when we came to a clearing among the trees we threw off our clothes, fell on the ground, and embraced so tightly that the air could not find any space between us.

I kissed her mouth and the underside of her arms—she smelled of lye—and pulled open her shift so that her small breasts could free themselves. She was as hungry as I was, biting my lips and making soft mewing noises. Then she pulled me roughly on top of her and wrapped her legs around me to draw me into her. When I looked into her eyes the sadness had disappeared.

Suddenly, Agnese pushed me off her and, sitting up naked in front of me, she turned to look at her two white moons. They were filled with small red bumps for we had, in our urgency, laid down on an insect nest and they were angrily repaying us. But we were both too overcome with lust to stop and, quickly crawling through the grass, found another spot where it was long and soft and, turning Agnese onto her hands and knees, I mounted her from behind.

O my soul! What pleasure we gave one another! It seemed as if, having taken so long for us to find each other, nothing could interrupt our joy. The cloud covered the sun but we did not notice. A wind sprang up and still we continued our cries. Drops of rain splattered onto us, slowly at first, and then as if no longer able to bear its own weight the cloud burst and the rain poured down, dripping from my face onto

Agnese's back and from her back onto the ground. We were still making love when the sun came out again and we exploded together like fireworks on Midsummer's Eve.

Later, Agnese lay in my arms and I spoke words of love to her. She furrowed her brow as if she did not understand. So I repeated them slowly one by one, and then it dawned on me that she was mocking me because she broke into a smile as wide as her face—it was the first time I had ever seen her smile—and kissed me with great passion. I caressed her breasts. I pressed my lips to her marks of childbirth.

"He would be seven," she said, the words chasing the smile from her face. Then she pulled me to my feet and made me dance round and round, trampling the memory beneath us.

She did a cartwheel. She squatted and pissed on the ground in front of me. She caught a butterfly and, showing me its beating wings, said, "That is my heart." Like a girl half her age, she climbed a tree, her strong arms and legs lifting her easily from one bough to the next. Then she sat on a branch and sang a sad song in a small, tuneless voice.

"*Che c'è di male?*" I asked.

"*Niente,*" she said, and jumped into my arms. She took my face in her hands and said fiercely, "You must not tell anyone about us."

"But I want to tell the world."

She shook her head. "The world has taken my husband, my son, and my country. I do not want it to take you."

"What about Miranda?"

"Only Miranda."

I lay her on the ground for I wanted to put my head between her legs to taste her sweetness, for except for the freshly laid eggs I sometimes stole, she was the only thing that I knew would not be poisoned. But no sooner had I knelt between her knees than ants crawled all over my face. Agnese laughed, a great honking gooselike laugh that rang across the hillside. She curled up her legs and laughed until she was out of breath. Then she reached her arms out to me.

We had almost arrived back at the palace when a horse cantered past us. "It is Giovanni, the hunchback," Agnese said, and hid her face in my shoulder.

"He returned yesterday. We have nothing to fear from him."

"But no one must know," she cried, her eyes filled with worry.

"He did not see us," I assured her. "Without his spectacles he is as blind as a bat. You go first and I will follow in a while and then we will not be seen together."

I walked back to the kitchen lighter than the air itself, humming Agnese's tuneless little song. My blood trembled with delight. The serving boys immediately guessed that I had screwed someone but did not know who. "It was good, huh?" they laughed.

Because of my promise to Agnese I said nothing but, fearing that my good feelings would undo my lips, I left the kitchen and went to my room.

Miranda was standing by the window talking to the birds. When she saw me she twitched her face like Piero and stammered, "W-w-where have you been?" Then she growled like Federico, blustered like Tommaso and made me laugh till I cried. I wanted to tell her of Agnese, but since it was the first time she had been so playful in so long I was content to let her speak.

"Do you like my hair?" she asked. She had plucked the hairs from her forehead as was the fashion for girls at that time.

In truth, I did not like it, because it made her head look like an egg, but I said, "It makes you look very pretty."

"I want my hair to be blonder, too," she said, looking in her hand mirror. "I have been in the sun every day but it has not changed. Maybe I should get some false hair."

She would have gone on like this all evening had I not interrupted, saying, "Miranda, I have met a woman."

"A woman?"

"Agnese. The washerwoman. From Bosnia."

"Ah, with the blonde hair. I wonder if she—" her body stiffened. She put down the mirror and turned to face me. "Is she going to live with us?"

"I had not thought of that—"

"No! No, I do not want her to."

"But—"

"No."

"Miranda—"

"No!" she shouted and stamped her foot. Her outburst so annoyed me that I shouted back, "If I want her to and she wants to, then she will!"

She glared at me and turned away. I put my hand on her shoulder but she shook it off. I grasped both her shoulders, turned her around and forced her chin up to face me. "Do you think I will forget your mother?" I asked.

She nodded slowly.

"I will never forget your mother, I promise. But you must promise me something, too. You must not tell anyone about Agnese."

Her eyes opened wide. "I promise," she said.

For the rest of the afternoon I wondered why Miranda had lied to me, for even a blind man could have seen she was not thinking of her mother.

At dinner that same evening, Giovanni showered gifts on everyone to celebrate the wool contracts he had made. He gave Duke Federico a gold helmet encrusted with jewels, little trinkets to the servants, and showed off his new clothes, especially an English jacket which had been cleverly made to hide his hump.

"I could only stay a week in London," Giovanni sighed. "The ambassador in Paris was giving a dinner in my honor, *n'est-ce pas?* A countess in the Netherlands wanted to marry me, but *s'blood!* It is too cold there, *n'est-ce pas?*"

Every sentence began or ended with *"n'est-ce pas," "voilà!"* or *"s'blood!"* and for weeks after the servants called him "Miss Nesspa" behind his back. Giovanni again told Federico it was time to pay his indulgence for his cardinalship. Federico chewed his food and said nothing, but as the saying goes, "His silence spoke volumes," and as it pleased God, that was the beginning of my journey through hell. It began like this:

Whenever Giovanni returned from a trip he brought back a doll which was dressed in the latest fashion. His sister, Emilia, gave it to her dressmaker to copy and when he was finished with it, Emilia gave the doll to a daughter of a courtier. That was how Miranda's friend, Giulia, had received hers. However, this time Piero's child was the fortunate one.

"I will never get a doll," Miranda sulked.

"How do you know?"

"Because you are a food taster." She spat out the words as if they were poisonous.

"Ungrateful child," I shouted, grabbing her arm. "Because of me you eat two meals a day, you sleep in a bed under a sound roof. You have lessons three times a week. I face death every day! Is that why you do not want Agnese to live with us? Because she is a washer-woman?"

Miranda bit her lip. Tears leaped from her eyes. "My arm!" she whispered.

In my anger, I had gripped her so tightly that the bones were crying out. I let go and she fled from the room.

She did not speak to me for several days.

"You have no reason to be silent," I said. "I am the one who was insulted, not you!"

She still refused to speak to me. It was Agnese who came to my rescue. "Did you not tell me you were a woodcutter?" she said. "Why not carve her a doll?"

It was typical of Agnese's goodness that even though she was the reason for Miranda's anger, it was she who soothed it. Climbing the hill that afternoon with Agnese I found an old branch of an alder tree, and while she slept I carved a little doll. With berry juice from the kitchen, I painted a nose, a mouth, arms, legs, and hair. Agnese rouged its cheeks and when it was finished I lay it on Miranda's bed and hid myself close to our room. I heard Miranda enter and a moment later the door flew open and she ran out, shouting, "Babbo! Babbo! It is wonderful."

She cradled it in her arms, kissing it over and over. "Felicita! That is her name. Felicita!" Her eyes sparkled as she twirled around and around as she always did when she was happy.

I remember that day well because at dinner Giovanni began demanding yet again that Federico pay the indulgence for his cardinalship. His voice grew so insistent and his manner so impatient that his glasses fogged up. Taking them off to clean them, he peered at Federico, his big bulging eyes filled with anger. Federico chewed on a bone until he had finished and then, throwing the bone to Nero, said, "I am not paying that miserable goat one *scudo* and that is that!"

"You humiliate us," Emilia screamed. "If it were not for my brother, this palace would be a swamp."

Federico rose slowly, wiping the grease from his chin with his sleeve. I was standing behind him and, as he turned, he stuck his fist into my face and pushed me onto the floor. He would have trodden on me had I not rolled out of the way. The courtiers followed quickly, no one wishing to be seen with Giovanni, who remained at the table brooding, his sister Emilia whispering in his ear.

*Potta!* How long can you keep the lid on a pot before it boils over? Something had to happen. I did not know how, I did not know when, but I knew it would. Worse still, I felt in my bones it would affect me. I could not sleep. Little things—a hole in my hose, a platter being too hot, a sharp word—which would not have bothered me before now worried me. So when Miranda cried that Tommaso had thrown Felicita to the ground, breaking her arm, I went looking for him with murder in my heart.

I found him just before Vespers in the little chapel of the Duomo Santa Caterina. "Ugo," he said, swallowing a piece of apple, "I have been waiting for you." He moved into the middle of a pew so I could not reach him easily. "I have something to tell you." He wiped his mouth.

I did not answer. He looked around to make sure we were alone. "Federico refused to pay for Giovanni's indulgence again."

If he thought I would fall for his stupid tricks he was mistaken. "Wait!" he said, as I climbed over a pew. "Did you know Giovanni's mother Pia is coming from Venezia?"

"So?"

"Venezia!" He said it as if I had never heard of the place. "The city of poisoners." He went on, "They have a price list. Twenty gold pieces to kill a merchant, thirty for a soldier. A hundred for a duke."

"How do you know that?"

He shrugged as if it was common knowledge. "Lucca told me."

"Is this Pia bringing a poisoner with her?"

"Who knows? But if you were Giovanni and she was your mother—" he hissed. He did not need to continue.

"I think you are making this up to save yourself from a beating."

He clapped a hand to his forehead, then waved his arms in the air as if I had done him a terrible wrong. "You were the one who asked me to be your eyes and ears," he spluttered. "All right!" He made his way to the aisle. "On your head be it." He pointed to me as he walked out of the church. "And do not say I did not warn you." Whether his story was true or not, he had got out of a beating.

I did not follow him because part of what he had said *was* true. Everyone knew there were more poisoners in Venezia than there were Romans in Roma. They spent their days concocting potions and were only too eager to try them out. Any lord, rich merchant, or person with money, which Pia was, could afford one. I closed my eyes to pray, but it was not the face of God, or Our Lord, or the Holy Mother who appeared to me, but the grinning mug of my brother, Vittore.

The evening meal was like the first banquet all over again. My mouth cracked like winter wheat. My stomach shrank. I suspected each dish more than the one before and became so afraid that when the milk custard was served, I sniffed at it, held it up closely to my eyes, turned the trencher around, sniffed at it again, scooped a tiny piece onto my finger, tasted it, and said, "The milk is off."

Federico's lower lip dropped to his chin. "Off?" he said. "What do you mean, off?"

"It is sour, Your Excellency, I fear it will upset your stomach."

I thought he would thank me, throw the custard away and eat some fruit, but he swept several platters off the table and called for Cristoforo the cook.

"Ugo says the milk is off."

"It is his head that should be off," Cristoforo replied, sniffing at the custard. "My Lord, Ugo is a fool who has grown too big for his breeches."

"I have tasted the duke's food for nearly a year," I yelled at him, "and I know the duke's stomach as well as my own. If I am a fool, then you are a villain and the truth will soon be obvious to everyone."

"Are you accusing me of doing something to the food?" Cristoforo said, waving a kitchen knife at me.

"I am neither accusing you nor not accusing you—"

"*Basta!*" Federico said. He passed the bowl to Cristoforo. "Eat it." Cristoforo blinked. His goiter swelled up.

"Your Excellency, should Ugo not—"

"Eat it!" Federico roared.

Cristoforo ate a spoonful of pudding. "It is delicious!" he said, and ate two more spoonfuls. He burped. "Your Honor, if you wish me to finish—"

"No!" said Federico, and grabbed the custard from him.

"Shall I make some more?"

"Yes," Federico grunted.

I wanted to slip out of the hall while Federico was still eating, but I had barely moved when Federico said, "Where are you going?"

"He is going to eat some pudding," Cecchi said, to much laughter.

The servant boys told me that after I left they continued to talk about me, saying that for a servant to speak out of turn the way I did could only mean I had lost my mind for the moment. Piero said I was lucky the duke had not killed me for my rudeness and Bernardo added that if the chairs kept jumping up on the table the whole world would come to ruin. I did not care what they said because Federico had replied, "The more he wants to live, the better for me. But the next time he does something like this I will make him eat it just to be sure."

Cecchi gave Cristoforo some coins to ease his humiliation. Although I had been wrong about the pudding, it had turned out all the better for me. I was so relieved I wanted to take Agnese into the hills and screw her until my *fallo* fell off. But it was night, the gates were closed, and she would not let me touch her in the palace.

If Federico was concerned about Pia's arrival he did not show it. True, he killed a man in a joust, and confiscated a village and burned the houses, but he probably would have done those things anyway. He found a new whore called Bianca, who was pretty and well formed. For some reason she always wore a scarf or a hat which covered her forehead and in a certain light this made her look like an Arab.

"He uses her like an Arab, too," Emilia shrieked, as they left the table.

I understood why Federico preferred whores to Emilia. I could have understood if he preferred sheep, goats, or even chickens. There was nothing attractive about her form, her face, or her voice. I was told that when she was younger she had been slender, with a pretty face and a keen sense of humor. But living with Federico had soured her, and I did not doubt that she had tried to poison his other whores and would try to poison Bianca if she could—even Federico himself.

Thoughts of poison plagued me. Lying in the glade with Agnese, I dreamed everything I ate was green with decay and filled with maggots or that my stomach burst open and snakes and dragons crawled out. When I awoke, Agnese was sitting in her favorite tree.

"I can see Bosnia," she said. She told me what her son would be doing if he were alive. This talk had never bothered me before, but now my mind was crowded with Giovanni's sulking, Emilia's shrieking, and the arrival of their mother, Pia, from Venezia and I turned away from her.

But what could I do? For days I racked my brain until my head hurt and then suddenly it came to me. I could test my amulets! Why that had not occurred to me before I do not know, but God in His wisdom gave me the answer just when I needed it. To do so, however, I needed poisons.

As soon as I could I walked down the Weeping Steps to Corsoli. The steps had been built by Federico's brother, Paolo, and it was said that after Federico poisoned him, water trickled down the steps like tears even though it was midsummer. The night was warm, the last rays of autumn casting an orange glow over the city. The shouts of children echoed lazily through the streets, a lullaby wafted from a passing window. I turned a corner and there sat Piero dozing in a chair, his head bowed. I wondered if I should wake him when his eyes suddenly opened as if I had walked into his dream.

"Ugo," he said sharply. "What are you doing here?"

Without hesitation I asked him to instruct me in the effects of poisons and their antidotes.

"Poisons?" he laughed. "I know nothing about poisons." Rubbing his head as if he expected to find some new strands of hair there, he picked up his chair and entered his shop. I followed. Every shelf was filled with jars and bowls of herbs and spices, bones, dried plants, animal organs, and other things I did not recognize.

Piero nervously moved a pair of scales on the counter. "If the duke knew what you had just asked, there would be a new taster standing where you are in less than an hour," he said.

"Piero, what harm would it do to teach me a few things that could save my life and that of my daughter? Maybe yours as well someday. Or will you not tell me because you do not know anything?"

Before he could reply, I added, "Every week you bring new potions to the duke and he still complains he cannot shit. He cannot screw either." This last was not true.

"The duke said that?"

"No, Bianca did."

Outside, it had grown dark. The bell was ringing to warn everyone the gates were closing. The voices of the watch came toward us.

"You are lying," Piero laughed.

The watch were walking past the door.

"No, I am not!" I replied loudly.

There was a knock. "Piero? Is everything all right?"

Piero stared at me. If I was found in the shop it could be trouble for both of us. I opened my mouth as if to speak again and he blurted out, "Everything is good."

"*Buona notte.*"

"May God be with you."

We stood in the darkness till the voices had faded.

"I could be killed for this," Piero said, "If people see us together they will think we are plotting against Federico."

I told him I was a spy for Federico; how else would I have dared to speak to him like that? I swore I would keep my visit so secret I would not even tell myself.

He hemmed and hawed. "If you want to know about hemlock then read the death of Socrates. That is all I can tell you."

"Who was Socrates?"

"You do not know who Socrates was? He was a Greek who was ordered to drink poison because of crimes he committed against the state. But before he drank it he asked if he could propose a toast. Now *that* was a brave man." I nodded although it sounded foolish to me. "In the middle of dying, he told his friends to pay off one of his debts."

That sounded even more foolish, but for once I held my tongue. "What is this?" I picked up a jar full of pink petals from a shelf. "I have seen it before."

"Leave it, leave it!" He took it from me with his fat little hands. "It is meadow saffron. Deadly. Very deadly. One bite and your mouth burns like the flames of hell. You suffer violent stomach pains for precisely three days. And then you die."

So he *did* know about poisons, and I could tell that with a little flattery he would be only too happy to teach me everything he knew. "You must be very brave to live among so much death. I would be scared."

"Ugo," he said, allowing himself a small smile, "Neither of us is a fool, huh? As long as you know what you are doing there is no danger."

"But do poisons always take days before they—"

"Kill someone? No," he said, carefully replacing the jar. "Bitter almonds take just a few hours and are even more violent. I have never used them," he added hastily, "but I was told a woman in Gubbio poisoned her husband in this manner."

"Is that what Federico used to kill his brother?"

"No, that was aconite." He stopped. "I did not—" he began.

"What about Lucca?"

"Lucca? Lucca was filthy. He did not wash enough, there was dirt under his nails. Federico just told everyone he tried to poison him to scare—" he stopped. His cheek twitched. "I have spoken too much."

"I have seen this, too." I said, and quickly held up another jar.

"Yes, dandelion. That is nothing. But this," he picked up another jar, "this is wolfsbane. You must have seen it, it grows everywhere. It makes the body tingle and the hands feel furry like a wolf. Then you die. You always die. Sometimes you bleed, sometimes you shit, sometimes you do both. But you always die. And it is always painful. This is henbane," he said, showing me a smelly green plant. "It grows best in human shit." Now that his excitement had been unbound he wanted to show me every page of his knowledge. "You have heard of Cesare Borgia? He invented a concoction called *la tarantella*." He closed his eyes as if he was making the potion. "It is the saliva of a pig hung upside down and beaten until it goes mad."

I asked how long he thought that would take. He giggled. "No more than three days, because is that not how long it would take for you to go mad if you were hung upside down and beaten? But all the poisons together are not as deadly as this." He held up a small jar of silver-gray powder. "Arsenic. Just half a fingernail can kill a man. What is more, it is tasteless and odorless. There is immediate vomiting and uncontrollable diarrhea, as well as sharp blinding pains in the head as if someone had drilled nails into the skull. Oh, yes, and terrible itching, too. Some people also experience a giddiness and bleeding through the skin. Finally, complete and utter paralysis."

He licked his lips, nodding to himself as if he was making sure he had not left anything out. "In ancient Romagna, emperors would eat tiny amounts every day to build up a resistance to it."

"Did it work?"

"Who knows?" he tittered, as he returned the jar to the shelf. "They are all dead."

"What would a poisoner from Venezia use?"

"From Venezia?" He faced me. "Is someone coming from—?" His cheek twitched again. He dipped his hand into a jar of fat, absentmindedly rubbing it on his head. "What have you heard?"

"Nothing. I was just asking. *Buona notte*."

As I returned to the palace, clutching the small amount of arsenic I had stolen, I could not forget the look on Piero's face when I said Venezia. If only for a moment, a ray of hope crossed his eyes like a bird flying across a setting sun; a fleeting ray of hope which served to remind me that even as I was trying to protect Federico, no one would be sorry to see him dead.

# xiii

Pia arrived on a crisp September afternoon with a train of courtiers and servants. She was wrinkled, plump, and even smaller than Emilia. From a distance she looked like a white raisin. She brought a horse for Federico, dresses for Emilia, and gifts for their sons, Giulio and Raffaello. She shared Giovanni's apartment, which she said was too small, and the first night demanded that Federico add a wing to the palace. "Use my architect. He is a student of Candocci. Everyone says my palazzo is the most beautiful in Venezia."

She wandered about talking to anyone she pleased, grabbing them by the elbow and asking them why they did what they did, and telling them how much better and easier it was done in Venezia. Her voice was as loud as a trumpet, twice as shrill, and could travel through walls. She played backgammon with Emilia and Giovanni or cards with Alessandro, her chief adviser. I studied her courtiers closely and was convinced that if any one of them was a poisoner it was Alessandro. He dressed in black from head to toe, had a huge forehead like a slab of white marble, and silver hair which swept back to his shoulders. There was always a golden toothpick stuck between his teeth like a twig of an unfinished nest. Once, when he, Giovanni, Emilia, and Pia were sitting together, I saw Death hovering about them.

Pia insisted her meals be cooked with butter instead of oil; she said it was fashionable in Germany where she had cousins, and she demanded nuts in everything. "They are good for the blood," she screeched. "Federico, why do you not eat calamari? Tell your cook to cut it into large pieces, boil it with some finely chopped parsley, fry it, and then squeeze a little orange juice over it. My cook, Pagolo—Oh, I so wish I had brought him—makes it twice a week without fail. I could live on it. Emilia tells me you do not eat peaches. Is that true?"

"He thinks they are poisonous," Emilia cackled.

"Just because an ancient king who could not overcome some Egyptians sent them all poisonous peaches," Giovanni said.

Federico's bottom lip fell to his chin. Pia, Emilia, and Giovanni did not notice or if they did they did not care.

Two days later, Tommaso told me he had seen Cristoforo whispering with Alessandro. "Christ! I knew in my bones that pig was treacherous," I said, and warned Tommaso to watch his vegetables carefully.

"You are the one who has to be careful," he replied.

He was right. I did not have the time to experiment with mad pigs. The days were passing swifter than a weaver's shuttle, and as the saying goes, "God helps those who help themselves."

I drank wine with Potero, the keeper of the duke's goblet, and when he fell asleep, I used his key to open Federico's cabinet. Federico's goblet was larger and more magnificent than any other. It had an elegant silver stem and a golden head upon which a lion, a unicorn, and a crab had been beautifully engraved. I filled it with wine and sprinkled in a pinch of arsenic. The arsenic dissolved and I waited for the rainbows to appear on the surface of the wine or for the wine to hiss and sparkle as if it was on fire. Nothing happened. I dipped the unicorn bone into it. According to Tommaso the wine was supposed to froth. Still nothing happened! Perhaps it was the arsenic. Maybe Piero did not know what he was talking about. More likely that fool Tommaso had misheard or misunderstood!

I found a half-starved tawny cat and offered her the wine. She lapped at it eagerly, stretched her front paws, and walked away, satisfied. She had not gone more than a few steps when she stumbled, her back legs crumbling beneath her. She looked up at me, her yellow eyes questioning me in the darkness. Then she lay down, whining pitifully, and her back stiffened into an ungodly shape. She gave a sigh, trembled, and then lay still. O blessed Jesus! There was nothing wrong with the arsenic. It was the amulets! The bone! The goblet! They were useless! They were worse than useless because they had filled me with false hope.

I held the goblet in my hand, uncertain what to do next. Then something occurred to me. What if I left a little arsenic in the goblet? And Federico drank it? How would my life change? If no one cared that Federico was killed, then I would be a hero. But if someone did, there would be a hunt for the poisoner. I wondered if anyone had seen me with Potero. Piero would say that I had asked him about poisons. I would be put on the rack. My limbs would be torn apart. I would be hanged or perhaps buried alive head first. Parts of my body would be cut off as Federico had cut out Lucca's tongue. Then I would be thrown over the mountain.

Fearful as these thoughts were, it was not they which deterred me. No, I did not leave arsenic in the goblet because Potero would surely be the first to die and he had never harmed me. Moreover, whatever ills Federico had brought on others, he had saved Miranda and me from starvation. Finally, I had promised to protect him and I could not betray my promise to God. So I washed and cleaned the goblet with the greatest care and replaced it.

I did not tell anyone what had happened. Instead, I told Tommaso I had taken the unicorn's bone to Santa Caterina during the full moon and offered it to the golden Madonna. I looked around, and after making sure we were alone, I whispered, "At the stroke of midnight it grew warm in my hands and glowed in the dark."

He looked up at me disbelievingly. "What happened?"

"The Madonna told me that she has made it so powerful that if someone even thinks of poisoning the food, the bone will crack in half all by itself."

He held out his hand. "Let me see this miracle."

"There is nothing to see," I said, showing him the dark brown bone.

"Then how do I know you are telling the truth?"

"Because God is my witness."

Like everyone in the palace, in Corsoli, in all of Italy, Tommaso loved to gossip. Even if he knew something was not true, even if he had been with me and seen that nothing I described had happened, he could not resist telling the story—unless he could make up a better one. Can any of us resist if the story is good enough? I was sure mine was good enough, just as I was sure that by the end of the day every servant would know about the bone and by tomorrow the rumor would reach Alessandro. Some of Federico's cunning had rubbed off on me.

That evening, Federico ate heated calves' brains mixed with eggs, salt, verjuice, and pepper and fried for a very short time with liquamen. He shared some with Bianca.

"You horse's *culo*," Pia shrieked. "You bring this whore to the table in front of my daughter!"

Federico lurched to his feet, snarling. Nero barked and Pia knew she had made a mistake. Federico pointed to her and, driving a knife into the table, roared in a voice that must have been heard in Urbino. "You dare to insult me, you ball of pig's fat! From now until you leave, you will live in the tower!"

Giovanni immediately stood up and pushed himself in front of his mother. Eager to make an impression, a young guard lunged at him, but quick as a snake, Giovanni drew a short thick dagger from his belt and stabbed him three times. The first blow went into his chest. He was already dead when the second blow struck his thigh. The third pierced his right eye, the ball spilling out onto the table. The man fell into a heap at Giovanni's feet. The other guards froze and looked at Federico, who, I believe, was as surprised as they were.

Speaking in very measured tones, his eyes never wavering from Federico's face, Giovanni said, "Duke Federico Basillione DiVincelli, I have served you faithfully for many years, but I cannot allow you to insult my mother and sister. It would be best for us to leave Corsoli as soon as possible. I ask only that you give us safe passage."

O my soul! Those are the moments by which men are remembered! The way Giovanni addressed Federico by his full title, the eloquent manner of his address. *Potta!* Who knew that little sodomite had such big balls! A most curious expression, almost a smile, came over Federico's face, as if he had finally found his match. He nodded to Giovanni, who, knife in hand, led his sister and his mother out of the hall.

We could not have been more shocked had an earthquake struck Corsoli. The palace talked of nothing else and everyone guessed as to what would happen next. One day Federico was going to burn them in the tower, the next he was going to massacre them in their beds. He did neither, but instructed Cecchi to arrange for Emilia's, Pia's, and Giovanni's departure. The children would have to stay to ensure that Giovanni would not harm the wool contracts. Emilia begged and wept but Federico would not change his mind. For their journey back to Venezia, Federico agreed to a train of twenty mules guarded by a battalion of soldiers as well as all the servants they needed.

"It is very generous," I said. "There must be some other reason."

"This is but a drop of Federico's gold," Tommaso replied. "He is just pleased to be rid of them."

The first storm of winter swept over the mountains tearing down trees, changing the course of rivers, and drowning animals where they stood. Soaking, starving peasants swarmed into Corsoli besieging the poorhouses and the churches because the hospital was already full of sick feverish people. It was impossible to keep warm. The fires were no use because the wood and the very air itself were damp. Winds whistled through the rooms and hailstones the size of a man's fist broke the windows. Rain poured through holes in the roof and Federico sent servants to fix them. Lightning struck one man, killing him.

After three days the courtyards were deep in mud. Federico could not hunt or joust, his gout pained him, and he cursed everyone. Bernardo said that according to the stars the rain would let up in two days' time on *Ognissanti* (All Saints' Day) and if Emilia left then she would have a safe journey home.

"There is to be a farewell meal," I told Agnese. "I will be glad when they have gone." We were standing in the courtyard, looking toward the hills where the bonfires spluttered weakly. Because of the rain, the parade for *Ognissanti* had been canceled.

Agnese took my hand and placed it on her stomach. "I am to have a baby," she said.

"A baby? O merciful God, what joy!" I pulled her to me and kissed her small button nose, her sad gray eyes, and wide mouth.

She pulled away from me and motioned her head to where Giovanni was watching us from a window in the tower.

"Why are you so afraid of him?" I asked.

She shrugged.

"Because he is a hunchback?"

She shrugged again, burying her head in my shoulder. "He is just a man. A little one. Screw him, he will be gone tomorrow." And to show that I did not care I made the sign of a fig at him, shouted "I am to be a father," and kissed Agnese again. "Now I must tell Miranda. Soon the whole world will know." I rushed off and passed someone slipping out of the kitchen. I was too busy thinking about my good fortune to notice who it was. I had to ask Cecchi if Agnese and I could have a room together. I had to ask Federico for a position other than food taster. It was only then that I realized the man coming out of the kitchen had been Alessandro, Pia's adviser. But surely, I thought, he was locked up with Giovanni? New fears so overcame my joys that I could not even remember what I wanted to tell Miranda.

Bernardo was wrong. It poured with rain on All Saints' Day, but the decision had already been made and Pia and her family were anxious to leave in case Federico changed his mind. All morning, servants loaded Emilia's and Giovanni's trunks into carts and onto horses. The soldiers polished their swords and festooned their horses with banners. At noon, looking pale but proud, Giovanni, Pia, and Emilia and their courtiers were led out of the tower. Some of Agnese's fear had rubbed off on me, so to be safe I told her to stay in the laundry until they had left. "Now we are to have a baby, you must be even more careful."

She smiled and kissed me. The other girls said I would be a good father because I truly loved her. I looked for Tommaso, but I did not see him until I entered the hall. He walked past me and, moving his lips silently, said, "Poison."

# xiv

Are we ever more alive than when we are faced with danger? Every sense—seeing, hearing, smelling, touching, tasting—is heightened. Every nerve is on edge. We see nothing but what is important; everything else falls away like well-cooked meat from a bone. My mouth was dry, my armpits stuck to my sides. I had examined my amulets, experimented with poisons, but I was as helpless as a rat in a dog's mouth. I wanted to tell Federico of my fears, but he had said that the next time I suspected something was wrong I would have to taste all the dishes, so I remained silent. Bile rose in my stomach. My heart beat faster. My throat closed up. I could hardly breathe!

Federico sat next to Bianca at one end of the table while Emilia, Pia, Giovanni, and her advisers, who were dressed in their traveling clothes, sat at the other. First, in honor of the dead, came a white bean soup made in the Tuscan style with olive oil. Then Cristoforo laid a platter of capons in front of Federico. Federico passed his trencher to me and stuck his tongue into Bianca's ear. I watched Cristoforo leave the room. His goiter was its usual pink which meant he was unconcerned. The meal looked delicious and smelled even more so. Cristoforo had used more oil than usual. That was it! More oil would hide the poison. I sniffed at the trencher. Was that poison? I turned it to the side and sniffed at it again.

Federico's voice came at me from out of a mist. "Is something wrong?"

"Nothing, Your Excellency."

Even though I had made up the story about the unicorn bone breaking in two if the food was poisoned, I prayed it was true! As I bit into the bird I called on God, Christ, the Madonna, and every saint who ever existed. Then I tasted the capon on my tongue. O Lord be praised. I have said before that I had lost all enjoyment of food, and it was true, but when I sampled that first bite the pleasure which had been stored up for so long exploded into my mouth.

The meat fluttered, yes, it fluttered on my tongue. The olive oil had browned the bird to perfection and Cristoforo had added just a dash of mustard. The combination was so unexpected that my taste buds surrendered. I waited for an unfamiliar taste, for something to burn my palate. There was none. I passed the trencher to Federico. He picked up a breast and shared it with Bianca. Emilia looked away in disgust. I watched Giovanni, Emilia, and Pia picking at their food. Could I have heard wrong? Perhaps Tommaso was just amusing himself at my expense. I left the hall to look for him. He was not in the hallways or the kitchen. Thunder cracked, the rain beat down even harder. No wonder that cursed Socrates had been able to make a toast! He *knew* his cup was poisoned. But I could not go to Cristoforo and say, "You sniveling coward, tell me which dish you poisoned or I will cut your balls off, fry them in oil and make you eat them. And by the way, did you use hemlock or arsenic?"

"You are wanted," someone said. "They are going to serve the second course."

The second course consisted of fried veal sweetbreads with an eggplant sauce, cabbage soup, Federico's favorite sausages, and stuffed goose boiled Lombardy style—that is, covered with sliced almonds and served with cheese, sugar, and cinnamon. The goose liver was soaked in wine and sweetened with honey, and looked very appetizing.

"Hurry!" Federico groaned, handing me his trencher.

My hands were shaking. I tried some of the sweetbread and a little of the cabbage soup and the sausage. I felt no ill effects. The goose! It had to be the goose. Of *course* it was the goose! Federico loved goose, everyone knew that. I glanced again at Emilia and Pia. They used to be loud and raucous, but today they were silent. I thought—it is because they do not wish to attract attention to themselves!

The goose was placed in front of Federico. The hall was quiet except for the slurping of food and the rain beating against the window. Giovanni had hardly eaten anything. Thunder crashed over the hills.

"More wine," Federico shouted. I was afraid if he asked me to taste anything else I would die of fright. I nibbled at the goose and kept a small bit under my tongue ready to spit it out if I felt the slightest sensation. I handed the platter back to Federico. He did not even look at me. Bianca gobbled her food down.

It occurred to me that if I died right now I would never see Miranda again. This so disturbed me that I interrupted Federico, saying, "Honorable Duke—" and here I made a face that indicated I would piss on myself if I did not leave.

"No," Federico said, belching loudly. "Wait till after the dessert."

Cristoforo carried in the platter of cookies himself. And then I knew. It was the dessert. What better place to hide poison? Everyone knew Federico loved sugar ten times more than he loved goose, capons, or anything else. Each person was served several cookies shaped like beans and a skeleton made of almonds and sugar. "Ah, *ossi di morto*," Federico smiled.

He passed the platter to me. "Quick," he said, his big bruised lips salivating in anticipation. There was a flash of lightning. Thunder crashed again. Nero barked.

I picked up the skeleton. Oh, how clever of that little hunchback to use a skeleton. I thought—I will not bite the head because that was what Federico liked and anyone who had been in the palace for a while, as indeed Alessandro now had, would know that, and would therefore put the poison there. Instead, I raised the tiny feet to my mouth. Suddenly, I saw Tommaso looking at me from across the hall, his face a mask. I sniffed at the figure and could not part my lips.

"Come on!" Federico snapped.

"Your Excellency, I have reason to think Cristoforo—"

Federico looked at me with such anger I could not finish. "Eat it!" he snarled.

Pia and Emilia were looking at their figures. Giovanni was pouring himself some wine.

"To Miranda," I whispered and bit into the skeleton's feet.

I no longer have any memory of whether it was sugary or not. I swallowed. Lightning lit up the hall, illuminating the yellow teeth, the sharp little eyes and haughty noses. Thunder shook the foundations of the palace and now all the dogs started barking. I gulped. My throat! I grasped my throat! My hands trembled. My body shook and twisted. Something shot through my body. I raised my hand and pointed, "Giovanni!" Cursing, I fell back, crashing into a servant and onto the ground, my legs curling into my stomach, my back arched in the air as the cat's had done. I gasped. My tongue begged for water! Oh, water! Water! I could not control my cursed legs! They jerked backward and forward. I screamed. Chairs were pushed aside. Tables upended. I heard Federico roar, "Cristoforo!" I heard Emilia and Pia shouting above the thunder. Then came the clash of swords, and such bloodcurdling screams as I had never heard before.

Wind raced through the hall and mixed with the gurgles of the dying. Hands struggled to pick me up. I fell into a pool of blood. I was picked up again and carried out of the hall and into my room. The servants ran out. I could hear shouting and wailing and people running back and forth. The door opened again. I heard two people.

"God in heaven, have you ever seen anything like it?" I did not recognize Piero's voice at first because it was trembling so much. "He must have stabbed her six times in the face alone."

"Her mother, too." That was Bernardo.

"But why Cristoforo?"

"If Ugo was poisoned, then Cristoforo must have changed sides."

"But why?"

"It does not make sense. What about Alessandro?"

"He is pleading for his life even now."

"And Giovanni?"

"Who knows?"

Footsteps moved closer to my bed. Piero must have leaned over me for suddenly I smelled the fat of his hair. His hand felt my throat. "He is still breathing." He opened one of my eyes and then the other and stared at me. He leaned down to hear my heart and the fat on his balding head was right up against my nose. I thought I would throw up, but as I did not know whether it was safe yet, I pushed him away, sat up and, remembering the story of Socrates, pointed to Piero and said in a trembling voice, "Pay Tommaso the ten *scudi* I owe him," and sank back down again as if dead.

"What did he say?" Bernardo gasped.

At that moment the door opened and Miranda ran in and threw herself on my chest, wailing, "Babbo, Babbo!"

Her cries were so pitiful and heart-wrenching that even if I had really swallowed poison I would have roused myself from the dead to comfort her.

"The devil is fighting for his soul," Bernardo said, "and the devil has won."

"No, Babbo, no!" Miranda cried.

"Serves him right. He spoiled everything," Bernardo grunted and left the room.

I heard Piero whisper to Miranda. "Come with me. I will give you some olive oil. If you pour it down his throat you may still save him."

"Oh, please hurry," Miranda cried.

"Do not worry," Piero chuckled, "he will live."

I could still hear footsteps running along the corridors, and people shouting and yelling. Servants ran in to look at me and then ran out so as not to miss anything. Soon Miranda returned, lifted my head, and poured olive oil down my throat. Moments later, I was retching so hard I could have expelled Jonah himself. Miranda was overjoyed, weeping and kissing me at the same time.

"Babbo's alive," she kept saying.

Just then Tommaso came in wrinkling his nose at my vomit. "What happened?" he asked, suspiciously.

"What happened?" I gasped. "You fool! I was poisoned!"

Tommaso frowned. "Federico's food was not poisoned."

"Yes, it was," Miranda said angrily. "How can you say that? Babbo nearly died!" She would have beaten him with her fists if I had not whispered, "Miranda, please get me a piece of bread."

As soon as she left the room, I said, "What are you talking about? You said poison."

His eyes widened. "No! I would have told you if Federico's food was poisoned. He poisoned *their* food."

Christ on a cross! The puzzle had been upside down the whole time! Now I understood why Federico was so generous with the gifts, why he acted so surprised when I had fallen sick. He had planned to poison Giovanni, Emilia, and Pia and my pretending to be poisoned had confused everyone. But I still could not let anyone know the truth. "But why did Federico kill Cristoforo?" I asked.

"He must have thought Cristoforo had tricked him," Tommaso shrugged.

"But Alessandro—"

"Alessandro has been working for Federico since the moment he arrived."

How did Tommaso know this? To be sure I was not being trapped, I said, "But I *was* sick. The bone grew warm in my hand."

"You had better hope Federico believes you," Tommaso snorted.

Dressed in his armor, Federico was seated at his desk, his sword by his side. I had never seen him in his armor before, but I understood immediately how fearsome he must have looked on the battlefield. Bernardo, Cecchi, and Piero hovered behind him. Alessandro was not with them—Federico had imprisoned him until he knew exactly what had happened. I walked slowly toward Federico, for the retching had exhausted me. When I was in front of him he suddenly stood up, grasped my neck with both hands, and lifted me right off the floor.

"Why in the devil's name are you alive and my best cook is dead?" he roared.

The room spun around me. "Your Excellency—" My air was cut off. My heart beat in my ears and I could taste my own blood.

"My Lord," Cecchi exclaimed. "This is a blessing."

"A blessing? How?" Federico let me go and I fell to the floor coughing and spluttering.

"If Emilia and her mother had been poisoned, the pope would have blamed you," Cecchi explained. "But because Ugo fell sick everyone will know an attempt was made on your life. You were forced to take action against murderous assaults. Giovanni's leaving is proof of his guilt!"

I could have kissed Cecchi's feet. No wonder they called him "*Il Cicero di Corsoli*." It was a brilliant idea and for the second time in my life I praised God that this honorable and noble man had come to my aid.

"It is a pity Ugo was not killed," that pig Bernardo grumbled. "That would have been the best proof of Giovanni's intentions. We could still kill him."

"But if anyone asks him, he will say he was poisoned," Cecchi said.

"But I *was* poisoned," I said, and, struggling to my feet pulled out the bone which I had broken into two pieces. "The Virgin Mary said if I was poisoned my unicorn horn would break in two—"

Federico knocked the pieces out of my hand with one blow. "Leave me," he ordered. "All of you. Except Ugo." They hurried out.

It had stopped raining, but the wind was whipping around the castle to make sure that no one could escape. Federico leaned back in his chair and lowered his chin to his chest. His eyes became small and hard. "Cristoforo poisoned three skeletons. One each for Emilia, Pia, and Giovanni." He paused, waiting for me to speak.

"He must have poisoned yours as well, Your Excellency."

Federico reached across the desk. "You mean this one?" He lay the footless skeleton in front of me.

"Yes, Your Excellency," I said, indignantly. "That is the one."

"Are you telling the truth?" His eyebrows raised questioningly.

"The gospel truth, Your Excellency."

"Because if you are not, the rack will make you confess."

"My Lord, if you put me on the rack I will confess to killing Jesus Christ himself."

Federico scratched his nose and licked his lips. "There is only one way to find out." He pushed the skeleton toward me. "Eat it."

I stared at the cookie. "My Lord, if it *is* poisoned, then you will lose the best food taster you have ever had."

Federico's eyes did not waver from my face. "You are either very smart or very lucky. Which is it?"

"I am very lucky to serve you, Your Excellency."

Federico's face soured. "I was hoping you were smart. I am surrounded by idiots."

I cursed myself for not being braver. Federico rose from the desk, took out a key, went to a door, and opened it. Even as he unlocked it, part of the wall on my right moved slightly. I thought that Federico's key was moving this wall, but Federico did not look up. An eye peered into the room, saw me, and retreated into the darkness; and the wall moved silently back into place again. I was about to say something, but my words were stilled by the sight of thousands upon thousands of gold coins lying in a heap on the floor of the closet Duke Federico had opened.

He picked up two gold coins and threw them to me. "Have some new clothes made. Tell Cecchi I said you should have a new room."

"*Mille grazie*, Your Excellency, *mille grazie!*" He held out his right hand and allowed me to kiss it.

I left the duke's chambers as if I had been crowned pope. "Look at me now, Vittore! You poxy goat! And you too, Papa!" I shouted, "Look at me now!"

Miranda was rocking backward and forward on the bed, cradling Felicita to her bosom. I tossed a gold coin into her lap and cried, "We are to get a new room and new clothes. And you will have a brother for I am to be a father again!" I pulled her to her feet and swung her around the room. "I must find Agnese."

"No, Babbo," Miranda said.

"You do not want a brother? Very well, you shall have a sister."

She squeezed Felicita's neck as if it was just a piece of wood instead of her precious doll.

"What is it? Speak up."

"Agnese is dead," she whispered.

"Dead? No, she is in the laundry."

She shook her head.

"Tell me," I cried.

Tears poured down her face. The words burbled out in such confusion that I made her repeat them three times before I could understand what had happened. "Giovanni killed her! When Agnese heard the screaming she ran into the courtyard. He was coming out of the palace. The stable boys said he struck her down for no reason."

*Oi me!* How many times can a man's heart be broken without killing him? My mother. My best friend, Toro. Elisabetta. Agnese. My unborn child. All dead. Everyone I loved except Miranda. What was God telling me? That I must not love? Did that mean I would lose Miranda, too? I prayed to God but He did not answer me so I cursed Him. I cursed all the times I had prayed to Him and then, fearing He would avenge Himself, I wept, asking for His forgiveness, and begged Him to protect Miranda from me.

I have not written for several days because I ran out of paper. Septivus would not give me any more until his order arrived from Fabriano. It came today and so I will hurry and catch my story up to these present events.

The palace changed after the killings. After convincing Federico that he had not double-crossed him, Alessandro was rewarded with Giovanni's rooms and his role as ambassador. Tommaso was put to work in the kitchen and I was thrown into a pit of despair. The archbishop offered to bury Agnese in the graveyard, but I insisted that it be the glade where we had spent so many happy hours. I crawled on the ground weeping and tearing at my hair even as my father had done when my mother died. I sang Agnese's sad little song in words I did not understand. I climbed into the grave and held her close to me to remember her smell and the feel of her body. I cut off a lock of her hair. Then I wept all over again for the child I never knew. Cecchi came to fetch me, for Federico was soon to eat his evening meal.

I cursed Federico and said I did not care if he imprisoned me. Cecchi said Federico would most certainly do that and forced me to go with him. He warned me to hide my tears because it would upset Federico, but even as I tasted a capon bathed in lemon sauce, I was overcome with sorrow. Cecchi whispered something to Federico, who looked at me and said, "Ugo, I did not know Giovanni killed your *amorosa*. He is an evil man and you will be avenged."

"*Grazie*," I sobbed, "*mille grazie*."

Then Federico addressed everyone at the table, saying in a solemn voice, "There is no pain that time will not soften."

Everyone nodded and pleased with this morsel of wisdom, Federico turned to me again and said, "So stop crying!" and bit into his food.

Agnese's face appeared to me in my dreams and in my waking hours. Her voice called to me from behind every pillar and doorway. I lit candles in the Duomo Santa Caterina and begged God to forgive me for the part I had played in the killings of Pia and her family, for as sure as night followed day, I knew Agnese had been killed for my sins.

So drowned in grief were my senses that it was not until some time later that I realized servants I did not know were calling me "Ugo," and asking if I had slept well. They complimented me on my appearance, offered to do favors for me, and asked me to speak to Federico for them. One morning, the new cook Luigi, a man with stooped shoulders and a goatee, took me by the arm and whispered, "I swear on my life I will never do anything to harm Duke Federico or you."

"They think you were saved by a miracle," Tommaso snorted. "If they knew that you faked it—"

"But you are not going to tell them any different. If everyone is scared of me it will stop them from trying to poison Federico."

Tommaso folded and unfolded his arms—his tongue flapped like a banner in the wind for it was against his nature to keep a secret. It was in that moment that I recognized that it was his eye I had seen in the wall. He was a spy for Federico! That was why the serving boys had warned me about him my first day in the palace. That was why he warned me against getting too close to Federico. That was how he knew Giovanni's food had been poisoned. I did not tell him I recognized him. Even if he could not keep a secret, I could.

He was fifteen now and growing taller by the day. He did not like working in the kitchen—the spices made him sneeze—but I needed him there so I flattered him, saying, "One day you will be Federico's chef."

"And then Miranda will have to respect me," he said.

*Oi me!* I had hoped he had forgotten about Miranda, but she was growing prettier by the day, the other boys commented on it, and no doubt this fired his passion.

Miranda and I were given a new room with two beds, a beautifully painted chest, and a solid oak desk. Our windows overlooked Emilia's garden which, now that she was dead, was abandoned to the roses, daisies, and other wildflowers. At night their fragrances drifted up to our window and scented my dreams.

The biggest change of all came because of Bianca, Federico's new whore. She acted as if she had been born a princess. She looked haughtily at everyone, but issued her orders in a voice as soft as a kitten's purr, so no one knew which was the truer self. Perhaps because she had been a whore for so long (they say she had started at twelve), she knew exactly what men were thinking the moment they set eyes on her. Consequently, she could coax them into doing anything she wanted. Luigi inquired daily if there was a particular dish she liked. Bernardo hurried to consult the stars for her every morning, even making up excuses so that he might see her more often. Even Cecchi ordered special wines from Orvieto, Urbino, and Roma for her.

Bianca bought new clothes and jewelry, rearranged the furniture, and held little parties for her old friends. The sound of the whores gossiping made the wives of the courtiers jealous, but the men never said anything. She was careful never to offend Federico, but if, for some reason, his lip fell down to his chin, Bianca took him by the hand and led him back to her room. I do not know what they did behind those doors but sometimes he was too exhausted to leave for days. And when he did, he was smiling! It is the gospel truth! He hunted, he falconed, he played tricks to amuse himself—he ordered a lame woman to dance with a blind man—and insisted that I be with him at all times. Not that he spoke to me unless it was about food, as when after tasting Luigi's specialty of veal wrapped in bacon and toasted on bread, he turned to me and said, "This is excellent. I should have killed Cristoforo long ago."

To be respected by Federico eased the pain of Agnese's death and so I took my task with even greater seriousness. I spent time in the kitchen learning how different dishes were prepared, how long they had to be cooked, which sauces to use, and so on. I learned from Luigi that too many turnips brought on phlegm and that fava beans were good for men because they looked like testicles. I was so over-flowing with knowledge that it spilled out before I could stop it.

One day I advised Federico the veal needed more pepper. Another time I said the chicken should have been marinated a little longer. And he agreed! Once, just by sniffing a venison sauce, I named all the ingredients: marjoram, basil, nutmeg, rosemary, cinnamon, celery, garlic, mustard, onion, summer savory, pepper, and parsley. Duke Federico was so impressed he often asked me to perform this trick in front of his guests.

Now I felt truly at home in the palazzo. Federico trusted me. True, it was only in small matters, but does the acorn not give birth to the oak tree? I was sure I would soon be promoted to a courtier and prayed for an opportunity to prove to Federico that I could be of greater use to him. However, God in His wisdom decided that I was not yet ready for such a post. But *potta!* Did He have to use that ungifted little dwarf, Ercole, to tell me?

The only thing Ercole and Giovanni had in common was their size. Ercole was as cowardly as Giovanni had been brave and as stupid as Giovanni had been clever. Where Giovanni had changed his clothes to suit his mood, Ercole wore the same brown jerkin and hose every day of his life. Had Giovanni been able to straighten his hump he would have been as tall as any man, whereas Ercole was a runt when he was born and will remain one till he dies.

I have hardly mentioned Ercole because, aside from wrestling a sheep to death at the first banquet, the little turd had never done anything worth mentioning; and, since Corsoli relied so much on its sheep, he could only perform that trick once a year. Most of the time, he hopped around in the corner of the hall trying to appear even smaller than he already was by bending his knees and bowing his head and banging softly on his little drum, praying Federico would not notice him.

One evening, Federico idly tossed away a half-eaten trencher which hit Ercole squarely on the head. Ercole rose up indignantly, the fury in his little lined face causing me to laugh louder than I had ever done at his tricks. He hissed at me because he thought I had thrown the trencher. Then, when he realized that it was Federico who had thrown it, he immediately picked it up. But as he did so something occurred to him. I could see the idea blossoming in his brain. He moved his head from side to side, examining the trencher as if he had never seen one before. He sniffed at it like a dog. He turned it upside down and sniffed it again. The little squirt, the little piece of shit was imitating me! Federico nudged Bianca. The diners stopped eating to watch. Aware of this, Ercole sniffed at the trencher some more and again turned it this way and that. Then he broke off a tiny piece and placed it on the tip of his tongue. He stood with his legs apart, hands on his hips, eyes pointed at the ceiling, his big wide mouth and thick lips pausing every other instant to chew and think, chew and think, until he swallowed it with a big gulp and traced its path with his finger down his throat and into his stomach.

I knew what he was going to do next. He clasped his throat, spluttered, and coughed. He sank to the ground, yelling and shrieking, thrusting first one part of his body into the air and then another, distorting his face, clawing at the ground and yelling, "My bone! My bone!" Then he arched his back and slumped to the floor, silent as if dead.

Bianca burst into laughter and could not stop. She covered her face with her hands, uncovered it, saw me and laughed again. Then Federico started snorting and laughing, and banging his fist on the table. Immediately, the rest of the court began braying like the asses they were. I wanted to plunge a knife into Ercole's neck and pull it down to his little balls. To have a dwarf mock me in front of everyone! After all I had been through?

Ercole bowed solemnly. The applause went on. He bowed again. He bowed four times. Good Christ! You would have thought he had conquered the French single-handedly! Federico wiped his eyes and said, "Bravo Ercole! Bravo! Do it again!"

The laughter and applause inspired Ercole. Contorting his face, he tried to imitate my haunted looks with his short squat body, making him look even more ridiculous.

"Do you not think he is funny?" Federico asked me.

"Since I have never seen myself eat," I said, "I cannot tell if it is accurate or not."

"Oh, it is accurate," Federico laughed. "Very accurate."

I left the hall, the laughter ringing in my ears. I found Miranda's mirror and watched myself eat in it. Ercole's moves were clumsy, but they were accurate. I wanted to kill him.

"You cannot," Tommaso warned. "Federico likes him. If something happens to Ercole, Federico will know it was you."

Soon Ercole was giving performances to anyone who would watch and the very same servants who had praised me the day before now sniggered when I passed. I tried different ways of eating, but how many ways can you chew a piece of food?

"Federico will forget, Babbo," Miranda said, trying to calm me.

But Federico did not forget and asked Ercole to perform his routine whenever he had guests. Once when I did not sniff the food, Federico said angrily in front of Duke Baglioni, "Do it the old way; otherwise it spoils Ercole's imitation."

So like the pet I had become, I had to sniff the food and then stand by while Ercole made a fool of me. Whenever Ercole did his imitation, Federico told the visitors about the killings of Pia and her family. They must have retold my story when they returned home, forgetting some things and adding others so that the tale became as varied as the roads they traveled. I became known in cities as far away as Roma and Venezia.

I cannot deny this pleased me and I told Septivus I would soon be the most famous food taster in Italy. He smiled, gnashing his little yellow teeth together. "Dante tells us that fame is like a breath of wind that is forgotten as soon as it dies."

"No doubt that is true. But while the wind blows everyone else is touched by it."

"Yes," he said, "some to praise and some to curse."

How right he was, but I am ahead of myself.

Of course, since I was *only* a food taster, none of the diners could believe *I* had thought of faking my death. No, they assumed Federico had told me to do it to justify his killing of his wife and mother-in-law. Soon Federico was convinced of it himself, and once, while I was standing right next to him, he boasted to the ambassador of Bologna that he not only had invented the plot, but also had shown me how to fake the death throes!

I remember thinking about this one winter's evening. The nights came with increasing swiftness and the rain turned the white walls of the palace gray in front of my eyes. Stories, it seemed to me, were like the walls in that someone seeing them for the first time would never have known they were once white, just as someone hearing my tale from Federico would have never known the true story. If the listeners enjoyed the story, they cared little for the truth. Perhaps, then, Jonah was not swallowed by a whale at all, but had eaten the large fish. Or maybe Jesus had never been killed, but had climbed down from the cross and hidden in the cave. Perhaps, too, Socrates had not joked before drinking the hemlock, but had begged and screamed for mercy.

This did little to comfort me. The rain beat down harder. I wondered where Miranda was; she had not returned from her classes, and so I searched for her. Outside a room where she sometimes played, I heard a voice say, "Oh, Miranda, do not be so upset."

I peered in. A few of her friends were huddled together in front of a large fire, their heads leaning against each other, their arms around one another's shoulders as girls will often do. They were laughing at Miranda, who was sitting a little way off, hugging her knees under her chin.

"Anyway," Miranda said sullenly, "you are not doing it right."

"*You* do it then," a girl teased and the others joined in. "You do it."

Miranda bit her lip. She stood up (my hand trembles as I write this), and imitated me tasting some food. Ercole was limited by his talent, but Miranda was gifted and knew things about me even I did not know. After she had mimicked me eating, which made the girls shriek with laughter, she pretended to examine her throat in a tiny mirror. She coughed and gargled and stuck her fingers inside her mouth as if a crumb had become stuck between her teeth, something I often did when I returned to our room after a meal. She did this with great earnestness, twisting her face, licking her lips, wiggling her tongue, and digging in her mouth as if she was mining for gold. One girl laughed so hard she wet herself.

Suddenly, Miranda looked in my direction, and when our eyes met she immediately ran out of the room. Her friends chased after her while I turned my face to the wall so they would not see me.

Later, I asked why she had made a fool of me.

"How do you think *I* feel?" she said. She did not say it, but I knew what she meant. It was because I was a food taster. "I will never have a dowry worth anything."

I wanted to laugh but I feared I would choke. I had done such a good job of raising Miranda to be a princess that she was now ashamed of me. I left her and went to Ercole's room.

"If you are asking me not to imitate you," he said, leaning back in the little chair he had made for himself, "I cannot. God has granted me a gift which Federico loves. If you were talented, you would be able to entertain him, too."

I put one foot on top of the other to prevent myself from kicking the chair out from under him. "Well then," I said, "You should do it correctly."

"I do do it correctly," he said hotly.

"Not according to Federico. From where I stand, I hear things."

"What things?" He frowned. "What have you been hearing?"

I pretended it was difficult for me to explain. I wanted him to get so interested that his eagerness would cloud his judgment. "Well, I overheard . . ."

"What?" he demanded in his squeaky voice.

"Federico thinks you are not as funny as you used to be. He thinks your movements should be bigger and grander."

Ercole raised the tip of his nose, which was already pointing straight up, and looked at me suspiciously. "Federico said I should make bigger movements?"

"That is what I heard. I wanted to tell you because you know if you do not please Federico . . ." I did not need to say anymore.

The next time Ercole imitated me he chewed and waved his arms as if he was having a fit. No one laughed. Federico's lower lip dropped to his chin. Ercole became so afraid he picked up his drum and started banging it for no reason.

"What are you doing?" Federico roared.

"Your Excellency," he stuttered. "You said—"

"What? Do it properly," Federico said.

By now, however, Ercole was so flustered he no longer knew what to do.

"Maybe this will help you remember," Federico roared and threw a bowl of soup at him, followed by several knives, spoons, and loaves of bread till Ercole was hunched up like a little ball on the floor.

"I think he should be hanged," I said loudly. "He was given a gift by God which he has abused."

"Shut up," Federico said. There was nothing more I wanted to say. I knew Ercole would never imitate me again and now others would think twice before they tried. But God had not finished with me, and worse was yet to come.

# xvi

Our second winter in the palace, the winds drove the snow into huge piles which dotted the courtyard and the streets of the city. The boys made lions and birds out of snow and one morning Tommaso made a wolf sitting on its haunches. He used almonds coated with saffron for its eyes and a piece of leather for its tongue. He wanted Miranda to see it, but she refused, saying she was too busy reading the Bible.

"She is going to become a nun," Tommaso said, forming the wolf's paws. "She says she has no time for foolish things."

"She will have changed her mind by dinner."

He nibbled his nails. "She gives her food to the poor."

"How do you know? Have you been following her?"

He told me he had watched her kneeling in the rain in the Piazza Del Vedura and that had he not pulled her out of the way a soldier on horseback would have trampled her to death.

"Did she thank you?"

He shook his head. "She said I had no right to interfere in God's will."


Miranda was in the Duomo praying to a statue of the Virgin Mary. In between her entreaties I asked her gently why she was punishing herself so.

"I am preparing for the *privilegium paupertatis*," she answered, her voice filled with anguish and heartache as if she had just climbed down from the cross itself.

"Miranda, you do not have to have the *privilege* of being poor. You *are* poor. I am poor. This is because of the dowry, is it not?"

She turned away and went back to her prayers.

"You think because you will never get married you might as well devote your life to the church: am I right?" She did not answer. "Miranda, those nuns you admire so do not have to be poor either. They spend all day making things for free and then they beg for alms so they can eat. If they charged the churches just a little for their work, they would not have to beg from people like me who can ill afford to give them anything!"

"Begging reminds them to be humble," Miranda admonished me.

"Hunger reminds you how to be humble," I yelled. "*Basta!*"

But she did not stop. She continued to give her food away and would drop to her knees and pray wherever and whenever she felt like it. The old half-blind washerwoman said she was a saint. It did not matter whether I was angry or kind to her, Miranda would not listen to me.

"This will kill you and then what good will you be?" I pleaded, after I found her shivering in the snow. Her lips had turned blue and her teeth chattered. She recited Hail Marys and novenas to drown me out.

Two nights later I awoke to find her bed empty.

"She said God told her to go to the convent at San Verecondo," the guard at the gate said. I swear the gate guards are the most stupid of all God's creatures. It does not matter which city you go to, if the city has a gate and the gate has a guard, then the guard is bound to be stupid.

"This is madness! How could you have let her go in this weather?"

"She looked holy," he shrugged.

The sky was covered in a blanket of gray clouds. Soft, fat snowflakes fell silently like goose feathers from God's pillows. I ran as fast as I could, calling, "Miranda, Miranda!" A wolf's howl answered me. I prayed it had not found her and that I would soon catch her and if I did not it was because she had already reached the convent. The snow grew deeper. Every bush, each tree, each blade of grass was white. My shoes and hose were soaked through, my hands and face numb with cold. I called Miranda's name again, but the night swallowed my voice. I could not make out the hills and no longer knew if I was going in the right direction. Exhausted, I fell to my knees. As I knelt there I realized I was in the same position I had seen Miranda in. I wondered if this was God's way of punishing me for forbidding Miranda to do as He had wanted. I threw myself in the snow, weeping for forgiveness and promising God that if I found Miranda I would deliver her to the convent myself.

No sooner had I said this than a light came toward me through the trees. It was the Virgin Mary herself. She reached out her hand to me, saying in a soft, sweet voice, "Sleep. Rest. Then I will lead you to your daughter."

But another voice said, "This is not the Virgin Mary, this is Death." I rose to my feet and stumbled onward, plunging into the snow up to my waist, crying out to God to protect me. And when I was at my last breath I tripped over a body—Miranda.

I do not know how I returned to Corsoli for it was God alone who guided my footsteps. I knocked at Piero's house and though it was past midnight he woke his wife and children and ordered them to boil hot water while he covered Miranda in blankets. He bathed her hands and feet, gave her medicines, and, when I had to return to the palace to taste Federico's breakfast, watched over her as if she was his own daughter.

I spent every moment I could at Miranda's bedside, for Piero said her life was in danger. Tommaso brought soups and pastries—it was her illness that inspired him to become a cook—and I prayed and wiped the sweat from her brow.

I had never been inside a Jew's home and was surprised to see it was much like anyone else's. Since Federico was always complaining of some ailment, I asked Piero why he did not live in the palazzo.

"Duke Federico does not allow it because we are Hebrews. Besides, here," he smiled, "I am closer to the citizens of Corsoli."

Just then Miranda, whose face had turned from blue to white, gave out such a racking cough that it rattled the very bones in her body. She became feverish and cried out in her sleep. Piero said that although it did not seem so, it was in fact a good sign.

At last, through God's good graces and Piero's care—for which I could not thank him enough—Miranda was well enough to be taken back to the palazzo. She stayed in bed, and although Tommaso still brought her food and her friends inquired about her, she refused to see anyone. She did not say so, but I knew it was because the two smallest fingers of her right hand had withered as well as two of the toes on her right foot. She would never recover their use and wailed that she would never be able to walk again. I told her of soldiers who walked with only one leg and of an aunt of mine who walked all her life even though she had been born without a foot. I said she should give thanks to God and Piero that she was alive. This did little to comfort her. Indeed, she said I should have left her to die. "I have failed Santa Claire," she wept, "I have failed Our Lord."

I did not tell her of my promise to take her to a convent because, having found her, I could not bear to part with her again.

In the midst of her weeping there was a knock at our door. I opened it and there stood Bianca, dressed in furs, a hood studded with diamonds covering her forehead. "Is this where the little saint is hiding?" she asked.

I was so surprised to see her that she said, "Are you not going to ask me in?"

"Of course." And I stepped aside to allow her to enter.

She smelled of bergamot and musk and as she passed me she slid her tongue over her lower lip and smiled as if she knew secrets about me which even I did not know.

"Ah, here she is," she said playfully, and sat on Miranda's bed. She wiped away Miranda's tears and patted her cheeks. "We will fatten up these little beauties so they outshine the sun." Then she said to me, "Miranda and I have much to talk about so go away for a while. And do not listen outside the door. They all do," she winked to Miranda. "They are worse than women."

I walked into Corsoli and back again, wondering why Bianca had come to see Miranda. Was it simply out of the goodness of her heart? Beneath all her furs and jewels Bianca was still a whore; but, I reminded myself, many wives and mistresses of famous men had been whores. Certainly they knew the ways of men better than men did themselves. Bianca was no fool. She was Federico's mistress. She could help Miranda in many ways.

When I felt I had waited long enough I returned to our room. Miranda was alone, sitting up in bed, regarding herself in her hand mirror. A necklace of beautiful pearls hung around her neck. "Did Bianca give you those?" I asked.

"Yes," she said, trying to hide her excitement. "She invited me to her apartment."

"That is wonderful."

"But I cannot walk, Babbo. Even if I could, I could not go," she added earnestly, as only the righteous can. "She is a whore."

I was tempted to throw Miranda back into the snow, but instead I said, "Our Lord Jesus Christ turned away neither sinners nor prostitutes."

Miranda frowned, her big dark eyebrows knitting together in the center of her forehead, her teeth biting her bottom lip.

"What did you talk about?" I asked.

She tossed the hand mirror onto a nearby chair and held up her frozen fingers. "Bianca said they were not made for work and this was God's way of saying that I should not do any."

"I see. And what else?"

"She said I was the prettiest girl in the palazzo and that one day I would have a line of suitors waiting to court me."

"That is good news indeed."

"She said I must change my hair because this style is old." She reached for the hand mirror, but it was too far away so she threw off the covers, climbed out of bed, and picked it up. Then she realized what she had done. "Babbo," she breathed. "Babbo."

I took her in my arms. "If Bianca can make the lame walk, then maybe you should listen to her."

Miranda returned from Bianca's the next day wearing a beautiful bracelet and a red shawl made of the finest wool. Her face had been brushed faintly with powder and her lips were rouged to match her cheeks. The day after, her hair had been combed so that it curled softly around the edges of her face. She wore a little tiara and a dress that swirled about her when she turned. "How do I look?" she asked.

"Very beautiful." As indeed she did.

"I spent all afternoon at the dressmaker's." She held up her wrist to show off another bracelet. "Bianca says it is from the silver mines in Germany. They are the best in the world. Do you see these stones? You can only buy them in Firenze or Venezia. Now I have to practice my lyre."

The next week she returned, waving a little fan. "I danced, Babbo! I can almost dance as well as I could before. Alessandro said I danced as beautifully as anyone he had ever seen."

"Alessandro was in Bianca's apartment?"

"Yes, he showed me how to hold the fan so that no one would see my dead fingers."

"Bianca is turning Miranda into a whore," Tommaso complained.

He was jealous and angry that Miranda had not thanked him for the soup and pastries that he had brought her.

"Two weeks ago Miranda was starving herself to death. We should kiss Bianca's feet."

I did not kiss her feet, but thanked her for her kindnesses.

"Anything to get her away from those nuns," Bianca smiled. "She is a beautiful child."

"You are the mother she always wanted."

For a brief instant her face seemed older and sadder; and in a voice that was neither sultry nor haughty she said, wistfully, "She is the daughter I always wished for." Then she walked away, her furs twirling about her. "Make sure she practices her lyre and writes her poetry," she called over her shoulder.

The next day Miranda returned wearing a beautiful fur jacket Bianca had made for her. "Alessandro showed me how they dance in Venezia," she said, and demonstrated the steps he had taught her. In her fur jacket, her head held high, the girl disappeared into a woman.

Suddenly, Tommaso's warning came back to me.

"Miranda, please, do not wear that in the palazzo."

"Oh, I will not. I am saving it for Carnevale."

After Elisabetta died, I used to go to Corsoli every year for Carnevale with my friend Toro. Did we have fun then! We got there in time for the parades because right after the olive pickers, came men dressed as priests who blessed us with curses. Toro always walked in front because he could curse better than any ten men together. Some other friends and I would wait on the roof of a house by the West Gate and as Toro walked by, his face red with cursing and swearing, we pelted him with eggs and flour! I remember a crazy woman who tore off all her clothes; we chased her through the streets till we caught her and took turns screwing her. And the food! *Potta!* We stuffed ourselves so full of sausages and polenta we could hardly move. A grocer used to sell truffles marinated in olive oil that were so good Christ Himself would have risen again just to taste them.

The day Miranda spoke about Carnevale, Bianca also mentioned it at dinner. She told us that in Venezia, the noblemen held magnificent balls inviting hundreds of people including princes and princesses and ambassadors from Germany, France, and England as well as all over Italy. They dressed in costumes of Roman gods, some made out of gold. She said that once she had dressed as Venus, another time as a peacock. She told us her lover had spent half the profits from one of his ships for this costume; it was made of jewels, had taken two months to create, and the train was so long two boys had to carry it. She was proclaimed the most beautiful woman in Venezia and the doge himself had danced with her. But, she said, compared to some women even this was nothing.

We had never done anything like that in Corsoli and sat spellbound at these tales, even Federico, although I could see it was making him jealous.

As if she sensed this, Bianca turned to him and said, "Federico, you should throw a ball."

"A ball?" Federico frowned.

"You are right, who would come? But we must do something! She tugged gently at her scarf which had ridden up her brow in her excitement. "I know, we could switch places!"

At this everyone began to talk at once. When I was small my father wore breasts made of straw and cooked polenta while my mother put on his hose and spent the whole day swearing and farting. Vittore laughed so hard he was sick, but I was too small to understand and begged my mother to be herself. I had not seen anyone do it since then.

Cecchi said that he had once changed places with his servants. "They ate and drank and made a terrible mess because they knew I had to clean it up."

Alessandro admitted he had once dressed as a young girl and an old priest followed him around all day offering him gifts and money. It was not till Alessandro had taken several hundred ducats from him that he revealed he was really a boy.

Federico listened, gorging himself on pine kernels dipped in melted sugar and covered with thin gold leaf.

"Why do you not do it, Federico?" Bianca said.

"Do what?"

"Change places with someone."

"The duke should not lower himself," Cecchi said, rousing himself from his memories.

"But when men of great standing do it, it inspires love among their citizens," Alessandro said.

"But the duke *is* much loved," protested Piero. "Duke Federico is—"

"Let me consult the stars," Bernardo said. "If they—"

"Yes, why not?" said Federico, beaming at Bianca. "But who shall I change with?"

"Me!" Bianca laughed.

"You are not my servant," Federico cooed. "You are my delight."

He looked around the room. Everyone stared at the ceiling or the walls, anywhere, but at Federico.

"Why not Ugo?" said Alessandro, picking at his teeth with his little gold stick.

"Ugo?"

"He is loyal and trustworthy."

"That is an excellent choice," Bianca said.

"What do you say, Ugo?" Federico asked, turning his great bulk toward me.

*Potta!* What could I say? I thought I was done with people imitating me, but Alessandro was right. If a servant was to switch places with Federico, who among the court had proved themselves more loyal than me? So I said, "I would be honored, My Lord."

"Good. We will exchange roles for the last breakfast before Lent. In the servants' hall. Have it made ready," Federico said, and Bianca clapped her hands with delight.

"If you are going to change places why wait till tomorrow morning?" Luigi said when I told the kitchen help what had happened. "Start tonight, then you can sleep in Federico's bed."

"And he can sleep in mine."

"He would need yours *and* Miranda's," Luigi said to much laughter.

"But then," Tommaso said, with a frown, "the duke would be sleeping with Miranda."

"Yes, and Ugo likes doing that," a boy sniggered.

I drew my knife, but the servants came between us. "It was a joke," they shouted.

"Does everyone think that?" I asked Tommaso later.

"Well," he said, carefully measuring his words, "all the other girls have boys who like them, but Miranda keeps them away, so they think, perhaps . . ."

"I keep her away only because I do not want her to get with child," I said angrily.

"You asked me and I am telling you."

I was so upset that it chased away a thought that had been nagging me like a broken tooth. Now I could not remember what it was.

For once the clouds parted and a watery sun celebrated Carnevale with us. Laying in my bed I could hear the city filling with people. The fountains were already running red with wine and soon everyone would be drinking and carousing. I had no desire to join them. I could not stop thinking about changing places with Federico. It was supposed to be an amusement, but it felt like a death sentence. How would Federico act if I ordered him to do something?

"No," I said to Tommaso when he asked me if I was going to the *palio*. "My stomach hurts. There is bile in my throat. I am sick."

"Ugo! Federico will not go through with this. It is just talk. Come on, we will make some money on the horses." His words tripped over one another in excitement. "Even if you do get killed, at least you will have had a good time!" So I allowed him to persuade me.

The valley must have been deserted for the streets were so crowded I could not see the ground beneath my feet. Revelers hung out of windows and sat on rooftops. The families who owned the horses marched through the streets, singing, blowing their trumpets, and insulting one another.

By evening, it was raining and the cobblestones of the Piazza Del Vedura glistened in the flickering light of the sconces. When the horses surged by us the crowd screamed, yelling so loudly that I forgot my troubles. I saved my money for the last race which was riderless and always the most fun.

The first time the horses galloped through the piazza, a dark brown stallion was leading, a gray horse hanging on its shoulder. Tommaso had bet on the stallion and I on the gray. As soon as they had passed, the people on our side of the square rushed to the other side and those on that side ran to ours. There was much pushing and shoving as we banged into one another and then came the yells, "They are coming! They are coming!" and we flung ourselves against the walls to get out of the way of the trampling hooves.

The third time the horses swept by, the stallion was still leading. Tommaso turned to me, his eyes shining, and screamed, "Pay me!" Just then the stallion slipped and crashed into the crowd across from us, knocking the spectators down like blades of grass. A terrible wailing arose. The horse tried to stand, but could not because a bone was sticking out through the flesh of its foreleg. It fell backward, its terrified neighs and whinnies mixing with the pitiful cries of the people trapped beneath it. Everyone leaped on the horse, stabbing it and kicking it, trying to get it to move, but the poor beast just lay there, its legs kicking in the air, its white, panicked eyes looking straight at me. It reminded me of my own helplessness and I could not turn away.

Then it was pushed aside and the poor souls who had been crushed were carried off, some to the hospital, others to the graveyard. Tommaso went to the Palazzo Fizzi to see who had won, but I stared at the horse, watching the life drain out of its eyes. While it was still warm, it was cut into pieces and the pieces placed on spits for the poor. Within minutes it had gone from being a hero to a villain and now in death it was a hero again. Would that happen to me?

The next night—that is, the last one before Lent—Cecchi gave me one of Federico's old green robes. "He wants you to wear this."

"I will look like a fool."

"How do you think he will look in your clothes?"

Miranda climbed into the robe with me, but there was still room enough for another person. She stood in front of me and insisted on combing my hair forward like Federico's. She had dressed as a princess and Bianca had given her silver earrings to go with the fur jacket. Tears of pride flooded my eyes. I wanted the world to see her, yet I feared she was slipping away from me.

"Walk like this," Miranda said, pushing her chest out. She strode around the room like a bull with an ache in its *culo*. Although she weighed a quarter of Federico and barely came up to his stomach, she had caught the very essence of him.

"Do it again," I laughed.

Smiling and then frowning like Federico, she walked around the room, stopped in front of me, opened her mouth so that her bottom lip sat on her chin and, pretending to pull out a *fallo* said, "Ugo, taste this."

The laughter stilled in my mouth. "What did you say?"

Her face flushed.

"Where did you hear that?"

"From the boys," she whispered.

"Which boys? The kitchen boys?"

"The kitchen boys. The stable boys. All the boys. They all say it."

Fearing that I would become enraged, she hurried from the room. However, it was not rage that overcame me, but humiliation. Is this how people joked among themselves when I passed by? Would there never be any end to the shame I had to endure to stay alive?

When Miranda returned a short while later I was still sitting on the bed. She knelt at my feet and leaned her head against my knees. We sat like that until the darkness pulled a blanket over our shame.

The sun was barely awake and yet the servants' hall was alive with the colors of a thousand costumes. Grooms, chamberlains, seamstresses, ostlers, secretaries, even scribes had dressed up; stable boys as young girls, washerwomen like soldiers—the old, half-blind washerwoman had a mustache and kept pretending to scratch her balls. No one could remember the last time Federico had come into their hall. Christ! No one could remember the last time *any* duke had come into their hall.

No sooner did I enter than I tripped over the back of the robe and fell down. This caused much laughter, but so many hands helped me up and pushed me forward that, encouraged by their good spirits, I lost my fear and swaggered up to the grand table at which Piero, Bernardo, Bianca, and several others were already seated. Bianca was dressed like an Oriental slave girl, her bountiful breasts tumbling out of her bodice.

"He is coming," Cecchi said. "Remember, just do what he says."

A moment later Ercole the dwarf snuck in, grinning from ear to ear, followed by Federico. Federico was wearing a white shirt and a pair of red hose, though they must have sewn three pairs together just to cover his *culo*. Usually, he pounded his feet into the ground as if he was trying to leave his mark upon the earth, but today he moved his feet in little quick steps as if he was gliding on a set of wheels. As I did. Everyone applauded. Federico beamed. Bianca whispered, "Sit in his chair."

I had not expected that, but since Bianca nodded so eagerly I did as she suggested. Federico had sat in that chair for so long it was shaped to his body and I could only sit as Federico did, slouching to one side. Again everyone laughed. The laughter was as intoxicating as wine and gave me great confidence.

"Well," said Federico, who was now standing behind my chair. "Ask for the food!"

Perhaps it was the way I was sitting, perhaps it was the robe, certainly the laughter, but when he said that, I lifted the left cheek of my *culo*, and farted and belched just like he did. I said loudly, "Get that bean eater in here with my breakfast."

Cecchi tugged frantically at his beard, Piero clapped a hand over his mouth, Bianca and the servants shrieked. But the loudest laugh of all came from behind me.

"Bean eater!" Federico spluttered. "Bean eater! Luigi *is* a bean eater." He waddled in front of me. "Say it again."

I lay back in the seat, farted, belched, licked my lips, and said, "Tell that bean eater to bring me my breakfast. Now!" And turning to Federico, I said, "Get back to your place."

As soon as I said that, I thought—*Sono fottuto!* I am ruined! But God strike me dead, if Federico did not waddle back to his position! The hall could not stop laughing. And Federico did not mind at all! He thought they were laughing at his impression of me.

The trumpets blared, the doors opened, and Luigi entered carrying trays of breakfast foods. He laid down a silver platter with fresh apples, a bowl of polenta with raisins, and some grilled eggs sprinkled with sugar and cinnamon. Everyone waited to see what I would do. But I did not do anything. *Jesus in sancto!* How could I? This was the finest meal that had ever been placed in front of me! I just wanted to sit there and look at it. I wanted to take the platter back to my room and chew each piece slowly.

"Are you not going to make me taste it?" Federico hissed.

"Of course," I muttered. I looked over the hall. Miranda sat on a bench in the front, Tommaso behind her, dressed like a knight. The kitchen boys were sitting on one another's shoulders. I said loudly, "Where is my taster?"

"Here I am, My Lord," said Federico, stepping forward.

I could not believe my ears. Federico had called me "My Lord!" I waved my hand. "The apple first."

Federico nodded. He picked up an apple, rolled it in his hands and sniffed at it. The hall was silent. No one could have been more surprised had Federico grown wings and flown out of the window.

He lifted up one finger as if to see which way the wind was blowing. This was something I never did.

"Quite brilliant," said Piero.

"Yes," said Bernardo, "The duke is so amusing."

"Well?" I said to Federico.

He took a small bite. Screwing up his nose, he put his hands on his hips and looked thoughtfully at the ceiling. Now I understood why Ercole was grinning. He had coached Federico. At first people giggled, but Federico did it for too long and the laughter died away. I had to be careful. If it did not go well for Federico he might blame me so I said, "I do not feel like the apple after all."

"The polenta," Bianca whispered to me. She too sensed it was best to forget the apples.

"I want the polenta," I said, pushing the bowl toward Federico.

Federico pulled out a wishbone. He broke it in two and held it up to the light. This brought great laughter once again, for of course everyone knew the story of my bone. He dipped it into the bowl, pulled it out and made a great fuss over it.

"Just eat it," a voice shouted.

"Yes, eat it," came more voices. "Eat it."

"Well," I demanded, "What are you waiting for?"

Federico dipped a spoon into the polenta and slowly raised it up to his lips. Then he looked out over the crowd. They were staring at him. Slowly he put the spoon down and turned to me. "You eat it," he said.

"Me?" I dropped my lower lip onto my chin. People started to laugh, but then stopped.

Federico's eyes turned into little black dots. *Oi me!* He thought the polenta was poisoned! Now I remembered what had nagged me. It all fit like a key in a lock! Bianca had suggested switching places and Alessandro had suggested that Federico change places with me. Miranda had seen them together in Bianca's apartment and they were both from Venezia. Body of Christ! How could I have been so stupid!

"Go on," Federico said, tearing off the shift. "Taste it!"

"Of course," I answered. A thousand thoughts crowded my mind. If I said the polenta was poisoned, Federico would want to know why I had not spoken earlier. He would think I was part of the plot and force me to eat it. I raised the yellow steaming mush dotted with raisins to my lips when, just as the polenta touched my tongue, I cried out, "There are seven raisins, Luigi! How many times do I have to tell you! Not seven!" And picking up the bowl, I hurled it into the fire, smashing it into a hundred pieces. The flames leaped and hissed like a sleeping cat that had been trodden on.

No one laughed. No one made a sound. Federico's eyes narrowed and guards appeared from nowhere. They grasped my neck and shoulders and slammed my face on the table. Federico picked my head up in one hand, the knife in the other. My life came to a halt. I saw Ercole, his squat little body standing on one of the benches. I do not know if it was my mind playing tricks but there seemed to be a glow about him. At that moment I knew God was everywhere. Not just in what was beautiful and good, but also in what was ugly and crippled. For this had all come about because I had laughed at Ercole all those months ago when Federico had thrown the trencher at him, and since Ercole could never have foreseen something like this, it had to be God's hand.

At the same time as I was begging God's forgiveness I caught sight of Bianca's eyes. Her face turned white. I knew I was right. "My Lord—" I gasped.

"Oh, Federico!" Bianca squealed. "He did it just like you! Just like you!" She put her hand on Federico's arm, the one that held the dagger, and said, "Do not upset yourself, my pet. He is just a *cantadino!*" To Luigi she said, "Bring Duke Federico's garments and another bowl of polenta with lots of raisins. We will be eating in his room."

The hall applauded. Federico let go of my neck and I quietly slipped out of his reach. *Potta!* I thought, as they left the hall, she is a master.

After Federico and Bianca left, everyone crowded around telling me how lucky I was that Bianca had saved my life. Even Miranda said so. They kept on and on till I fled and walked up the hill to Agnese's resting place to be alone. It was not till that afternoon that I was able to return to the hall and search for the remains of the polenta which I had thrown in the fire.

Alas, it had vanished and all traces of the broken bowl had disappeared. I asked each of the boys if they had swept it away, but they denied it, thinking it might lead to trouble. When I said I would give ten ducats to whomever it was, they all claimed to have done it.

That evening, a boy a year or two younger than Miranda complained of a terrible bellyache. I hurried to his bedside. He was sweating and in such pain that his voice had become hoarse from screaming.

"He is pretending," Luigi said. "They all do it to get out of work."

The boy was holding his stomach. His eyes were sunken and peered fearfully out of their sockets. "Death waits for me by the door," he whispered. "Tell him to go away."

I gave him olive oil to drink, but it was too late. The poison was in his blood and the vomiting took away what little strength he had left. "Did you throw away the pieces of the bowl?" I asked.

He nodded.

"And the porridge? Did you taste it?"

He was about to answer when a wave of pain surged through him, shooting its claws into every part of his body, erasing his memory forever.

I waited for Bianca inside the doorway to the Duomo and as she entered I thanked her for turning Federico's anger away from me.

"Do not thank me. Thank God for your good fortune."

"As you are going to thank Him for yours?"

"I always do," she smiled.

Strangely, I no longer feared her or Alessandro. Soon after, Alessandro left for Germany where he was killed in a brawl. I could not blame Federico for his actions for he was right although he did not know it. Nor could I tell him without endangering myself or Bianca. As for me, it was neither the conspiracy nor my own cleverness that lingered in my memory, but the terrible face of the dying boy that appeared every time I closed my eyes.

After Carnevale, Bianca no longer entertained Miranda, saying that she had taught her everything she knew. Now, when Miranda practiced her lyre, I had to pretend to be a duke and clap and shout, "Brava!" when she finished.

She practiced the way Alessandro had taught her to walk and to dance. She practiced the art of kissing on her doll, Felicita. She wrote poems in writing as neat as Cecchi's.

"You try," she said, placing the quill in my hand. It is the same quill I am using now.

"But these are farmer's hands."

"So were mine."

I did it to please her and, by the end of the week, I could write the letters A and B as well as any scribe. Then I learned the other letters and as soon as I could I wrote my name. I had heard it so often, I wanted to see what it looked like and when I started writing it I could not stop.

"That is good, Babbo," Miranda said. "Now you will be a scribe as well as a taster."

If she had said that to me earlier the words might have stung, but not anymore. I had almost lost my life twice as a taster and as Miranda was becoming more beautiful every day, she deserved to have a real suitor and a dowry. Sometimes when I looked at her, thoughts came to me that I had to banish from my mind. Tommaso shared them, too.

Not long after, we were pissing when we saw Miranda walking in the courtyard below us, her pigtail bobbing gently on her behind. "In two years she will be fourteen and . . ." Tommaso grinned, and waved his *fallo* in the air.

"Perhaps," I said.

"What do you mean?"

"What I said."

"Those who break their word get their heads broken."

"Then watch your head. I was almost poisoned."

Someone was shouting to us from the courtyard. "Poisoned!" Tommaso exclaimed. "No one was trying to poison anyone. That was Federico! You know how he is."

"And what about the kitchen boy? You were supposed to be my eyes and ears in the kitchen."

"I was, and anyone who says I was not is a liar."

"*You* are the liar," I said calmly. "Because you were not there. You were in your room putting on your costume. Luigi said everyone was wearing costumes so anyone could have slipped poison in the porridge."

There was more shouting now. In the town below us people were running to and fro. One of the kitchen boys was running toward us.

"You just want to break our agreement," Tommaso said, pulling out his knife.

I pulled my knife out. "You already broke it. I am tired of your lying and boasting."

The boy ran up to us, panting. "The plague. The plague is coming."

# xviii

The plague had already visited Genoa, Milano, Parma, and Bologna. The week before, the first cases had been discovered in Arezzo. The gates of Corsoli were closed, but what is a gate to the plague? A few days after my argument with Tommaso, a merchant sent his servant to the hospital with swellings in his groin and armpits. He died the next day. Three more people had died by the end of the week. At first, each death was given a burial, but then the gravedigger died and there was no one to do the burying so the corpses piled up in the streets. There was no wind to chase away the smell of death and it rose slowly until it reached the palace. Two kitchen boys fell ill. Giulio, Federico's youngest son, died, but his other, Raffaello, did not. Bernardo's wife perished. He did not shed a tear for her. Piero did what he could, running from one family to another, but after his eldest child died, he was so overcome with grief he could not go on.

Giulia, Miranda's friend and Cecchi's youngest daughter, died. Miranda wept, but the sight of Giulia's mother running through the halls screaming terrified her even more. A tall, thin woman, who until then hardly spoke to anyone, now could not stop talking to her dead daughter. Her hair turned white overnight and she shrieked when anyone, even Cecchi, came near her. She died a week later.

We were helpless. This was not an enemy we could fight or even see to run away from. Besides, where was there to go? Corsoli was the highest point in the valley.

"I am afraid," Miranda whispered, as she pulled the covers over her. She awoke in the night, tearing her clothes off, looking for boils. Fear overtook her modesty. She made me look under her arms, on her back, and on her buttocks. She imagined she saw marks and spots between her thighs and I had to comb away the soft hair and show her there was nothing there. Then she hunched into a ball and wept. I promised her she did not have to worry, but in truth I was as scared as she and when she slept I pulled down my hose and examined myself as closely as I had inspected her.

If a boil appeared on anyone in the city, they were driven out of doors, left to fend for themselves, and often starved to death. Houses which had been visited by the plague were boarded up and the tenants forced to stay inside, even those who were not sick. The markets were canceled, and so was the feast of San Giovanni. The archbishop and a few boys waved a burning torch over the fields to bless them, but they were afraid to carry the saint's head through the streets as was the custom. The same boys believed the cats and dogs were to blame so they hunted them down and burned them. Husbands deserted their wives, and wives their children. The screams of abandoned babies rose into the night air and hovered about the palace to remind us of their suffering.

In the third week, two boys in Miranda's class died. The archbishop said our wickedness was to blame and that we could only purge ourselves by fasting. Then he issued a proclamation forbidding blasphemy, games, sodomy, and prostitution. All the things that Federico liked best. Federico said nothing because he, too, was afraid. One night when the moon hovered above us, all of Corsoli's children paraded through the streets carrying pictures of the Holy Mother and San Sebastian. Even little ones who were too small and too sick to walk begged to join in. Some died even as they marched. Every day we flocked to the Duomo crying, "*Misericordia, misericordia!*" and begged God's forgiveness.

Women flogged themselves till the blood ran down their backs. It made no difference. The dying went on. The stench of death lodged in my nose even as the screams of the living rang in my ears.

Two weeks after his first sermon, the archbishop died. Now the fear of the plague was as bad as the plague itself. A servant whose master swore he was perfectly well was so afraid that he threw himself down a well. Miranda sat in the corner of our room wringing her hands. Her fingernails had been bitten to the quick and she had scratched the skin off her thighs and the underside of her arms. I feared she would lose her mind; and even though my mother had died of the plague in the country, I believed Miranda would be safer there.

"You can stay with my father. You are his grandchild. He will look after you."

"You are not coming with me?"

"No, Federico will not allow it." Cecchi had told me Federico asked every day if I was still well and would not eat otherwise. A surge of pride had rushed through me. Duke Federico Basillione DiVincelli *needed* me. He could not eat without me. He could not *live* without me!

"But I am your daughter," Miranda cried.

I asked a few courtiers, but they had their own lives to attend to and I knew their answers before the question left my mouth. It pained me more than having nails driven into my eyes, but I had to ask Tommaso.

Tommaso was making a cherry torte. Although he had not been in the kitchen very long, his hands already bore the nicks and burns of his new profession. His fingers were not thin and well formed like Miranda's, but they were quite skillful and it was a pleasure to witness them darting over the pots and pans like a bird weaving its nest.

He blended a bowl of ground-up cherries with crushed rose petals, added some finely grated cheese, a dash of pepper, a little ginger, some sugar, four beaten eggs and mixed them all together. Then he carefully poured the mixture into a crust and placed the pan over a small flame. I remembered that when he had made the snow wolf he said he wanted to be a sculptor and I said aloud, "You already are."

"Are what?" He whirled about. His cheeks were thinner and his eyes pained and sad.

"A sculptor. You said you wanted to be a sculptor. Now you are. Except you use food instead of marble."

He turned away to attend to the pan. "What do you want? I am busy."

"Miranda is not well." He looked up sharply. "She does not have the plague," I added quickly, "but she will go mad if she stays here. I want to send her to my father's house in Fonte."

"Why are you telling me?"

"She cannot go by herself and Federico will not let me go with her." I took a breath. "I want you to take her. I do not trust anyone else. I know we have had our differences, but I beg you to put them aside—if not for my sake, then for Miranda's. If you love her, you will do this."

He snorted. He snorted often now, thinking perhaps it made him more manly. A rat scurried past and he threw a pot at it which hit it on the head, stunning it.

"This means our agreement is on again?" He beat the rat to death and threw it into the courtyard.

"Yes."

"I want it in writing."

"You will have it so."

"Before we leave."

"Before you leave." He took off his apron. "Will you get into trouble with Federico?" I asked.

"Federico? Why?"

"Because you are his spy. I saw you in the doorway after the killings of Pia and Emilia."

"I do not do that anymore. Now I have this," he said, indicating the kitchen.

Septivus wrote the agreement, signed Tommaso's name for him, and then I signed mine. I packed a small bundle of Miranda's clothing, Tommaso brought some food, and we met by the stable at dawn.

"Tommaso will take care of you," I told Miranda as she mounted the horse I had bribed from the stable boys.

"With my life," Tommaso said, and swung himself up behind her. He unbound his sword and took the reins.

For a moment I felt jealous that I was not going. To be away from Corsoli, away from the plague. "Godspeed," I said. Miranda did not look at me. Tommaso jerked the reins and the horse moved toward the entranceway. I ran alongside, clutching at Miranda's foot. "May the Lord bless you and keep you. May He make His face to shine upon you and be gracious unto you. May the Lord lift up His countenance upon you and grant you peace."

She still did not look at me. "Miranda," I cried, "say something to me. We may never see one another again."

She looked down at me. "Take good care of Federico," she spat. Then she dug her heels in and the horse trotted through the entranceway to the palazzo, down the Weeping Steps, and disappeared into Corsoli.

I watched them ride through the streets, past the bodies of men and women, the piles of babies and children, until they reached the gate and passed through it. It came to me that my brother Vittore might be at my father's house and my heart froze. I wanted to ride after them and bring them back, but then I heard wailing from inside the palazzo and I was glad they had left.

That night I dreamed Tommaso had raped Miranda and I rose from my bed, shouting, "I will kill you," so loudly someone knocked on my door but did not come in for fear I had been stricken.

Cecchi said that a merchant in Firenze had told him that the scent of herbs such as fennel, mint, and basil, and spices like cardamom, cinnamon, saffron, cloves, aniseed, and nutmeg, prevented the evil odors from affecting the brain. The next day Emilia's garden was picked clean. Christ! The whole hillside behind the palace was picked clean. The spices in the kitchen were stolen. None of it helped. Potero, Federico's cup bearer, covered himself in spices and died the same day.

Spring slid into summer and the heat increased daily. Dogs and servants fought one another for shade. Federico and Bianca seldom left their chambers and I had to taste Federico's food while he watched me from the doorway. "You are still well?" he would say to me.

"Yes, My Lord. I am well."

He grunted, "Me and the food taster."

Another time when he opened the door, I could see all the way into his bedroom. Bianca was kneeling naked on the bed, her head bowed down, her *culo* in the air. She was wearing a mask and sobbing softly. Federico did not care if I saw or not. He just wanted to know if I had caught the plague.

One day Septivus wore a bag around his neck which contained snake venom. He had read in the *Decameron* that such bags had been worn to ward off the plague in earlier times so he had gone into the woods and killed a snake. He offered to sell other bags with snake venom. Those who were old or sick bought them, but everyone else went into the woods to hunt for snakes for themselves. Several people were bitten, including Raffaello, Federico's oldest son, and one man died in a fight with another over a snake that had no venom. Then Septivus was accused of putting ordinary ointment into the bags to make money.

Servants left the palace under cover of night for the countryside, but within days they returned, saying that wherever they had gone they had seen suffering and that it was the end of the world. I pleaded with God to forgive my sins and if He could not, not to avenge Himself by taking Miranda. I do not know why I bothered. God did not care who prayed and who did not! Most of the dead were children who had not lived long enough to harm a fly and did not know what a sin was. How can a merciful God snatch children from their mothers' arms?

One evening, Federico called some of us into the main hall. We were ragged and weary with fear, afraid of our shadows, afraid of ourselves. Federico said, "I never won a battle by being afraid. We have cowered too long and if I am going to die it will be on my feet."

He ordered food and drink and called whores from the city. He told the stable boys to paint their faces, Ercole to clown, and the musicians to bang drums and blow trumpets as loud as they liked. We cheered him as if he had delivered us. We ate and drank till we were sick, then ate and drank some more. Septivus leaped onto the table and recited obscene verses of Aretino. Federico told crude jokes and Bianca did a wild dance she had learned from a Turk. The Carnevale masks were brought out. I wore a bull's head. When Bernardo crept away with a whore, we threw open the door and cheered them on.

As the night came upon us, we pushed the food onto the floor and screwed on the tables. Soon we were all so drunk that men copulated with men, women with women, all of us grunting like wild beasts. Two boys were on their knees in front of Federico. I was crazed with drink and desire. I grabbed a woman with large breasts and a hawk's mask and pulled her into an empty room.

"Ugo," Bianca laughed.

Even though Federico was in the next room, I did not care. Bianca threw herself across the bed on her back and spread her legs. "Taste me," she yelled, and when I hesitated, she laughed, "I am not poisonous."

I was right, she *had* tried to kill Federico. But I liked her spirit. "I always wanted to fuck you," she said.

She had big lips the color of ripe cherries. She kissed my face, pulled my shirt off, and licked my body. I ripped open her bodice, and buried my face in her big breasts. One hour passed into another, one day into the next. Corpses rotted in the hallways while our lovemaking grew fiercer and fiercer as if it would help us outlast Death. The whores brought wooden *falli* and showed us how nuns entertained themselves. I wanted to sodomize Bianca, but she pleaded, "No, Federico makes me do it. I do not like it."

There were cries from the main hall. I ran in as the painted boys stumbled out weeping. The tables had been overturned and dogs were gobbling up the food. A boy lay bleeding on the ground, a sword stuck in his belly. Federico sat on the floor covered in sweat. His clothes were torn and in disarray, revealing his huge white belly. "Piss," he said, through parched, cracked lips. "We must drink piss. That will save us."

The few of us who were there looked at one another and laughed. Federico crawled across the table, overturned a bowl of food, took out his great fat snake, and pissed a dark yellow stream into it. He turned to me. "Taste it."

"But you just pissed it," I laughed. "How can anything be wrong?"

"You are my taster. Taste it."

"Duke Federico, why do you not taste Bianca's piss and then she can taste yours?"

Federico pulled the sword out of the dead boy. It dripped with blood and guts. "Are you forgetting who I am?" he said.

I *had* forgotten. In the madness which had seized us I no longer thought of him as our prince, but as just another man driven mad with fear. I picked up the bowl and looked at the dark yellow liquid. The odor was sharp and stung my nostrils. I said to myself—I need only drink a little and since I have trained myself not to taste anything, what harm can there be? I raised the bowl to my mouth, but my lips would not open.

What lies we tell ourselves! For over two years I had believed that although I could tell the ingredients of a meal, the taste meant nothing to me. But if that was true then why could I not drink this? Federico's sword pushed against my ribs. Big, fat bitter drops of Federico's urine sat on my lips. I wanted to swallow them quickly, but once inside my mouth they ran everywhere like a naughty child, between my teeth, up the sides of my mouth, under my gums, over my tongue. I was going to be sick, but then the point of Federico's sword broke my skin and blood trickled down my stomach. My throat had closed up. I could feel the piss burning on the back of my tongue, waiting to plunge into my stomach.

"Look at his face," Federico laughed. "Swallow it!"

*Potta!* The bastard! He knew his piss was not poisoned. I thought—if I am to die, then I will spit it in his face. I gathered the liquid in my mouth, when a scream froze me. A door swung open so hard it smashed against the wall and bounced back again. Bianca stood in the doorway. She was not wearing her mask. She was not wearing anything.

I thought she was going to tell Federico we had made love. I wanted to run, but something about her stopped me. It was not her full, heavy breasts with their huge pink nipples which I could still feel in my mouth. Nor was it her soft round belly, or her fleshy thighs, or dainty feet. Nor was it her eyes which were wide with fear, nor her mouth forever shaped by the agonizing scream which had been torn from it. Nor her hair which fell around her head like the pictures I had seen of Medusa.

It was the mole on her forehead. It looked like a large round plum, and far from being ugly, it was so big and beautiful, like everything else about her, that it was a shame she had hidden it for so long.

"Look!" she screamed. Her right hand was pointing to her groin and there, protruding from her blonde hair, was a huge black boil. She lifted one arm and then the other and in her armpits were two more boils as large as eggs. I swear had I not seen this I would not be writing it down, but as we looked more boils appeared on her body in front of our very eyes! First on her stomach. Now on her thighs, her ankle, her belly. An evil spirit had laid its eggs inside of her and its young were hatching all at once. More boils appeared. We backed away in horror. She opened her mouth and shouted in a strangled voice, as if something in her throat was growing there, "Help me!"

Federico stepped toward her—I thought to take her in his arms and comfort her. Instead, he stabbed her through the heart with his sword, the thrust pushing her back into the room and onto the floor. Then he closed the door, leaned on it and wept.

We tiptoed out of the hall and fled as far away as we could. I never saw Bianca again. Nor did I want to. I was terrified that because I had lain with her, I, too, had caught the plague. It was not till much, much later that I realized I had swallowed Federico's piss.

The deaths in the city slowed and when I had not fallen ill after two months I stopped worrying that I would die. The plague had spent itself out. Federico, Piero, Bernardo and his infernal fennel seeds, Cecchi, and Federico's son, Raffaello, were also spared although Raffaello was affected in the head and had to be looked after day and night from then on. Nearly a quarter of all those living in Corsoli died and many more in the palace. I feared I would never see Miranda again and I was planning to ride to my father's house when Tommaso entered the courtyard leading a lame horse on which Miranda was sitting.

I ran to her, but Tommaso, who had an angry wound across his right cheek, would not let me near until he had gently lifted her down. I covered her face with kisses and told her how much I missed her. Then I embraced Tommaso like a long-lost son and thanked him for returning Miranda safely to me. He listened, never taking his eyes from Miranda and, from his tender expression, I guessed that much had happened between them. I led Miranda to our room where I arranged water for her to bathe and oils and scents with which to freshen herself.

"Do you have a screen?" she asked.

"A screen? Why?" We did not have one and had never needed one even when she had her monthly courses. Bernardo saw his daughter naked and she was seventeen.

"I want a screen," she repeated.

I borrowed one from Cecchi, and while Miranda bathed I sat on the other side and told her of the sorrows that had overtaken the palace in her absence. She listened quietly, only interrupting once to ask about her friends. I told her that several of them had died, Bianca, too, although I did not say how. Miranda sobbed softly. I wanted to comfort her, but because of the screen I stayed where I was. The anguish of her weeping made me weep, too. Death had become so common I was sure my tears had dried up, but now we sat on either side of the screen mourning for all we had seen and for those we had lost.

Eventually, Miranda emerged, her dark brown hair resting gently on her shoulders. Her eyes seemed older, her lips fuller, her body more formed. In short, if she was not yet a woman, she was no longer a girl. I asked her if she had seen my father. She shook her head, showering droplets of water onto her shoulders like golden sunbeams. "He left with his neighbors." She screwed her face up with disgust. "We could not stay in his house. It was disgusting."

"Did you stay with the abbot Tottorini?"

She snorted, the same way Tommaso did. "With that fat pig? If all priests are like him, then God is in trouble!"

"God is good despite man, not because of him."

She stared at herself in her little mirror, examining her hair, her eyes, her mouth, first from one side and then the other. "All we wanted was some bread and cheese, but when we said we were from Corsoli he shut the door in our faces."

"The bastard!" I cried.

Miranda began to brush her hair. "So we kept on riding."

"To Gubbio?"

She shrugged. "I suppose. We just rode." She looked down at her feet. There was a scar across the top of her left foot. "A piece of burning wood fell on it," she said. "The plague was everywhere, Babbo. Men and women were lying in the fields, on the paths, in their houses. I saw a man and woman who had hanged themselves and their baby next to them. The birds had plucked their eyes out." She stopped brushing her hair as if the memory had suddenly appeared in front of her. "I did not know so many people could be dead at the same time." Her lips trembled and her body began to shake.

"What is it?"

"And then . . . then . . ."

I knelt beside her, grasping her hands.

"Two men . . ." she dissolved in tears. I stroked her hair and held her close. At last she sobbed, "Two men . . . raped me."

My heart tore in two. "Oh, my Miranda. My angel. My angel." I rocked her backward and forward. "Where was Tommaso?"

"They nearly killed him! If it were not for him I would be dead!" Again tears overcame her.

I did not question her any further. My ears, which hungered for the details, were at the same time reluctant to hear them. At last, Miranda continued. "Tommaso told them he was escorting me to die in my father's house."

"Where was this? In the valley?"

She furrowed her brow.

"At the bottom of the valley or on the way to Gubbio?"

She screwed her face up impatiently, "On the path going away from the house. What does it matter?"

I promised I would not interrupt her again.

"Tommaso said I had the plague and that he was escorting me to die in my father's house," she repeated. "They did not believe him. They wanted to see my boils. I told them that even in the time of a plague a lady must be respected. They said the plague did not care who was a lady and who was not and neither did they and if I did not show them the boils they would look for themselves."

"One attacked Tommaso, and the other—" She broke down, pressing her face into my chest. "Tommaso killed the first one and drove off my attacker, but not before . . ." The rest was lost in weeping.

I did not say anything. What was there to say? I had sent her away. "*Mi dispiace, mi dispiace*," I whispered.

I was blind with rage. I wanted to hunt down the criminals, scoop out their eyes, cut off their *falli*, and burn them at the stake. I dreaded what else I might hear, but I needed to put my mind at ease. "Are you . . . with child?"

"I do not know," she whispered.

"My angel, my Miranda. I will take care of you." I waited a moment longer and then I said, "What happened after that?"

"We found a hut. Just like the one we used to live in. Remember?" Her face brightened briefly. "Tommaso could not do anything because of his wounds. I was afraid he might die so I bathed them in urine."

I tried not to imagine what this had looked like. "What did you eat?"

"There was plenty of fruit—apples, peaches, and pomegranates— because no one had picked them. I swear I never want to see another pomegranate as long as I live," she laughed. "I made polenta and Tommaso killed a pig."

"He was better already?"

"No, when he got better. He is such a good cook, Babbo. One day he will be the chief chef. He is better than Luigi is even now, I swear it!"

She told me how they had eaten the pig for three days, how Tommaso had cut slices of ham and salted them and had even made a sausage. "He has wonderful hands, Babbo. Have you ever looked at them? They look so small and stubby and he is so tall and thin. But they are strong. He can crush a nut between his fingers!"

"Really!"

"Yes, it is true." Tommaso had also killed a chicken and a squirrel, built a fire, plucked a goose, and repaired part of the hut. It was a wonder he had not made the rains come.

Miranda held out her own hands and studied her long, thin fingers. "My hands are too long."

"You have the hands of an artist."

"But Tommaso's are tender." She rose and went behind the screen to dress.

I could not help myself. I said, "Where did you sleep?"

"In the hut."

"Did you sleep . . . ?" I could not finish.

"Of course not, Babbo! Tommaso said he could not betray your trust." She came out from behind the screen and placed her hand over her heart. "I swear by all that is holy." In that moment I knew as sure as sparks fly upward she was lying.

I stood up. "Where are you going?" she asked, alarm flickering in her eyes.

I did not answer.

She grabbed my arm. "You do not believe me?"

"I believe you."

"Babbo, if you hurt Tommaso, I will kill myself."

"Why would I hurt him?"

Her eyes filled with tears. "I love him, Babbo. I love him."

"I know. Now eat and sleep. And Miranda, do not tell anyone of this rape."

Tommaso was lying on his pallet. The wound on his right cheek made him appear older and, together with his hair, which had grown longer and curlier, he looked like the disciple Peter in a painting in the Duomo Santa Caterina.

"I want to thank you for saving Miranda's life."

"You asked me to take care of her and I did as you asked. It was nothing, *niente*."

"*Niente?*" I smiled. "The Tommaso I used to know would have bragged about it from the rooftops." I did not add "because you have never won a fight in your life." "What started it?"

He shrugged. "We met these men on the path. I told them to let us pass because Miranda had the plague but they wanted to see her boils. I said, no. I said . . . a lady . . . a lady . . ."

"Must be respected."

"Yes, yes. Exactly so. But they said if she did not show them the boils, they would force her! So I attacked them."

"That was very brave."

"But as I was fighting one, the other one ravished Miranda." He carried on as if he was afraid he would forget what he was supposed to say. "I killed the first one and drove the other one off."

"Miranda said you killed the second one."

"No. Maybe . . . no . . . I do not remember." He frowned, turning away. He was such a bad liar. "They cut me," he said. "I am lucky to be alive."

"I see." I had been looking at the wound on his cheek which was not as deep as it first appeared. Indeed, it seemed as if someone had inflicted it carefully so as not to cause too much pain. "Then you found a hut."

"If Miranda told you, why are you asking me?"

"She said that you cooked wonderful meals."

He tossed his hair out of his face and puffed his cheeks out. He was so easy to flatter. "I caught a pig if that is what you mean. I cooked it with some herbs and mushrooms. At night we prayed to God. And we prayed for you, too," he said earnestly.

"Me? Why?"

"Because Miranda missed you. We knew people in Corsoli were dying and that you had to look after Federico. She was worried about you."

"What else did you do?"

"We sang songs. We danced . . ." He stopped, the memory overtaking him. "It was . . . crazy."

"Crazy, why?"

"Why?" He waved his hands about, becoming excited like the old Tommaso. "All around us the world was dying, but we were living in this hut like . . ."

"Like what?"

"Do you not see?" he cried. "We were all alone . . . we could have been the only two people living . . . in the world—"

"Living like what?" I grasped his throat.

"Like man and wife!" His eyes stared into mine. Unafraid. "I cannot lie to you, Ugo. Kill me if you wish. I do not care. I love her. *E mio l'amor divino. L'amor divino*," he repeated.

She loves you too, I said to myself. So much so that she would pretend to be raped in case she got with child. How could I do anything to Tommaso? He had brought my Miranda back safely. I told him he could no longer sleep with her. "Our agreement is for one more year. If you love her you can wait."

Miranda woke each morning with Tommaso's name upon her lips. She whispered his name in her prayers. She wrote little poems to him and declared that they would get married and go to Roma so that Tommaso could cook for the pope. She swore she would be in love with him till the day she died.

Because Tommaso had won her heart, the other boys stopped teasing him. Now he walked around the palace with Miranda on his arm, as proud as a peacock. He worshiped her and brought her combs, ribbons, and other trinkets. He made pastries for her, little delicacies of sugar and fruits in the shapes of birds and flowers. Sometimes they sat for hours on the wall outside the palazzo entwined in one another's arms, caressing one another's faces, stroking each other's hair, saying nothing. She would take his short stubby hands in hers, kiss each nick and burn, press her face against his cheek, and sing to him.

Watching them, I sometimes wondered if there was not some invisible twine linking them together like the one Ariadne gave Theseus, for no sooner did they stray from one another's grasp than their fingers blindly searched for the other until they met again. I often overheard their conversations; most of them I do not recall, but this one I remember for it showed the gentleness of their nature. They were saying good night to one another when Miranda said, "You must sleep on your right side with your left arm extended like this. I will lie on my right side, too, and then I will know you are lying behind me and your arm is across my body and I will sleep well."

I smiled to myself and thought no more of it until I saw them together the next day. From the way they were standing I knew he had done as she asked. They were, in a word, as happy as doves who, having found a mate, remain together for the rest of their lives.

Miranda and Tommaso were not the only ones who embraced life after the plague. I could now read and write and took great pleasure in recording my experiments with plants and herbs. I also amused myself with a servant girl. In Corsoli, men took new wives and women found new husbands. I do not know where they all came from, but a few months later there seemed to be as many people in the city as there had ever been and all the women were with child.

I heard that after surviving the plague, some princes, like the duke of Ferrara, devoted themselves to the church or charitable works. Federico was the opposite. "We survived the worst God could send us," he said, stroking Nero, who now sat in Bianca's chair at the table. "Why should I believe in Him? Ugo does not believe in Him, do you, Ugo?"

Christ on a cross! Arguing and cursing God was something I did when I was alone, but Federico was asking me to denounce God with the new bishop of Santa Caterina sitting right there and everyone staring at me. I stumbled over my answer, afraid to speak and yet pleased that Federico had called upon me for my opinion. Fortunately, Federico did not wait for an answer, but said that from now on he was going to enjoy life even more.

He ate twice as much as he used to, took up with new whores, and increased the number of his hounds to a thousand—the dog shit around the palace was ankle deep. He spent huge sums on new silks, satin robes, rings, and other jewels. Sometimes when he dressed up he looked like an altar at a festival. But though he never mentioned Bianca's name again, her death affected him deeply. As the days grew shorter and the skies filled with melancholy clouds and angry, biting rains, he moped around the palace, Nero by his side.

"I want a wife!" he shouted at us one morning. He ordered Cecchi to write letters to the d'Este's, the Malatesta, the Medici and other courts stating his intentions. When the replies came, if they came at all, they said all the eligible women and girls were spoken for. Federico decided the only way to get a new wife would be to journey to Milano where he had once served Duke Sforza. Everyone in the palazzo was beside themselves with excitement. To leave Corsoli and go to Milano! They begged and lied, pleading with Cecchi for a place in the retinue. I did not have to raise my voice. I knew I would be going with Federico. He could not afford to go anywhere without me.

Going on a journey with Federico was like going to war. Lists were drawn up of who should go and who should stay, then more lists were made of what to take. These lists changed every day, sometimes from hour to hour. Cecchi hardly slept for months and those parts of his beard which were gray turned white and those which were white fell out.

To begin with, there were to be no more than forty of us, but then three boys were required to look after the horses, and the cart master said he needed at least three servants and so did Federico's dressers. The number grew to eighty. The whole palace wanted to leave, but since few monasteries or palaces could house that number, carpenters, laborers, and sewers were added to build tents wherever we stayed. We were now a hundred. When Federico saw how much this would cost, he threatened to castrate Cecchi, burn his body, and then behead him. Cecchi reduced the number to sixty. By now Federico had grown so fat, and his gout so painful, that a special cart had to be built to carry him. It was lined with silken cushions and sheets, and pictures of jousting knights were painted on the sides. Federico tested it twice a day to make sure it was comfortable.

Since Miranda and Tommaso were not going to Milano, they paid little attention to the preparations. Besides, they were too much in love to care. Although Miranda had not been with child, I feared that could happen while I was away and since she often spoke of marrying Tommaso I was tempted to tell her of the pact I had made with him. In truth, I was surprised he had not mentioned it, but I guessed this was because he now loved her and wanted to respect me. This changed my feelings toward him and in this mood I went to the kitchen intending to say that although the four years were not yet up I would be happy to announce their marriage.

Tommaso was placing pieces of spit-roasted thrushes onto slices of toast. He had mixed up some spices, which by smelling the bowl I could tell included fennel, pepper, cinnamon, nutmeg, egg yolks, and vinegar. He poured the mix over the birds, placed the slices of toast in a pan, and put them over the flames. I told him it was fit for a duke and there was no doubt that he would one day be cooking for the pope.

"I could be a chef in Roma or Firenze right now if I wanted to," he boasted. He told me about new recipes he had invented, of special foods and spices from India he wanted to try, even ways of improving the kitchen. Never once did he mention Miranda. The longer I listened, the more uneasy I became. I thought—he has grown tired of Miranda, but does not know it yet. So I said nothing about the marriage contract.

Miranda spoke of him with as much love as ever and wandered about the kitchen wanting to be close to him, but where they had once walked side by side, now Tommaso walked a little ahead. He no longer brought her ribbons or combs and looked away when she spoke to him. He yawned when she sang and once when I was watching from the window, I saw her lead his hand to her breast. Laughing, he pulled away and strode off.

Septivus told me that Miranda had missed her lessons and had been seen weeping in Emilia's garden. I looked for her there and in the stables, but could not find her. I sought out her friends, asking them if they knew the cause of Miranda's distress.

"Tommaso," they answered, as if the whole world knew. "We warned her his word was not to be trusted."

I found Miranda in our room tearing at her hair, beating herself about the breast, and scratching her face like the shrieking harpies in Dante's *Inferno*. "He no longer loves me," she wept.

"No. It cannot be true."

"It is!" she screamed. "He told me. He told me!"

I sliced a mandrake root into tiny pieces, fed her a little, and she fell into a restless sleep. Then I sharpened my knife and went looking for Tommaso.

He was putting on a tight-fitting, green velvet jacket over some deep red silk hose. Rings twinkled on his fingers and the chains around his wrist glinted in the moonlight. I asked him where he was going at this late hour.

"What is it to you?" He pulled on a pair of black boots.

"You have upset my daughter."

"Your daughter." He shook his curls so that they sprayed out across his neck. "Your prisoner. She cannot pee without you watching over her."

"That is because I do not want her to become a whore like the girl you are going to see."

"I am not going to see a whore," he said hotly.

"You told me you loved her."

"I did not tell her of our betrothal so I did not break my promise to her."

"In the Bible, Jacob waited for Rachel for fourteen years."

"That was the Bible." He adjusted the feather in his hat. "This is Corsoli. My name is Tommaso, not Jacob. And tonight I am going to hunt the hare."

"What happened to your love?"

He shrugged as if he had lost a cheap coin. I threw myself at him, grasped his throat, and slammed him into the wall. I pulled my dagger and pressed the point into the crevice by his neck bone.

"I will teach you to taste the peach before you buy it." I drove my knee into his stomach. "You think I will carefully cut your face like Miranda did?" I pierced the skin and could feel his flesh quivering around the point of the knife. Blood spurted over the blade. "Tell me, what happened to your love?"

"I do not know," he begged, "I do not know."

"You do not know?" I pulled the knife across his neck. I wanted him to feel as much pain as Miranda felt.

"Who knows where love goes?" he gasped in bewilderment.

I was about to drive the knife into Tommaso's throat when a voice said, "No, Babbo!" with such power that I stopped.

Miranda was standing behind me, her head lifted high, her face as white as chalk. "He is not worth dying for."

"But he—"

"If you kill him and are hanged, what will happen to me?"

I lowered my knife. Tommaso pointed to Miranda and cried, "If you believe this will put me in your debt, then kill me now."

Miranda replied. "It is I who owe you. For you have closed my heart and opened my eyes." She reached her hand out to me, "Babbo, come. Anger shortens our lives and we have much to be grateful for."

I told her to come to Milano with me. "You will see wonderful palaces. There will be balls and parties and many fine young men."

"I do not want many fine young men."

I asked if there was any way I could be of comfort to her.

She said, "I am comforted by God. It is Tommaso who is restless.

He always has been and always will be. That is his nature. That is why he needs me."

"You still love him? After what he has done to you?"

"Does the shepherd stop loving the lamb who strays? I am his balm, Babbo. Without me he is lost."

Then she lay down on her bed and in a few moments was sleeping the sleep of the dead, while I stared out at the hillside wondering if I would ever be as wise as she.

Federico wanted to leave at the end of Lent, but Nero was sick and we had to wait three days. Then Federico would not leave on the seventh of the month, so it was not until the following Tuesday that the bishop blessed the journey and wished Federico "*buona ventura*" in his desire to find a wife.

As we emerged from the Duomo Santa Caterina into the bright spring morning, the bell rang joyfully and the most beautiful rainbow I had ever seen embraced the heavens, each color so clear and vibrant that we knew God was watching over us.

Twenty knights dressed in full armor climbed upon their horses, their red and white banners waving from their lances. Then came Federico's cart (pulled by eight horses), twenty more knights, carts containing Federico's clothing, and another cart bearing gifts. After that were the falconers, chamberlains, grooms, clerks, kitchen staff, dressers, whores, and more carts containing everything else.

Miranda watched from our window as we gathered in the courtyard. The night before I had urged her to practice her lyre, fulfill her duties cheerfully, and promise to take several drops of a potion for her humors before she went to bed. In truth, it was the juice of apple mixed with the powder of a dead frog and it dulled all feelings of romance. Although Tommaso was no longer in love with her, I feared that because she was a woman she might fall in love with someone else just to show him she no longer cared.

"Women are different than men," I counseled her. "They are weaker in the face of love, yet they are braver in their pursuit of it and I do not want you to get with child."

"Nor do I," she had yawned.

Now she suddenly ran out of the palace and threw herself into my arms. I held her close and whispered I was sorry she was not coming and that I would miss her. She said she was sorry for her rudeness and, putting on a brave smile, said that I had no need to worry on her behalf; she would discharge all of her duties faithfully and with good cheer.

There was a fanfare of trumpets, Federico's carriage stirred, and then we were moving out of the courtyard toward the Weeping Steps like a long colorful snake. All of Corsoli watched us leave. Federico threw a few gold coins to the cheering crowds though I swear the cheering became even louder after we passed through the city gates.

A brisk wind chased the puffy white clouds across the bright blue sky. The green hills were dotted with patches of yellow violas and blue lupines. Everywhere the sound of running water accompanied us, dripping from trees, spilling over rocks and rushing in little streams underfoot to the bottom of the valley. I felt the same as I did when I first left home: this journey would change my life!

Halfway down the valley, Federico's cart bounced over a boulder, the back left wheel snapped off, and the cart crashed to the ground. Federico emerged like a mad bull, tangled up in sheets and blankets, red in the face. "Who built this piece of shit?" he screamed.

Cecchi said they were Frenchmen who had been hired for the task, but who had since left Corsoli.

"Then we declare war on France," Federico shouted.

"Is that before or after the cart is fixed?" I muttered. A chamberlain next to me laughed. Federico ordered him killed. Instead, he was taken back to the palace and thrown into the dungeon. Cecchi said he knew some Italian workmen who could fix the cart and while Federico was carried back to the palace, Cecchi sent for the men who had built it—they were from Corsoli—and warned them if they did not repair the cart correctly they would be hanged. Two days later the procession started again. This time no one watched us leave.

The second day Federico complained that the path was too bumpy and any rock or stone larger than a ducat had to be removed before we could continue. Every servant, soldier, and minister—even Cecchi—had to get down on their hands and knees and clear them all away. By the end of the morning the road was so smooth you could have rolled an egg on it. Cecchi said at this rate it would take five years to get to Milano. Federico cursed and ordered all the geese from the nearby farms killed, and their feathers stuffed into his cushions. From then on many farmers drove their livestock into hiding when they heard we were coming. The abbeys were not so lucky.

At the bottom of the valley, we stopped at the abbey of Abbot Tottorini, the same one who had turned Miranda and Tommaso away during the plague. I remembered that he made his own wine and cheese and thought it only right to tell Federico how wonderful they were. Federico agreed with me. Indeed, he liked them so much we stayed for a whole week.

On the fifth day, I rode to my father's farm. Although my last visit had been a bitter one, I hoped that time had softened his heart toward me. I wanted him to see what I had made of myself. His house looked as if the slightest wind would blow it down. I looked about but could not see him, so I called out his name.

"In here," he cried out.

I no longer remembered if the house had always stunk like that or if it was because I was now used to the perfumes of the palace, but I could not enter and stood in the doorway. At last, my father's shrunken frame limped out of the darkness. He was bent over almost double now and he smelled of decay and death. He squinted at my new leather jerkin and brightly colored hose, but although I said my name I was not sure if he knew who I was. I put my arms around him and offered him a few coins. He could not open his hands properly so I pushed the coins into the spaces between his fingers. I told him I was accompanying Duke Federico to Milano and asked if he wanted to see the procession.

"What for?" he croaked.

"The knights, the duke's carriage. They are magnificent."

"Magnificent? Spain! Spain is magnificent."

"Spain? What do you know about Spain? You have never been out of the valley!"

"Vittore tells me," he said. "Spain is magnificent."

"Oh, so Vittore has fled to Spain."

"He is commanding a ship!"

"Yes, and I am the king of France."

He waved a finger at me. "Jealous," he shouted. "You are jealous. Jealous!"

"And you are a fool!" I said, climbing on my horse. "And I was a fool to come here."

He tried to throw the coins at me, but his hands could not let go of them.

The abbot Tottorini was waiting for me when I returned, his fat face sagging around his jowls. He hissed that all his wine had been drunk, and his cheese and fruit eaten. He said he prayed that all my children grew tails, my blood would boil, and that I caught the French disease. I told him he should wait until we had left before he insulted me or I would tell Federico about some of the tricks he liked to perform with the nuns. Then I made sure that whatever wine and cheese we had not drunk or eaten, we took with us.

I almost forgot! Just before we reached the abbey, we passed a peasant standing in his field. His skinny body was lost inside his shift and his naked legs protruded into the stony soil like sticks of wood which had been left out in the sun. When some of the soldiers laughed at him, the peasant ran alongside Federico's carriage, screaming that he had lost his children in the famine while Federico ate like a pig. He ran between the horses and before anyone could stop him, leaped onto Federico's cart just as Federico stuck his head out to discover the cause of the yelling.

*Oi me!* I do not know who was more surprised, the peasant or Federico. Before the peasant could harm Federico, the knights slashed him to pieces with their swords and he fell onto the ground where the knights continued to lance and slice him long after his soul had left the earth.

Federico was eager to reach Firenze and stay with Bento Verana, a wealthy wool merchant who traded with Corsoli. Most of the servants remained on Verana's estate in the country, but a few of us stayed in his palazzo overlooking the Arno. Verana was a thin-faced, stern-looking man who dressed as a priest and regarded his wealth as something to be hoarded and not enjoyed. But because he treated everyone with dignity and was said to be honest in his business dealings, he had no need of a food taster. He said at our first meal that since he considered Federico a friend he would be offended if Federico used a food taster in his house.

Federico licked his lips, not knowing what to say. I said, "My Lord, it is not that Duke Federico fears being poisoned. He has a tender digestion and as mine is the same as his, by tasting his food I am able to spare him any discomfort before it arises."

Federico nodded and said that was exactly so. Unfortunately, I could not soothe the other discomforts so easily. The Firenzani ate differently than we in Corsoli did. They liked more vegetables— pumpkins, leeks, broad beans—and less meat. They ate spinach with anchovies, baked fruit into their ravioli, and made desserts in the shapes of emblems. They used less seasoning and considered the uses of spices a gaudy display of wealth, employed squares of cloth called napkins to wipe their mouths, ate from gold plates instead of trenchers, and covered their mouths when they belched.

"There are so many things to remember," Federico complained at dinner. "I cannot enjoy the food!"

"But conversation is the real food, is it not?" Verana answered. "Too much food leads to gluttony, and gluttony slows the brain just as too much drink dulls the senses. Because the body is forced to expend energy to digest the meal, conversation is forgotten and the diners are reduced to animals who gorge themselves in silence. In my house, conversation is first on the menu."

Septivus chimed in. "The joy of eating is like the joy of learning, for each feast is like a book. The dishes are words to be savored, enjoyed, and digested. As Petrarch said, 'I ate in the morning what I would digest in the evening. I swallowed as a boy what I would ponder as a man!' "

"Indeed," cried Verana. "To be a slave to the stomach instead of acquiring knowledge at the table is, in my reckoning, to fail as a man." Verana must have seen Federico's face, for even from where I was standing I could see that Federico's bottom lip was now lower than his chin. "But come, let us eat. Forget the seasoning, Federico. Truly the best seasoning is the company of good friends."

O my soul! I prayed for his sake that Septivus would not say another word for as surely as there are stars in the sky, one of Federico's black moods was coming on. So when Verana recommended a thin pancake stuffed with liver called *fegatelli,* I took a small bite and suggested Federico not eat it because his stomach was too delicate. Federico loved that.

"Did you see Verana's face?" he roared afterward. "Well done, Ugo." I hoped he would instruct Cecchi to give me a gold coin but he did not.

Verana said much of what he learned came from a book by a Dutchman called Erasmus, which had just been translated into Italian, and after dinner he presented a copy to Federico. No one had ever given Federico a book before and he held it in his hand as if he did not know what to do with it. When he returned to his room he threw the book at Cecchi and told him to burn it. We left Verana's palazzo soon after because Federico said he would starve if he stayed another day.

I was sorry to leave Firenze. While it is true the Firenzani have "sharp eyes and bad tongues," they live in a beautiful city! I saw the blessed Duomo and the statues in the Piazza della Signoria and best of all, the stupendous David by Michelangelo next to City Hall. I wanted to kiss that magnificent sculptor's hands and kneel at his feet, but his servant said that unfortunately he had left for Roma that very morning. I saw many fine palaces built by wealthy princes and merchants, but the ones I liked best belonged to the guilds. As we journeyed on to Bologna, I could not stop thinking about them and soon an idea began forming in my head. I had never had an idea such as this one before and it thrilled and excited me. The hills on either side of us were covered in a rich tapestry of red, blue, and yellow flowers. I was sure that God Himself must live here since harmony and beauty are the truest aspects of His soul and my idea was in keeping with these surroundings. Thus I was sure my idea had been blessed by God. It was as follows:

Of all the servants, be they chamberlains, grooms, scribes, cooks or so on, surely the food taster is the bravest of all. What other servant risks his life not once, but two or three times a day just in the service of his work? In truth, we are as brave as the bravest knight for if a knight is outnumbered in battle he runs away—I have known many that fled before the battle even started—but does a food taster run away? No! Every day he does battle and every day he stays until the battle is ended. Why then, if there are guilds for goldsmiths, lawyers, spinners, weavers, bakers, and tailors, should there not be a guild for food tasters? Are we not as important as they? The very existence of our princes depends on us! Of course a food tasters' guild would be smaller, sometimes only one person to a city, but we could still meet, discuss new foods, poisons, antidotes, even assassins.

Thinking about this helped pass the hours of travel. Even as I was hunting for boar I was planning our initiation rites. I thought they should not only be severe, but useful. I listed them as follows.

1. An apprentice food taster should be starved for three days, after which he should be blindfolded and made to taste tiny amounts of poison which would be increased until he identified them correctly. If he survived he would have proven his ability. If he died, then he was obviously not suited for the task.

2. To make sure his heart was strong, he should be told after eating a meal that there was poison in it. If he immediately clutched an amulet and began praying to God, he should be thrown out the window, for if there had been poison in the meal, he would soon be dead anyway. But if he immediately found a woman and made sport with her, then he should be admitted with full honors. For a food taster must remain calm at all times: calmness will save a life, whereas a man who dabbles in superstition will act on the first thing that comes to his mind, which is usually wrong!

3. Most importantly, the examinations must be held in summer and in the open air since the emetics would cause such a foul odor in an enclosed room as to make a pig sick.

Having made these rules, I looked forward to meeting other food tasters to discuss my ideas with them.

But I met very few tasters on the way to Milano. A clown who claimed that he had faked his death was too stupid to change his story even after I told him who I was and so did not deserve to be in my guild. I also met a thin, nervous man with white hair, a pronounced nose, and thick lips. He sat in a chair in the sun and did not answer my questions, but every so often licked his lips with his tongue. When I asked him why, he said he was not aware he did so. Later, I saw other tasters do the same thing. They said they had been doing it ever since they could remember and were of the opinion that wet lips could better detect poisons.

In Piacenza, I met a taster who was convinced Federico had told me to fake my death; since *he*, the taster, was not capable of such cunning, how could *I* have done so?

Federico had planned to arrive in Milano in time for the feast of San Pietro. The guests included princes, merchants from Liguria, Genoa, and Savoy, as well as cardinals and an ambassador of the emperor. These many men of importance would ensure that many women would be there, too. However, we had traveled so slowly that the feast was already in progress the night we arrived. Federico was in a bad mood. Outside Parma, the cart had lurched unexpectedly while one of his whores was sitting on top of him. She had hit her head on a wooden beam, her eyes had become glassy, and she had muttered strange things. Fearing he would catch her madness, Federico left her on the side of the road. His gout had also been plaguing him badly. The gatekeepers allowed him and a few servants, including me, into the *castello*. The others were to follow in the morning.

I must say something in praise of Milano. If a finer city exists then they must invent new words to describe it. To begin with, the roads in the center of the city are not only as straight as gun barrels but also paved too, so that the carriages, of which there are many, may have a smoother ride! Is that not a miracle? And the castle! If a more magnificent one exists I have not seen it. It is almost as big as Corsoli itself and has an enormous moat around it. They told me the pig-swilling French stole many of its treasures, but *potta!* Everywhere I looked I saw the most beautiful paintings and the most exquisite sculptures! I remember a painting of Mary Magdalen by Il Giampietrino, which was so beautiful and tender it was no wonder Our Lord had reached out to her. By now I could write well enough to record things like this.

One staircase, designed by Leonardo da Vinci, was so magnificent I walked up and down it several times because it made me feel like a prince. Bold, colorful carpets of Oriental designs lined the hallways. A hundred scenes were painted on the ceilings and from the center of each room hung a chandelier with a thousand candles. Servants scurried to and fro, beautiful women entertained themselves, and from every room came the sound of laughter and music. If one is going to die in the service of a prince, I said to myself, then let it be for Duke Sforza.

Then I found the kitchen! Oh, what better sanctuary is there for a weary traveler than the hiss of boiling pots, the sight of steam curling up from the oven, and the warm smell of pies cooking? And what a kitchen! Compared to this, the kitchen in Corsoli was like a mousehole. There were three times as many ovens, five times the number of cauldrons, and more knives than in the Turkish army. I ate quickly because I wanted to visit the servants' quarters, for I was sure that such a magnificent prince would have extended his generosity to those who worked for him. I should have known better.

Just as in Corsoli, the servants' rooms were smaller and uncared for. Since French and Swiss soldiers had recently lived here, the stench was almost unbearable. As I wandered the hallways, my disappointment increasing with each step, the sound of voices pulled me to an open door. I peered in.

Six or seven men sat drinking and playing cards. One, a dandy with a careless attitude, wore a large feather in his hat and lounged with one leg over the arm of his chair. Another was a man with a bulbous onionlike face whose right eyelid was half closed from a knife wound. He was arguing with a fat man who looked as if he might have been a monk. "But if he sides with Venezia, then what?" the onion-faced man said fiercely.

The Fat One shrugged. "It depends on the pope."

The onion-faced man spat. "The pope changes sides more often than the weather."

"Who does not?" said the Fat One. "Besides I heard—" He saw me in the doorway. "What do you want?" he said brusquely.

"I have just arrived with Duke Federico Basillione DiVincelli," I said. "I am his food taster."

The others stopped their conversation to look at me. "Welcome," said the dandy in a smooth high voice. "We are all tasters here."

"Yes, come in," they cried.

At long last, I was home.

They sat me down at the table and a small, drunk man with bad teeth and a mouth that turned down at the corners like a frog poured a goblet of wine. I seldom drank wine, but since I was among friends I saw no reason not to enjoy myself. He handed me the goblet and said, "Mind the arsenic."

We laughed loudly. "*Salute!*" I said.

"*Salute!*" They cheered.

The wine swirled around my mouth like a spring river washing away the weary taste of my journey. "*Benissimo!*" I said. "*Benissimo!*"

"You do not have this in Corsoli?"

"We do not have anything in Corsoli."

"*We* do not have anything here either," the small man laughed, from which I gathered the flask had been stolen. They clapped me on the back and introduced themselves. Onionface served Duke Sforza, the small drunk a Cardinal of Ferrara, the Fat One a rich Genoese merchant. I believe the others were German and French.

"What is Federico like?" asked the drunk.

"Fat."

He laughed. "No, to work for."

"I have never worked for anyone else so I do not know."

Onionface jabbed me in the ribs. "Have you seen the food taster for the archbishop of Nîmes?"

"No," I said. "Is he here?"

"A he!" they laughed. "He is a she!"

"A woman?"

"As God is my witness," said the Fat One.

"I would like to dip my bone into her bush to see if it is poisoned," a German said, and we roared with laughter and drank again.

My heart soared. Here at last were men who risked their lives as I did. Who understood not the dangers of war, but the evil hidden in a leaf of lettuce. Here were men who would understand my guild! We spoke of which foods we liked and which we hated, which cooks we trusted and which to beware of. Oh, I could have talked like this forever and I would have done so had not the dandy suddenly slapped his thigh and said, "You are *that* Ugo DiFonte."

"Yes, that is me. Ugo DiFonte. Ugo, the magnificent!" I was a little drunk by now.

"Ugo the magnificent?" the Fat One said.

The dandy leaned across the table toward me. "Tell us what really happened."

"What happened when?" the Fat One asked.

"Yes, when?" I said.

"When Federico killed his wife and his mother-in-law because he thought the food was poisoned—"

"That was you?" said the drunk. The others murmured excitedly and crowded around me. They were younger than they had first appeared, some no more than boys. The drunk climbed onto a chair and, cupping his hands like a trumpet gave three loud blasts, shouted, "I salute you!"

Onionface knocked him to the floor.

"Why did you do that?" whined the drunk. "It is time one of us survived." I wanted to help him up, but Onionface stopped me.

"Never mind him," he said. "Tell us."

"Yes, tell us, tell us," the others pleaded, their faces desperate for any story of triumph.

"Ah, there will be time enough for that. Tonight, let us just drink and forget our cares."

No one moved. Perhaps I needed to be coaxed, one said, and called for more wine. They filled the goblets and shouted, "A long life."

"Tell us!" Onionface repeated. "We are all friends here." For all his bullying he seemed more anxious than the others.

"Wait," the drunk appealed, "he has just arrived. We cannot expect him to give away his secrets before we show him some of ours." He dug his hand into his pouch. "Ever seen one of these?" He held up a small, yellow stone dangling on the end of a chain. "It is a bezoar stone. From the belly of a cow. It saved my life."

"The only thing that saved your life," said Onionface, "was you were so drunk you threw up."

The drunk ignored him. "It gets hot in your hand if there is poison around."

"We all have them," said another, and, pushing the cards aside, spread a handful of stones on the table like a jeweler showing off his wares. The others did the same and in a moment the table was covered with objects of every size and color. As well as bezoar stones there were amulets of gold and silver, an earring which had belonged to John the Baptist, a stone from Jerusalem that threatened to crumble at the touch, a lock of Samson's hair, a fingernail of Saint Julian, a bee stinger locked in amber, finger rings of ivory. There were also ancient plants, the brain of a toad no bigger than my thumb, shells, pieces of ruby and topaz.

They picked up each piece in turn, told how it came into their possession, and boasted of its powers, each tale grander than the one before. Each time the owner swore to the Virgin Mary the tale was true—they had seen it with their own eyes or knew someone who had—and anyone who disputed them was a liar and should have their tongue cut out. No one doubted any of the stories and I saw for all their passions and boasts they were nothing more than ants, ants blindly marching forward without knowing why.

"I bet no one has one of these," said Onionface, holding out a dagger with a brown bone handle. "It is made from an African snake's fangs. It is the only one in the world."

"Then what is this?" said the Fat One, pulling out a knife with the same handle.

"This is the real one," Onionface said darkly, "I paid two hundred ducats for it."

"Then you were cheated," the Fat One smirked.

Onionface flicked the dagger around so the point was facing the fat man. The others hastily grabbed their stones and put them away.

"Neither of them are as good as a unicorn's bone, are they Ugo?" said the dandy, stepping between them.

"You have a unicorn bone?" Onionface asked.

They turned to me, the fight forgotten.

"I had one," I said, "but not anymore."

"What do you use, then?"

"Yes, show us," said the drunk.

"If you are hiding something—" The Fat One pushed me in the chest.

"I am not hiding anything."

"Then open your pouch," Onionface demanded.

I heard the door close behind me. Before I could pull my knife I was grabbed from behind and thrown to the floor. The Fat One sat on my chest. Onionface tore off my pouch, untied the string, and turned it upside down so the contents would spill out, but nothing did. It was empty.

A week earlier, just outside Cremona, it had rained for three days and three nights without stopping. The carts stuck in the mud and a child of a serving girl wailed so loudly that the knights wanted to kill her. I gave her my amulets to play with and told her stories of poisonings and hangings and other tragedies which befell noisy children. She listened quietly, hiding her face with her hair, so like Miranda when she was that age that I was about to tell her they were just tales when she suddenly snatched up my amulets and threw them into the darkness.

Although I had lost faith in them long ago, it had not occurred to me to throw them away so I jumped down into the pouring rain to search for them. By then, however, a dozen horses had already passed over that spot and unless the amulets themselves could have spoken I could never have separated them from the hundreds of stones beneath my feet. Since they did not mean anything to me I was not angry and I did not think of them again until the dandy turned my pouch upside down.

"Where are they?" Onionface said in bewilderment.

"I do not use them." I pushed the Fat One off my chest.

"You do not use talismans?" Onionface repeated. "But everyone uses them."

"Do they?" I brushed the dirt off my new, red velvet jacket.

They stared at me, waiting for me to explain myself.

I wanted to tell them that their charms and bones and stones were worthless, but they were too superstitious to give up their little shreds of hope. For the same reason, if I told them I relied only on my wits, they would not believe me and would accuse me of hiding something from them. No, they wanted me to give them a miraculous solution which would banish all their fears. So that is what I gave them.

"Magic," I said. "That is what I use." I was only half expecting they would believe me. Indeed, if only one of them had laughed I might have told them it was a joke.

But instead the Fat One said, "Only witches use magic."

As one they took a step backward, gaping at me as if I was the devil himself. Christ! What fools! What little respect I had for them vanished in that instant. In the end it mattered not. The word had fallen out of my mouth and I could not put it back.

"Then he must be a witch," Onionface said, pointing at me. His stupid bullying face annoyed me and I snapped at his finger with my teeth, catching one of the tips before he could pull it away. If they did not think I was a witch before, they did now. Some stumbled over themselves to get away from me, others pulled their daggers. I knew I must not show any fear so I bowed my head, wished them all "*Buona notte*," and very calmly walked into the hallway.

On the way back to Federico's quarters I could not help laughing at Onionface's stupidity. "*Ha il cervello di una gallina!*" as the saying goes. No, a chicken had *more* brains than he did, but as I lay down I was overcome with disappointment. No wonder there was no guild of food tasters. Nor, I saw now, was there any chance of there ever being one.

The next morning I cursed my mouth for running away with itself. Overnight my victory had become tarnished. I had never given any thought to the Inquisition, but now the word flew into my mind and nested there. I had not only said I knew magic, but also that I was a practitioner of it. If one of the tasters told his master or a priest, I could be hanged. I prayed that the tasters were as stupid as they looked and would believe that I would do them harm if they told anyone. And then, as quickly as my fears arose, they melted away for that evening I saw the woman the tasters had been talking about— Helene, food taster for the archbishop of Nîmes.

It had been nearly three years since the death of Agnese and during that time my heart had lain as dormant as a sleeping squirrel. Now it woke as if it was the first day of spring. O my soul. O blessed saints. The tasters had been far too modest in their praise. Helene was perfection itself. All of summer's flowers blended into one. She was slight of stature, yet there was a sense of sureness about her, like a young tree that bends in the wind but does not break. The French sun had tanned her skin to a light shade of brown, and her blonde hair was cut short in the French style. Everything about her—her hands, her feet, her breasts—was small and in perfect proportion, except for her nose, and her blue eyes, which were large and deep as spring pools. She dressed simply and did not paint her face, but when she smiled, her face seemed to light up from the inside and all the gold and jewelry in the world paled beside her. Not that she did anything to attract attention. And yet for that very reason I could not take my eyes off her.

Her movements were small and purposeful; she did not so much disturb the air as glide through it like a melody. All night long I repeated her name for it was the most beautiful I had ever heard. I borrowed paper, ink, and quill and wrote it over and over. I formed it out of stones, flowers, and leaves.

Helene remained closer to the archbishop than his shadow, assisting him in everything he did, whether it was arranging his platters, playing cards, or reading to him. I cursed him for condemning her to such a dangerous task, but it was hard to dislike him. He was filled with good humor and his big, red face creased in laughter when he told stories of the pope and other cardinals. At the serving table, I tried to tell Helene that she had slipped into my heart and I could not remove her. But I blushed when she looked at me and could not speak. I imagined her voice would be as musical as that of a thrush, but the sound which came out of her small pink mouth was low like a man's and sent shivers down my back. She caressed each word she spoke as if it was a precious child she hated to lose and, as I listened to her utter the most simple things, I suddenly wanted to hear her say my name more than anything in the world. I tried every trick that would give her reason to do so, but almost as if she knew what I wanted, she found ways of answering me—that is, if she answered me at all—by not saying it. To hear her say my name became my one desire. I could not sleep because of it.

I wrote her a sonnet. I had never written one before, but if Miranda could write poems to Tommaso why could I not write one, too? I rose early to be inspired by the beauty of the sunrise. At night I studied the mysteries of the moon. I remembered poems Septivus had read to Federico. I labored over my creation every waking moment, writing and rewriting it. Each hour I spent with it renewed my love for her. Thus, when at last I completed it I was both pleased and sad. It is as follows:

> When first my eyes your radiance did behold
> No breath, no sound, no movement could I make

> Long had I slept, but now I was awake
> Gazing on wonders no dream had foretold.
> Your hair, ashine like summer's wheaten gold
> Your eyes, twin pools of Como's blue lake
> And oh, your cherried mouth my heart did break—
> So soft it was, so kind, and yet so bold.
> Then when you spoke, such music did cascade
> As would make angels move from their addresses
> To sail for Earth in Heaven's winged ships.
> Life Eternal would I have given in trade
> And all the bliss of Eden's sweet caresses
> To hear my name drop once from your sweet lips.

I wanted to give it to Helene right away, but I was afraid she might not like it. Then we would never speak and that would drive me to despair. "Courage," I said to myself. "Courage."

When at last I did speak with her I did not have the poem with me so all my stored-up questions and desires burst forth in my eagerness to express myself. I spoke of the food, the wine, the ceiling, and then interrupted myself to praise her beauty. I talked of walking up and down the staircase da Vinci had built and of the straight roads in the city. I could not stop talking for I feared that if I did I might never be able to start again. And, when I could think of nothing more to say I told her that, too. She waited until I was out of breath and then said, "I must serve the archbishop." I had not realized she was holding a platter of food the whole time.

In my dream that night, Helene was walking barefoot through a garden of yellow and blue flowers. Her dress was blood red and embroidered with gold. No matter how fast I ran I could not catch her. She did not look over her shoulder and yet I knew she wanted me to pursue her. After running through a bower of bushes she descended a flight of steps which led to a small piazza. Fearing she would escape me, I called her name. She stopped on the bottom stair, turned and looked as if she would speak, but instead of words, nightingales flew out of her mouth, all of them singing so sweetly that I was mesmerized by the beauty of their song. When I looked again, Helene had vanished.

I awoke with such longing and desire that I could not move. I prayed to God that Federico would find a woman so I might stay longer in Milano. I was drunk with love. So drunk that when the Fat One purposely jogged my arm I nearly dropped the platter of fruits I was carrying.

This was the second time the tasters had tried to hurt me. After our first meeting they avoided me. If I saw that lout Onionface in the hallways, I lowered my eyes and muttered, pretending to cast a spell. He shouted and pulled his knife, but he was too cowardly to do anything. The Fat One and the dandy were more dangerous. Before the Fat One jogged my arm, the dandy had tripped me and I had fallen into a German knight who beat me round the head for my pains. Now I would make them pay for their foolishness.

The next day as the dandy reached to pick up a bowl of meats, I poured a boat of steaming hot sauce over his hand. He screamed— not too loudly, for the banquet was starting—and accused me of burning him deliberately. I said he was lucky I was not holding a knife or I would have cut his hand off. After that I snuck up behind the Fat One and whispered, "If *you* try anything, I will carve your fat *culo* into more slices of bacon than you can count."

He gave a shriek and waddled away as fast as he could.

I learned that Helene and the archbishop walked the same path through the gardens every day at noon. I made it a practice to be there at the same time, my eyes half closed, as if writing poetry or studying the flowers, but all the while conspiring to bump into them as if by accident. Several days later I did just that, but because my eyes were half closed I trod on the archbishop's toe by mistake.

"A thousand pardons," I said. "I was consumed with my own thoughts."

"May I ask," said the archbishop, rubbing his injured foot, "What thoughts concern you on such a beautiful day?"

"I was thinking that all man has to do to be aware of God's grace is to look at the beauty around us." I said this to the archbishop although I was looking at Helene.

"Perhaps then," the archbishop snapped, "it would be better to keep your eyes open so you could *see* them!"

I did not mind that he was angry because this would give me reason to address him again. However, when that day came, I was again pretending to be deep in thought and so missed my path and tripped over that oaf Onionface and two other tasters who were hiding behind a bush. They were armed with cudgels and had obviously been waiting for me. It was only because they were as surprised as I that I avoided most of their blows. From then on I stopped walking in the garden and resolved to meet Helene in some other way.

While all this was going on, Federico was having no better luck than I in his pursuit of women. Every woman in Milano who was young or pretty or wealthy said she was betrothed. A few fat women with mustaches as thick as hairbrushes flounced around in front of him, but one look from Federico, or at him, and they left as quickly as they had come. He was sure the other dukes and princes, particularly Duke Sforza, were laughing behind his back, and so he avenged himself by beating them at cards. He soon amassed a small fortune and delighted in taunting Sforza, claiming the duke owed him enough to pay for his journey three times over. Cecchi pulled at his beard, urging Federico to leave before Duke Sforza regained his losses by force. Federico replied, "Did Caesar run? Did Marc Anthony run? Did Caligula run?"

I did not know Caligula played cards. *Potta!* I did not know who Caligula was. I did not care whether Federico won or lost as long as he stayed in Milano.

We had been in Milano for almost a month and the *castello* was again filled with dukes, princes, and rich merchants from Savoy, Piedmont, Genoa, and Bergamo who had come to celebrate Sforza's birthday.

"New blood," Federico muttered. His gout was causing him pain and he looked for anything that might take his mind off it.

I, too, was looking, not only for ways to speak with Helene, but also for ways to avoid the other tasters.

What a feast we had on Duke Sforza's birthday! Eel, lamprey, sole, trout, capon, quail, pheasant, boiled and roasted pork and veal, lamb, rabbit, venison, meat tart with cooked pears! Caviar and oranges fried with sugar and cinnamon, oysters with pepper and oranges, fried sparrows with oranges, rice with chopped sausage, boiled rice with calves' lungs, bacon, onion, and sage, a wonderful sausage called *cervellada* made of pork fat, cheese and spices, and pigs' brains. And that is just the food I remember!

At every banquet there had been a subject for discussion which had been decided upon beforehand. I did not listen to these any more than I listened to the speeches. Every orator thought he was the best in Italy, if not in what he said than in how long he took to say it, so after a few words my ears became deaf. I do remember that honor had been discussed as well as love, beauty, laughter, and wit. At this banquet the subject decided upon was trust.

There was talk about the treaty Venezia had signed with the emperor and how it would affect Milano. How Venezia could not be trusted any more than Firenze or Roma and that each state could only be concerned with its own interest and that was always changing. Someone said that the only true trust was between a man and his wife. This brought much laughter and everyone told of women who had deceived their husbands and the other way around. This talk went on for quite some time and then the archbishop said the only true trust was between God and man. A German soldier argued that God could not be trusted since no one knew what God was thinking. Someone else said that other than a dog, a prince could only place his trust in a faithful servant.

I was tasting some gorgonzola, cheese made from cows' milk which Federico loved, when a chill ran through me. It was not the cheese, but the conversation.

Duke Sforza said, "Federico places his greatest trust in his food taster, is that not so?"

Federico slowly moved his aching foot and replied that he did indeed place great trust in me.

"Would you sell him?" the duke of Savoy asked.

"Sell him? No. I need him. He advises me on the balance of humors and he anticipates poisons."

"Anticipates poisons?" said a Genoese merchant. "You exaggerate."

"I do not," Federico replied.

"He is the one who survived the poison that was meant for you, is he not, Federico?" Duke Sforza inquired.

Everyone craned their necks to see me. And that is when I noticed those traitorous, rat-shit dogs, Onionface, the dandy, and the Fat One, smirking and rubbing their greasy hands with glee.

"Yes," Federico said, "I can point to any dish and just by one taste he can tell me the ingredients in it."

"Then he must be able to identify every taste that exists," someone said.

"Every one I have come across," Federico answered.

"That is impossible," Sforza replied, gobbling a piece of veal shank covered in a gremalada sauce.

Federico's face turned red. "It is not," he said slowly.

"Well then," Sforza smiled, and, pointing to an uneaten platter in the middle of the table, said, "Will you wager he can tell us the ingredients in this dish?"

I tried to remember who had brought that platter to the table.

"What is it? Polpetta?"

"I do not know. But if he can identify all of the ingredients, I will double your winnings," said Duke Sforza. "If he cannot, you lose everything you have won."

My throat closed up.

"How shall we prove it?" Federico asked.

"My cook will write down exactly what he used."

The cook must have been waiting outside the door because he scuttled in like a cockroach. Someone magically produced some paper and a quill. The cook wrote down the list of ingredients and folded the paper, and it was placed on the table next to the polpetta. I looked to Cecchi for some guidance, but he was tugging at his beard. Everything had happened so fast we were taken unawares.

"I will join that wager," said the duke of Savoy, throwing several rings and medallions onto the table. They were joined quickly by golden earrings, goblets, silver necklaces, headbands, brooches.

The Fat One poured more wine for the duke of Savoy. Onionface licked his lips and I swore he winked at me. The dandy smiled coyly from behind Duke Sforza's chair. Suddenly, there in the midst of the magnificent paintings, the chandeliers with their thousand candles, the golden platters filled with delicious food, I saw myself writhing on the ground with Duke Sforza standing over me saying, "You lose, Federico. He guessed everything but the poison."

The polpetta was poisoned! I knew it! I wanted to tell Federico, but how could I? I could see the pile of jewels reflected in his eyes; he already possessed them! His determination spurred me on. If he wanted to win, then so did I! It was a moment in which the spirit of God spoke through me as it had when I rose from my dusty bean patch and said, "I will take Lucca's place." Now I turned to Duke Sforza, who was sitting at the table opposite Federico, and said, "I am willing, if your taster is."

"*My* taster?" said the duke.

"It would make the bet more exciting, if while I am tasting the polpetta, your taster could tell us," and here I pointed to a bowl of ripe blueberries, "what is in this bowl?"

Onionface's mouth dropped open.

"The bowl of berries?" Duke Sforza frowned.

I nodded. The dukes, merchants, knights, and princes looked at one another. Onionface looked to the dandy and the Fat One, but they were as stunned as he.

Duke Sforza laughed. "Yes, why not?"

I picked up the bowl and walked slowly toward Onionface. Halfway between the two tables, I stopped. Closing my eyes, I muttered something that sounded like a curse in Arabic just loud enough for Onionface to hear. In truth, I was praying silently to God, imploring Him that if He rewarded those who were righteous, brave, and honorable, to come to my aid.

Then I raised the bowl to my face and turned slowly in a circle. I pretended not to see the faces staring at me, some in bewilderment, others in surprise. The archbishop was frowning and Helene was looking at me with wide open eyes. I remember thinking, now she will know I exist.

When I had turned a full circle I blew slowly over the berries and then placed the bowl in Onionface's hands. Beads of sweat appeared on his brow. I could smell his fear. I turned my back on him and walked to my place. "Let us eat at the same time," I said, lifting a piece of veal from the platter.

Onionface looked at the berries and then at me. "He is a witch," he whimpered, pointing to me. Cecchi and Bernardo burst into laughter.

"He is scared," Septivus said. The others repeated, "He is scared!" The whole of Corsoli was behind me!

"Go on!" Federico suddenly roared. "Take one!" Others, too, added their voices, shouting, "Yes, take one."

It was as if Onionface had been challenged, and not me. I picked up a piece of veal. Sforza said something to Onionface. Onionface reached for one of the berries, then he withdrew his hand. Sweat trickled down his cheeks.

"Pick one!" The Genoese merchant shouted.

"No, do not touch it," someone said. "He has put a spell on it."

"By God! I will eat one," said a German knight.

"No," shouted Cecchi.

Federico rose to his feet, his face twisting with pain because of the weight on his gouty foot, and leaned his massive great body toward Onionface. This made everyone stand, even the archbishop. The dogs barked and a candle fell from the chandelier onto the pile of jewelry. No one was looking at me. Onionface reached into the bowl and picked up a berry.

"Taste it!" shouted Federico.

"Now!" I called out, and lifted the veal to my mouth.

Onionface raised the berry to his mouth. His hand seemed to be at war with itself, one force pushing it toward his lips, the other pulling it away. The berry touched his mouth and as soon as it did, he dropped the bowl. His eyes bulged out of his head as he staggered backward, lurching about like a ship in a storm, clutching at his heart. Then he crashed to the ground, spit drooling from his mouth. For an instant no one moved. Then the archbishop pushed his way to Onionface's side and, in the time it takes for a fly to beat its wings, someone behind me pulled my arm down and replaced the piece of veal with another.

"I am ready to taste," I said loudly, and bit into the veal. Everyone turned around.

Federico grabbed the paper in the middle of the table.

"I taste mozzarella cheese . . . raisins . . . parsley," I said loudly, "Garlic, salt, fennel, pepper, and, of course, veal."

"That is right," said Federico, reading off the paper, "although not in that order. But that does not matter, does it?"

Onionface was forgotten as Duke Sforza snatched the paper from Federico. The dandy and the Fat One were looking at me, waiting for me to scream, to shout out, to fall down. I knew I would not, but pretending I did not know they were watching, I took another bite, chewed it a little, furrowed my brow as if there was something wrong with it, coughed slightly, finished chewing, swallowed and belched loudly. "It is delicious!" I said, "I compliment the cook."

"I win!" Federico exclaimed, and scooped up as many jewels as he could in his fat, pudgy hands. Cecchi took the rest. Leaning on my arm, Federico walked out of the banquet hall, clenching his jaws, but refusing to acknowledge the pain his gout was causing him.

"Now," Federico said, as soon as we reached his quarters, "what was that about the polpetta?"

"My Lord, the polpetta was poisoned. I am sure of it."

"Poisoned!" His small eyes became like arrow points. "How do you know?"

"The other tasters have attacked me from the moment I arrived. Two weeks ago they lay in wait for me in the garden. They must have told Duke Sforza because if you recall he suggested the bet. They wanted to kill me and win back your winnings at the same time."

"Then why did you eat it if you knew it was poisoned?"

"Because you changed it, Your Honor."

"I changed nothing."

I looked to Cecchi. He shook his head, as did Piero, Bernardo, and Septivus.

Could I have imagined it?

"Triple the guards outside my door," Federico barked. "Cecchi, we leave in the morning."

The courtiers hurried to fulfill his commands. I wondered whether I had lost my senses and I tried to recall if I had touched the flesh of the hand that held the other piece of veal, but I could not.

"Ugo," Federico said.

"Yes, Excellency."

He ran his hands through the pile of jewels. "I do not know what happened. I do not care. But here." He tossed me a most beautiful silver ring sparkling with precious gems.

"*Mille grazie*, Your Excellency." I said, and kissed his hand.

"Be careful," he said roughly. "The Sforzas do not like to lose."

"*Mille grazie*, Duke Federico, *mille grazie*."

Septivus and Piero congratulated me as I entered the hallway, but Bernardo spat out some seeds and said, "You must have been born under the sign of the lion."

"Because of my boldness?"

"Because you have as many lives as a cat."

"To the winner go the spoils," Cecchi murmured, and told me to go to the bottom of the stairs.

Remembering what Federico had said, I took out my knife and slowly descended the steps, carefully looking all around me. The voices of other guests drifted toward me as I reached the bottom stair. But there was no one there except for the portraits staring at me from the walls. A voice whispered. "Ugo!"

I turned around and there she was, standing beside a column, her blue eyes shining in the light of the sconces. Helene. My Helene, calling my name.

"Are you all right?" She asked, raising her hand toward my throat.

"It was you! You switched—"

Footsteps came toward us. Helene pulled me behind the column and we waited until they passed. I would have been happy to remain there, feeling her warmth, smelling the sweetness of her hair. Motioning I should follow, she led me down staircases, through darkened hallways, and into the palace gardens. The stars were bright; the moon hung low over us.

"You saved my life, Helene." I needed to say her name aloud.

She shook her head so that her hair flew around her face. "Phppft! Those fools! What did you do to the berries?"

*"Niente."*

She smiled. "I did not think so. But he is dead."

"Onionface?"

"Onionface?"

"That is my name for him."

"Yes, Onionface." She smiled. "That was a good name for him. His heart stopped. I tried to explain to the archbishop, but he does not care."

"What concern is that of mine?"

"Because he investigates all suspicious activities for the Inquisition. He will not do anything tonight, but tomorrow . . . ?"

"But why?"

"You blew on the berries and Onionface died!" She shrugged as if no more explanation was necessary.

*Oi me!* How could I be thrust from heaven into hell so quickly? Helene paced in front of me, tapping her cheek with her finger. "How long are you staying in Milano?"

"We leave tomorrow."

"By which road?"

"I do not know—"

"Avoid Ferrara," she frowned. "The bishop has friends there."

"They do not ask me which way to go." I grasped her arms. "Why are you telling me this?"

She tucked her head to one side and looked at me. "I never believed those stories the other tasters said about you any more than I believed you poisoned the berries."

"How could you be so sure?"

She laughed. "If you knew magic you would not have said those stupid things in the garden or at the serving table."

I could not have stopped smiling had someone sewn my lips together. Every word from her mouth delighted me. I slid my hands down her arms till I felt her hands. They were soft and warm as I knew they would be. "But if the archbishop comes for me tonight—"

"He will sleep till morning. He drank a lot of wine."

Staring into her eyes I could see right into her heart; I saw myself walking beside her. I saw her bearing my children. I saw us old, unable to leave one another's side. I saw us in death, two branches of a tree entwined like Baucis and Philemon.

"Do you see our future?" she asked.

"You read minds, too?"

"Only yours, Ugo." She leaned forward and pressed her lips to mine.

Oh, Helene. Oh, my glorious Helene. My delight, my happiness, my Helene. To hear her call my name. Had any word ever sounded so sweet? I asked her to say it again and again. I wanted to memorize the sound of her voice in my heart. Joy surged through us, causing us to laugh for no other reason than we were alive. I could not keep from touching her, kissing her lips. I thought food was the sustenance for which I hungered, but again I was wrong. Holding her in my arms, I wept because I had found my strength, my rib, that part of me I did not know was missing. Even now I feel her skin upon mine. I smell her. Taste her sweat. I see her eyes, round and clear, I feel her breasts, her thighs, her small, strong feet. I hear her voice in my ears and in my heart. Oh, that my fingers could transfer her softness to this paper and my quill could capture her passion! The very thought of her illuminates my darkness even as the moon brightens this room. Everything I am cries out for her. O saints preserve me! To be overcome by such longing on the eve of the wedding. The past has reached into my present and captured my soul and I cannot write anymore.

# xxiii

When Helene pressed her lips against mine I was lifted beyond the skies to a place where all dreams are possible. I wanted to lie with her, but the sky was growing lighter and the servants would soon be rising to prepare our departure. I took Helene's hand and hurried to the stable. We mounted a stallion, whose impatient snorting woke a stable boy. He opened his mouth, as if to shout, but instead yelled, "Courage!" and threw us a bundle of bread and cheese.

At the gates, Helene told the guards that we needed wild parsley to soothe our princes' stomachs.

"Where are we going?" I asked as the *castello* faded from view behind us.

"France," Helene said, as if this was something we had both decided on.

I nodded. France. Why not? What was there here for me?

Our horse galloped with great speed. Soon the *castello* and Milano were no more than memories. Everything aided us in our journey. The grass lay down as we approached, the birds cheered us on, and the green hills beckoned us forward.

I imagined how Federico would gnash his teeth when he discovered I was missing. At first he would think I had been killed. He would surround himself with guards and leave hurriedly, clutching his winnings. But perhaps a horse would be reported missing. Then it would be known that I had left. I could be hanged just for taking a horse. Christ! I could be hanged just for leaving! But when I felt Helene's arms around my waist and her head against my back, I did not care. O, God in heaven! The devil take Federico and Duke Sforza and the whole lot of them. I was free! I could not contain my excitement and shouted with delight and wonder. For the third time in my life I had been reborn.

The snowcapped mountains lined up on our right like northern kings. Two travelers rode ahead of us and I called out to them, wanting to be certain that this path led to France. But as we galloped toward them, they grew frightened and raced away.

In the heat of the day we rested in a glade of beech trees and gorged ourselves on the bread and cheese. How good it tasted, each bite a blessing from heaven. I wanted to remember to tell Septivus that the most important thing about eating was not the food or the conversation but who you ate it with. We lay down amid the wildflowers and loved one another until we fell asleep.

When we awoke, the setting sun had ignited the mountaintops. We rode swiftly for several more hours before we stopped at an inn. The first people we saw when we entered were the travelers we had seen on the path. I assured them we had not intended them any harm. The smaller one clapped his hand to his heart and said, "*Ecco!* I thought I would die of fright. You looked like the avenging angel the way you rode toward us."

Helene told the innkeeper she was employed by the archbishop of Nîmes and offered to cook his favorite meal in exchange for a bed. The innkeeper, a fellow with bushy eyebrows and a runny nose, happily agreed, in part I believe to annoy his wife, a large buxom woman with the arms of a blacksmith. We soaked two chickens in wine, added vinegar and spices, and while they baked, Helene made polenta *cocina*—a polenta sprinkled with grated cheese and truffles—a Sunday delight in Piedmont.

After the first mouthful, the innkeeper said, "If you cook like this every day, I will hire you as soon as my wife dies." To which his wife replied, "I promise you however long you live I will live one day longer."

It was in these good spirits that we ate and drank, surrounded by good company and good food. Suddenly, Helene started to laugh, softly at first, but soon louder and louder and with great abandon. She pointed to my trencher where my polenta lay half eaten. Hers was, too. Only then did I understand why she was laughing. Food tasters both of us, we had not tasted our food before eating it. We had not sniffed at it, nibbled it, or tested it in any way, but had enjoyed it just as our companions were doing.

I pulled Helene from the bench, held her tightly in my arms, and kissed her. Even tired and weary from our journey, she was the most beautiful woman I had ever seen. "This moment," I told her, "will be carved in my heart forever."

Our companions cheered and the smaller man said it was easy to see we were deeply in love. Thus, we were fulfilling God's most divine law, for He had sent love to ease man's path through life, and the sicknesses and wars which plagued us existed because man had forgotten this divine commandment.

Three soldiers entered the inn and for a moment my heart stopped, but since they were not wearing Federico's colors or those of the archbishop I thought no more about them. The innkeeper brought the soldiers some wine and when he returned to our table he said, "Those soldiers keep looking at you."

I said I did not know why they should, but even as I was speaking two of them approached our table. The captain, a man with broad shoulders and a rough beard, said, "What is your name and where are your passports?"

I said, "Ugo DiFonte. I am traveling with Duke Federico Basillione DiVincelli of Corsoli, but I have left him." I do not know what excuse I was about to give, but it did not matter for as soon as I said Corsoli the soldiers looked at one another and the other interrupted, asking, "Is that close to the Convent Verecondo?"

I replied it was no more than half a day's ride. He asked if I had heard of a Prince Garafalo. I said I had not, but only because I had never been in this part of Italy before. At this he eagerly laid a hand on my arm. "You must come with us right away to see our prince."

When I asked why, he said he could not tell me. Well, I had not left one prison to be thrown into another! I pushed his arm away, and leaping up, I knocked him backward over the bench with a blow to the head. Then I grabbed the carving knife and, pulling Helene behind me, shouted, "Though we are strangers here we hoped that we would be treated with respect. But if you or the prince are intent on harming us, then be prepared to die for I will not exchange the liberty God has given me for the chains of man."

He quickly rose up and said they were not here to harm us. The innkeeper cried out, "Prince Garafalo is a good man who loves every living thing. He often comes here to eat just to be with his subjects."

The soldier I had knocked down said they had simply been charged to take me to the prince, adding that if they had frightened me they were sorry. I wondered how this Prince Garafalo could have already known about me. However, trusting to God, I put down the knife and said that as their prince seemed to be a peace-loving man, I would be happy to accompany them. So without finishing the meal we had so lovingly prepared, Helene and I bid farewell to our gentle hosts and allowed ourselves to be led to Prince Garafalo's palace.

Fireflies lit our way through vineyards and orchards of perfumed orange trees till we arrived at the prince's palace. Peacocks roamed the grounds, their colors blending with the many beautiful flowers. We were given water to refresh ourselves and clean clothes to wear. Suddenly, I was overcome with fear and seeing me tremble, the servant asked the reason for it. "If this leads to another job like that of a food taster," I replied, "I would prefer to take the poison now."

Again I was assured that Prince Garafalo was a good man and intended neither of us any harm. I was led to a small room with beautifully carved chairs and a writing desk where Helene soon joined me. She had also bathed, washed her hair, and now wore a red gown exactly the same as she had worn in my dream. Not a moment later the door opened and a servant announced Prince Garafalo.

The first thing I noticed about him was his bowlegs which made him rock from side to side as he walked. The next was his good-natured spirit, for although he had a head of white hair like a sheep waiting to be shorn, he had the energy of a man half his age. I understood immediately why the soldiers and the innkeeper worshiped him so highly.

He came right up to me, staring into my face. Holding me at arm's length, he peered at me from head to toe, examining my hands and legs. Then he squinted at my face again. The soldier offered something to the prince, but the prince said, "I do not have to see it. I know. This is he! This is he!"

Although the prince had a manner about him which made me love him immediately, I disliked being prodded like a chicken so I said, "I am who?"

The prince laughed and, throwing his arms around me, cried, "My son! My son!"

You cannot imagine how I felt. The walls swirled around, the blood rushed to my head, and I fell to the floor as if I were dead.

Servants roused me by making me sniff pepper and when I had sneezed out all my brains, I assured the prince that although I was in the best of health, his news had rendered me helpless. However, if this was a jest he had performed it with great wit, but I begged him now to tell me the truth. The good prince insisted Helene and I join him at his table where he would explain the reasons for his belief. So we gave up a wonderful meal at the inn for an even greater one with the prince.

I hardly remember what we ate because I was so entranced by the prince's tale which I shall relate as best I can. He said that in his youth he had been a sergeant in the papal army of Pope Julius. They had been marching through Umbria on their way to attack Bologna when the pope instructed him to stop at the Convent Verecondo to make a donation. Close to the convent, he had met a young woman who was so distressed that the whole countryside could hear her weeping. Since the prince was then a young and handsome man and the girl was very beautiful, her tears touched him deeply. In answer to his questions, the girl said her husband had cruelly taken their small son with him to tend the sheep and she missed him terribly.

The prince continued to Verecondo where he spent the night, but the woman's weeping invaded his dreams. The following morning he went to her farm and declared his love for her. She had fallen in love with him the moment she saw him and so great was their passion they threw off their leaden shoes and danced the songs of love until the next day. The prince begged the woman to accompany him to Bologna, but she could not leave her child. With a heavy heart he left her and hurried to meet the pope. However, his absence had not gone unnoticed, and his enemies so maligned him to the pope that he was forced to flee to Firenze and then to Venezia for his safety.

Many years went by before he was able to return to the village, by which time the woman had died. The neighbors told him she had given birth to a second son, which he realized might be his own, but that child had since grown and left for Gubbio some years earlier.

I had been listening with astonishment to this tale and when the prince mentioned Gubbio I could contain myself no longer, throwing my arms around his neck and calling him my own dear father. I fell into such a weeping the like of which I had not done since my mother died. The prince did likewise and everyone at the table was so moved, the tears flowed like the sweet rain of spring, for beneath all of our sorrows, hope had blossomed again.

My father said he pursued a career trading olive oil which had made him very prosperous. He had never married, the remembrance of his love coming between him and every other woman, until one day it had burst forth into a painting which he held up for us to see. It showed with simple delicate lines a woman with dark hair and a somber face, with full lips just like mine and the left eye slightly larger than the right.

"Blessed be the Holy Virgin," I cried. "It is the mirror of my mother!"

The prince smiled. "When I was very young I studied with Leonardo da Vinci for a short while in Milano."

"You are a most worthy pupil," I said.

The prince said he had instructed his servants to remember my mother's likeness from the painting and to bring any man who resembled it to the palace. This they had done several times, but the prince had known immediately they were not his offspring. He despaired of ever finding his son until the moment he saw me. Now, as Death approached, he could die happy at last.

I pleaded with him not to speak in this manner ("God would not have waited so long to bring us together only to tear us apart"), and I told him the incredible journey that Helene and I had just undertaken had now resulted in our meeting. The prince said he would commission a new altar to be built on his grounds to celebrate our reunion. Thus with much rejoicing we continued until the chirping of the birds heralded the approaching dawn. Then my father led us to our bedroom whose walls and floors were covered in luxurious carpets and tapestries and to our bed covered with the finest linen sheets and pillows. I could not believe my good fortune. To have found my heart's desire and be reunited with my father all in the space of a few days! What had I done to deserve this? I reached out to Helene. Her softness, her goodness, her beauty and courage overwhelmed me. I see her even now as she bends her head toward me, her hand reaching for mine, her lips beckoning me. I see it as clearly as the day it happened.

Oh, but why go on with this? None of it happened. None of it. I did not run away with Helene. We did not stay at the inn, cook a meal, meet my real father or a thousand other fancies. I dreamed them all. I dreamed them by night and I dreamed them by day. I dreamed them so often they became servants to my desires and so real that I remember the food we ate, the clothes we wore, the words we spoke with greater passion than the things which really did happen. And now it is written down which makes it true. I do not know why that is so, but it is.

All my life I believed the stories of the Bible or of Greece or Roma were true just because they were written down. Now, as I read over what I have written, I see how easy it is to make up a story where none existed. To stir the humors, to make the reader weep, laugh, or clutch his heart—surely that is a gift more valuable than all the gold and silver that exist. Truly the man who succeeds in this is god of his own world.

In truth, Helene and I clung to one another every moment of the few hours we had together. Sometimes the words poured out and at other moments there was no need to speak. I recited my poem and she kissed me, repeating my name a hundred times so that whenever I heard it from then on, it was her voice I heard saying it. We loved one another standing against the walls of the *castello*, not caring if anyone saw us. Then I had to leave for the sun was beginning to rise and the servants were packing the mule carts.

When I returned from tasting Federico's breakfast, Helene was weeping and cursing her pride for the time she had wasted by not speaking to me. I kissed her again and again and told her to return to the archbishop because I was afraid she would get into trouble if she was seen with me. She refused to leave my side.

Then Federico was climbing into his carriage and the knights and ministers were mounting their horses. The mule carts were led out of the courtyard. Helene tore at her hair and began wailing loudly. I climbed down to comfort her while behind us the procession rode through the gates. The dandy and several other tasters had gathered by the stables, and were watching us.

"Go," Helene said, wiping her tears. "Go, before they harm you."

The guards were closing the gates, but I did not want to leave

Helene—had I not lost Agnese in a similar way?—but she assured me they would not dare to hurt her because she was the archbishop's taster and there were guards everywhere.

I told her that one day I would come back for her. It did not matter if she was in Nîmes, Milano, or Paris—I would find her. It might take the rest of my life, but without her my life was not worth living. She clung to me, laid her soft, small finger against my lips and said, "If God wills it, so it will be. But go now, please, Ugo. Go."

I mounted my horse. The tasters rushed at me, swinging their swords and clubs. I reared my horse, scattering them, and galloped out of the *castello* grounds just before the gates closed.

It was during our return to Corsoli that Cecchi named me *Il miracolo vivente*—a living miracle. But I was hardly living and my life was far from miraculous. Although I had every reason to rejoice, I was filled with melancholy. It was not just that I had found the love of my life only to have lost her again, but I was weary in mind and body. My bones ached, my blood was sluggish, and I did not sleep well. And when I did, my sleep was invaded by dreams of death and deception. I was given to looking over my shoulder and licking my lips like the food tasters I had met. Yes, I had triumphed over Onionface, but he had made a ghost of me. I finally understood what Tommaso had meant when he had warned me about becoming too close to Federico. I had taken on all of his fears as well as my own.

Thus, when on the third day of our journey Cecchi said that Federico had invited me into his carriage, I did not wish to go. Cecchi said although he was sure my reasons were good, he could not think of one that was good enough to disobey Federico's command.

The others were already there listening to Septivus read about a Roman emperor who had defeated the French and German hordes.

"And he was loved, too?" Federico asked.

"He was a stoic."

Federico's mouth puckered up. "A stoic."

"To a stoic, virtue was the highest good," Septivus explained. "They believed that to attain freedom, true freedom over their own lives, they had to set aside all passion."

"I can do that," Federico said, biting into a peach.

We nodded in agreement.

"And also put aside unjust thoughts," Septivus continued.

"I never have unjust thoughts," Federico said, wiping the juice from his chin.

Again we nodded.

"And live with nature and give up all indulgences," finished Septivus.

Federico swallowed the last of the peach. "*Basta*. We will read again tomorrow."

Septivus hastily closed the book and left, quickly followed by

Piero and Cecchi. Bernardo grasped my shirt and tried to pull me with him.

"Go," Federico said to him, and as Bernardo left, Federico hurled the peach stone at the back of his head.

"*Scusi*," Federico said, when Bernardo turned around. "An unjust thought." Then he turned to me and said, "Did you know Marcus Aurelius persecuted Christians? I wish they would have had popes then." He rearranged the cushions behind him and bit into another peach. "Did you like Milano?"

I replied that I had, although not as much as Firenze.

"Do you like the paintings and sculptures better in Firenze or Milano?"

I had to be careful how I replied because I did not know the reason for his questions. "I liked the painting of Mary Magdalen."

"With the book in her hand? Yes, I liked that one, too. Who painted that?"

"Il Giampietrino."

"Giampietrino." Federico nodded his head. "Did you see the da Vinci in the tower hall? The tree with all those golden ropes? Magnificent. Just magnificent. But you should see the paintings and the mosaics in Istanbul." He told me of the magnificent mosques, mosaics, and jewelry he had seen while he was employed by the sultan. I was surprised, not only that he remembered, but also that he was confiding in me. "I want to do something like that." He parted the curtains. "Look at the clouds. Do they not look like sculptures?"

I sat next to him and peered through the curtains. It was most peculiar talking to him as if he was just another man. "Yes," I said, "That one reminds me of the head of the David in Firenze.

"So it does." Christ on a cross! He was agreeing with me! I added, "I liked the Duomo in Firenze, and especially the statue of David. It has an unearthly beauty."

Federico stared at the clouds for a long moment and then closed the curtain. "You mentioned Milano, Firenze, but not Corsoli. Not even once."

"Your Excellency, that is because it is—"

"A shit hole," he said angrily.

"If I may beg to differ—"

"You may not. But I will change that." His eyes squinted with ambition. "I am going to build an altar to the Virgin Mary in the Duomo Santa Caterina."

"To echo the golden Madonna on the front?"

He must have forgotten about the golden Madonna. "Yes," he snapped, as if the idea now disappointed him. "I want to add something to the palace, too."

"A tower?"

"No. A new wing to go across the back to hold a library. A place for scribes to translate my manuscripts."

I did not know he had any manuscripts. I said, "To make a square out of the palace courtyard."

"Exactly. Make a square out of it."

"It is a bold and excellent idea, My Lord."

"Yes, it is bold. And excellent. The courtyard will be enclosed and the scribes can look upon it while they work. I spoke to a student of Bramantino while we were in Milano." He began to plump up his cushions and then looked at me, which meant that I should do it for him. I have since taken on that task whenever I see him. "But I do not wish to lose the garden," he continued. "A palace must have gardens. They are good for contemplation."

"Maybe if it were planted into the hillside."

He looked at me as a hawk does when it spies a rabbit. I was about to apologize when he said, "You mean like the Hanging Gardens of Babylon?"

Since I had never heard of the Hanging Gardens of Babylon, I said, "Yes. But bigger."

"Bigger! Of course, bigger." He rubbed his hands together. "I want to wake up and see the hillside covered in flowers. The Hanging Gardens of Corsoli. That would make those fools in Milano sit up! Do you know what they said about Corsoli?"

I shook my head although I could have guessed.

"Backward! They called it backward!"

I could see the storm brewing, and, as I was the only one in the carriage with him, I knew I would be the one to suffer, so I said, "But, My Lord, that just shows their own foolishness because when it comes to cleanliness and neatness they do not compare to Corsoli."

"You noticed that?" he cried.

"They were like pigs. The servants' quarters would have horrified you."

"I knew it! That is because of the Germans! And the Swiss. And the French. They are all pigs! I will build Corsoli to be the envy of Romagna and it will be clean. And neat, too!" He was excited again.

As soon as I emerged from Federico's carriage the others hissed at me. "What did he say? What did he want?"

I told them Federico had spoken to me as a trusted servant and I could not betray that trust.

Later, Cecchi took my arm and we walked a little ahead of the carriage where the clopping of hooves would bury our words. "Federico cannot rebuild Corsoli—"

"But why not? Some new buildings and statues will be good for the city."

Cecchi tugged at his beard. "But the *contadini* are already starving. If we raise the taxes again they will die. Then there will be no one to feed the palace."

The next day, Federico called me to his carriage again. I had been warned by Cecchi not to encourage his ideas, but when an idea seized Federico nothing could change his mind. Septivus sat in a corner trying to write as the carriage jolted up and down.

"I am inviting sculptors and painters to Corsoli," Federico said. "They will compete to design the back wing, the Hanging Gardens, a statue of me, and some paintings." He snatched a piece of paper from Septivus and read it with his thick bruised lips.

"To the most modern of ancients, my illustrious brother and Lord, Michelangelo Buonarroti, I thank the Virgin Mother that those of us who look upon your wonders are not required to be as gifted as you since then you would only have God Himself for company. For a man such as I, whose hands unfortunately have been *immerse in sangue,* it is not only a revelation, but also an absolution to know that man is capable of such magnificent deeds. Your statue of David, which I recently saw on my way to Bologna, so overwhelmed me that I was rooted to the spot, unable to eat or drink, unable to do anything but gaze upon this vision and give thanks to Almighty God that I was allowed to witness such unearthly beauty."

Those last were *my* words! There was another page of praise until, finally, Federico invited Michelangelo to paint Federico in one of three poses which he believed would be a challenge worthy of Michelangelo's talent. The first was Federico as Hercules strangling the lion of Nemea, the second as Alexander cutting the Gordian knot, and the third as Caesar crossing the Rubicon. Federico was prepared to pay a thousand gold coins and added that, knowing how promptly the pope paid his artists, he thought Michelangelo could use the money. When he finished reading he looked up at me.

"I cannot see how he will fail to come," I said.

He grunted and read another letter—this one to Titian—promising exactly the same amount, except he changed Hercules to Perseus slaying the minotaur.

"Federico as the minotaur is something I would pay to see," Cecchi growled after I told him.

Letters were also written to Piero Bembo and Matteo Bandello, inviting them to Corsoli, which Federico claimed was like the Garden of Eden and where inspiration was as common as dirt. He also wrote to Lorenzo Lotto, Marco D'Oggiono, and to the sculptor Agostino Busti, whose works he had admired in the cathedral in Milano. "I would like a statue of me on a horse," he wrote.

The third time I went into the carriage, Septivus was reading aloud from Verana's book. Fortunately, Septivus had not thrown it away as he had been instructed, for now Federico made him read from it every day. Septivus was reading a passage which said that after blowing one's nose it was not wise to look into the piece of cloth as if it contained the pope's jewels, but to place the piece of cloth in a pocket.

"That's easily solved," Federico boasted. "I always use my fingers."

Federico now ordered me to play backgammon with him while Septivus read from *The Odyssey*. Every now and then Federico would look up and say something like, "Who got turned into hogs?"

"Circe turned Eurylocus's men into hogs."

"Why?"

"Because she hated men."

"And where was Odysseus?"

"By the ship."

"Which ship?"

"The ship they were on when they left Laestrygones, no I mean . . . Aeolus . . . no . . . no . . . Telepylus."

"No wonder I am confused," Federico said. "Start again."

"From the beginning?" Septivus squeaked.

"Where else?"

Although it was often difficult to follow Septivus's reedy voice reciting the journeys of Odysseus or Dante, I found it pleasing to rock backward and forward as the rain drizzled lightly on the carriage roof and the wheels crushed the stones beneath us. Sometimes Federico fell asleep, sometimes I did, and once, Septivus himself began to snore even as he was reading.

It was only when Septivus explained that Beatrice had only been fourteen when Dante had fallen in love with her that I thought of Miranda. I wondered how she was, if she had fallen in love with another boy, if she had taken her potions, if she was with child. My heart ached to see her and I felt such a weariness that I said to Federico, "Your Excellency, I am so grateful for the many honors you have given me. As you must know my sole desire on earth is to serve you faithfully as Our Lord wills me to."

"I can always tell when someone wants something," Federico said. "They praise me as if I was Jesus Christ Himself. But you, Ugo? You disappoint me."

"It is only because I wish to serve you in an even greater way that I ask you to consider my request."

"What is it?"

"As a food taster I serve you twice a day. If, however, I were a courtier I could serve you every moment of the day."

"But what would you do?" Federico replied. "Piero's my doctor, Bernardo is my astrologer, Cecchi my chief administrator, Septivus my scribe and tutor."

"Perhaps I might assist Cecchi—"

"He does not need assisting. And besides," he frowned, "who would be my food taster?"

"I could train someone. It would not—"

"No," he laughed. "*Tu sei il mio gustatore*. You will *always* be my food taster. Let us hear no more about it."

"But, My Lord—"

"No!"

I could not stop myself and after a moment I said, "Your Excellency—"

"No," he roared. "Leave me!" I was never invited into his carriage again.

We had just passed the village of Arraggio, south of Bologna. A fine mist covered the hills and the smell of rain was in the air. A wind slipped through the trees, disrobing them of their red and brown leaves. Chestnuts clothed in their green, bristly armor stabbed at my feet. Across the valley a flock of sheep clung to the hillside. A shepherd and a girl huddled together beneath a tree. Michelangelo can have his thousand florins, I said to myself, all I want is to live here on a small farm with a flock of sheep and my Helene. I will love her. I will take care of her. We will sleep together at night and together we will wake in the morning. I made this promise to Helene, to myself, and to God, and I carved our names in a tree as a sacred covenant.

It was cold and wet when we entered the valley of Corsoli, but when I saw the jagged hills, the trees bunched together like broccoli tops, the palace rising like a sepulcher from the mist, I was so overcome that I kissed the ground, thanking God for returning us safely. Halfway up the valley the Duomo bell began to ring. We sang to encourage our weary feet, boys rode out to greet us, and no sooner had we entered the city than we were besieged by wives, husbands, and children. I wondered where Miranda was when suddenly, as I climbed the Weeping Steps, a woman shrieked, ran out of the crowd, and threw her arms around me, crying, "Babbo, Babbo!"

Oh, what joy to feel her in my arms again! "Mia Miranda, mia Miranda!" I barely recognized her. Her hair was in a coif, revealing her elegant swanlike neck. She wore earrings and a necklace lay on her soft white bosom. When I left she was a girl and now she was woman!

"Is that your *amorosa?*" said a voice behind me. I turned around. It was Federico. His carriage had stopped and he was looking out of the window at us.

"No, My Lord," I bowed. "This is my daughter, Miranda."

Federico stared at her in a way that made me feel uncomfortable. Miranda blushed, bowed her head, and said, "Welcome back to Corsoli, Your Excellency. Each day without you has been like a summer without a harvest."

Federico raised an eyebrow. "Did you hear that, Septivus?"

Septivus poked his head out of the carriage. "A summer without a harvest." Federico repeated. "Write that down. I like that."

The carriage moved on. I took Miranda's hand and we followed into the palace. As Federico climbed out of the carriage I saw him turn around as if looking for us.

I gave Miranda a comb, some rose water, and false hair made of blonde silk I had bought in Firenze. I did not tell her about the ring Federico had given me for I had given it to Helene. Miranda sat on my lap as she had done when she was a child, and I told her all that had happened to me. She looked at me with horror. "But Babbo, what if Onionface had eaten the berries and nothing had happened to him?"

"I trust God would have taken care of me."

She put a finger to her chin thoughtfully and asked, "Since I am your daughter, will God take care of me, too?"

"Of course," I cried, "of course." I told her about Helene and how one day I would marry her and that we would all live together in Arraggio.

Miranda pursed her lips. "I would not marry a food taster."

"And why not?"

"Because I would always fear for his life."

This thought had never occurred to me and after my disagreement with Federico I did not wish to think about it, so I said, "And who would you marry?"

"A prince."

"A prince, indeed. Is he anyone I know?"

"In Corsoli?" she said with wide eyes.

I smiled. "But it is good to aim high, Miranda. Birds that fly too close to the ground are the first to be shot out of the sky. How is Tommaso?"

"I neither know nor care," she shrugged, but I could hear mischief in her voice.

It was more complicated than that, which I discovered when I went to the kitchen. Tommaso, who was skinning some eels to put into a torta, barely nodded his head, but Luigi and the other boys crowded round, wanting to hear about the journey, and especially the story of Onionface, from my own lips. When I had finished I looked about for

Tommaso, but he had slipped away. Luigi said that two weeks after I had left, Tommaso had suffered a change of fortune.

Not content with seducing a merchant's wife (it was his first such conquest), Tommaso had boasted about to it his friends. Knowing how easy he was to tease, and also because he sometimes stretched the truth from here to Roma, they pretended to disbelieve him. "*È un impetuoso!*" Luigi said to much laughter.

So Tommaso had insisted the boys follow him the next time his lover's husband was in Arezzo to prove he was not lying. Unfortunately, he had not warned the woman's chambermaid that he was coming and so was unaware that the husband had returned. When Tommaso arrived in the dead of night, the husband and his brother were waiting with cudgels. They beat him, stripped him naked, locked Tommaso's balls in a chest and placed a razor in his hand. The husband said that if Tommaso was still in the house when he returned in an hour he would kill him. Fortunately, Tommaso's friends had heard the commotion, and when they saw the husband leave, they broke in and rescued him.

"He was in the hospital for more than a month. By the time he came out everyone in the valley knew what had happened."

Tommaso returned to his duties in the kitchen but when he was not working he sulked in his room. He refused to go outside because he could not stand to see the other boys pursuing Miranda through the palace. Since the four years to their betrothal passed without Miranda knowing, I saw no reason to tell her, and after what had happened even Tommaso could not insist upon it. As I had foreseen all along, God in His wisdom had known what was best.

As indeed God had known what was best for me. I turned my disappointment at not being given another position into good use, gathering herbs, mixing them, and taking small amounts to see what effect they had on me. Indeed, recording those effects was how my writing improved, and, watching Cecchi scurrying about at Federico's bidding, I was glad I had not been rewarded. I spent so much time with my experiments I resented each moment away from them. I did not tell anyone about them, and although Miranda and I shared the same room, she was too concerned with making her lips redder, her hair straighter, and her skin softer to notice. She cried when she thought boys did not look at her and acted aloof when they did. She practiced her lyre one day and the next refused to leave her bed. Within the space of a sentence she could be as sweet as sugar or as bitter as wormwood and many were the times I was glad there was a screen between us.

Federico's invitations to the painters and sculptors went unheeded, but *potta!* Some wit must have posted them in every piazza in Italy, for that summer artists swarmed over Corsoli like mosquitoes! They came from Roma, Venezia, and every town in between: students thrown out by their masters for laziness or thievery, beggars looking for free meals, debtors running from creditors. Half of them had never heard of a poem, did not know which way to hold a brush, and the only thing they had ever carved was a piece of bread. They got drunk, fought one another, and pestered the women.

Miranda and her friends walked arm in arm around Corsoli while these idiots wrestled one another to walk beside her. Sometimes she sat in the window, remaining there all morning, neglecting her lessons and duties, while the louts stood below serenading her. "They are like cats in heat," I said, and pissed out the window on them.

When Federico was told the artists were living for free he said, "Have them killed."

Instead Cecchi ordered the gatekeepers to forbid any more artists from entering Corsoli. He also announced a competition to design a new crest for Federico; the winner could stay but the rest had to leave. The first drawing showed Federico holding two cheetahs on a leash. He dismissed it with a wave of his hand: "It is too tame."

I was there when the second drawing was submitted. This time Federico's lip dropped to his chin. "Why," he asked the mealy-mouthed artist from Ravenna, "am I sitting next to a cow?"

"That is not a cow," the artist said, a little too haughtily. "It is a bear."

Federico had the man tied to a cow for a week to show him how mistaken he was. The competition was interrupted when a caravan arrived from Levantine carrying a lion and a giraffe—a gift from the sultan Federico had served. All of Corsoli thronged the streets singing and dancing. A great feast was held to which I wore my first silk shirt.

"Even the Medici did not have a lion *and* a giraffe," Federico boasted at the table.

Finally, another painter, Grazzari from Spoleto, designed a crest of Federico strangling a lion with his bare hands. Federico loved it. He ordered the other painters to leave before nightfall and commissioned Grazzari to paint a fresco of him. The fresco, which is in the main hall, shows Federico, as handsome and young as Michelangelo's David, sitting astride a white horse in the middle of battle. The horse is rearing on its hind legs while Federico, his black armor shining in the sunlight, leans over the horse's left flank to plunge a sword into a soldier's breast.

"Grazzari is a master," Federico said. "He captured me in my youth."

Federico took an interest in everything. He complimented Tommaso on a castle he was making out of sugar and marzipan. "Make a drawbridge," Federico said. "And make the turrets a little bit bigger." Like the fool he was, Tommaso resented Federico's suggestions.

One evening, I was standing in the courtyard before the evening meal. I had tasted a little too much juice of henbane and my head was spinning. I swore the clouds lying on the horizon were really sleeping dogs and I was about to warn everyone in the palace not to wake them, for fear they might attack us, when Tommaso came and stood next to me. He was almost eighteen in years and as tall as I. His hair, which had been cut into bangs, still refused to obey his comb, but his mouth had grown and his teeth now looked as if they belonged there rather than as if some devil had switched them with someone else's while he was asleep. But it was his eyes that had changed the most. They were melancholy and made him appear even older than he really was.

He said he knew that God had punished him for the way he had treated Miranda and that he was more sorry than words could say. "I still love her," he said quietly. These were the most words he had spoken to me since I had returned and very unlike the old Tommaso. He raised his head and, looking me boldly in the eye, said, "I beg you to find it in your heart to forgive me."

I said I forgave him. "Then please, speak to Miranda for me."

"You must speak to her yourself."

He shook his head. "I cannot."

"Then you should find yourself another girl. There are plenty in Corsoli. You are a fine young man—"

"No. I love her more than life itself."

Perhaps it was the henbane, but his sorrow reminded me of the loss of my Helene. "I cannot promise you anything," I replied, "but if the time is right and the occasion presents itself, I will press your suit with her."

He thanked me and wanted to kiss my hand, which I might have allowed him to do except that I felt, because of the henbane no doubt, that my hand would float away if I gave it to him. He said although we no longer had a contract, he would look out for me in the kitchen again. He was now assisting Luigi, and if I ever wanted any special food he would be happy to make it for me. Then he started boasting how he knew better than anyone else what was going on in the kitchen, and even though he was no longer a spy, he was in Federico's favor once again, and so on and so forth till I had to tell him to shut up! He was the same Tommaso after all!

The artists, the wild animals, the promise of new buildings gave Corsoli a festive air. Each day brought some new surprise, and so when Tommaso came to my door waving his arms in excitement, saying, "Come quick, there is someone you must see," I pulled my robe over my silk shirt, put on my new hat since it was raining, and followed him out of the palace.

"He has been to the Indies," Tommaso said breathlessly, as we hurried to the Piazza Del Vedura, "and seen men with three heads!"

The day was gray and the wind and rain spattered their marks all over it. As we entered the piazza I was surprised at the number of servants who were silently standing in a circle. Pushing my way to the front, I saw a tall thin man, with long gray matted hair covering the right half of his face. The part of his face I could see was deep brown and wrinkled like well-worn leather. His clothes were rags, his feet encased in old boots. A mass of charms and amulets hung from his neck and I could smell him from where I stood.

He dug his long grimy fingers into a pouch hanging from his waist and pulled out a piece of dark root. He raised it in the air, the rags falling away to reveal a thin, muscular arm. He lifted his face to the rain and cried out strange words in a hoarse, raspy voice. Then he opened his left eye and, looking us over, said, "Whoever places this root beneath their pillow will capture their heart's desire as surely as the fox captures the hare."

He walked to the half-blind washerwoman, placed the root in her hand, covered it with his own, and muttered in her ear. She clutched at his chest crying, "*Mille grazie, mille grazie*."

"I want some," Tommaso blurted.

Ignoring the driving rain which was beating down, the magician placed his hand on Tommaso's brow. "I have more powerful potions for you." He pulled out a dove from inside his shirt. "Give this to Duke Federico and he will reward you with a long life; for this bird is descended from the one which brought the olive branch to Noah."

Tommaso thanked him over and over and promised to feed him and arrange for an introduction with Federico. "I will take you now," he said eagerly.

The magician smiled. In a moment he had gathered up his charms and potions and was striding toward the Weeping Steps.

"Are you not coming?" someone asked me.

I shook my head. Bile had risen in my stomach, phlegm had formed in my mouth. My knees trembled. I stood in the rain clenching my fists and asking God why He had yet again raised me up only to tear me down. Blood of the Antichrist! Just when my life was floating like a feather in a breeze, my brother, Vittore, had to show up!

# xxvi

"I thought about you often, little brother," Vittore said. He had not been granted an audience with Federico yet, but he had been fed, and bathed, and given new clothes and was now lying on my bed eating an apple and stinking of perfumes. Even though I was the one who lived in the palazzo, who worked for Duke Federico, dressed in velvet, and was admired and respected all over Italy, and Vittore was just a thieving, lying tramp, the old fears still welled up in me.

"What do you want?" I snapped.

"Me?" he said, with the innocence of Christ. "Nothing. A roof over my head. A meal."

"I could have you hanged."

"Oh, Ugo. Is this still about those sheep?" In the light of the candle it was difficult to see his face—his hair still covered most of it, except for his one good eye. "Ah, my poor little brother."

He rose like a snake from the bed and began snooping about my room. "You should thank me. If it were not for me you would have spent your life running up and down Abbruzi chasing your flock. Now look at you. A silk shirt, a dagger with a bone handle. A fine room. A reputation. What is this?" He poked his finger into a cabinet. "Henbane?"

I snatched the leaves from him.

"And aconite? Who else knows about this, little brother?"

"No one," I said, pulling my knife.

"Ugo." He raised an eyebrow in mock surprise. "You would kill me for this?"

"No, but for killing my best friend Toro on the way back from the market."

Vittore sank to the floor in front of me. "Ugo, please!"

"Please what?" said a voice. The screen was moved aside and there stood Miranda, her dark brown hair mussed up, her small white teeth shining in the pale light of the candle, her soft plump feet sticking out of the bottom of her nightshirt.

"Miranda?" Vittore said, rising immediately. "*Che bella donzella!* Remember me? Your uncle Vittore?" He opened his arms as if to hold her and the thought of that bastard just touching her made me crazy. I stepped between them.

"Go to bed. Go to bed!"

"Ugo, let her stay! Aside from our father there are only us three DiFontes in the world. We should cherish these moments. Tomorrow we may part forever."

"Are you Vittore, my father's brother?"

Vittore bowed. "At your service, my princess."

Miranda saw the knife in my hand and her eyes widened in alarm. "What are you doing, Babbo?"

"He was showing me his knife," Vittore smiled. "As I was showing him mine." A long thin dagger appeared in his hand from out of nowhere. He smiled. "Two brothers showing one another how they keep the devil away. Nothing more."

I put my knife away and his dagger disappeared up his sleeve. Miranda sat on my bed.

"She is as beautiful as Elisabetta," Vittore smiled.

"You never knew her mother."

"Well, she does not get her looks from you." He winked at Miranda. "I remember when Ugo used to hide in his mother's skirts whenever there was a thunderstorm."

"You told me not to be afraid," Miranda accused me.

Vittore laughed. "We used to cut down long sticks and fence with them as if we were knights. Did Ugo not tell you?"

"Babbo hardly ever mentioned you. Where have you come from?"

"Everywhere." Vittore sat beside her.

Miranda stared at the twinkling amulets hanging from his neck. "Have you been to Venezia?" she asked.

"For a year I lived in a palazzo on the Grand Canal, one of the best years of my life."

"I wish I could go," Miranda sighed, hugging her knees to her chin. "Somebody once wanted to take me there."

"I have been to France, Germany, England too!"

"Is it true the English have tails? Papa said so."

"I did not!"

"Yes, you did!"

Vittore roared with laughter, and turning to me, said, "She is delightful. No, Miranda, they do not have tails. At least not the women I met. And I looked very carefully."

Miranda blushed.

"I have even been to the Indies."

"The Indies?" Miranda gasped.

"Yes, where men eat other men."

Miranda's eyes opened so wide I feared her pupils would pop out. "You saw them eat men?"

Vittore nodded. "They also smoke fire through their noses and walk naked all day long." He reached into a pouch and took out a tube with a small bowl at one end and which split into two small tubes at the other. From another pouch he withdrew some brown flakes which he placed into the bowl and then he put the two thin tubes into his nostrils. Using a taper, he lit the flakes and sucked in through his nose. Miranda and I watched as a second later, a long stream of smoke came out of his mouth. Miranda gasped in horror. "Is your stomach on fire?"

Vittore shook his head.

"What is it then?" I asked.

"They call it tabac. It cures whatever ails man. The stomach, the head, melancholy. Every illness known to man. In the Indies men and women smoke it all day long."

He puffed several more times until the bowl was empty and then put it away. "I have seen so many wondrous things. Countries where the sun shines every day and it rains only long enough to water the flowers. And flowers! Oh, Miranda! Flowers larger than a man's hands and all the colors of the rainbow!" He pointed a long arm toward the ceiling. "Trees that reach to the very top of the heavens and bear more fruit than in all of Eden." He sighed. "And yet wherever I am, I always come back to Corsoli."

"Why?" Miranda asked. "It is so boring here."

"Corsoli is my home. I want to die here." He crossed himself.

"Are you going to die?"

"We are all going to die someday."

"How true," I said. "Vittore, tell us what happened after you became a bandit."

"You were a bandit?" Miranda gasped.

Vittore shrugged. "Only to eat. Then they started paying me to rob people."

"Who did?" Miranda frowned.

"The duke of Ferrara, the Swiss, the emperor, the French. I became a soldier and I fought for whoever paid me." He leaned forward, his raspy voice dropping to a whisper. "I have seen horrors such as no man should ever witness." He shook his head as if a nightmare had suddenly risen in front of him. "After I stopped fighting I wanted to become a priest and devote myself to God."

"What stopped you?" I asked.

"I have a greater gift."

"Selling love potions?"

"Babbo, what is wrong with bringing love to people?"

"Exactly," said Vittore, gently patting her knee. "What higher calling can there be than spreading love?"

"Is that how you got the pox?"

"Babbo, why are you so mean?"

Vittore put his fingers to his lips. "Do not be angry with your father. He was trying to shield you from the bitterness of life. I only wish someone had done it for me." He turned to me. "I got it from a woman. I forgave her."

Slowly he moved his hair covering the one side of his face. Miranda cried out. Vittore's eye socket had fallen and twisted so that his eye peeked out between mounds of rotting flesh. The cheek was puckered and marked by deep lesions and his jaw had crumpled as if some spirit was eating his face from the inside. "I do not have long to live. I only ask to spend the rest of my days with those I love and those who love me."

"I think I am going to cry," I said.

"Two of my fingers are useless," Miranda said, holding out her right hand to Vittore, "and two of my toes."

With great solemnity Vittore took her hand in his, murmured a prayer and gently kissed the limp, withered fingers. Then he knelt on the floor and kissed her toes. Miranda watched him as if he was the pope himself. Still kneeling, he lifted a silver amulet from around his neck and placed it over Miranda's head so that it fell between her breasts. It was shaped as a hand in which the thumb and first two fingers were open and upright and the last two fingers were closed.

"For me?" Miranda exclaimed. "What is it?"

"The hand of Fatima. To ward off the evil eye."

"It does not appear to have done you any good," I said.

"It is so beautiful," Miranda breathed.

"Now it will protect both of us."

"I shall always wear it," she said.

I might as well have not been in the room!

"Is that rue?" Miranda pointed to a silver wildflower also hanging from Vittore's neck.

"Yes, rue and vervain, the flowers of Diana."

"And this one?"

Vittore caressed the silver, winged *fallo* softly between his fingers. "My love charm," he said.

What is it that makes evil so attractive? The uglier it is, the greater the mystery, the more attractive it becomes. I know people who would not dream of entering a lion's den and yet they think nothing of talking to the devil. Do they think they can overcome evil? That it will not touch them? Do they not see it is their very goodness that evil feeds on?

So it was with Miranda. "How can you be so cold to your brother?" she asked, after Vittore had left. "Can you not see the suffering he has endured?"

Christ on a cross! I thought I would pull my hair out! I told her of the times Vittore had beaten me when we were young. Of the lies he had told to get me in trouble with our father. How he refused to give me a few sheep to start my flock after I had looked after them in winter and in summer day and night, night and day, while he had been drinking and whoring. I told her how he had killed my best friend.

She nodded as if she understood, but then said, "Are we always to be judged on what we did yesterday? Did Christ not forgive those who had sinned?"

"A wolf is always a wolf, Miranda."

"But you are his brother and he is yours. I never had a brother or a sister. Or a mother."

She seemed to have forgotten everything I had just told her! I opened her hands, wanting to know if he had slipped her a potion. I pulled the necklace off her neck to make sure he had not rubbed something on it. How could he have turned her against me in a few short minutes? I became so enraged I said, "If I ever see you speaking to Vittore again I will beat you!"

Whenever the courtiers emerged from Federico's chamber they usually could not wait to speak ill of each other, but after Vittore's audience with Federico they were united in their fury.

"He said," Bernardo spluttered, "according to the stars Federico will have a new wife. He drew a circle on the ground, blabbed something in Latin, consulted a chicken leg, stared into Federico's eyes, and said, 'in two months and no longer than three!' "

"He gave him potions, too," Piero twitched. For once he was not laughing.

"Surely Federico did not believe him?" I asked.

"Not believe him? He has appointed him the court magician," Bernardo spat. "He will sit next to him at the table."

"When Federico does not get what he wants," I told Vittore, "he kills people."

"That will be my problem," he answered.

"Not just you. He will kill others—"

"Then pretend you do not know me. We are not brothers. We are not related at all."

"I will remember that," I replied.

From the day Vittore arrived the valley was covered with black clouds. The rain lashed the palace walls; the winds howled through the courtyard, shaking stones loose and uprooting trees older than time itself. In Corsoli, the peasants said that at night demons flew from the palace into the clouds and back again. An evil fungus spread through the hallways. I awoke with the smell of rot buried in my nose and I could not rid myself of it no matter how many perfumes I put on. I knew it was all because of Vittore.

At first, women were afraid of him, but I saw him take them softly by the wrist and pull them behind a pillar. When they emerged a moment later they were smiling and calm. It was not what he said because whenever I asked them to repeat it they could not. "It is the *way* he speaks," a woman shrugged, "his voice is like cream."

"He holds me with his eye," the old washerwoman sighed.

Holy Mother of God! To me his voice was like the bray of an ass mixed with the hiss of a serpent's tongue. Could they not see the evil riding on the back of his words? No, they shrugged, they could not. Or would not! Stupid, ignorant cows! It made no difference whether they were young or old, unmarried or married. Nor was it just the women, but the men, too! Only for them his voice lost its creamy softness and rang with the sounds of battle against the French or Germans. He told of sailing to the Indies and seeing nothing but sea for months on end. He spoke of whales as tall as ships and twice as long. Of a wave that rose out of the ocean and roared over the ship, swallowing all the men and disappearing again in less time than it took to tell it. He told of native women who went without clothes and were happy to do nothing but sport with sailors. He spoke of kings richer than the pope but who lived like peasants. Of brown men to whom gold was as common as grass. The servants listened to his tales and begged for more.

"They are in need of love," Vittore said.

I do not know what Vittore told Federico—he was careful not to speak when I was close by—but it must have been what Federico wanted to hear. Sometimes Vittore whispered something to make Federico laugh aloud. Then everyone else sat in silence, their eyes on the table for fear they were the objects of Vittore's ridicule.

Vittore advised Federico to eat ginger with every meal. My poor tongue hung out like a thirsty dog and I could taste nothing else. I wondered if Vittore was doing this so I would not be able to detect poisons. I woke up in the dead of night convinced he was working for Pia's relations in Venezia or perhaps Duke Sforza in Milano or some other prince Federico had injured. But I had not protected Federico with my life to have that sheep fucker kill him!

I asked Tommaso if Vittore ever came to the kitchen. "Why should he?" he said, annoyed that I had disturbed his sleep. I shook him angrily. "Does he give you anything to put in Federico's food?"

"No," he said indignantly. "He is *helping* Duke Federico."

That was all I needed to hear. Ever since Vittore had given Tommaso the dove, Tommaso worshiped Vittore because he hoped Vittore could help him win Miranda back.

"He will not," I said.

"Have *you* spoken to her?"

"The time has not been right."

He snorted and I must admit that even to my own ears my words were not convincing.

That evening, as Miranda was playing her lyre, I asked her if she ever thought of Tommaso. "No," she answered lightly, but the tremor in her voice betrayed her.

Within a few weeks, Vittore became as important to Federico as his cane, which he always used now because of his gout. I heard Vittore urging against the plans Federico had made on his way back from Milano.

"I think it would be more fitting for you to have another palace," Vittore said.

"Another palace," Federico mused as he chewed on a capon leg smothered in ginger.

"With your permission, Your Excellency," I said, "this excess of ginger is not good for your humors."

"Oh, Ugo," Federico said, "What do you know? What have you seen of the world? How many times have you been out of the valley? Once? And going to Milano does not count."

I stepped back as if I had been struck by lightning. Federico nudged Vittore and laughed, not seeing the rage welling in me. But Vittore did, and from the look in his eye, I realized he was afraid I would tell Federico we were brothers. The world had turned upside down! A few weeks ago, I was the one who did not want anyone to know, but now it was Vittore who felt I was a burden to him! I knew then he would not feel safe until he had killed me.

The morning after the full moon, the old washerwoman was found wandering naked in the yard muttering about Diana. No one knew which Diana she was talking about, and although there were several among the servants, they all denied it was them. Piero bled her and gave her some ointments but she would not say what had happened and kept falling to her knees, begging everyone's forgiveness. It was only one of many things which disturbed me. Miranda often fell asleep during her lessons. She was lax in her duties to Isabella, a courtier's wife. When I tried to speak to her she answered in a dull voice that she was doing as she always did. Tommaso refused to look me in the eye. Cecchi sulked about the palace. Bernardo did not leave his bed, claiming he was ill, and Piero was so afraid that he jumped at his own shadow. The palace was falling down around me, and it was all Vittore's doing.

Two boys stopped me at the stable entrance demanding to know what business I wanted. I was about to crack their heads when Vittore called out, "Let him in."

The horses looked at me with drowsy eyes as I walked past them. Vittore had made a home for himself at the back of the stable among the straw. Strange objects hung from the rafters—a jawbone of an ass, a lock of hair, a broken piece of a sculpture. The stony, gray palazzo was cold and drafty, but here the warm smell of horses and hay mingled in a pleasant manner and the odor of a sickly perfume made me want to lie down and sleep.

Vittore was sitting on a pile of straw. His hair was still matted, amulets and charms still hung from his neck, but his black robe was new as well as his boots and cape. It had taken me months to get new clothes and years before I had a new robe and boots. "You have done well for yourself," I said.

He leaned back, sucked on his *tabacca* and blew the smoke toward me. "God has been kind."

I was annoyed at the way I had to stand in front of him as if I was in his court. "What have you been giving Miranda?"

"Ah, Miranda, *mia angelica,*" he smiled.

"What have you been giving her?"

"What I give everyone, Ugo." He paused to suck his *tabacca*. "Love."

"Do not give her anything. I forbid it."

"Are you threatening me?"

"Yes, I am threatening you."

"It is too late for that."

"It is not too late," I said. I heard a noise and glanced around. The stable boys were approaching me, knives in hand.

"But it is, Ugo," Vittore said. His voice had changed. He sprang to his feet and pulled his dagger. "It is much too late."

The boys looked at one another, unsure of what to do. "He is the taster," one said stupidly.

I yelled loudly, and fortunately someone in the courtyard shouted back. As the boys turned I knocked them down and ran out of the stable, not stopping till I reached my room. With a pounding heart I sat by the window. From now on I had to be more careful; the next time I might not be so lucky.

It rained for seven days and seven nights. Clouds filled the sky until the day was as dark as night. A blanket of moss climbed the palace walls and a thin gray mist slipped through the corridors. Puddles formed in the dining hall, in the kitchen, and in my room. Fevers struck. Cecchi took to his bed, Bernardo moaned all day, and Federico had bad attacks of phlegm. I, too, caught a cold and could not shake it. Only Vittore did not fall ill. He had less than a month to fulfill his promise to Federico, but he did not seem concerned. Every night I prayed he would fail and that Federico would drive him out of the valley or throw him down the mountain.

Miranda ate little and stared at the rain for hours. She was no longer interested in boys and did not comb her hair. Sometimes when I was not experimenting with my herbs—I took small doses of arsenic every day as well as meadow saffron—I tried to follow her, but she slipped away from me and my head would grow so heavy I had to lie down. I asked Bernardo if the stars were affecting her.

"When was she born?"

"Three days after Corpus Christi." I remembered because Elisabetta had picked wild roses to throw in the procession, but the petals had caught in her hair and she had looked so pretty I had begged her to leave them there.

Bernardo grunted. "The crab. Behavior like that is to be expected. She will probably live to be at least seventy years old. Then again she might not."

Piero said it was probably her monthly courses and that he would know better when the moon was full in three days' time. He said he would be happy to bleed her.

"I will die before that pig touches me!" Miranda shouted.

"He saved you when you almost died from the cold."

Whatever I said caused her to be angry, even little things. When I remarked I had seen her talking to Tommaso, she cried, "You are spying on me!" Her voice trailed off and she averted her eyes from the window. Below us in Emilia's garden, Vittore was talking to the old washerwoman.

"It has to do with Vittore, has it not?" I said.

"No."

"It has!"

"No!" she screamed. "No! NO! NO! NO!"

Just then Vittore looked up at me and smiled.

The night of the next full moon, I slipped away from the table while Septivus was reading Dante's *Purgatory*, and into the stable. The stable boys were still eating in the servants' hall. At the back, where Vittore had made a space for himself, I climbed to the top of a pile of straw near the roof and waited. Amulets and charms hung everywhere, and that strange scent which had made me drowsy was there again.

I must have fallen asleep for I was awoken by muttered voices. It was dark except for the dim light of a candle. Several people sat on the ground with their backs to me sipping from a bowl which they passed to one another. Vittore sat facing them, stroking something in his lap. He spoke to it in a low voice and rubbed its back as one might pet a kitten. Then he held it up for all to see. It was not a kitten, but a toad! He *was* an *incantatore*. A witch! And this was a witch's sabbat. I wanted to tell Federico right away, but I stayed, for I had never seen a sabbat before.

One by one the men and women leaned forward and licked the toad. I have done some things that God will judge me for, like screwing a sheep, but I have never ever licked a toad. After a moment or two, a man stood up and jumped around as if the devil had entered his soul. It was Tommaso! That fool! Then the others rose to their feet stumbling about like newborn calves. They tried to walk, but the space was so small that they all bumped into one another. One woman turned around and around till she fell down, her eyes wide open, her mouth in a twisted smile. Another man raised his arms above his head and cried out. Vittore clapped his hand over his mouth with such force the man sank to the ground and did not speak another word. The woman lying on the ground turned her head and was staring straight at me. She raised her arm and pointed, but no one noticed.

I do not know how long they stumbled about like this till Vittore, who had turned his back on them, raised his arms in the air, and hissed, "I renounce Jesus Christ!"

"I renounce Jesus Christ!" they repeated. Then Vittore said, "The Madonna is a whore! Christ is a liar. I deny God!"

*Potta!* Even if God had not spoken to me, I had never denied Him. I prayed that if He was looking down on us that He would see that although I was here in the stable I was not part of this. Vittore said other blasphemies and each time they repeated his words with more fervor. A woman giggled and sang, "The Madonna is a whore. The Madonna is a whore."

Vittore called out softly, "*Diana, bella Diana.* Bring your horse."

Was this the Diana the old washerwoman had talked about? I wondered who she was and how she was going to get a horse in there because it was already so crowded.

Then Vittore asked them if they saw his mighty head. They said they did, but how could they? No one had left and the horses were still on the other side of the straw. They were under his spell!

"Obey him!" Vittore said and turned around. *Jesus in sancto!* He was wearing goats' horns on his head! I wanted to laugh, but then he lifted his shirt and showed himself. "*Sarete tutti nudi,*" he said, and they began to take off their clothes! Suddenly I saw that one of the women was Miranda! I am ashamed to say I could not look away. She was so young, so beautiful. Her breasts small and upturned, her stomach so flat, her thighs fully formed and her buttocks round and full. I was seized with rage. Yet I waited.

The old washerwoman with sagging breasts and thighs like tree trunks knelt in front of Vittore and kissed his *fallo.* He turned around and presented his *culo* to her. She pulled his cheeks apart and gave him the "*Osculum infame.*" Vittore turned around and laid his hand on her brow. She moaned and fell to the ground. I could not believe my eyes! Could this be happening here? Here in Duke Federico's stables while the rest of the palace was fast asleep a few yards away? But there was more.

Tommaso knelt in front of Vittore, kissed his *fallo* too, and then paid homage to Vittore's *culo.* Six of them did this and when they had finished they fell on one another and made love like wild beasts. Then it was Miranda's turn and there was no one for her to make love to except Vittore. He put his hand on the back of her head. I had seen enough and no longer cared if he conjured up demons or if he was the devil himself. Shouting the names of God, Jesus Christ, and the Holy Ghost, I threw myself down from the straw and ran at Vittore with my knife aiming for his good eye. The others screamed when they saw me, but I was past them before they could stop me. Vittore spat and raised his arm. His eye was completely black. He *was* the devil! My hand stopped as if some force was pushing against it! Vittore grasped my wrist, but I stabbed him! I stabbed him in the chest!

We fell on the ground. Other men threw themselves on top of me and I slashed at them with my knife. Someone pulled my clothes, another bit my wrist. The candles must have fallen over for suddenly flames were licking at the wet straw and smoke filled the stable. I caught hold of Miranda, but she fought me with the strength of a man so I was forced to crack her about the face and bang her head into the wall. I threw her over my shoulder. Now the flames were arching toward the roof. The horses—whinnying, bucking, and shrieking with fear—broke from their ties. Everyone was fighting to get past the flames and the horses. The fire shot through the roof, leaped over us, and now we were in hell itself! A man was trampled by a horse in front of me and I tripped over him. Miranda fell out of my arms. Part of the roof collapsed and the burning embers fell on the panicked horses. I pulled Miranda up, knifed another man in my way (I prayed it was Vittore), and staggered out of the stable, imps of flame clinging to my hose and Miranda's hair.

The air was filled with wailing, the crying of men and women, and the neighing of horses. The hounds were howling and barking, the fire bells chimed, and the great bell of the Duomo Santa Caterina added its frantic voice to the noise. Servants poured out of the palace. I carried Miranda through Emilia's garden to the back entrance of the palazzo and up the stairs to our room. Her eyes were clouded over; she was calling to Diana and singing songs to the devil. I stuffed rags in her mouth, tied her down to the bed, and hurried back to the court-yard where the fire roared, its flames fanned by a black wind.

Cecchi organized the servants to throw water onto the blaze, but Federico kept forcing them into the stable to rescue his horses. Then just when it appeared that the stable would be destroyed, lightning struck the palace, the thunder rolled, and the rain poured down. The flames hissed and sizzled till at last they shrank and withered into sodden defeat.

More than half the stable was destroyed as well as ten horses. Their pitiful cries and the smell of their burning flesh lingered for days.

When guards had not arrested me or Miranda by early morning, I decided to tell Federico what I had seen. He was already awake in his chamber and to my surprise Vittore was there as well. One of his hands was bandaged, but otherwise he appeared unharmed. Even more confusing, Federico was in a good mood.

"My Lord," I began, "permit me to say what a terrible trial you have been through—"

"Ugo, horses can be replaced. The Jew Piero will pay. Vittore says he was conducting sabbats in the stables."

"Piero?"

"Yes, he is on the rack. He will confess." I wanted to laugh; Piero conducting sabbats? "But, I have good news," Federico went on. "Vittore said the woman I have been looking for has been living here the whole time."

"Here in the palace?" I repeated. Each new pronouncement was crazier than the last. "Who is it?"

"Your daughter," Federico smiled, "Miranda."

# xxvii

"You are not pleased?"

"Pleased? I am honored. Heaven has blessed me," I cried.

"Her moon complements the duke's perfectly," Vittore smiled. "I want her to sit at my table tonight," Federico said.

"Yes, Your Honor."

"Make sure she rests well," Vittore added.

I walked back to my room, my head whirling as if I had ingested meadow saffron, belladonna, and henbane all at the same time. Miranda, my daughter, Miranda my child, was to sit at Federico's table. I knew why Vittore had done this. He had promised to find Federico a bride in two months and now those two months were almost up. If he could not have Miranda then he would give her to Federico. But would Federico really take my precious Miranda for his mistress? Surely not. She is too young, I said to myself, but what did that matter to Federico? She was no longer a virgin, but he did not know that, nor would he care. How would Miranda feel? What if she disappointed him or said something rude or screamed or laughed at the wrong time? The man who had laughed at my joke on the way to Milano was still in prison. The whore who had banged her head in Federico's carriage was dead in a ditch for all I knew. A peasant who had sung obscene verses at Carnevale had been beheaded. And what about me? Was I going to have to taste Federico's food while my daughter sat at his table? Surely, Federico would not allow that to happen.

Miranda had fallen into such a deep sleep that instead of waking her I walked through the palace and listened to the rumors of magic and witchcraft. Two stable boys and the old washerwoman had burned to death. Another body had been burned so badly no one could tell if it was a man or a woman. I passed by the kitchen where Tommaso was baking bread. So he had also escaped. He caught my eye and started to say something, but there were servants everywhere. Instead he followed me down the hallway, whispering, "Ugo, I must speak with you." I did not stop to listen. There was nothing he could say that was of interest to me.

Later in the day, Vittore advised Federico to spare Piero from more torture. "It is because Vittore does not know how to cure Federico's gout or any of his other diseases," Cecchi said. I heard that with bleeding fingers, the nails of his right hand had been removed, and, jabbering like a fool, Piero knelt in front of Vittore, kissed the hem of his robe, and swore allegiance to him.

I wanted to convince Miranda once and for all of Vittore's wickedness, but when she woke she remembered nothing! *Niente!* She stared at me, her pupils huge and round, as if she did not know me. She chewed on her lips, complaining of a metal taste in her mouth. I poured a basin of water and washed her face.

"What is that smell?" she asked.

She was still so young, so innocent. "It is nothing. Do not trouble yourself."

"What is it?" she said impatiently, and, pushing my hand away, went to the window.

"There was a fire in the stable. Some horses were—"

Her body stiffened. Her memory was wakening. She looked at me fiercely. "Vittore? I must—"

"Miranda—"

She pulled away. "Is he well? I must find him!"

I followed her to the door. "Forget Vittore."

She whirled around. "Is he dead?"

Christ on a cross! It was my father all over again!

She flew at me and beat me with her fists. "I hate you," she screamed, "I hate you."

"Vittore does not care about you!" I cried.

"He is alive then?" And seeing my face, she laughed. "He is alive!"

"He sold you," I said, grasping her arms. She did not understand. "He said you would make a perfect wife for Federico!"

Who knows the mind of a woman? In Castiglione's *The Courtier*, which Septivus sometimes read to Federico, the ideal woman is gracious, knowledgeable, prudent, generous, virtuous, remaining free from gossip, and is beautiful and talented as well. *Potta!* Are they talking about women made of flesh and blood? Did those women work in the fields like Elisabetta until the hour Miranda was born?

Did any of them witness the joy of a naked woman turning cartwheels like Agnese? Did any of their women have Helene's courage or Miranda's strength? No, they lived in a different world.

All afternoon Miranda studied her hair in the mirror. It had always been a source of great pride, but because of the fire, the ends were ragged and of different lengths. Here and there were bald patches where an ember had singed her. Something had to be done, but I feared saying anything lest I upset her even more. At last I could not stand it and I said, "Perhaps you could wear a wig or maybe a scarf the way Bianca—"

As if to silence me, Miranda took a knife and began hacking away at her hair as if she was possessed by a devil. I tried to stop her and after a struggle she allowed me to wrest the knife away.

"Are you mad?" I cried. "You are to sit at Federico's table tonight."

She was not upset at all; indeed, she smiled at me as if I was a child and said, "Tell Lavinia and Beatrice to come here quickly."

These were her closest friends, who, when they heard what was going to happen, came at once. They were horrified at the sight of her hair, but Miranda cheerfully said that she had tried to cut it herself, but had made some mistakes and needed their help. They were only too happy to do so and, laughing and giggling, they cut it quite short except for a small curl that hung down over one eye. Then they painted her face and rouged her mouth. Miranda cleverly questioned them to see if they knew she had been part of the sabbat—they did not. Beatrice lent her an exquisite blue *camora* with pictures of colored birds woven into the sleeves. Miranda borrowed a necklace from Isabella and when she laid it against the top of her breasts I would have defied any man in Italy not to want to place his head there.

In the midst of this, Tommaso came to the door. "You cut your hair," he said, unable to hide his surprise.

Miranda turned from her dressing table. "You do not like it?"

"No. Yes, I—I am not used to it," he stammered. "Forgive me."

"And my dress?" She stood up and turned around for him. Tommaso grew red in the face. He said he had never seen anything so beautiful. But she was not finished. "What about my shoes?" And as her friends giggled, she stretched her foot toward him, displaying one of her slender ankles. Fearing the poor boy would faint, I asked him why he had come.

"Luigi wants to know if there are any particular dishes Miranda would like this evening."

*"Mangiabianco,"* Miranda replied without hesitation.

"There is not time enough," Tommaso said.

"Hmm . . ." she frowned. "Then . . . some . . . veal . . ."

He nodded. "Sprinkled with salt and fennel?"

"Yes," Miranda replied.

"With marjoram and parsley and herbs," Lavinia laughed.

"Yes. Yes, like that," Miranda said, clapping her hands with delight.

"And rolled and put on the spit," Beatrice added.

Tommaso stood in the middle of the room staring at the floor. "And for dessert?" he asked.

Miranda raised her head, showing off her long white neck. "Cheesecake. And prosciutto."

"With the cheesecake?"

"No," she said, with disdain. "Before the cheesecake."

Tommaso nodded again and was about to leave when Miranda added, "With melon."

Tommaso stopped. "Prosciutto with melon?"

"Yes," she said. "With melon," as if everyone knew that was the way it should be. Then she turned back to the mirror as the girls burst into laughter once again.

Even though she was ready in time for dinner, Miranda arrived just late enough so that everyone would see her entrance. She apologized to Federico but offered no explanation, sat opposite him and adjusted the front of her *camora* bringing attention to her breasts as Bianca used to do. Then she smiled at Federico. I had seen her practice that smile in the mirror—her lips parted slightly, her eyebrows furrowed, and the dimples in her cheeks revealed themselves like two soft pearls.

Federico beamed. "A little princess."

The dinner continued as all dinners did. Federico was consumed with his food. Every now and then he glanced at Miranda, but did not say anything. The courtiers spoke to one another, but since Federico did not speak to Miranda, nor did they. I had been afraid that she might say something out of turn; now I worried that she might cry out of neglect. However Miranda felt, her face remained calm as if she had attended dinners like this all her life. Then Tommaso served the prosciutto with melon.

"An excellent combination," Cecchi said.

"Yes," Federico agreed, sucking on his fingers. "Luigi is a far better cook than Cristoforo ever was," he said, and called Luigi to the table.

Miranda's face still did not change. Luigi must have thought something was wrong—that was the only reason the chef was ever called—and, rushing to the table, said, "Your Excellency, if the prosciutto with melon does not please you I can easily change it. It was not a dish of mine and I—"

"Whose was it then, Tommaso's?"

"No, My Lord. Your Illustrious Highness, it would not be seemly to betray one whose beauty cannot compete with her experience—"

"It was your idea?" Federico asked Miranda.

She bowed her head modestly. "Yes, Your Excellency."

"Forgive her ignorance," Luigi chuckled, "I will prepare—"

"You will prepare nothing," said Federico. "It was excellent. Make some more."

For the rest of the meal Miranda was included in the conversation and her opinion asked on every subject. Most of the time she said she had no knowledge of such things, but once she quoted from Dante and another time from Polizian. Septivus had taught her well. She said she preferred the poetry of the people to that of the courts.

"Could you favor us with such a poem?" Federico asked.

"If it would please the duke."

"Yes," Federico said, "it would please me."

Carefully laying her spoon next to her trencher, Miranda closed her eyes and folded her hands. "My favorite poem in all the world goes like this." She cleared her throat and recited.

Although the sun burns hot above
I shake and shiver with the chill of love.

The table was quiet. "Is that it?" Bernardo laughed.

"It does not take many words to win a lover's heart," Miranda replied lightly. "Just the right ones."

"*Brava!*" Federico applauded, and, pointing to Septivus, added, "That is true of everything."

Miranda blushed, "Excuse me, honored duke, if I have spoken too much on a subject which women have no place—"

"No, no, no," said Federico. "Please honor us with your presence whenever we dine," and farted loudly to seal his announcement. Miranda thanked everyone, especially Duke Federico, patted Nero on the head, and left the table. She had not glanced even once at Vittore throughout the meal.

Federico followed her with his eyes until she had left the room. "I traveled all the way to Milano to look for a princess and she has been here the whole time."

Afterward, Miranda rushed up to me asking, "Babbo, what did Duke Federico say?"

I assured her that he had spoken highly of her and that she had conducted herself well. She was delighted and chitter-chatted with her friends, discussing what she had said, what had been said to her, what she had said back and so on and so on, the telling of which took three times longer than the event itself. When at last they left, she said, "Babbo, when I become a rich woman in the court, I will take care of you."

I held her in my arms and wondered what Federico had in mind for her. So much had happened in one day—the sabbat and the fire were already distant memories—that my thoughts were as jumbled as leaves in a storm. Later that evening, I stood in the courtyard looking up at the stars when Tommaso came to my side. We leaned over the wall looking down at the huddled houses of Corsoli bathing in the light of the moon. He said, "I swear I did not tell Miranda to go to the sabbat."

It amused me to think that he thought that he could convince Miranda to do something. "No," I laughed, "you cannot make Miranda do anything she does not want to do." He nibbled his nails. "Then why did you give Miranda to Federico?"

"I did not give her to Federico. Vittore did."

"What will you do about it?"

"Nothing. Why?"

His eyes became as round as the moon. "But Miranda cannot be with Federico!"

"Why not?"

"But she is—" His eyes closed, he gripped the wall.

"You may not have told her to go to the sabbat," I said, "but you did not stop her."

He hung his head. "It was she who made *me* go," he replied.

That night I had bad dreams. I do not know if it was because of the pinches of arsenic I had been taking, but I dreamed Corsoli was drenched in blood. No matter how many times I awoke I always fell back into the same dream. Blood flowed from everywhere. From every mouth, from every vessel, from the pores of my skin, and from the walls of the palazzo.

"We must leave," I said to Miranda the next morning. "I can find work in Firenze or Bologna. Maybe we could go to Roma."

She looked at me as if I had lost my senses. "Why, Babbo?"

"Something terrible is going to happen. I feel it."

"Babbo, you were dreaming again."

"Yes, but I dreamed it in the morning when the truth speaks clearer because it is farther away from the body."

"Then you must pray that you do not have bad dreams, Babbo."

"No, we must leave."

"But how can I?" she cried. "Duke Federico has ordered the dressmaker to make some new dresses for me." She stood up and danced around the room. "I am going to be a princess!"

"You are doing this to make Vittore jealous."

"Vittore?" she answered. "Who is Vittore?"

From then on Miranda ate at Federico's table every night. On the third meal, Federico pushed Nero off the seat so that Miranda could sit next to him. Soon she was imitating birds and animals, even some of the courtiers. Within a week, she was the life of the dinners and I could not have been happier. Even so, I was not prepared when a servant knocked on my door while Miranda was taking her lessons and said, "Federico is on his way to see you."

I did not have time to ask why. Like a madman, I pulled the large chest over to my table and in one sweep pushed every potion, herb, poison, antidote, all my experiments and all my writings into it. I had just lit some incense and spices and piled up the cushions on the bed when Federico entered.

I bowed. "I am honored, My Lord."

Federico coughed and waved his hat at the wisps of smoke. I snuffed out the candles and opened the window. He sat down on the chest. In my haste I had not closed it properly and part of my writing was sticking out.

"What does Miranda like?" Federico asked. "Vittore said you would know."

I might have known that bastard was behind this. "She likes to sing and play the lyre."

"I know that."

"When she was younger she used to stand in the window when the sun was setting and sing."

"What else?"

I could not think of anything because I was so worried that he might see the writing sticking out of the chest. I said on the farm she spoke to the animals as if they were her friends, and that she liked to ride on my back.

"I do not want to know what she liked when she was three! I want to know what she likes now! What sort of jewelry? What kind of perfumes? What styles of dress?"

"She likes all manner of jewelry and perfumes."

"She does not like rose water."

"All except rose water," I agreed.

He said, "You have known her all your life and I only a few days, yet I know her better than you do."

He stood up, sniffed the air, put on his hat and left. I opened my chest and rescued my experiments, but I could not work on them. Something Federico had said disturbed me. How could he know Miranda better than I? It was not possible. *I* knew Miranda's moods. I knew how she jumped up and down when she was happy. How she sang to stop her loneliness. How she bit her bottom lip when she was upset. What else was there to know? What father knew more about his daughter than I did? Did Cecchi know more about Giulia? Did Federico know more about his sons? No! Miranda would like any perfume because she had never had any of her own. She had never owned jewelry and her dresses had always belonged to someone else. She would be pleased with anything Federico gave her.

The next day Federico gave Miranda a gold bracelet and a peacock feather. The day after a statue and a tiara. The day after that a diamond-studded hand mirror. By the end of the week, we were so flooded with gifts we had no room to sleep. Federico evicted three clerks from the room next to ours and gave it to Miranda. A door was made between our rooms. Federico told Miranda to decorate her room however she pleased. She wanted the ceiling painted with stars, the floors covered with carpets, and on the wall opposite her bed, she told Grazzari to paint a picture of the Madonna and child.

"Ask her if I can paint something different," Grazzari complained. "I have painted the baby Jesus sitting in the Madonna's lap, standing on her knee, and lying in her arms. I have painted him with blond hair, black hair, curly hair, and no hair. I've drawn him asleep and awake, smiling at the sky, pointing in a book, and blessing a lion. I am tired of painting the Madonna, too. I want to paint something else."

Miranda insisted on a Madonna and child and so that is what Grazzari painted.

Miranda rose late and spent hours arranging her new furniture. She ignored her lessons. Federico said, "She does not need any more schooling. She is already cleverer than the rest of the court put together."

I hoped he would continue to think so because even though I loved Miranda more than life itself, sometimes she had no idea what she was talking about and when she became upset, her voice squeaked. Federico did not care. "She has the neck of a swan," he said at the table. "Her hair is like a dark river. Her eyes glow like fireflies." He asked me if her pee smelled like bergamot.

"Her pee? I do not know."

"You are her father. How can you not know what her pee smells like?"

And do you know, I wanted to ask him what his son's turds smell like? But I said nothing. It did not matter what I or anyone said. *Completamente in adorazione!* He worshiped her. He hid behind columns to watch her walk by while the servants carried on as if he was not there. He ordered his barbers to tease his wispy hairs into different shapes to please her. Piero made sweet-smelling potions for his skin, and two tailors worked day and night sewing him new robes and hose and hats.

"Federico is in love," the palace tittered. Just how deeply in love I saw one evening at dinner when Miranda related how she used to serenade her goats. Federico had just lifted a heaping spoon of finely chopped salted tongue mixed with spices and vinegar to his mouth when Miranda stayed his arm and began to sing.

*Oi me!* I thought, she is separating Federico from his food! But Federico did not say a word. He sat there, the spoon inches from his gaping cave while Miranda sang three verses of her little song. Then, when she had finished, she let go of his arm.

"Wonderful," Federico clapped.

"She has a voice," Septivus mused, "which is not so much like a bird, but an angel."

"Yes, but not any angel," Bernardo chimed in, "an angel who has been close to God."

"Surely all angels are close to God," said Vittore. "That is why they are angels." He was wearing a handsome green velvet jacket and matching hose, although his hair was still unkempt and his chest still covered with charms and talismans.

"That is it, Vittore," Federico said. "She *is* an angel."

Every day for a week Federico ate a soup of cloves, laurel, celery, and artichoke followed by a baked pie of layered ham and mince lambs' kidney doused in wine. There was something else in it, too.

"Sliced goats' balls," Tommaso said, as we stood in the courtyard watching the sunset. "Sprinkled with salt, cinnamon, and pepper."

That was all he had time to say because just then Federico rushed up to us and, pointing at the band of fire scorching the mountaintops, cried, "Do you see? The sun!" He took a deep breath and spouted:

> My heart is like the sun
> For when you leave the room
> Then I am filled with gloom
> And . . . and . . .

We waited. He took a breath, closed his eyes. Tommaso was standing next to me, and Federico was standing slightly in front of us. Tommaso's hand moved to his dagger.

"My heart is like the sun," Federico said again.

The dagger was halfway out of its sheath.

"For when you leave the room—"

I put my hand on Tommaso's arm to prevent him from pulling the dagger out any farther.

"A sonnet," Federico roared. "I want to write a sonnet."

He whirled around. My hand was back in its place and so was Tommaso's dagger. "I think it will be a wonderful expression of love, Your Excellency."

"So do I. I must find Septivus." And he rushed off.

Tommaso's face was white with rage. "I could have—" he began.

I inclined my head to the three guards standing in the doorway of the palace. "We would have both been killed and I will not die for your foolishness!"

"And I will not let Miranda die because of your selfishness," he cried, with such determination that for the first time I believed him.

Later that evening, I walked by Septivus's room. He was working by candlelight, his hair in disarray, muttering those same lines over and over again:

> My heart is like the sun
> For when you leave the room
> Then I am filled with gloom. . . .

Septivus has not slept since Federico fell in love. No one has. Love has changed Federico so much that even those who know him well do not know what to expect. He pulled Cecchi's beard and made fun of Piero's giggling. He no longer believed the world was in the shape of a triangle, but in the shape of a heart. He surprised us by saying,

"Surely, it is as Cicero said: 'There is nothing that cannot be achieved with a little kindness. Dare I say love?' "

We cheered and applauded. Federico quoting Cicero! He neither raped Miranda nor forced himself on her in any other way. He wanted her to love him. Love had bloomed in him, and although the walls of anger and cruelty were hardly collapsing in the face of its power, here and there a small hole appeared. As if she knew this, Miranda did her best to open them wider. "I want to go to Venezia, ride a camel, and meet the Holy Father," she announced, during a game of backgammon.

Federico's eyes crinkled with delight and disappeared between the fat folds on his face. "I will take you to Venezia next year and I will buy you a camel."

"And the pope?" Miranda asked. She removed several of Federico's pieces and clapped her hands with glee.

"Not the pope," Federico answered.

"Why not?" Miranda demanded.

"Because I said so!" Federico snarled. Miranda continued to play as if she had not heard him. Then she looked up and, smiling innocently, said, "The Federico I heard about as a child used to spit out popes as if they were fennel seeds. Oh, look," she said, moving a piece on the board. "I win. Again. Now can we go to Roma?"

Federico stared at her. I could see he wanted to smile, but his anger would not allow him. "We will see," he said gruffly.

He doted on Miranda's every word and sometimes found meanings in them she did not intend. When she said in passing that the other girls had mocked her when she first came to the palace, Federico ordered them into the hall—some were now married with children—and threatened to cut out their tongues if they ever spoke badly to Miranda again.

I pleaded with her to be cautious. Federico had once given jewels to a whore only to accuse her the next day of stealing them. "Are you comparing me to a whore?" Miranda asked.

"Of course not. I just beg you to be careful."

She rolled her eyes. "You worry too much."

Because Federico was in love with my daughter, women wanted to seduce me. *Potta!* It had been a long time since I had been with a woman, but by keeping the vision of Helene in front of me, I was able to resist them.

One night I saw Federico and Vittore standing beneath a tree in Emilia's garden. As I watched, Vittore raised his arms to the moon and uttered a prayer which Federico repeated. Then Vittore uncovered a bowl he was carrying, and Federico, after first looking around to make sure no one was watching, dipped his hand into the bowl, took out some paste, and rubbed it on his testes. I hurried to the kitchen maid and told her what I had seen.

"What is Federico eating?" she asked.

I told her about the soup with cloves, the pie of layered ham, and the sliced goats' balls.

"Aphrodisiacs," she giggled.

But they cannot be working, I thought to myself. Now I knew why Federico had not tried to rape Miranda or force himself upon her. He could not get it up. I prayed that this would not alter his love for her or change his good humor.


There was still reason to fear Federico. At breakfast, Miranda mentioned that roses were her favorite flower. Federico ordered twenty servants to gather all the roses in the valley and present them to Miranda at dinner. "I want to surprise her."

But roses were no longer in bloom. Enraged, Federico ordered the servants imprisoned and the eldest one put on the rack.

"Ask Federico to release them," I said to Miranda. "It is not their fault."

Miranda refused. "I cannot. He is doing it for me. To show how much he loves me."

"You will make enemies."

"Me?" She picked up a hand mirror and brushed her hair. "But I have done nothing."

"You have forgotten where you came from."

"Why should I want to remember?" she laughed.

"This is not how I raised you."

"Really?" She held up the mirror so I could see my face in it next to hers. "You think you are so different from me? Everything I am, I have learned from you. For the first time in my life someone is giving me everything I want and you are jealous."

"I am trying to protect you."

"Who from?"

"Yourself," I answered.

She laid the mirror down. "I did not think you would say who you really meant."

I grasped her shoulders. She glanced at my hands as if they were not worthy to touch her. I struck her and she fell to the ground holding her cheek. Picking her up, I begged her forgiveness. She got up slowly, her eyes cold, her cheek red from the mark of my hand.

"If you ever do that again, I will tell Federico."

I walked out and closed the door between us.

Every day the world changed a little more. Miranda spent her time becoming a princess, Federico spent his chasing Miranda and left the running of the palazzo to Vittore. Vittore supervised the wool contracts. He banned Bernardo from giving astrological readings and forced Piero to show him how he made his potions. He forbade Septivus from reading to Federico and argued with Cecchi. Guards accompanied him wherever he went. First two, then four.

Not long after, I heard a shuffling outside my door. When I opened it, Cecchi and Septivus entered quickly. "Candles are hard to come by," Checchi said, and snuffed mine out. We stood in the darkness, the moonlight casting our faces in shadow. Cecchi cleared his throat as he always did before he said something important. "We are concerned about the fate of Corsoli. We feel because Duke Federico is preoccupied, he is not listening to the best advice."

"Whose advice is he listening to?"

"Vittore's." Cecchi tugged at his beard.

"He has made friends with the soldiers," Septivus said. In other words, he was too well guarded for an ordinary assassination.

"Why are you telling me this?"

"You have served the duke well," Cecchi said carefully. "He is marrying your daughter. You are close to him. Maybe you can think of some way to save Corsoli."

A bat flew in the window and around the room, its wings beating frantically in the darkness. "An omen!" Septivus said.

But what sort of omen? I wondered, when the bat flew out again. "If I did something to help Corsoli—"

"We will be forever in your debt." Cecchi replied. We grasped one another's arms.

After they had gone I sat by the window. It was not raining as it is at this moment, but the stars were low enough for me to touch and the hills cutting into the dark, velvet sky looked more like a painting of nature than nature itself. Indeed, nothing was real anymore. Something had just happened that I was only just grasping. I, Ugo DiFonte, food taster to Duke Federico Basillione DiVincelli, was being treated like a courtier.

I had always tried to *save* lives, be it Miranda's, my own, or Federico's. Now I was being asked to become an assassin. Even though I had tried to kill Vittore in the stable, planning his death disturbed me. I wondered if God was watching. I found myself looking over my shoulder, smiling for no reason other than I was afraid that my face would betray my thoughts. Then, I remembered how Vittore had killed Toro, my best friend, how he had almost raped Miranda and . . . things, roused me . . . to . . . a passi—

I cannot write after I have drunk henbane juice. My eyes become confused, things grow bigger and smaller, and nothing is what it appears to be. My head aches. I will continue later.

The abbot Tottorini used to say God sees everything, but if that is so then why had He allowed Vittore to curse Him and not avenge Himself? Is He waiting, and if so, for what? He could avenge Himself at any time. But, if it was as I thought, that God does *not* see everything, then surely it is the duty of those who *do* see, to take up arms on His behalf. If Vittore was the devil, as he said he was, then I was a soldier of Christ. Besides, if Vittore was planning to kill me, I knew he did not concern himself if God saw him or not! Vittore did not care if there was a God. So whenever the scepter of doubt hovered above me, I contemplated the worthiness of my task and was filled with pride that God had selected me to achieve it, and I swore I would not abandon my effort unless I died doing so.

As we had agreed, ambushing Vittore was impossible because of his guards, and to poison him would have been equally difficult. So I watched and waited and asked questions of the servants, some of whom were so in love with him that they told me far more than I ever wanted to know. *Jesus in sancto!* What stupid women they were! But it was through them that I discovered that Vittore never allowed anyone in his room and whenever he left it, he not only locked the door, but also posted a guard outside until he returned. That had to be because there was something he wanted to hide and I was determined to see what it was.

I dared not bribe a guard because the guard might take the money and tell Vittore, so for two weeks I plotted, and at the end of them I was no closer to a plan than I was at the beginning. I had fallen into despair when God Almighty blessed my mission by providing me the answer. It came about in this manner:

Federico could not shit and Piero, who was taking care of him again, ordered an extra plate of fruit with the juice of several lemons squeezed over it to relax Federico's bowels. It worked so well Federico barely had time to get out of bed before he shit like a horse. When I heard that, I asked Cecchi to have a key made which would fit Vittore's room and once he had given it to me, I instructed Luigi to give Vittore's guards the same breakfast as Piero had given Federico. They ate it greedily and all I had to do was wait. It took several days, but, when the guard outside Vittore's door had to relieve himself, I slipped inside the room.

*Potta!* May I never see another room like that one. It smelled as if a flock of bats had died in there. Nor was it just the smell. Vittore must have prowled the streets of Corsoli, Venezia, and Roma, collecting every piece of refuse he could find. The floor was littered with battered chests, soiled pallets, cracked vases, torn baskets, and cleaved helmets with the dried tissue of brain still clinging to them. Bloodied clothing lay piled on the floor beside worn-out saddles, crippled chairs, and broken swords. Where he had found all this I did not know. Nor why he had kept it. Perhaps being a soldier and a bandit had caused my brother to lose his senses.

A large desk cluttered with books stood on one side of the door and three full spittoons on the other. I tried to move the books, but they fell apart at my touch. The spittoons were so heavy the slop slipped over the sides, and the stench made me sick. I crawled under the desk, then climbed over mounds of clothing and broken furniture until I came to the far wall close to the bed. I stood up and opened a shutter. A thousand wretched smells flew out and fresh air rushed in. I closed my eyes and breathed deeply for several moments. And then I smelled it! An odor so faint that only a food taster such as myself would have noticed it. I traced its path to the back of the bed and there, hidden under the sheets, were six small bottles of ginger, crushed beetles, cinnamon, and mercury. No wonder Federico was acting strangely. They were aphrodisiacs and probably no more useful than my amulets, but ten times as deadly.

I put tiny amounts of arsenic into each bottle and placed them back where I had found them, all except for one. Then I raced out of the room, knocking over chairs, armor, and books. The guard, who had since returned, was so startled that I rushed by him before he could stop me. Running down the stairs, I shouted, "*Salvate il Duca!* Save the duke!"

Doors opened as if I had announced the second coming of Christ. I kept running and shouting, "*Salvate il Duca. Salvate il Duca!*" I passed through the courtyard and rang the stable bell. Guards came, their swords drawn.

"Is Federico dead?" they yelled. They grabbed my arms, but I pulled away and ran up the marble steps to the palace, through the hallways, past the kitchen, up a flight of stairs and down another, through the garden, gathering people like monks to money. And all the time I cried out, "Save the duke! Save the duke!"

Those following me joined in even though they did not know why. Their faces flushed, their blood surged, their cries echoed off the palace walls. I saw Cecchi. "Save the duke!" I shouted. Immediately, he ran behind me urging on the others. "Save the duke! Save the duke!"

Now there were guards, washerwomen, scribes, footmen, kitchen help, and grooms all following me. More than fifty voices and twice as many arms. I led them up the stairs to Federico's chambers. The guards outside his apartment drew their swords, but they were confused for we were not coming to attack the prince, but to save him. I had not been running and yelling like a fool all this time for my health—running is *not* good for the health—but because I prayed that Federico would hear us, and God granted my prayers. Federico opened the door himself.

"Save the duke! Save the duke!" I gasped.

"Save me from what?" Federico asked. He carried a sword in his hand and he pulled his nightgown around him as he pushed his way through the guards.

"From being poisoned!" I held up the tiny bottle. "By him!"

I pointed to Vittore, who was standing in the doorway behind

Federico. Until then no one knew what I had been shouting about. Now Vittore's guards drew their swords and knives. Vittore ran at me, but could not reach me because the passageway was too narrow and the guards were in the way.

"He is mixing arsenic in your aphrodisiacs," I said, and whiffed the bottle under Federico's nose. He jerked his head back as if he had been stung.

"Someone stole arsenic from my apothecary!" Piero exclaimed.

"Kill him!" Cecchi said.

"Burn him!" Bernardo spat.

"This is a conspiracy," Vittore shouted. "I do not have any arsenic. Ugo is the one who has poisons in his room."

The blood drained from my face as Federico whirled on me. "You have poisons in your room?"

Time crawled. So many things rushed through my head, each crying to be recognized. "My Lord," I said calmly. "You have seen my room. You came at a moment's notice. You sat there, we talked, you saw no poisons."

"He is lying," Vittore cried.

"It is a trick to divert your mind. Look first in his room. Then look in mine." I prayed Federico would listen to me because if he went into mine first he would see enough poisons to kill Caesar's army!

Cecchi said, "Ugo has served you loyally. You can always look in his room afterward."

Vittore tried to protest but the servants, whose loyalty changed as quickly as a summer breeze, shouted, "Look in his room!"

Federico marched to Vittore's room with everyone crushed behind him, pushing, shoving, and yelling. Vittore's guard disappeared the moment he saw Federico. I unlocked the door. Federico did not crawl under the table or over the soiled clothing. He did not move a spittoon. Just the sight of the room enraged him as I knew it would.

"My Lord—" Vittore began.

Federico ignored him and said to me, "How did you know about this?"

"With due respect, Your Excellency, since you have appointed Vittore as your adviser you have sometimes said and done things which are not always in your best interest."

"What have I done?" Federico's eyes narrowed.

"You have been eating fish which, if one eats too much of it, brings about black bile."

"That is not true," Vittore snarled.

"It is!" Piero answered.

Cecchi interrupted, "You have allowed a man who has no experience in finances to become involved with the wool trade. We have been losing money."

"That is not true!" Vittore shouted.

"The people of Corsoli have long loved you for your wisdom, your fairness, and your goodness, My Lord—"

"Is that also not true?" Federico turned to Vittore.

"But we hardly know you anymore," I continued.

"*La cospirazione*," Vittore snarled.

Federico struck him so hard with the handle of his sword that Vittore fell to the ground. "Imprison him," he roared.

As I watched the soldiers take Vittore away I marveled how easy it had been. Just like that Vittore had been imprisoned and would likely be put to death. I did not feel sorry for him in the least. That he was my brother made no difference to me. Perhaps I was a better assassin than a food taster.

Piero bled Federico, examined his phlegm and his shit, and said since we had stopped the poisoning, he thought Federico would live till the next century. Federico pushed him away and rolled out of the bed.

"I am going to boil Vittore in oil," he said, pulling on his hose. "Then I will put him on the rack." As he was pulling on his shirt he said, "I will make him eat his poison and cut his heart out." By the time his shoes were on he wanted to cut out Vittore's heart, feed him poison, and *then* put him on the rack. I glanced at the others and knew what they were thinking—this is the Federico of old. Suddenly, a smile spread slowly across his face. "Did you hear that?" he asked.

All I could hear was the lion roaring.

Federico smiled. "We will have a *caccia* at my wedding. We will throw Vittore to the lion."

We stared at Federico. "Your wedding?" Cecchi said, tugging at his beard.

"Yes, my wedding," Federico replied, as if he had just decided to go hunting. "I will marry Miranda."

Marry Miranda!

"That is a brilliant idea!" the others cried. "A decision inspired by God! It will produce male children. She will make a worthy mate." The compliments came faster than a hailstorm.

"And you, Ugo?" Federico asked. "What do you say?"

"I am speechless, Your Excellency. You do me too great an honor. How can I ever repay you?"

"Your service to me is enough."

"But surely I shall not have to wait on my own daughter?"

"And why not?"

"And if I refuse?" I said, before I knew what I was saying.

"Refuse?" Rising like Neptune from the sea, he lurched to the fire and pulled out the poker. He had completely forgotten that I had just saved his life! Guards grasped my arms and turned me around so that my *culo* was pointing to Federico.

"My Lord," Cecchi cried, "If you kill Ugo you will have lost the very reason you wanted to keep him as a taster. Let Ugo have his own taster, but he will still taste your food. That would be enough, would it not, Ugo?"

I could feel the heat of the poker, smell my hose burning. My bunghole tightened up so much I did not void for three days.

"Yes," I gasped.

"Let him go," Federico ordered.

I fell to the floor, drained of all senses.

Federico kicked me with his foot. "His own taster," he laughed and, turning to the rest of the room he said, "He has the courage of a lion."

If God Himself had praised me, I could not have been in greater bliss. Federico had finally recognized my worth. I kissed the hem of his robe muttering, *"Mille grazie, mille grazie."*

"You must want to die," Cecchi said, shaking his head when we were outside Federico's chambers.

"No, I want to live! Vittore is imprisoned, my daughter is marrying the duke, and now, after almost five years, I will enjoy food again."

How could he understand how I felt? How could anyone understand? Now at long last, I would be able eat again. No, not just eat, but chew, gobble, suck all without fear of being poisoned! I could nibble as quickly as a rabbit or as slowly as a tortoise. I could munch as silently as a dormouse or chomp as noisily as a hog. Oh, what joy! What joy! I danced through the palace even though everyone could see my *culo*, but I did not care! Oh, that my father could see this. I could not wait to tell Vittore.

That was the night I began writing this manuscript. God had answered my prayers and it seemed as if all my tribulations were finally over. Now I will write what has happened since the announcement of the marriage three months ago, for just as a heavy rain will change the course of a river, so God in His wisdom saw fit to change the course of my life yet again.

I wanted to be the one to tell Miranda. She would be the princess she had always dreamed of becoming and have everything she wanted. But the news of the wedding had spread so fast that even as I was making my way to our room, courtiers and washerwomen and stable boys ran to congratulate me. Everyone was happy except Tommaso.

"This is what you always wanted," he accused me.

"You had your chance."

"And I will have it again."

I wanted to know what he meant, but first I had to tell Miranda of her good fortune. As it was she already knew. Her girlfriends were brushing her hair, kissing her cheeks, and reading her fortune. "Federico will invite all of Italy to the wedding. He will take you to Venezia. He will build you a new palace," they predicted. They claimed the wedding would take place next month, at the midsummer's festival. There would be two hundred guests, then three hundred, then six.

That evening, Bernardo consulted his charts and said the best day for the wedding would be when Jupiter and Venus were aligned with the sun, which would be on the last week of June, in four months' time. Federico decided the wedding should last eight days with four banquets, a play, a pageant, and the *caccia*. It would be the most expensive and greatest wedding Corsoli had ever seen.

What power there is in words! I had seen their effect on the palazzo when Federico had said, "I am going to Milano to find a wife." But when he said, "I will make Miranda my wife," *oi me!* The whole valley was transformed. Each house was to be cleaned, painted, and hung with banners. Four matrimonial arches flanked with statues of Harmony, Love, Beauty, and Fertility were to be built leading from the Main Gate through the town to the Palazzo Fizzi. All the cracked marble in the palace was to be replaced, Emilia's flower garden uprooted, and the hillside behind the palace re-created as the Hanging Gardens of Corsoli!

"I want a fresco of Miranda opposite mine," Federico told Grazzari. Grazzari was also instructed to design the pageant.

I cannot express how important I felt to sit at the same table with Duke Federico, Septivus, Cecchi, and Grazzari and make plans for Miranda's wedding. At the first meeting, an argument broke out between Bernardo and Septivus. Bernardo thought Federico should be portrayed as Justice because he was born in late September, but Septivus said, "A wise man is *master* of the stars," and that Hercules would be a better choice because of Federico's strength. "We could show Hercules and the twelve labors."

"Cleaning the stables?" Bernardo sneered.

"Hercules also captured a deer," Septivus retorted. "He killed a lion, and a monster, and captured a bull and a boar. In the tenth labor he captured four savage horses, in the eleventh—"

"*Basta!*" Federico said, "This is a wedding, not a zoo."

"Or a hunt!" Bernardo added.

"But it could be a hunt." Grazzari thought for a moment. "Miranda is a virgin, is she not?"

"Of course," I replied.

Grazzari leaned back, stroked his beard, and stared at the ceiling. "Since a unicorn symbolizes virginity, why not have a dance through the trees in which Hercules captures the unicorn."

"Hercules captures the unicorn," Federico mused.

"I do not think it becoming," Bernardo said.

"I do," said Federico. "It is a marriage of strength and beauty. We can use the same piazza for the *caccia*."

"That is an excellent suggestion," Cecchi smiled.

"And then she turns into Venus," said Septivus.

"Venus?" Federico turned to Septivus.

"Whose only duty was to make love," he explained.

"Perfect," said Federico. "Hercules hunts the unicorn, he captures her, she changes into Venus, and they make love."

"But Venus comes ashore naked in a scallop shell," Grazzari said. Again Federico turned to Septivus.

"Well then," Septivus said, biting his little yellow teeth together, "Hercules comes upon a lion about to ravage a unicorn. While Hercules kills the lion, the unicorn flees into the sea. We think for a moment she has drowned, but she emerges naked in a shell and comes ashore into his arms."

Federico loved it, even though it meant building a cave where the unicorn would change into Venus and damming up a mountain stream to create a small flood.

As soon as the plans were announced, peasants from all over the valley poured into the city. Grazzari and Cecchi set them to work, building, painting, digging, planting, sewing, and polishing. Actors were hired from Padua, singers from Naples. Every moment of the day was devoted to the wedding, and everyone, whether they were courtiers or peasants, strove to fulfill Federico's dream and make Corsoli the envy of Gubbio, Parma, Arezzo, Perugia, and every other city in all of Italy.

Nor was Miranda left out of the preparations. Federico sought her opinions on everything. At first she delighted in making suggestions and was amazed to see her words transformed into colorful costumes or dresses. But one morning she came back to the room stamping her feet and cursing Septivus. "He still treats me as if I was one of his students! He smiles when I say something and yesterday he patted me on the head! If he does it again I will tell Federico." Because of this she threw herself into the plans with even greater urgency.

I discussed the menu with Luigi, for since I would have my own taster I wanted all the dishes I had ever longed for: quail, sausages, veal in garlic sauce, and a dessert shaped like the Fizzi palace made out of marzipan, sugar, and many kinds of fruits.

At mealtimes, Federico instructed Septivus to read aloud passages from the book Verana of Firenze had given him so that we might uplift our behavior. Septivus read a passage which said that even though breaking wind was rude, to hold it in could be bad for the stomach.

"So what should we do?" asked Federico, drowning out Septivus's next sentence with a fart.

"Muffle it with a cough," Septivus repeated.

As the wedding drew closer, Federico rose early and checked on the progress of the fresco or watched the laborers replacing the marble. He inspected the costumes for the pageant and wanted to know which desserts Tommaso was planning for the banquets.

I prayed Tommaso would accept the marriage, but his eyes became haunted and he started biting his nails again. When I tried to talk to him, he turned away. He hated me as much as he hated Federico, but as long as he kept away from Miranda I did not care.

In the midst of the preparations, I heard that my father was dying. Duke Federico gave me permission to visit him, which I did one morning after breakfast. It was a relief to be out of the city and all of its activity, riding through the long grass, smelling the flowers, and the trees, and the freshness of spring.

When I was a child my father's house was as tall as a tower, but every time I had returned it appeared smaller. Now it was but a rude bump on the landscape that would soon be ground into the earth again. My father, who had also stood tall and proud, now lay on a bed of soiled straw, blind, barely able to move, crippled with pain, and covered in sores. A racking cough tore from his ribs and the smell of death was everywhere.

All my anger disappeared and I knelt beside his bed and took his hands in mine. "Babbo," I whispered, wishing that, if only for a moment, I could do something to relieve his agony. His mouth trembled, and his foul stinking breath covered my face.

"Vittore?" he whispered.

Vittore! Christ! Would he never think of anyone else? But when had he ever? When the flock died because Vittore had not taken care of it, my father blamed it on a neighbor. When Vittore was accused of rape, my father said the girl lied because he would not marry her. When Vittore became a bandit and stalked the highways, my father pretended he was a courier. When he fled to Spain, my father said he was a general in the army. My father worked in pouring rain, in burning heat, in swarms of mosquitoes, when he was well and when he was sick. He was robbed by his neighbors and deceived by those he served. Vittore avoided work, cheated, robbed, and raped, and my father loved him for it. What should I tell him?

"He prospers," I said.

My father raised his head a little from the bed. Parting his thin lips that revealed two sorry black stubs against the pale pink inside of his mouth, he croaked, "I knew, I knew." Then he sank back into silence.

"He asks about Vittore every day," the villagers told me, bringing me a bowl of *minestra* and some bread. They stared at me while I ate, feeling my clothing, especially my new hat with the feather. They wanted to know about my life in the palace. "Are the women as beautiful as they say?" the men asked. "Do you have your own bed? How many sleep in a room?"

"Do not let my clothes mislead you; I am no better off than you are."

A man said loudly to another, "It is not enough that he leads a better life, but he lies about it, too."

So I told them the beds were cool in summer and warm in winter. "Not only can we eat as much as we like, but we drink wine with every meal," I boasted.

"I knew it!" the man said.

I told them Federico gave jewels to his favorite servants at Easter and that I only worked enough to keep the blood moving. I bragged that Federico often asked my opinion on different matters. I made up stories about princes from India and strange animals from Africa. "We have a unicorn which is both male and female."

When they had brought the *minestra* to me, the muscles in my neck had tensed and my throat narrowed as it always did when I ate. But I became so swept up in my lies that it was not till I had eaten half the broth of grains, broccoli, fennel, and basil—the same broth my mother had fed me when I was young, the same broth which had left a gnawing in my stomach—that I sighed with satisfaction. When I realized that the sigh had come from my own lips, I burst into tears. The villagers, who had been staring in amazement, now looked at me with bewilderment, and the woman who had made the broth protested that she had made it with love; if I was crying it was not her fault.

My father coughed and I turned to him, my cheeks wet with memories, my heart overflowing with forgiveness. "Babbo," I cried, thinking perhaps that we might even now become friends and be kind to one another as all families should be, but he did not see me. He was staring past the empty nests tucked into the ceiling beams, past the cracks in the roof, to a paradise in the sky.

Ever since the wedding was announced I had desired to bring my father to the palace so that he might see how Vittore was awaiting death while I was giving my daughter in marriage. But God did not grant me that wish. My father withheld his eyes from me and this time they remained closed forever.

I sobbed as I dug his grave. Despite the day's warmth my body was frozen as if my soul was already in that ice reserved for traitors. My father was dead and I had triumphed over Vittore, but my victories were small and I even smaller for thinking them victories. How many hours, weeks, months, years had I wasted in hatred?

After I poured the last of the earth onto my father's body I rode home, weeping until there were no tears left inside me. It was only then that I saw how great was God's infinite mercy. At last I understood why He had given me Helene only to take her from me again. Had I never met Helene, then my mother's words—those who carry a grudge will be buried beneath it—would have come true. But now a millstone had been lifted from my neck. Since my anger for my father and brother was all spent, I was cleansed. From now on I could be inspired not by hatred, but by love, my love for Helene. Even as Dante had been inspired by Beatrice, Helene would be my inspiration. I would lead my life so that I might be worthy of her. Tears of joy replaced my sorrow and I dismounted and knelt in the sweet-smelling grass, praising God for showing me the way.

As soon as I returned I went to Miranda's room, intending to tell her of my father's death and of the miracle that had happened to me.

Her friends were there talking excitedly. One of the girls told me breathlessly that the actors from Padua had arrived that afternoon and Federico had told the leader that Miranda was to sing with them.

The leader had laughed and said, "The bride? It has never been done. People will talk."

"That is why I want it!" Federico said, poking a fat finger into his chest.

Miranda was seated on the bed in the midst of all this merry-making, smiling and laughing with the others, but I could tell from the way she was biting her lip that something had frightened her. Until now, bewitched by all the gifts and attention, she had thought it was all a game she could stop whenever she wanted. Even after the marriage was announced she was so flattered that she was to become a princess, and Federico had been so nice to her, that she had not considered it could be any other way. But now I suspected she was not so sure.

Suddenly, I remembered things about her I wanted to tell Federico. She had been raised without a mother. Although she laughed easily she was often scared. True, she was wise beyond her years, but she was still a girl. I wanted to silence the silly laughter that surrounded her. I wanted time to march backward. To when she first started bleeding. To when her hands were as plump as her cheeks. To when I told her stories of her mother. To when she sang to the sun and played with the goats. To when I carried her on my shoulders and wiped the sleep from her eyes. To when she was no bigger than a loaf of bread and could fit into both of my hands. I wanted to cross the room to her bedside and hold her in my arms and tell her that I would always care for her, but the way had become so crowded with our ambition that I could not get through.

That night I dreamed that Miranda and I and Helene were living in Arraggio; the rain was falling and the sheep were grazing on the hillside. When I awoke in the morning I saw I was still in Corsoli and my pillow was soaked with tears. I rose, dressed, and knocked on Miranda's door. It was open as it always was between us, and there, sitting on her bed, was Tommaso! He did not even stand up when I came in. "What are you doing here?" I said to him.

Miranda sprang out of bed and pushed Tommaso out the door.

"Do you want to get us all killed?" I hissed.

She said, "How could you betroth me to Tommaso without telling me?"

"Miranda, that was five years ago. We had just arrived in the palace. I was trying to protect you. I—"

"What else have you been keeping from me?"

"Nothing."

"You told Federico I was a virgin."

"Yes, of course."

"And when were you going to tell me Federico has the pox?"

"Who told you that? That fool Tommaso?"

"Vittore told him."

"And you believe Vittore?"

"Tommaso is willing to lay down his life for me!"

As if I had not! "Miranda, you encouraged Federico—"

"You should have stopped me. You should have spoken for me."

*Oi me!* Now *I* was being blamed? A banging interrupted us.

All day long Corsoli echoed with the sound of workmen sealing the marriage contract. They have finished the arches by the Main Gate, the Piazza Del Vedura, the Palazzo Ascati, and the last one leading to the entrance of the Palazzo Fizzi. They have decked statues of Diana with olive branches and doves. Every building, no matter how small, has been cleaned and decorated with banners. The fountains are being filled with wine.

And then, just as a soldier collapses with weariness once the battle is over, so did Miranda fall into my arms, weeping, "I cannot marry Duke Federico, Babbo. I cannot. I love Tommaso. I have always loved him. I will always love him."

My heart tore into pieces, each breath coming like fire. The moment I had long dreaded was upon me and I was no more prepared for it than when Federico had asked me, "What do you say, Ugo?"

I bathed Miranda's head with water, pressed a sponge dipped in mandrake root boiled in wine with crushed poppy seeds against her nose, and held her in my arms.

"What shall I do?" she wailed. "What will become of me?"

She sobbed until she fell asleep. What could I do? How could I tell Federico, five days before the wedding, when hundreds of animals are being slaughtered, music composed, actors rehearsed, poems written, and frescoes completed? When thousands of yards of cloth have been made into gowns and jackets, pantaloons, hats, and dresses? When princes are traveling for days with their retainers and servants, cavaliers and footmen? When an emissary of the pope is expected, and the lion has been starved to make him more savage and Federico has spent every penny so that the rest of Italy, if only for one week, will sit up and take notice of him? If I were to tell Federico now that Miranda does not wish to marry him, he would behead her, burn her body, cut her into pieces, and parade the parts around the city. I remembered the new poem Federico had ordered Septivus to finish:

> Your voice so soft so filled with pain
> Your looks so wounding to my eyes
> Your heart it breathes a thousand sighs
> Your soul—

He knows—the words screamed in my head—he knows about Miranda and Tommaso.

"You must be careful," I pleaded with Miranda.

But the next day I found Tommaso in Miranda's room again. I was so incensed at his boldness that I drew my knife, but Miranda said, "Federico ordered him to be here."

"It is true," Tommaso smiled. "He suspects Miranda has a secret lover so I am to guard her."

"You fools! It's a trick."

"I will tell him we are in love," Tommaso said boldly.

"You will not say a word!" I said, and forced him out the door.

Now I have caught up with my story, for this happened this very same evening. I have been sitting in my room ever since. Just now a star shot across the sky. It is a favorable omen. But for whom? Federico? Miranda? Tommaso? Me? Alas, it streaked with so much speed that I did not see a name attached to it. I will drink some mandrake juice. It helps me sleep and I must sleep to think clearly about what must be done. Not only that, but the guests began arriving two days ago, for tomorrow is the first day of the wedding.

# xxix

The first day.

The first day is over but there are still six more! Thank God for henbane, although it plays tricks on me, for I can only hope that what I recall did happen and is not what I wanted to happen, because, if that is so, then I do not know what happened, and my life, which is already confusing, will become even more so.

Even though my eyes were weary after I had finished writing last night, they refused to close and so I wandered around the darkened palace. All day long, laborers and servants had been making sure that every detail had been attended to, but now all was silent except for the snoring and farting of those same weary servants sleeping in the shadows.

The kitchen was empty, the stoves glowing softly. Pots and cauldrons were lined up like soldiers' helmets. Vegetables were piled in every corner along with mounds of cheese, vats of milk, oil from Lucca, wine from Orvieto, Sienna, and Firenze, all of them waiting, like everything else in the palace—indeed in all of Corsoli—for the wedding to begin. From the kitchen I entered the inner courtyard. On three sides the marbled, white columns gleamed in the moonlight and facing me was the hillside which had been transformed into the Hanging Gardens. O blessed saints, as long as men can speak they will talk of it. For two months, fifty men stripped the hillside of its weeds and scrubs and planted flowers and bushes, trusting to God that He would smile on their plans. In His infinite mercy He heard their prayers and now the hillside is a flowered tapestry of blue, yellow, white, red—a painting sprung to life. "We have improved on nature herself," Grazzari said.

Oh, Helene, how I wish you could see this. I asked Duke Federico to invite the archbishop of Nîmes, but he refused, saying that he did not like Frenchmen. Where are you, Helene? Does your blood run faster at the thought of me as mine does of yours? Do you stretch your hand out at night hoping I might be by your side?

I walked through the palace to the Piazza Fizzi and the last of the four matrimonial arches. What a wonder! It stands three times the height of a man and is flanked on either side by statues carrying garlands of flowers. The figures of Virtuosa and Fortuna look so real they could spring to life.

From there it was but a short walk down the Weeping Steps to Corsoli. Like the palace, the town was silent except for the lazy flapping of red and white banners from the rooftops. Even the most decrepit house has been cleaned and repaired and the Piazza San Giulio is so changed with trees and bushes and flowers that it is hard to believe that during the plague you could not see the ground for dead bodies. It is from here that we will watch the pageant and the *caccia*.

Truly love, Federico's love for Miranda, has changed him. On our return from Milano, he wanted to build statues and sculptures of himself. Now he sees the beauty of a sunset, he wrestles with poetry, he appreciates Tommaso's artistry in the kitchen. The thought of Tommaso pierced me like an arrow and, whereas a moment before I had wanted to bang on every door and shout in every window, "This is all for my daughter, Miranda!" now I hurried back to the palace to be certain Tommaso was asleep in his bed and Miranda was in hers.

Tommaso lay on his side, his mouth open, his face frowning slightly. He murmured something and stretched his head forward as if trying to reach someone lying next to him. I hurried to Miranda's room. She was also asleep, lying on her side, her face pale against her black hair, her lips parted, and her hand pressed against her breast as if she was holding someone's hand there. Anger rose in me because of the foolish way their love refused to be cowed. I could have cut off their offending hands but what good would it have done? Their passion mocks every obstacle between them. I returned to my room and, exhausted by the heaviness of my heart, fell into a restless sleep.

This morning, Duke Federico was sitting on the side of his bed—his feet in a bowl of vinegar, his gout had returned unexpectedly—yelling at Bernardo, "But what does it mean?"

Bernardo looked at me sharply, as if my entrance had disturbed him, when we both knew that he was grateful for it. "Miranda is running away," Bernardo said slowly, "and she wishes you to pursue her even as the hunter pursues the game."

Federico must have been dreaming again. "But whenever I caught her," Federico said, "she slipped through my hands."

"If I may interrupt, Your Excellency, it means that her spirit can never be captured. Everyone knows that just as dreams are not real, the people in them are only spirits." As I had no idea what I was saying, I went on quickly, "I have apples and figs with honey for your breakfast, My Lord."

"Her spirit cannot be captured," Federico repeated to himself.

Relieved that he was off the hook, Bernardo hurried from the room. I shifted the cushions behind Federico. He lay back and asked, "How is Miranda this morning?"

"Resting," I said, and carefully lifted his gouty foot onto the bed. I reached for the bowl of figs and honey. Federico's head was turned away from me, looking out at the Hanging Gardens. His eyes darted toward me, then turned away again. I thought perhaps he wished to be alone, but he waved his paw and said, "*Reste!*"

Once more he looked out at the gardens and back at me. His mouth opened, words formed, but he did not speak. His eyes were wounded, not from the fiery pain of gout, but from a deeper, more powerful ache.

I had never seen Federico weep; indeed, until then I did not think he was *capable* of weeping, but I swore I could see tears in his eyes. Then, as if I had spied upon the sacred ark itself, a veil descended and he sat up, dipped a fig in honey, and ate it. "The night before a battle," he licked his lips, "my senses are sharper than my sword. I can see in the dark. I can hear grasshoppers fucking in the next field. I can smell the fear of the enemy."

I waited, certain he would ask about Miranda, but he did not. Instead he asked, "Has Princess Marguerite of Rimini arrived?"

"She is expected this morning."

He nodded. Gritting his teeth, he threw the covers off the bed and lurched his full weight onto his good leg and the rest onto my shoulder. Sweat formed on his brow, but as in Milano, he would not admit he was in pain. "The Hanging Gardens are beautiful," he grunted.

"Yes, Your Excellency. They are magnificent."

He stared at me. I did not blink or turn my head away even though his breath was fouler than a sewer on a hot day. I helped him to the chair so he could shit. Then I waited until he had finished and gave him my arm so he could return to his bed. He sat down and waved me away. I wanted to say something to ease his mind, but I was afraid that whatever I said would only arouse his suspicions further.

When I returned to my room I could hear Miranda's handmaidens giggling as they helped her dress. "As thick as my arm and twice as long," a girl tittered.

A moment later, Miranda knocked on my door. She was wearing a gown of blue silk and velvet. Precious jewels had been sewn into the design to compliment her necklace of rubies and emeralds. She seemed thinner and moved slowly as if her head might fall off her neck. Her pupils were still large from the potion I had given her earlier, but the paleness of her face set against the darkness of her hair only enhanced its beauty. "I need some more potion." Her voice cracked when she spoke.

"Your lips will bleed if you do not stop biting them."

"Give it to me!"

"Only a sip."

Her huge, dark eyes looked at me over the edge of the bowl.

"Miranda, you must not listen to stories about Federico. He loves you, deeply. For your own sake, I beg you—"

She swallowed the potion in one gulp, wiped her mouth with her hand, and then threw the empty bowl against the wall. She pretended to stagger as if she had suddenly become drunk, laughed too loudly, went back to her ladies, and together they walked down the hallway. I followed, fearing the potion might make her say something she would regret, but I lost her in the courtyard amid the colorful confusion of the carriages of the arriving guests.

The women were dressed in traveling clothes, but the men paraded around like peacocks, admiring themselves and congratulating one another on the safety of the journey. They wore goatees—it is now the fashion in Venezia—and two-colored hose. They had slits in the back of their jackets as if their tailors had forgotten to sew up the seams.

No sooner did their feet touch the ground than their tongues started wagging. "Federico has spent a fortune." "Not as much as the Estes in Ferrara." "But more than the Carpuchis!" "Corsoli looks splendid!"

"The matrimonial arches are wonderful!" "To have spent all this money, he must truly be in love!" "But with the daughter of a food taster?" a prince from Piacenza sniggered, as if food tasters had six legs or a *fallo* where their nose should be. I mentioned to the prince that it was my daughter, Miranda, the duke was marrying. He looked at me as if I was an idiot. Christ on a cross! He insulted food tasters and then he did not believe I was one! What did he think food tasters looked like? Oh, but he would soon find out, I would make sure of that. Indeed, they all did later that afternoon.

We had gathered in the entrance hall for the unveiling of Miranda's fresco. By now the palazzo was so crowded with guests and their servants that the very air tingled with excitement. Grazzari made a speech in which he praised Federico for being the sun from which he had drawn his strength, and Miranda the moon from which he had taken his inspiration. Then he pulled the curtain aside. I had watched Miranda pose several times and each time I had been astounded as Grazzari transferred her beauty to the wall. But now that the fresco was finished I was astounded all over again. The fresco is as tall as I am and twice as wide. In it, Miranda flies through the air from left to right, her dark black hair streaming behind her. She is dressed as an angel and the sun's rays form a halo around her head. Her face, which is turned toward us, is aglow, the ends of her mouth turned up as if she carried within it the secret to happiness. Grazzari had finished it that very afternoon—the colors were not yet dry—and it seemed so alive that I was sure that if I had pressed my head against the wall I could have heard the beat of her heart. I had always known she was beautiful, but to see every mole, every eyelash, every dimple larger than life was to behold the very essence of beauty itself.

I thought everyone would cheer, but no one said a word. "Are you all blind?" I wanted to shout. "This is the best painting I have ever seen! Better even than the Mary Magdalen in Milano!" Then I saw it was not that they did not wish to speak, but that they could not. The loveliness of the painting had stolen their breath away.

*"Magnifico!"* someone sighed at last, and then, like a damn bursting its sides, the praise poured out. *"Stupendo! Meraviglioso!"* over and over again, as if only a mountain of words could express their admiration. They surrounded Miranda, heaping praises upon her.

"But it is Grazzari you must applaud," Miranda said. "He has improved upon nature a second time."

"No," Grazzari replied. "When God saw how ill prepared I was to complete this task, He assisted me Himself."

He explained how the doves flying next to Miranda symbolized peace which could be seen by the lion and lamb lying together in the grassy foreground. "The necklace around Miranda's neck is the same one Aphrodite gave Harmonia at her wedding. It gives the wearer irresistible beauty."

"Maybe she needs it in the painting," Federico said, "but not in real life."

The guests agreed heartily. Miranda blushed. I did not hear what she said because just then I saw Tommaso in the doorway.

"I came to see the fresco," he said. His eyes were red from weeping, his face drawn from lack of sleep.

"If you do anything foolish," I whispered, "you will be killed!"

"I have nothing to live for!" he cried, and dashed away.

I could not follow because just then Federico led the guests into the main hall for a small dinner. Because many of them were weary from their journeys they went to bed soon after and I returned to look at the vision of Miranda once more.

I remembered that Grazzari had begun painting Miranda's face the day after the marriage was announced, when it was all still a game to her, which was why her face appeared so playful. Gazing at it again, I understood the madness of Tommaso's desire. Did I not feel the same for Helene? Did my heart not ache when I thought that I might never see her again?

Behind me, someone whispered, "Who is that?"

I turned around. Miranda was pointing to the fresco. "Why is she smiling when her heart is breaking in two?"

I reached out to comfort her, but she brushed my hand away. What could I say? It has been decided she will marry Federico. The wedding can only be canceled if something were to happen to him. But nothing will. Tommaso cannot stop it. What could he do? Stab Federico? He would never get through his guards. Poison him? Not as long as I am Federico's food taster. He had his chance. As Miranda had hers. Time marches forward not backward. What is done is done.

Federico will marry Miranda and I will no longer be a food taster. That is the way it is and that is the way it will be and if Tommaso even thinks of doing something about it, by the beard of Christ, I will cut his balls off!

The second day.

I do not know if it is the potions I have been taking, my anger toward Tommaso, or the excitement of the wedding, but I woke this morning wearier than when I had closed my eyes. I went to the kitchen, intending to speak with Tommaso. It was already crowded with servants chopping and mixing and boiling and frying, each one inspired to best the other. Luigi confided to me that over the next week two hundred sheep, fifty cattle, and fifty deer will be eaten, as well as two thousand doves, capons, and woodcocks. No wonder so many peasants have flocked to work here: there is no food anywhere else.

Tommaso was pouring cinnamon, verjuice, and ginger onto a bowl of berries. The berries reminded me of that oaf Onionface and I became furious that berries, which had once saved my life, could now bring about my death. "A perfect place," I said, as Tommaso poured them into a crust.

He jumped. "What do you want?" he shouted. I wanted to talk to him quietly, but he yelled again, "What do you want?" as if I was a peasant who had just wandered in from the country. I picked up a heavy ladle and would have cracked him over the head had Luigi not pushed me out of the kitchen, chiding, "What devil has got into you? We have work to do."

In the courtyard servants were lighting fires beneath vats and cauldrons. The smell of roasting meat filled the air. Giggling girls hurried past, clutching garlands of flowers. I should have been happy, but I was nervous and the roaring of the lion only agitated me further. The lion has not been fed for over a week to prepare him for the *caccia* and the smell of fresh meat has excited him. I was suddenly reminded of Vittore, for with so much going on I had forgotten about him.

When he heard my footsteps descending the steps to his cell, he stood up eagerly like a child expecting a treat. Then he saw who I was and sat back against the wall as if he had not a care in the world. His nails had grown and were thick with dirt, his clothes were black with filth, his hair was more matted than ever.

"Are you going to let Federico put me in the piazza with the lion?" he said, rubbing his poxy eye.

"I cannot stop him."

"Tell him I am your brother."

"But you did not want me to tell him, remember?"

He leaped up and clutched hold of the bars as if he could tear them apart. "You will not be satisfied until Papa and I are dead, will you?"

"Papa is already dead," I said.

He stared at me. "You are lying."

"A week ago, I heard he was sick so I went to see him. He died while I was there."

"Why did you not tell me?"

Why had I not told him? "I am sorry. I forgot. I—"

"You did not forget!" he yelled. "You are jealous. You have always been jealous." He spat out the last word as if it could hurt me.

"If you had truly loved him you would have visited him yourself or brought him to the palace," I answered.

"You . . . ass shit!!" He was no longer listening. "ASS SHIT!" He banged his forehead against the bars.

"He asked after you," I said. He stopped his pounding. "I told him you prospered."

He looked at me, and after a moment sneered, "Am I supposed to thank you?"

"No."

The air seemed to leave his body. He had always been taller than me, but now, standing in the middle of the cell, tugging at his hair, muttering to himself, he reminded me of that thin, feeble peasant who had attacked Federico's carriage on the way to Milano. He leaned his head on the bars again. "*Grazie*," he whispered. "*Grazie*."

A small ball of light glowed between us. It was filled with memories of what might have been—two boys playing together, two young men, their arms linked in friendship, two brothers, companions in life. Then it was gone and an emptiness overcame me. "I have to go. Cardinal Sevinelli is arriving from Roma."

As I reached the top of the stairs I heard a cry like the tearing of a soul. I crouched down and could just see into Vittore's cell. He was lying on the floor, his face in the muck, his hands grasping at the soiled straw, sobbing, "Babbo! Babbo!"

I took my place on the balcony behind Federico and Miranda and next to guests from Perugia and Spoleto. Below us, the crowd was singing and dancing around the matrimonial arch. Trumpets sounded some way off and a whisper spread through the crowd, "Here he is! Here he is!" and then twelve knights dressed in shining armor and green and white sashes rode into the piazza. They carried olive branches in their right hands and sat tall in the saddle as if their heads were attached to heaven. Behind them came twenty magnificent white horses without riders, each outfitted with golden saddles and bridles. Then came three nobles, each carrying a banner. One bore the sign of a cross, the next the keys of the church, and the third, the five crescents—the imperial flag of the Holy Church of Roma. Then came knights wearing papal robes and between them servants carried a canopy of blazing gold.

The procession stopped in front of the balcony and a figure stepped out from under the canopy. Holy Christ! I could not believe my eyes. It was not Cardinal Sevinelli, but that damned hunchback, Giovanni! I could tell those ears a mile away! My stomach heaved into my throat. I looked again to make sure I had not been mistaken. But no, it was him! He was wearing a robe of beaten gold and that dammed little red hat on the top of his head! The piazza fell silent! Everyone looked to Federico. I thought he would throw himself off the balcony and attack Giovanni, but instead he stood up and said, in a strong clear voice, "We welcome Cardinal Giovanni to Corsoli and pray that his stay finds us all in God's good graces." The crowd cheered; the procession moved into the palace.

The guests hurried away, buzzing like a thousand bees. I could not move, my *culo* was rooted to the chair, my legs as solid as a stone sculpture. Perhaps I am dreaming, I said to myself. I asked Cecchi if he had known that Giovanni was coming but he shook his head. Septivus swore he had not written to invite him. Who else could it have been then?

The guests gossiped about nothing else all afternoon. "Surely Giovanni would not have come unless he was invited!" they said. "Even so, one cannot deny he has the balls of a giant!" "And the dick of a horse, so I hear," someone joked. Rumor fell upon rumor until they piled so high they blotted out the sun.

That evening, we gathered in the courtyard for the first performance by the actors from Padua. The air was heavy with the scent of roses. Fireflies darted here and there, eager to play their part in the celebration. The chairs were lined up so that they faced two columns of scenery depicting clouds and birds and flowers which blended perfectly with the Hanging Gardens behind them. Miranda was dressed all in white except for a necklace of dazzling emeralds and a dainty golden crown. Whatever she was feeling, maybe even because of it, she had never appeared more lovely. As she took her place next to Federico, the sconces were lit and we beheld the most sparkling sight we had ever seen. There were so many exquisite women, so many shimmering jewels, so many handsome men all enhanced by the magnificence and splendor of nature, that we were not the pale imitators of heaven, but its very inspiration! Everyone sighed, honored to be part of such a wondrous spectacle.

I leaned back in my chair, drunk with the wine of goodness, and saw Tommaso's face staring down from a palace window. I was so startled I almost lost my balance. Just then, the flutes and drums commenced to play and I wrenched my eyes away from him to watch the stage. First a huge cloud suspended between the two columns slowly descended to the stage. When at last it came to rest, actors dressed as gods stepped out from it and called upon nature to show her pleasure. Thereupon more actors dressed as lions, lambs, cats, and dogs ran onto the stage and danced together. They sang love songs to Federico and Miranda and beseeched the gods for a fruitful union.

Then they left the stage and the columns of scenery were turned, displaying a series of paintings which would unfold throughout the evening. This one showed a convent's cell for a performance of a Boccaccio story about a nun who lost her wimple or something, I do not remember exactly. My mind was so distracted. I could not stop wondering why Giovanni had come or if Tommaso was planning something foolish. More dancing followed, another comedy, and, finally, two huge griffins pulled a golden chariot onto the stage in which Miranda was seated. It had all been planned so smoothly that I had not seen her leave her seat. She was seated in front of a painting of a hillside filled with trees which blended so well with the Hanging Gardens that it was perfection itself.

I looked to see if Tommaso was still watching; he was not and I cursed him for spoiling my enjoyment. Good God in heaven! Magnificence such as this only happenes once in a lifetime and I wanted to remember every detail. I wished my father and my dear mother could have seen it! *Potta!* I WANTED THE WORLD TO SEE IT! I would have even released Vittore just to show him how his poisonous words had been turned into gold.

Miranda strummed her lyre and notes spilled out like a gentle stream. She closed her eyes and sang of a love so great it could not be contained by the human heart. It burned so fiercely that it consumed not only the poet, but also her *amoroso*, and only in death, unhindered by flesh, could the lovers unite. As the last notes rose into the night, she opened her eyes and raised her head slightly, as if she could see the souls escaping into the starry blackness above us. Then she dropped her head, the griffins pulled the carriage off the stage, and the last thing we saw was the ghostly pale of Miranda's neck. I looked up at the window. Tommaso was weeping.

The guests cheered and shouted as Federico rose from his throne and turned to face us. "She is better than all the actors from Padua!" he beamed. Everyone cheered again. Federico shouted, "*Mangiamo!*" and with Miranda by his side, led the way into the banquet hall. No one mentioned the song.

If I had not seen the hall every day for the past five years I would never have recognized it. Chandeliers bearing hundreds of candles hung from the ceiling. Fine linen cloths covered the tables and at every place setting there were gold plates instead of trenchers. Grazzari had designed everything, even ensuring that the napkins were folded like delicate flowers. No sooner had the guests seated themselves than trumpets announced the serving of the food. I have already mentioned the first course. The second course consisted of fried veal sweetbreads, liver covered with the sauce of eggplant and served with slices of prosciutto and melon, as well as hot foods from the kitchen. Since it was early summer, the meat was tender, especially the rabbits, which had been raised for the occasion, and were served with pine nuts. The slices of spit-roasted veal were bathed in a sauce of its own juices. Of course, Septivus had to make a speech.

"Keep it short," Federico said.

Septivus said that although Corsoli could not boast of the grandeur of Roma or the splendor of Venezia, the three cities were sisters in spirit. Each had their virtues and, since Corsoli was situated midway between them, it benefited from both. If Corsoli's reputation in art or commerce was lacking, that was due to its geography for which only God Himself could be faulted, and who would fault God for placing Corsoli where it was? This made no sense to me, nor anyone else or perhaps even to Septivus, because he stammered and said that Corsoli would make amends for its geography by being the first city in Romagna to use the fork! Then the servants presented each guest with a silver fork. *Oi me!* You would have thought they were nuggets of gold! Luigi had to stand on a table to get the guests' attention.

"Grasp the fork like this," he said, holding the fork in his left hand. "Now spear the meat on the platter and carry it to your plate."

Everyone immediately stabbed at the bowls of meat. "Be firm," I heard Giovanni say.

"Now," continued Luigi, "holding the meat securely on the plate with the fork, and picking up the knife in the right hand, cut off a slice."

He cut a small piece of veal to demonstrate, stuck it on a fork, and offered it to me as if I was a dog! I tasted it, pronounced it free of poison, and returned the plate to Federico. Federico immediately stabbed the veal as if there was still life in it and cut it into three slices. "It is easy," he boasted.

Everyone did as they had been instructed. The women giggled and shrieked, "Blessed Holy Mother! The fork is a gift from heaven. Oh, how could we have lived without it."

Septivus, who as usual was talking as he ate, stabbed himself twice in the mouth. The stabbing reminded me of Tommaso and I wondered if he had tampered with the berry torte. All around me guests laughed and joked. Even Miranda! What was she laughing at? Unless it was because she KNEW the berries were poisoned and did not care.

"My pastry chef," Federico said, as Tommaso entered, carrying Federico's torte on a golden plate. Federico spooned out some torte, but instead of giving it to me, he gave it to Miranda! Why did he do that? Did he know something was wrong? Should I shout aloud? Throw myself at her? Tear the food from her mouth? I looked at Tommaso. His face was as blank as a stone wall.

"Your Excellency," I said, "should I not try the berries first?"

"There is no need, is there?" Federico asked, holding the spoon in the air.

"No, but as I will not be your taster much longer—"

Miranda calmly took the spoon from Federico and, before I could do anything, swallowed the torte and sighed with pleasure. Tommaso walked out, looking at me with such disgust that I trembled with rage. Actors sang, clowns juggled, musicians played. My shirt was soaking with sweat, my knees would not stop shaking. There was a hole in my stomach. I wanted to die.

I have just come back to my room. The first rays of dawn are sliding over the mountains. Some of the guests walked into the garden to watch the sunrise but I am wearier than Job and need to sleep. As I crossed the courtyard, Cardinal Giovanni passed me with four of his guards. I bowed and said, *"Bouna notte,* Cardinal Giovanni."

Giovanni stepped in front of me, blocking my path. "Ugo DiFonte, Duke Federico's food taster." He looked me up and down as if I was a piece of meat he might wish to buy. "Tell me Ugo, will you still be Duke Federico's taster after your daughter becomes Duke Federico's wife?"

"No. I am to have my own taster."

"Your own taster?" The little twat turned to his guards. "Did you hear that? Ugo is going to have his own taster." The guards smirked and Giovanni turned back to me. "When will that be?"

"At the last banquet."

"In five days' time?" His eyes bulged from behind his spectacles.

"Yes." I could hardly believe it myself.

"Well, we will see," he smirked, and strode off without a backward glance.

What did he mean by that? Who cares what he means. He can think what he likes. He cannot harm me. Not here in Corsoli. This is Federico's court and Federico is marrying my daughter and even if Giovanni is an emissary of the pope and Jesus Christ Himself, he cannot do anything to me here.

*   *   *

The third day.

*Oi me! Sono fottuto!* My life has been overturned! The jaws of hell gape below me and devils grasp at my heels. How can this have happened? I was sitting in my room . . . no, no. I must start at the beginning. This morning in the Duomo Santa Caterina, Giovanni gave a sermon in which he talked about rendering to Caesar what was Caesar's and to God what was God's. I was sure Giovanni was talking to me because of the conversation we had last night and this afternoon I knew I was right! As soon as mass was over I came here to write the very words I have just written, when there was a knock at the door.

*"Un momento!"* I called out, because I wanted to hide this manuscript. A voice said if I did not open the door it would be broken down. I was outraged that someone would talk to me like that. Me! A courtier! The father of the bride! In the middle of the wedding! "I will give whoever it is a good thrashing for disturbing me," I shouted, as I opened the door. There standing before me were the same four soldiers I had seen with Cardinal Giovanni the night before. The captain said Cardinal Giovanni wanted to see me. I replied that Cardinal Giovanni must have forgotten that my daughter was getting married and that I had many things to do and if Cardinal Giovanni wanted to see me could he please come to my room. The captain warned me that if I did not come immediately I could be thrown in prison. *Potta!* What could I do?

Giovanni was bending over his desk writing when I entered. His hair had been cut short and without his hat his head looked like a big pot and his ears handles to pick it up with. I waited for a moment and then said, "Cardinal Giovanni, if you will pardon me for interrupt—"

"No, I will not," he snapped, and went on writing.

The fool was acting like the pope himself! After a few moments, he put down his quill, sat back in his chair and said, "Do you know why I am here?"

He was obviously playing a game, but since I did not know the rules I replied quite innocently, "Surely, it is to give the pope's blessing to this holy marriage."

He said, "I am here by authority of Pope Clement to investigate anyone who has sinned against the church."

"What has that to do with me?" I shrugged.

He did not answer but continued to look straight at me.

I said, "Cardinal Giovanni, I swear by la Santa Madre Vergine, *I* have never said anything against our Lord Jesus Christ, the Lord God, the church, or a saint. Not even the pope!"

Giovanni picked up a piece of paper from the desk, adjusted his spectacles, and read, "The Imperial Church of Roma hereby accuses Ugo DiFonte of Corsoli of practicing witchcraft."

"Me?" I laughed. "A witch?"

"This is a serious charge! The penalty is death!"

"Cardinal Giovanni, you have the wrong DiFonte! My brother Vittore held sabbats in the stable. He cursed Christ. He made his followers kiss his *culo*—"

"It would be better if you confessed."

"To what?" I replied hotly.

Someone hit me in the back of my head and I fell to the ground. I was kicked in the ribs, then picked up, and stood in front of Giovanni again as if I was nothing more than a doll. My head was ringing and blood flowed from my mouth, for a tooth had come loose.

"You should control your temper. We have a witness."

"I would like to see who it is," I shouted.

Cardinal Giovanni nodded to a guard who opened a side door— *Jesus in sancto!* O my soul!—in stepped the dandy from Milano! "Perhaps you remember Battista Girolamo," Giovanni went on. "He used to be the food taster to the Duke of Savoy. He says he saw you perform witchcraft at a banquet last year given by Francesco Sforza."

"He put a spell over a bowl of berries that killed Antonio DeGenoa," the dandy said slyly.

"I never killed him—"

"Quiet! You saw this happen, Battista?"

"Yes, Cardinal Giovanni."

"Had you ever met Ugo DiFonte before?"

"Yes, Your Excellency, Cardinal Giovanni. The night he arrived a group of us food tasters were drinking and talking about amulets."

"What did he say?"

"He said he did not use any amulets."

"What *did* he use?"

"He said he used magic."

"*Magic?*"

"Yes, Cardinal Giovanni, magic!"

*Potta!* They were even better rehearsed than the actors from Padua!

"You may go," Giovanni smiled. The guard opened the side door. The dandy walked through it but paused in the doorway, turned to me, and drew his hand across his throat.

"Now what do you say?" asked Giovanni, adjusting his spectacles once more.

What could I say? If I told him that no one was more surprised than I when Onionface had died he would not believe me. If I told him I could not perform magic if my life depended on it he would not believe me. It did not matter what I said. He wanted revenge for the killing of his sister and mother.

"Cardinal Giovanni, if I could really do magic, why would I have remained a food taster here in Corsoli risking my life twice a day, every day of the week, for all these years? Would I not have gone to Roma or Milano or Venezia and made a fortune? Indeed, if I knew magic why would I be standing here right now?"

Giovanni's face turned as red as a beet. "How dare you mock this court," he shouted. "You could be beheaded for your insolence. That is all. Until I call you again."

The guards marched me back to my room, telling me I was lucky to be alive because Giovanni had ordered other men to prison and some to death on far less evidence. Now here I sit, trembling. Why did Giovanni not put me to death? Or at least in prison? Why is he taunting me? Is he afraid of Federico? Perhaps he is waiting till after the wedding. O merciful God, what shall I do? Where can I go? For the moment I must remain calm. Above all I must not let Giovanni see I am afraid. Oh, why did you have to come now, you little bastard, hunchback sodomite dwarf! Ugo, calm yourself. Courage! Something will come to me.

Whenever there was something I did not understand in the Bible, such as why God allowed saints to be killed and sinners to live, the abbot Tottorini said that God's ways were mysterious and not to be questioned. The more I thought about this, the more it seemed that what people thought were God's mysteries were really mistakes. When I told this to the abbot he replied angrily, "God does not make mistakes!"

"If they are not mistakes, then he must not care," I answered.

This made the abbot angrier still. He said God had sacrificed His only Son for the sins of mankind, which showed how much He cared. And because we are His children He watches over all of us.

"Then His eyes are bad," I replied. How can He watch over me and also watch over everyone else in Corsoli? As well as everyone in Venezia and Roma and Milano and France and all at the same time? We pray and beg Him to favor us, praising Him when He does and blaming ourselves when He does not. The truth is I do not think He sees us. And if He does, I do not think He cares. I remember the first time I looked down from the palace walls and saw the villagers making their way to market. They appeared no bigger than ants and I could not tell one from the other. Surely that is how we must look to God. Thousands upon thousands of ants, each struggling to overcome the twigs and stones in their lives. But for what? If there is some reason why I must overcome these twigs and stones, why does God not give me a sign? Does He think I am too stupid to understand? I, who have overcome Onionface and my father and Vittore? Does He think I have no more brains than an ant? Why give me a brain at all? I would rather be an ant and not think. Then I would be at peace.

Truly, the world has gone mad. Guests stand below my window watching the rain—it started earlier today—while just above them I burn in hell. I must speak to Federico. I have served him well. I have saved his life. He is marrying my daughter. He will protect me against Giovanni. He must. It would not look well if the father of the bride was arrested for witchcraft at Federico's wedding.

I have just returned from Federico's chamber. The guard said Federico was resting and did not wish to be disturbed. I swear if Giovanni locks me up in the same cell as Vittore I will go mad! Now I must prepare for the jousting.

I have returned from the jousting. Miranda was cheering and laughing as if she did not have a care in the world. I wanted to ask her why, but I did not feel well. The walls of my room sway up and down like a boat at sea. My paper refuses to lie still on the desk even after I threatened to tear it into pieces. Ugo, Ugo, Ugo. U U U U. The quill has sharp claws. Giovanni has claws. Everyone has claws. Even I. I cannot scratch my face unless I am very careful so my face does not see. Someone is standing by the door. They are calling me. They have the mouth of a rat. I shall ignore them because I cannot be seen with a rat. I cannot go to the banquet with a rat. I do not care how many times it calls me, I am not going. I am not . . .

The fourth day—midafternoon.

My senses have deserted me! I *am* mad! It is the afternoon of the fourth day and I am a bowstring pulled to its tautest point. Federico did not go on the hunt—what horse could carry him?—and neither did Giovanni. As we prepared to leave I saw them talking together. What were they talking about? I asked Cecchi but he did not know. The hunt was abandoned because of rain. I am going to see Federico again.

Early evening.

Federico was still resting. Why? He never rested before. Perhaps he does not wish to see me. But how would he know why I was coming to see him? I wandered around the palace. The guests were gossiping about Federico marrying a peasant girl and not just taking her as he had done with so many others. "I would kill myself," a woman said. Another man wondered how I could have allowed Miranda to marry the duke, for he would never have agreed to such a match. It is jealousy. I see it in their faces. I hear it in their voices.

Thunder clapped just now, lightning rent the sky and the rain falls with a vengeance. Some moments ago the actors returned from the Piazza San Giulio. The actress playing the unicorn said if the ground became any muddier Hercules would not be chasing a unicorn but an elephant.

After Federico refused to see me I went to the kitchen to make sure Luigi was making my favorite little rolls of tame game as he had promised. The game is finely cut, mixed with fat of veal and spices, wrapped in a crust, and baked. Then the yolks of two eggs are beaten together with a little verjuice and dripped gently over four rolls. It was just as well I went, for when I arrived Luigi was not making the rolls, but mixing ground-up breast of chicken with ground almonds and soft bread.

"We are having *mangiabianco* instead," he said, looking at me as if I should have been cleaning out the cesspool. Christ on a cross! Three years ago he did not know pork from chicken and now he thinks he has invented cooking! "I changed it because after so much feasting the stomach is saturated with food and it is necessary to tease it."

"But we have not had that much feasting."

"What did we do two nights ago?" he asked indignantly.

I looked at Tommaso but he pretended not to see me.

"As a taster you are not acquainted with the many different types of appetite," Luigi said.

I, Ugo, the food taster, not acquainted with different types of appetite?

"The appetite of an empty stomach is not the same as one which has enjoyed a meal." He added a handful of ginger and sugar, mixing it with the chicken and almonds. "Once the appetite has been aroused, it is not so curious. It says, 'Surprise me.' "

I will surprise you, I thought, taking out my knife. "Whose idea was this?"

"Tommaso's."

So that was why he had ignored me.

"I cannot talk now," he shouted, waving his arms in the air. He was making a chariot and horses out of sugar and marzipan. I wanted to smash it into pieces. He must have sensed this because he stood in front of it. "What do you want?" he yelled.

Everyone in the kitchen stared at me. Luigi said, "You cannot keep coming in here while we have work to do!"

"I will come in whenever I like!" I shouted.

I found Miranda, but she would not listen to me either. Now my head hurts and my skin prickles. I have scratched it till it bleeds but it will not stop. Why does it not stop? I must prepare for the banquet.

*   *   *

Dawn.

I am barely alive. There is no reason for me to go to hell for I am already there. O God in heaven, what are you preparing me for?

After the banquet, which I can no longer remember for I have aged a thousand years since then, I fell into a deep sleep. I do not know how long I slept, but suddenly I was dreaming of Federico. He was walking along a corridor, his cane in one hand, his sword in the other. He was walking slowly at first, but then faster, down one corridor and along the next. I knew he was coming to my room. I knew I had to hide something, but I did not know what it was. I ran around the room, searching under the bed, behind the chairs, all the time knowing that Federico was coming closer and closer. I tore the curtains from the windows, tears streaming down my face, crying for my mother to help me, when all of a sudden I knew what I was looking for. I shot up out of my sleep, sprang to the door Miranda and I shared, and banged on it.

"Who is it?" she answered.

"Your father!" I hissed. I could hear the shuffling of feet. "Open the door! For the love of God, open the door!" The door opened and there stood Miranda and Tommaso, clutching sheets to their nakedness. "Are you mad? Federico is coming!"

Miranda said, "I will have Tommaso's child."

"I will tell him we are betrothed," Tommaso said. They stood there, grains of sand before an onrushing tide.

"He will kill you both!"

"Then we will be together in heaven," Tommaso replied. *Oi me!* I could hear Federico's three-footed walk in the hallway! Tommaso ran toward the door as if to confront Federico himself. With a cry, I flung Miranda back into her bed and with a strength I did not know I had, pulled Tommaso by the back of his head into my room, closed the door and leaned against it. He tried to pull me away. I put my hands over his mouth and wrestled him to the ground. We heard Miranda scream, the clanking feet of Federico's guard and then Federico's harsh voice, demanding, "Where is he?"

Only then did Tommaso emerge from his dream state. I let him go, pointed to the window, and threw myself against the door of

Miranda's room as it opened. I was pushed to the ground as the guard strode past me and in the doorway stood Federico as I had pictured him in my dream. "Who are you?" he roared, his face twisted with rage, his sword at my neck.

"Ugo DiFonte, Your Excellency. Your food taster. Your faithful servant. I heard Miranda scream—"

Behind me the guard tore my room apart, searching through the bedclothes and overturning my desk.

"I smell it!" Federico hissed. "I smell it." He slashed the air with his sword and stabbed my bedclothes over and over.

I wanted to say, "Your Excellency, it is not Miranda's fault but that ass, Tommaso. Kill him and your worries will be over!" But as I raised my head I saw Miranda's pleading, terrified eyes—so I said nothing. Besides I could not say anything without implicating her.

Federico hobbled into the hall, his footsteps echoing on the stone floor. When I could hear them no longer I went into Miranda's room. She was sitting up, trembling and shaking. She reached out her arms to me. "Babbo," she wept, "Babbo."

I told her that God has plans for all of us and that we must trust in Him. Even when the world is against us, when darkness and evil overtake us, we must have faith in Him. For the blackest clouds disperse in time, revealing the sun. So it is with God. For those who believe in Him, He is the sun and like the sun He will heal us when the clouds of dismay have vanished.

Miranda did not say anything; she did not have to, for she knew, that it was not her I was trying to convince, but myself.

The fifth day.

Dear God, why do you not listen to me? I pray for your guidance but YOU GIVE ME NONE! My world is shattered. Giovanni's guards came for me again. This time they just burst into my room and dragged me to Giovanni. As soon as I stood before him, Giovanni asked, "Ugo DiFonte, do you believe in God?"

"Of course," I made the sign of the cross. "God the Father, the Son, the Holy Ghost. Our creator. Our Father."

"Our Father?"

"Yes. Our Father, that is to say, we are made in His image."

Giovanni chewed the end of his quill. "If we are made in His image, ipso facto, He must reflect us, *n'est-ce pas?*"

"I am sorry, Cardinal Giovanni, but I do not know what you mean."

"If we are made in His image then He must be like us," he repeated. "Our strengths are His strengths and our weaknesses His weaknesses."

"Cardinal Giovanni, your words are sharper than your sword. I am just a peasant—"

"If you were a peasant you would not be wearing those clothes and be sitting at Duke Federico's table tomorrow night with your own taster," he snapped. "So," he carried on, "according to you, God can be caring and yet uncaring. Merciful, but cruel—"

"Cardinal Giovanni—"

"Selfish, arrogant, a thief, a murderer—"

"We are made in God's image, but our failings come because we stray from His teachings."

"What is the worst failing?"

I was afraid to answer for no matter what I said I knew it would be wrong.

"Pride, Ugo."

"It is as you say then."

"Are you not proud of your daughter?"

"But is that a sin?"

He ignored me. "You are proud of your daughter. You are proud you have risen from a food taster to a courtier. You are proud you have cheated death. Your pride is like a stench around you. You walk about in your fancy silks, but you are still a peasant. And a witch. That is all."

He waved a hand and I was thrown out of the room. Still he did not arrest me. Why? On the way back I saw Miranda talking to Tommaso in Emilia's garden.

"This is madness," I said to them. "You were nearly killed last night and now today—"

"We were discussing the dessert for the banquet," Miranda said coldly, and walked away.

Tommaso followed her with his eyes and I stepped in front so no one might see. "There are guests everywhere! I cannot believe you would sacrifice her life so."

"I?" he cried. "You have already done so," and he too walked away.

They lie. They are planning something. That is why they stopped talking when they saw me. They plan to poison Federico, and me, too. I know it. I know it. I, who persuaded Tommaso to become a chef, am going to be poisoned by him. And my daughter is going to help him. That is a comedy even Boccaccio would envy.

I wanted to tell Duke Federico about Cardinal Giovanni and Tommaso, but after last night I no longer know if he will listen to me. Besides, whenever he eats or wherever he goes he is surrounded by guests. Even when I taste his food in the morning there are people around him. This time he was playing cards with the duke of Perugia and Marguerite of Rimini. I waited for the game to finish, but he started another immediately. I know he saw me, but he avoided me. Is it because of Cardinal Giovanni? I do not care anymore. I will speak with him at the banquet even if I have to yell.

The actors will perform more plays tonight because the pageant has been canceled because of rain. It is a shame. I looked forward to seeing Hercules chasing the unicorn and the unicorn changing into Venus. Now the Piazza San Giulio will only be used for the *caccia*. I pray that will not be canceled. Now I must dress. I tried to talk to Miranda, but she was surrounded by guests and friends. There is no banquet tonight. After everything we ate last night, it is a wonder anyone will ever want to eat again.

The fifth night.

Tommaso! That stupid, hot-headed ignorant fool! If he wants to kill himself, then let him do so, but he will cause Miranda's death, too. I knew they were planning something. Miranda was smiling and talking with the guests and clutching Federico's hand, but I did not believe her for an instant. Then, while the actors were performing the piece about the nun again, I suddenly thought of Vittore. Perhaps it was the nun's cell which alerted me, I do not know. Whatever it was, I slipped away from the performance and looked for Tommaso. He was not in the kitchen nor in his room. Like a madman I ran all over the palace. Then suddenly I knew. I raced to the prison. The guard was not at the top of the stairs, and as fate should have it when I came to the bottom I saw someone struggling with the lock of Vittore's cell. I called out. "In the name of Duke Federico, stop what you are doing."

Tommaso turned round. He was trembling and panting, his mouth open, his hair in disarray.

"Open it!" Vittore commanded. Tommaso fumbled with the key again.

I pulled out my dagger. "Do not make me kill you, Tommaso."

"He does not have the balls," Vittore hissed.

"He will take Miranda and murder you. Remember what happened after the sabbats," I pleaded.

"I cannot live without her," Tommaso cried.

He turned the key. I ran at him and that bastard Vittore pushed the cell door open so violently that Tommaso fell backward onto my knife. He screamed as the blade sank into his thigh. I staggered back. "Ugo!" he cried.

I collapsed under his weight and he fell on top of me. His cry brought the guards. I pushed Tommaso off me and as he rolled over, blood poured from the wound. His hand grasped my shirt.

"Why did you not listen to me?" I pleaded.

"I will try . . ." His eyes rolled to the back of his head and he fainted.

"Ugo killed him!" Vittore shouted. He had slipped back into his cell and was holding the door closed. The guards tried to arrest me, but I fought them, yelling that it was Vittore who had stabbed him.

"But he is locked in his cell," said the guard. "And this is your knife?"

"Put him in here," Vittore shouted.

I tried to explain what I had seen, but in my anger and despair I made no sense.

"Where is the key to the cell?" the guard demanded.

"Vittore must have it."

"He is in the cell," the stupid guard repeated and started to drag me up the stairs. "He will escape!" I shouted.

Fortunately, Cecchi had become alarmed at my disappearance and came by at that moment. He ordered the guards to search the cell and they found the key buried beneath the straw. Tommaso was carried away and Piero attended to him. Shaking, I went to my room and waited for Miranda.

She arrived, pale and trembling, with Cecchi by her side. "What is it?" she kept saying, "what is it?"

Cecchi said, "Tommaso was stabbed trying to release Vittore."

Miranda would have fallen to the floor had Cecchi not caught her and slapped her about the face. He said if Federico discovered that she had been involved trying to free Vittore he would kill her himself. He said she had endangered not only herself, but me and others in the palace. He told her to put away all memory of Tommaso and never think of him again. Then he took her by the hand and led her away.

I think now, finally, she has grasped that there is nothing she can do. I pray the wound in Tommaso's thigh will remind him, too.

The sixth day—midday.

I have not slept. I look at my hands and do not recognize them. Although I tell myself that it was Vittore who pushed Tommaso onto me, I would have stabbed him to death in the next moment. Although the wound is deep, Tommaso will live. Even now he is making the pastry for the last banquet. I remember hearing that brown eyes mean that their owner is clever and wise, but Tommaso has brown eyes and he is foolish. Brave but foolish. Is he brave *because* he is foolish? How could he have believed Vittore would help him?

Miranda dressed in a gown which showed her breasts to the nipples. She painted her face with so much rouge that a fly would have left a mark had it landed there.

"Why are you doing this?"

"Since I am a whore, I am dressing like one."

"Miranda, listen to me!"

"Or what? You will kill me?"

I walked toward her but she clutched a knife and screamed "Guard! Guard!" so loudly that I left.

It is astonishing how this tragedy unfolds unnoticed amid all the festivities. Even now the bell of Santa Caterina leaps out of the vestry, its chimes joyfully tumbling into one another. The golden Madonna glimmers in the sunlight. Banners hang from every window and loggia, people sing and dance. They know nothing of this. Even if they did, it would not stop their merrymaking. Nothing can prevent today's celebration. The wedding *will* take place. I wish my mother could see it. My father, too. But both are dead. Soon my brother

Vittore will join them. He, above all, deserves to die, but this afternoon I was filled with remorse. I wanted to ask Federico that since the rain has stopped and death is not a good omen for the marriage, perhaps the *caccia* should be postponed till after the wedding. But Federico will not listen to me.

Night.

It was a shame the pageant was canceled because by the light of the sconces the Piazza San Giulio was more beautiful than anyone could have imagined. When Miranda appeared the crowd embraced her, calling her an angel and the queen of Corsoli. They praised Federico for choosing her and wished them many children. It was such an outpouring of love that even Miranda was surprised and moved. A man shouted that our patron saint, Santa Caterina, could be seen in the stars smiling down upon us. The bishop prayed that we would always be worthy to be held in the palm of God's hand. Then cats and dogs were thrown into the piazza and immediately there was barking and mewling as they bit and scratched one another to death.

The crowd shouted and yelled for the next event. After a flourish of trumpets a cart carrying a cage was pushed into the garden. It held three men: the first, a thief who had scraped gold leaf from the Madonna on the Duomo Santa Caterina; the second, the prison guard Tommaso had bribed when he tried to free Vittore; and the third was Vittore. More trumpet blasts announced another cage bearing the lion. The keepers freed the lion and then hurriedly clambered onto a platform. The thief tried to climb up after them, but the crowd pushed him back into the mud. The guard fell to his knees and prayed. Vittore stood next to a tree, his jacket and hose as torn and dirty as the day he arrived.

The lion walked slowly out of the cage, its knotty tail flicking back and forth. It had a large head and a huge mane, but it was so thin you could see its ribs. "It must be from Corsoli," a woman shouted to much laughter. I wondered if the lion thought it was at home in Africa. Did it know all these trees and bushes had been brought in for its benefit? The crowd cheered and whistled. A star shot across the sky.

Suddenly, Vittore shouted, "*Io sono vittima di una cospirazione! Cospirazione! Cospirazione!*" He said it over and over, turning round and round and beating his chest with his long thin arms.

The crowd mocked him, beating their chests and wailing, *"Cospirazione! Cospirazione!"*

The lion stood quite still, patiently waiting for his cue to begin.

"Yes, I gave Federico a potion," Vittore shouted, "but not arsenic."

"No one is interested in your lies," I cried.

The lion padded behind a bush. Vittore pointed at me and said, "He does not want you to know the truth."

"You would not know the truth if you spoke it," I shouted, and the crowd laughed.

"I gave Federico mercury," Vittore shouted. "Do you know why?" *Cristo in croce!* Why was the lion taking so long?

Pulling his hair away from his face, Vittore ran toward the balcony where Federico was sitting with Miranda. "This will be your fate—"

Even as it occurred to me that Vittore had been telling the truth about Federico, the lion leaped over the bush, caught Vittore's back leg in his jaw and pulled him to the wet ground. Vittore screamed. The lion clubbed Vittore's head with his paw. Vittore's legs jerked violently and his cry was silenced.

Miranda collapsed and Federico lifted her up in his arms and carried her away, her handmaidens running after him. The crowd did not notice for they were too busy watching the lion. It tore Vittore's left shoulder from his body and bit into his chest. Blood shot into the air, covering the lion's face. Vittore's bones snapped like twigs and with each bite a part of me snapped until I wondered if I was not dying, too.

"Tell all witches to come to Corsoli," someone shouted. "We have a hungry lion."

The crowd cheered. I was silent. Exhausted. Weighed down by the blood on my hands.

As soon as the *caccia* was over I went to Federico's chambers, telling the guards that Federico had summoned me to tell him of Miranda's condition. Federico was standing by the window when I entered. "How is Miranda?" he asked. His face was pale and worried.

"She is recovering, Your Excellency."

He sighed deeply. "Good. Good!" He clapped his hands together in a praying motion and then blew a kiss to heaven.

I did not wait for permission to speak. "Your Excellency, Cardinal

Giovanni has accused me twice of witchcraft in Milano." As if he had not heard, Federico turned his back on me to look out at the hillside. I did not let that stop me. "He is talking about the time I blew on the berries. But I did not use any magic. As you know it was only by the grace of God that Onionface died."

Federico did not answer. Was he still thinking about Miranda? Perhaps he was hoping I would go away.

"Your Honor—"

"Ugo." He turned toward me, and with a smile such as a parent uses to calm an anxious child, said, "How long have you been my taster?"

"Five years, My Lord."

"And you have served me faithfully."

"It has been my honor, Your Excellency."

"And now you are giving your daughter to me in marriage." He laid a heavy hand upon my shoulder and stared straight into my eyes. "Do you really think I would allow anything to happen to you?"

"But—"

"Think no more about it."

"Your Honor—"

"And say no more about it."

I knew then, as sure as my name is Ugo DiFonte, that he was lying. But I had not served him for five years without learning anything, so I heaved a sigh of relief and said "Your Excellency, you have given me new life and made me eternally grateful." I kissed his hand. Then I hurried out of the room before I vomited.

The poxy bastard has deserted me! Me! Who serves him faithfully. Who eats his food and saves him from poison! Who gently lifts his gouty foul-smelling leg! Who fluffs his pillows. Who stands by his chair when he shits! It has to do with Giovanni. But what is it?

Night.

I have found out why Federico lied to me! At the banquet I was as close to him as my quill is to this paper and yet he refused to look at me. Miranda also refused, but I do not blame her. I would beg her forgiveness for I have wronged her terribly, but I do not have time.

Halfway through the banquet, as golden platters stacked high with crests of hen and roast pigeon were being served, Cardinal Giovanni made a speech.

"Love is the seed of life," he said. "There is love for one's family, love for mankind, and love for God. When one inspires the other, the windfall of happiness knows no bounds. Because of his great love for Miranda, Duke Federico has agreed to take his new bride on a pilgrimage to Roma to receive a blessing from the pope!"

Everyone cheered Federico, who was beaming proudly! I looked at Miranda, who seemed as mystified as I was. And now, finally, I understood why Federico had not spoken to me! He has betrayed me! Betrayed me to satisfy a whim of Miranda's that she cannot even remember! Federico thinks by taking her to Roma as she had asked months ago, she will love him. And in return for safe passage Federico will allow Giovanni to arrest me. And I thought Federico would protect me! What a fool I have been! Federico will not protect me! Why should he? He no longer needs me. He will be married to Miranda who is loved by everyone. The peasants love him. The guests praise him!

Giovanni sat down and everyone congratulated him for making peace with Federico. It was then that I lost control of all of my senses. What need had I for them anymore? Voices echoed inside my head like the shouting of giants. My eyes glazed over and I could not see. The power of my nose, which I used to control as finely as Grazzari controlled his paintbrush, no longer obeyed me. Suddenly, I could smell not only the garlic, the lemon, the smoked cheeses, and the fennel, but also the perfumes of ambergris, musk, and rosemary. I could detect the whiff of velvet in the robes of the guests, their woolen shirts, the beaten gold trimming on the dresses. While everyone around me was talking about Miranda meeting the pope, I was overcome by the stink of their unwashed hair, the damp sweat under their arms, the dirt between their toes, the shit in their *culo*. My eyes watered at the overpowering aroma of Federico's lust. I gagged on Giovanni's choking smugness. I was overcome by the stench of Miranda's despair. Holy Mother of God! What have I done to my daughter? I have sacrificed her so that I might eat again.

There rose then still one more odor. One which had lain buried beneath the others but now snaked its way out of the bile of my stomach and up into my throat. It was my fear. My betrayal. My cowardice.

I sat there suffocating while all around me the guests celebrated. I prayed to God and He spoke to me, saying, "I help those who help themselves." No sooner had I heard those words than I knew what I had to do. I turned to Miranda, but she was not at the table.

"She left the hall," Duke Orsino said.

Miranda was in the courtyard standing on the ledge where the bodies are thrown down the mountain. In the moonlight she looked so like my mother that at first I thought it was her ghost. "Miranda!" I called.

She did not answer.

"Miranda, it is not over yet."

She looked down the mountain. "Not quite. But soon."

"Where there is life, there is hope."

She turned to me. "My champions have all been beaten."

"I am your champion."

"You?" she sneered.

"We have been in difficult times before. Miranda, I promised your mother I would always take care of you."

"Please . . ."

"I have a plan. As soon as you marry Federico, you must complain of an ache in your stomach." I moved closer as I was talking. "You must tell Federico that I have a potion that will cure it." I moved closer still. "Then you will come to my room and drink a potion I have prepared."

"What will it do?"

"You know I have been experimenting with potions—"

"What will it do?" she repeated angrily.

"It will make you appear as if you are dead." I did not have such a potion but I could not tell her that.

"How will that help?"

"Like this." And grasping her hand, I pulled her off the ledge.

"You tricked me," she hissed. She spat in my face and tried to scratch me. "Oh, why will you not let me die!" she wailed.

"Because I am your father and you will do whatever I tell you!" I led her back to the hall. I had to do that. I could not stop my mother from killing herself, but I would die before I let Miranda do the same.

*　　*　　*

Soon I have to taste Federico's breakfast and prepare for mass. Today is the day Miranda will be married and I will enjoy food again. I must do that at least once, otherwise this has all been for nothing.

The last day—morning.

Tommaso was fast asleep so I put my knife to his *fallo* and my hand over his mouth and when he woke I whispered, "Lie still or by God you will die here and now." Then I said, "Do you still love Miranda?"

His eyes flitted from side to side as if he was hoping to wake one of the other boys sleeping in the room.

"Will you marry her and take care of her for the rest of your life? Answer me!"

One of the boys raised his head, grunted and went back to sleep.

"Answer me!" Tommaso nodded. "Then get up. We have little time."

Outside the room I said, "You must make three cookies. One of Miranda, one of the duke, and one of me. The figures must be good but not great, for it must be as if I made them. Miranda's will be only marzipan and sugar, but in the duke's you must mix in the contents of this bag." I held it up. "Place the figures on the turret of the cake. This is the only way you and Miranda will be free."

He frowned angrily. "But they will know that *I*—"

"That is why they must be clumsy. Then everyone will believe me when I say *I* made them."

Questions dashed to the front of his mouth only to be overtaken by more pressing ones.

"Tommaso, I have inflicted great wrongs on you and Miranda. Allow me to heal them. I have but a few hours."

He was so confused that it was easy to lead him to the kitchen. There I persuaded him to make three small piles of dough and flavored them with sugar and marzipan. I poured the contents of my bag into two of the piles. "Make this one look like Federico and the other look like me."

Tommaso's head jerked up. "But—"

"Giovanni is going to kill me anyway for what happened to his sister and mother. That is why he is here."

He stared at me in disbelief. "Does Miranda know?"

"Of course," I lied. He had stopped working and I had to jog his arm. "Hurry!"

"I will put less in yours."

"No, Tommaso. You will put *more* in mine."

He stopped.

"Do what I say! I have my reasons."

He rubbed the poisons into the dough and began to shape the figures. In no time they took on the forms of Federico, Miranda, and myself. "Do not make them perfect," I warned him.

He placed them on the fire. There were voices in the hallway. "Go," he said. "I will finish them."

"You will take care of Miranda?"

"With my life. You have my word." We grasped arms and kissed one another on the cheek.

I prayed all day though I realize that my praying has made little difference to what has followed. That is not to say that I doubt God's existence. When I look out of my window and see the valley in springtime, when I see Miranda's face when she sleeps, when I close my eyes and imagine my Helene, I know that God exists. I believe He watches me. Not over me. But watches me. He leaves omens for me. For instance, I thought that I had overcome so many obstacles to Miranda's happiness when the biggest obstacle was myself. I am grateful to Him for allowing me to understand this.

Now I am going to the wedding feast. I am wearing a white silk shirt, a doublet of blue velvet trimmed with gold brocade puffed at the wrists, and my velvet hat with a jeweled brooch in its center. A medallion of pure gold, a gift Cecchi gave me, hangs around my neck. I have silver rings on three of my fingers. When I look in the mirror I see a courtier who would be at home in the palazzos of Firenze or Venezia. A man who was once afraid of Death, but is no longer, for in facing Death he has given purpose to his life.

Night.

I will try to complete this in the time I have left to live. Tonight, I was seated at the table between Miranda and Princess Marguerite of Rimini. I laughed and joked with everyone and even ate with a silver fork. Septivus could not finish Federico's poem, so I offered him the one I had written for Helene. I am glad to say everyone loved it.

The trumpets sounded—I am tired of trumpets, they are shrill and noisy and I am glad I will never have to hear them anymore. The servants marched in carrying platters of food. O my soul! Has it truly been five years since I was in that line? On each platter sat a swan wearing a golden crown, its eyes shining brightly, its wings spread out in flight, its beak casting out fiery sparks. Luigi placed the largest platter in front of me! Me! Ugo the food taster! He raised the long fork.

"Where is your taster?" Federico asked me.

I told him I did not want one.

"You are not going to use a taster?" He turned to the guests. "I told him he could have his own taster. Why do you not want one?"

I stood up. Septivus had given a speech, so had Giovanni, the bishop and nobles from Urbino and Spoleto, so why not I? Everyone quieted down. I cleared my throat. "Magnificent Prince," I began. "On this day, Christ in His Glory, the Holy Mother, and God Himself have all blessed Corsoli and all who dwell within her gates. In such a sacred house, the spirits will not allow anyone to harbor thoughts or deeds against you, Miranda, or anyone else." Then I sat down.

"Amen," the bishop said, and everyone echoed his blessing.

Federico leaned across Miranda (he was holding her hand as if she might escape) and whispered to me, "You are still going to taste my food."

"Your Excellency," I said looking into his eyes, "I am still your taster."

Luigi stuck the fork into the swan, raised it to the height of his chest, cut six slices off its breast, and poured the juices over it. I speared a piece with my fork and lifted it to my mouth. The odor made me dizzy. Luigi had used just the right amount of fennel. I opened my mouth and placed it on my tongue. It was warm, rich, tender.

"Ugo is weeping," Federico shouted, and the hall rocked with laughter.

"They are tears of joy," Cecchi said.

"It is not only free of all poison," I declared, "but it is delicious!"

"Now *you* must eat!" Federico said.

The evening I had been waiting for was here at last. I began with the spit-roasted quails. They were heavenly. The skylarks and pheasants were even better. The kid cooked in garlic sauce, superb. I ran out of words of praise before the first course had ended. There were also eggplants, capons in lemon sauce, platters of pasta, and sausages browned to perfection. The salted pork was succulent, if a little salty, but the fried broad beans were crisp as spring frost. I ate an entire platcful of calves' brains and had not one, but two helpings of Turkish rice with almonds.

I chewed over every bite, savoring every morsel, making up for all the meals I had missed.

"He is eating as if it was his last meal," Bernardo grumbled. Cecchi looked at me and raised his glass in my honor. I drank many goblets of wine and even smiled at Cardinal Giovanni, addressing several remarks to him. Miranda flashed her eyes and adjusted her dress so that more of her breasts showed.

I seized a moment when Federico was not looking at her and, squeezing her arm, whispered that although she hated me I loved her more than life itself. "If I could suffer a *thousand* deaths in your place, I would do so. I beg you, do not judge me. It is not over yet." She pulled away as more trumpets announced the wedding cake— Tommaso's sugar and marzipan extravaganza.

It was so large that two servants had to carry it on a tray. They held it aloft and walked around the hall as everyone marveled at how brilliantly Tommaso had copied the palazzo. Then they placed it in front of Federico. I prayed Tommaso had done as I asked and I was not disappointed. On the turret were the three figures of Miranda, Duke Federico, and myself.

"It is better than anything Bramante ever built," Federico said. The windows and columns were made out of cheeses, sweets, and nuts, the marble courtyard out of pieces of glazed orange and lemon.

"But what are these figures?" Marguerite of Rimini asked.

"Your Excellency." I stood up again. Everyone quieted again to listen to me. "I prepared these three figures myself. They are of Your Honor, Miranda, and myself.

"You are becoming a cook now?" Federico said, as everyone laughed.

"Why not? Who knows more about food than me?"

I could see Miranda looking at me, trying to shake off the effects of the wine.

"Why did you make them?" Federico said, his eyes narrowing.

I had spent so much time planning this that I had not thought that

Federico would question me, but once again God put the words into my mouth.

"My Lord, you have everything a duke could wish for. The valley of Corsoli is known for its beauty. Your city is prosperous and wealthy. Your reputation as a fearless *condotierro* is well known. As a lord you are admired, feared, and loved. You have distinguished friends and loyal citizens. Your walls are decorated with the finest works of art, your stables blessed with magnificent horses. Now you have the love of my daughter, the most beautiful woman in Corsoli. You do me the greatest honor of my life by allowing my family to join yours. Since there is nothing I can give you which can compare to all that I have mentioned, these cookies are simple tokens of the sweetness and the undying love which will now exist between our two families."

"He should be an orator," Septivus announced. The guests applauded loudly. Federico said nothing. He was thinking, as I knew he would, of the cookies of the Day of the Dead.

"Therefore," I went on, "let us partake of this symbol and so be united forever."

Again the guests applauded loudly. I reached for the three cookies and gave Miranda hers, Federico his, and I took mine. The hall was silent, waiting to see what Federico would do. He looked at Tommaso. I feared Tommaso would say something, but for the first time in his life, he remained silent. Ah, I thought, he has grown up at last. Then Federico turned to me and said, "Since I am taking over the responsibility of Miranda's protection, would it not be right for me to eat *your* cookie and for you to eat mine?"

I acted as if I was surprised, but I replied cheerfully, "If the duke wishes, he can exchange his cookie with mine or Miranda's."

Federico looked at Miranda, and then at the cookie in her hand. I prayed I was right and that he loved her as much as I thought he did.

Patting her hand gently, Federico turned to me and said, "No, I will exchange my cookie with yours."

"Then let it be so," I said. I gave him my cookie and took his. "Now let us eat." I bit down hard into my cookie to show everyone how much I enjoyed it. Miranda, thinking perhaps that I had poisoned hers, ate it greedily. Federico did the same.

Ah, now comes the fire. I did not think the poisons would take effect so quickly. I must hurry.

After the cookies and the cake were eaten, the bishop led Federico and Miranda through the palazzo to his bedchamber. The guests walked behind singing hymns of praise. Men sighed and women wept. At Federico's bedchamber, the bishop said a prayer. I kissed Miranda and placed her hand into Federico's. They went inside and closed the door.

Oh, but it hurts. I was blind but now the veil is lifted, the mist disappears. Septivus, you were right. Food together with the spirit creates a hunger only God can satisfy.

Ah, *potta!* But this is quick! Oh, my stomach! Claws of fire. The griffin's beak rips my flesh. It spreads through my bowels like a flaming sword.

Cardinal Giovanni, you think I am a coward for taking my own life, but my mother was not a coward.

O God! It comes again. Oh, . . . Oh, *potta!* I have shit myself! Oh, Helene. My darling, Helene, love of my life. We will not meet in this world, but I will wait for you.

My door is open, I must hear Federico fall! DEATH CANNOT TAKE ME FIRST.

My hands itch. My face bleeds.

Oh, fire! Helene, forgive me.

O my God,

Purify

Your servant.

I did not die. Cecchi once called me "*Il miracolo vivente*," and now I deserve the name. Truly it is a miracle that I am alive. I did not plan to live. Indeed, I was prepared to die, but God in His wisdom has spared me.

I did not hear what happened in the duke's chamber because after he closed the door I returned to my room. Cecchi told me that soon after the door closed, the guests, who were waiting outside for Federico to declare that he had taken Miranda's virginity, heard strange noises. At first, they thought it was the duke making love, but Miranda came running out crying that the duke was vomiting and complaining of burning in his throat and palpitations round his heart.

The courtiers, Cardinal Giovanni, and the bishop immediately went inside. Federico was crying, screaming, throwing himself around the room, smashing into the walls and furniture as though possessed by a thousand demons. Blood and vomit spilled from his mouth. He was shitting blood and feces. He tried to stab himself but his hands kept dropping the dagger. Teeth fell from his mouth. Howling like a madman, he rolled on the bed and tried to strangle himself. The courtiers threw themselves on top of him and after much fighting he sank to the floor, clutching Miranda to him. She screamed but he would not let go. He tried to bite her, but could not close his mouth. Afraid that he might squeeze her to death and distressed at seeing the duke in such agony, Cardinal Giovanni thrust his sword through the duke's heart to end his suffering. Federico shuddered, heaved like a huge dying whale, and then was still. Nero lay beside him, licking his face. They were forced to cut Federico's fingers off to release Miranda.

Then they came running to my room. By this time I was also screaming, bleeding, and shitting. I could only see shapes but I remember Cardinal Giovanni waving his bloody sword. Miranda knelt down and picked up my head in her hands. There was confusion and fear in her eyes. She was remembering the cookies of the Day of the Dead, the breakfast at Carnevale, the stories I had told her of Onionface. She wanted to embrace me, but I could not let her do that, for Giovanni was waiting to kill me and I could not let anyone think that she was part of the plan, so I spat in her face.

She jerked away and dropped my head to the ground. Turning to Giovanni, she said, "No, Cardinal Giovanni. Do not kill him. Let him suffer! Let him suffer a *thousand* deaths for the crimes he has committed this day."

Oh, bless her. Bless her! All the actors in Padua should take lessons from her! Cardinal Giovanni hesitated, but there was no question that I was poisoned, and in great pain. He put his sword away and agreed that I deserved the slowest of deaths. So did the courtiers. By this time I no longer knew what was going on. All I know is that they must have left the room because someone raised my head (I was told later it was Piero) and poured olive oil down my throat. I threw up, retching everything up that I had ever eaten, but it did no good. The poison was in me. I fell violently ill and was expected to die.

All of the guests, including Giovanni, left the palazzo as soon as it was light. Federico was buried the day after. Only a few courtiers attended his funeral. The city took a holiday. I was too ill to know any of this and lay like a dead person. Sometimes I slept and sometimes I was awake. It made no difference. Although I could hear people I could not speak or move any part of my body, nor could I see them. I was sure I was in purgatory and that God had not yet decided whether I should go to heaven or hell.

Tommaso was the soul of kindness, for every day he brought fresh cakes for me in case I should wake. On the other hand, Bernardo said my illness was a bad omen and I should be buried immediately even though I was not yet dead! Fortunately, Cecchi insisted on waiting.

Miranda spent hours by my bedside praying and singing. She imitated her birds and animals, put her arms around me, and whispered she loved me. I wanted to cry out, but could not. I tried to move my fingers the width of a fly. I could not and wept from exhaustion. Luckily, Miranda saw my tears and told the others.

One morning several weeks later, I awoke hungrier than I had ever been in my life. Piero said I had survived because of all the poisons I had taken for so many months. My recovery was cause for celebration, but in the middle of the festivities, Cecchi said that as soon as I was strong enough it would be best for Miranda, Tommaso, and me to leave before Giovanni found out that I had recovered. Bernardo had been seen riding out of the city and it was known he intended to tell him.

The following week everyone bid us farewell. I embraced Cecchi, Piero, and Septivus; truer friends I have never had. Tommaso, Miranda, and I mounted our horses and with the Duomo bell ringing joyfully in our ears, and tears in our eyes, we rode out of the court-yard, down the Weeping Steps through the Piazza Del Vedura and the West Gate, and out of Corsoli forever.

Miranda is truly a woman now—beautiful, brave, and wiser than many twice her age. I could not be more proud of her. With my blessing, she and Tommaso have ridden on to Venezia where Tommaso intends to find work as a cook. Before she left, I kissed her apple cheeks over and over and held her close to me. Although it broke my heart to see her leave, I am comforted knowing that Tommaso is ready to take care of her.

I have purchased a small piece of land here in Arraggio. The soil is rich and perfect for grazing. I am still thin, I suffer from cramps and throw up for no reason. I have lost some teeth and others have become loose. I am not as strong as I once was. Perhaps I will never be again, I do not know. I *do* know that God has given me one more chance to change my life.

My clothes are bundled beside me. My horse waits by the door. As soon as the sun rises I will ride to France. To Nîmes. To Helene. No matter how long it takes, no matter where she is, I will find her. And I will bring her here, to Arraggio, to be my love.

# Renaissance Recipes

# Rafioli Commun de Herbe Vanzati
## (Mint and Spinach Ravioli)

This is plain old spinach ravioli, but with exotic flavorings. The pinches of spice at the end are important. From the fourteenth-century anonymous work *Libro per Cuoco*.

1 (10-ounce) bag spinach leaves, chopped, about 6 cups, loosely packed
¼ cup chopped fresh mint
¼ cup chopped parsley
2 tablespoons olive oil
1 egg, lightly beaten
½ cup shredded mozzarella cheese
Ground cinnamon
Ground ginger
Ground cumin
Salt, pepper
Ravioli dough
Boiling salted water
Parmesan cheese, grated

Sauté spinach, mint, and parsley in olive oil until spinach is wilted. Let cool. Stir in egg, mozzarella, ⅛ teaspoon cinnamon, ⅛ teaspoon ginger, and ⅛ teaspoon cumin, and salt and pepper to taste.

Divide ravioli dough into 8 portions. Roll each piece through pasta machine on successively finer settings into thin sheets, about 4 inches wide and 16 to 18 inches long. Spread 1 pasta sheet on floured work surface. Place filling by teaspoons at 8 regular intervals about 2 inches apart, 1 inch from right-hand long edge of sheet. Lightly moisten pasta around fillings. Fold left half of pasta over filling, carefully squeezing out all air pockets. Seal between fillings by pressing firmly with sides of hands. Cut into

8 (2-inch) squares with filling in center of each. Transfer to floured cloth. Repeat with remaining sheets of dough.

Cook ravioli in boiling salted water until they float to surface, about 5 minutes. Remove with slotted spoon and drain in colander. Serve sprinkled with cinnamon, ginger, cumin, and grated Parmesan cheese to taste. Makes 8 servings.

**Ravioli Dough**

2 cups unbleached flour
2 extra-large eggs
1 tablespoon olive oil

Place flour in food-processor bowl fitted with metal blade. Beat eggs and olive oil in small bowl until blended, then add to food processor with motor running. Process until dough forms ball and is very smooth. Turn dough out onto lightly floured work surface. Knead well, adding small amounts of flour as needed to keep from sticking to hands and surface, until dough is smooth and very elastic. Let dough stand 20 to 30 minutes before rolling out.

Each serving contains about 224 calories, 137 mg sodium, 110 mg cholesterol, 9 grams of fat, 26 grams carbohydrates, 9 grams protein, 0.5 gram fiber.

# Torta Bononiensis (Chard Pie)

Taken from the famous 1446 *De Honesta Voluptate* (*Dishes of Lawful Pleasure*) by Bartolommeo Sacchi. Better known as Platina (Dish) because of the cookbook, Bartolommeo wrote it to impress two cardinals he had run afoul of. He was a librarian and a scholar, but not a cook; this was one of the dishes that he lifted unchanged from Maestro Martino, who *was* a cook. Martino called it plain old Torta Bolognese.

6 tablespoons butter
1½ cups flour
¼ teaspoon salt
4 to 5 tablespoons ice water
Chard filling
1 egg
1 teaspoon water
⅛ teaspoon saffron threads

Cut butter into flour and salt until particles are size of small peas. Sprinkle with ice water and quickly stir with fork until dough is evenly moistened and will form into a ball. On lightly floured board, roll out about ¾ of dough to fit bottom and sides of 9-inch tart pan. Trim edges. Roll out remaining dough and cut into about ½-inch-wide lattice strips. Fill tart with chard filling. Arrange lattice strips crisscross on top. Blend egg with 1 teaspoon water and saffron threads and brush on pastry.

Bake at 350 degrees 30 to 35 minutes or until filling is puffed and crust is browned. Remove tart from pan to baking sheet during last 5 minutes. Brush sides with remaining saffron-egg mixture and finish baking. Makes 6 servings.

## Chard Filling

1 bunch Swiss chard, tough stems removed, chopped, about 5 cups
2 tablespoons butter
1 teaspoon saffron threads, loosely packed
¼ cup chopped parsley
2 tablespoons minced fresh marjoram leaves
Salt, pepper
3 eggs, lightly beaten
½ cup ricotta cheese
½ cup mozzarella cheese, shredded

Sauté chard in butter until tender. Crush saffron and stir in. Stir in parsley and marjoram. Season to taste with salt and pepper. Let stand until just warm. Mix with eggs, ricotta and mozzarella cheeses.

Each serving contains about 371 calories, 491 mg sodium, 230 mg cholesterol, 23 grams fat, 27 grams carbohydrates, 14 grams protein, 0.4 gram fiber.

# Polpette Grigliate (Spiced Scaloppine)

To the modern taste, the most appealing part of this recipe is probably the pan juices fragrant with garlic and fennel. Use the Salsa Camclino sparingly; it's very sweet. This recipe comes from *Libro Novo nel Qual s'Insegna a Far d'Ogni Sorte di Vivande,* by Cristofaro Messisbugo, published in 1557.

12 thin slices veal for scaloppine
3 cloves garlic, crushed
1½ teaspoons fennel seeds, ground
Salt, pepper
6 tablespoons white wine vinegar
6 tablespoons butter
Salsa Camelino

Pound veal to flatten. Rub garlic, fennel, and salt and pepper to taste over all sides of meat. Place in shallow dish, sprinkle with vinegar, and marinate 30 minutes.

Heat butter in skillet until sizzling. Add meat and sauté quickly on both sides in several batches until lightly browned, about 1 minute per side.

Remove to platter. Spoon pan juices over meat. Spoon some Salsa Camelino on top, if desired, and serve remaining on side. Makes 4 servings.

**Salsa Camelino**

½ cup golden raisins
½ cup Marsala wine
2 to 3 tablespoons white wine vinegar
3 tablespoons fresh bread crumbs

1 tablespoon honey
⅛ teaspoon ground cinnamon
⅛ teaspoon black pepper
Dash ground ginger
Dash Ground cloves

Chop raisins coarsely. Add to small saucepan with wine and vinegar. Heat to boiling. Stir in bread crumbs, honey, cinnamon, pepper, ginger, and cloves. Simmer 1 to 2 minutes. Makes about ½ cup.

Each serving contains about 362 calories, 327 mg sodium, 124 mg cholesterol, 19 grams fat, 23 grams carbohydrates, 22 grams protein, 0.42 grams fiber.

# **Polpette Grigliate** (Grilled Saltimbocca)

Another scaloppine recipe from Messisbugo, again sweetened with raisins and fragrant with fennel and garlic, but this time with a rich cheese filling.

8 thin slices veal for scaloppine
2 tablespoons white wine vinegar
Salt, pepper
Cheese filling

Marinate veal with vinegar and salt and pepper to taste 1 hour. Pat dry with paper towels. Spoon about 2 tablespoons cheese filing on each slice and roll up. Grill quickly over high heat, turning to cook evenly, until meat is browned and cheese filling is melted. Makes 8 appetizer servings.

## Cheese Filling

1 cup shredded mozzarella cheese
½ cup seedless raisins, chopped
2 tablespoons chopped parsley
1 clove garlic, minced
1 teaspoon fennel seeds, crushed
2 egg yolks, lightly beaten
Salt, pepper

Mix mozzarella, raisins, parsley, garlic, fennel, and egg yolks. Season to taste with salt and pepper.

Each serving contains about 119 calories, 164 mg sodium, 102 mg cholesterol, 4 grams fat, 9 grams carbohydrates, 12 grams protein, 0.2 gram fiber.

# Pollo Fricto con Limone
## (Chicken Fried with Diced Lemon)

A strange but surprisingly tasty dish. Mentioned in a banquet menu recorded by Messisbugo.

1 chicken, cut up
Salt
3 tablespoons olive oil
4½ lemons
3 tablespoons sugar
1 tablespoon peppercorns, freshly ground

Rub chicken with salt to taste and brown in olive oil. Drain off excess oil.

Squeeze juice of 3 lemons and cut remaining 1½ lemons into ½-inch dice. Add lemon juice and diced lemons to pan, cover and simmer 15 minutes. Uncover and simmer 5 to 10 minutes longer, turning chicken to glaze all sides.

Combine sugar and ground peppercorns and pass with chicken for diners to season to taste. Makes 4 servings.

Each serving contains about 393 calories, 158 mg sodium, 90 mg cholesterol, 28 grams fat, 13 grams carbohydrates, 22 grams protein, 0 fiber.

# Verze Piene (Cabbage Stuffed with Walnuts)

Not your ordinary stuffed cabbage—here, only meat is in the sauce. From Messisbugo 1557.

2 cups ground walnuts
½ cup grated Parmesan cheese
2 cloves garlic, minced
1 teaspoon ground ginger
1 teaspoon minced fresh sage
¼ teaspoon crushed saffron threads
⅛ teaspoon ground cloves
½ teaspoon black pepper
3 eggs, lightly beaten
6 large cabbage leaves
5 cups chicken broth
1 cup diced cooked ham
¼ cup minced parsley

Combine walnuts, Parmesan cheese, garlic, ginger, sage, saffron, cloves, pepper, and eggs. Blanch cabbage leaves until tender in boiling water. Drain leaves. Spoon about ¼ cup filling into each leaf and roll up.

Combine chicken broth, ham, and parsley in large pot. Bring to boil, reduce heat, and add cabbage rolls. Cover and simmer 30 minutes. Serve in shallow bowls with broth and ham. Makes 6 servings.

Each serving contains about 413 calories, 1,143 mg sodium, 127 mg cholesterol, 33 grams fat, 11 grams carbohydrates, 21 grams protein, 2 grams fiber.

# Torta de Cerase (Cherry Cheesecake)

Cheesecakes have been made in Italy since Roman times. This one seems almost modern. From Maestro Martino's *Libro di Arte Coquinaria,* mid-fifteenth century.

2¼ cups flour
¼ cup sugar
½ teaspoon salt
¾ cup butter, cut up
3 egg yolks, lightly beaten
¼ cup Marsala wine
Cherry-cheese filling
Fresh Bing cherries for garnish, optional

Combine flour, sugar, and salt. Cut in butter until particles are size of small peas. Combine egg yolks and Marsala wine. Stir in quickly with fork until dough is evenly moistened and will form into ball.

On lightly floured board, roll out dough to fit bottom and sides of 9-inch springform pan. Place in pan, bringing sides up to about 1 inch below top edge. Chill until dough is firm.

Spread cherry-cheese filling evenly into crust and smooth top. Bake at 350 degrees 50 to 60 minutes or until center is set. Remove and allow to cool. Remove from springform pan. Garnish with fresh cherries. Makes 20 servings.

## Cherry-Cheese Filling

5 cups ricotta cheese
½ cup grated Parmesan cheese
½ cup sugar
3 eggs

2 tablespoons minced crystallized ginger
¼ teaspoon ground cinnamon
¼ teaspoon white pepper
1 (1-pound) can dark sweet pitted cherries, drained and
halved

Beat together ricotta cheese, Parmesan cheese, and sugar in large mixer bowl or food processor. Beat in eggs, 1 at a time, until blended. Beat in ginger, cinnamon, and white pepper. Fold in drained cherries.

Each serving contains about 274 calories, 263 mg sodium, 112 mg cholesterol, 14 grams fat, 25 grams carbohydrates, 11 grams protein, trace fiber.

# **Suppa Dorata** (Saffron "French Toast")

The luxurious ancestor of the French *pain perdu* or *pain doree*; really quite golden in color when you add the saffron-colored syrup. From Maestro Martino, mid-fifteenth-century.

3 eggs, lightly beaten
2 tablespoons sugar
½ teaspoon rose water
4 slices bread (½ inch thick), crusts removed and quartered
1½ to 2 tablespoons butter
Saffron syrup

Combine eggs, sugar, and rose water. Soak slices in mixture just until absorbed. Heat butter in skillet. Fry toast until golden brown on both sides. Serve with saffron syrup. Makes 4 servings.

**Saffron Syrup**

1 cup water
1 cup sugar
Dash saffron threads
¼ teaspoon rose water

Cook water, sugar, and saffron to syrup stage, 230 to 234 degrees. Let cool and stir in rose water. Makes 1¼ cups.

Each serving contains about 366 calories, 218 mg sodium, 172 mg cholesterol, 9 grams fat, 66 grams carbohydrates, 7 grams protein, trace fiber.

Recipes used by permission of Charles Perry.

# ACKNOWLEDGMENTS

Many people contributed to this book, but none more than Bill Berensmann and Dulcie Apgar. For their suggestions and guidance, I am deeply grateful. I must also thank Charles Perry for his advice on Italian cuisine, Carla Balatresi for correcting my Italian, and Garry Goodrow for his knowledge of all things poetic.

The book was started in Jim Krusoe's writing class at Santa Monica City College, and without his continual encouragement and criticism, and that of his class, it would never have been completed.

Finally, it might never have seen the light of day had it not been for the faith, persistence, and enthusiasm of my agent, Julia Lord, and my first publisher, Martin Shepard. To all, my deepest thanks.